Clay Ghosts in Sicily

Clay Ghosts in Sicily

Angie Voluti

BANK HOUSE BOOKS

First published in the United Kingdom in 2011 by

Bank House Books

PO Box 3

New Romney

TN29 9WJ UK

www.bankhousebooks.com

British Library Cataloguing in Publication Data
A catalogue record for this book is available from the British Library

ISBN 9781904408918

Typesetting and origination by Bank House Books

CONTENTS

Part Two: Sicily, 1955

HIGH FLIGHT

By John Gillespie Magee Jr
(457th Bomb Group)

Oh, I have slipped the surly bonds of earth
And danced the skies on laughter-silvered wings;
Sunward I've climbed, and joined the rumbling mirth
Of sun-split clouds – and done a hundred things
You have not dreamed of – wheeled and soared and swung
High in the sunlit silence. Hov'ring there,
I've chased the shouting wind along, and flung
My eager craft through footless halls of air.
Up, up the long, delirious, burning blue
I've topped the windswept heights with easy grace
Where never lark, or even eagle flew.
And, while with silent, lifting mind I've trod
The high untrespassed sanctity of space,
Put out my hand, and touched the face of God.

SICILY, 1943

Chapter One
AXIS AND ALLIES IN PALERMO

R osalia! Rosalia! An honest chair! Give me an honest chair, *maledetto Mussolini e le sue donnacce,* to hell with Mussolini and his whores!'
     She hears him call her name, and runs to the family home's inner courtyard, which is soaked in Sicily's midday sun.

Don Antonio Bellino Muggifalco's old leather slippers shuffle on the ancient stone tiles, as fast as his gout will allow. A tired yellow silk dressing gown opens indiscreetly on the solicitor's varicose legs.

'*Papá, papá,* do not trouble yourself. I shall go and find one,' she says, before scuttling back into the cool darkness of the palazzo's rooms. Wooden shutters frame doors like mascara-laden eyelashes.

'If he trips over again and stubs his bad toe, he will swear even louder about Signor Mussolini.' Rosalia bites her bottom lip, dragging the skin through her front teeth.

An asthmatic breeze coming from many an unsealed window cools her skin and runs down her back, lifting the light summer dress. She has thin, long legs, born to chase after lizards and swim in the Mediterranean seas.

Past the silent ballroom and the empty morning room, a couple of steps up here and one step down there, Rosalia follows the eccentric architecture of Palazzo de' Muggifalco's ground floor, which echoes in its layout the urban landscape and secret crypts under it.

Rosalia's home is an important historical building: the Muggifalcos' Christian ancestors, many generations before hers, came back victorious from the Crusades, and were given property and wealth by the conquering Normans.

Once in the dining room, Rosalia starts shaking the chairs, dragging wooden feet from under the huge dinner table, to check their solidity. 'An *honest* chair, he says. One which will not collapse under his guest's weight,' she muses. 'Did we not keep a couple of the original dining chairs?'

Thump, bang, thump, bang, Rosalia goes through the entire set. She discards the cheap imitations, one by one, and does not bother to tuck them under the table. Out in the courtyard, her father is thundering away, bringing down both known and unknown saints of a Paradise in which he no longer believes.

Thump, thump. A deep creaking rather than shrill squeaking: Rosalia has jolted the last chair's great ancestry.

'Ah! Here you are,' she cries, grabbing the polished mahogany legs. The antique linen presser in the corner seems to look down at her, with disapproving brass eyes. 'Watch it, old thing, or we'll sell you for kindling!' admonishes Rosalia, but she is glad to be out of the room, glad to be going back to her shouting father and the sunny courtyard.

'Put it in my study, that's a good girl,' growls Don Antonio; he points at one of the balconies above their heads. In the middle of the courtyard a solitary palm grows inside the parched flowerbed, stroking the balcony's ironwork with dry fingers.

Rosalia obeys, swinging the chair in front of her with difficulty as she climbs the marble steps of the main staircase. She steals a look at her father as he shifts his weight from one foot to the other, uncomfortably.

Once upstairs, and out of breath, Rosalia slows down. The narrow corridor runs along the inner courtyard; one, two, three, four windows flash past her right shoulder.

Rosalia knows that her father is following her progress through the dirty glass panes, until she reaches the heavy oak door at the end of the corridor.

There are secrets hidden in his study; the chair is for one of his mysterious friends, anonymous faces under white Panama hats who visit regularly, voices fading behind the study's closed door. The room smells like Don Antonio himself, musty and acrid behind the rich tones of an old-fashioned aftershave; in these war times of sacrifice and deprivation, his gold-and-blue label bottles make up for the lack of clean water. Signora Muggifalco, brought up like a lady, would never dream of querying her husband's preference for perfume over soap. Signora Muggifalco has not slept in the marital bed for a few years now and her interest in her husband's personal hygiene is minimal. The only thing Rosalia's mother and father have in common, apart from their daughter and a rambling palazzo in the middle of Palermo, is night-time solitude. Lying in their beds and pulling at linen sheets that have seen a brighter white, they no longer remember the last marital activities conducted, with dignity and still wearing their nightdresses, around sixteen years earlier.

The adjacent rooms where Signor and Signora Muggifalco retreat for the night are similar in size and layout, both with white walls and heavy, dark mahogany bedsteads. By tacit agreement, they have claimed a bedside table each, splitting the matching pair. The top drawers smell of lavender and something else, age and candle wax perhaps, the scent of cold nights and recent power cuts.

Rosalia looks around her. Her father's visitor will need the chair to face the antique oak desk. She puts the chair down on the Oriental rug, where the sun's rays, stealing through the window, have carved a big square of faded colours. The girl angles the chair this way and that way, trying to find the most sensible position. The heat trapped inside the study dulls her brain.

'Rosalia, Rosalia! What are you still doing there, *che' ti sei imbambolata,* have you become catatonic?' shouts her father from the courtyard, as if on cue.

Rosalia flicks her apathy off like an irritating insect on one's arm, and turns around to leave. Secrets. Her father does not like anyone prying around in his private retreat, and is clearly impatient to see her out of the study.

'What on earth could he possibly have in there?' she wonders, coming down the stairs quickly, out of obedience rather than fear.

In Rosalia's young eyes, her father's musty study, full of documents, files and books, is there to provide reassurance and stability.

Excitement is something Rosalia seeks outside her family home. Like her mother, sultry Signora Muggifalco, Rosalia has her own very secret life and interests, safe in the knowledge that Palazzo de' Muggifalco and her father's study will always be there, her own childhood haven.

'I need some *caffé* brought to my study in about an hour, *dolcezza,* sweetie,' Don Antonio says, his voice mellower now, when Rosalia joins him in the courtyard.

'For two,' he adds, still shuffling uncomfortably.

'*Papá,* the maid is down to her last scoop of ground *carruba,* and I'm not really sure ...' Rosalia starts, guessing that she won't be allowed to complete the sentence.

'*Carrube* are food for Arab horses!' cries Don Antonio, thumping his good foot on the tiles. 'I am sick and tired of that black piss. What am I supposed to give to my visitor?'

Rosalia pauses, biting her bottom lip. Carobs, also known as St John's bread, are already difficult to find in poverty-stricken Sicily, especially during this horrid war that nobody wants or understands. The black pods of the carob tree can be turned into a passable imitation of cocoa, but making the jump to fully fledged coffee is a tall order, even for a resourceful maid like the Muggifalcos' faithful Anna.

'Do you think Signor Mussolini has carob juice after his sumptuous lunch, in his Rome offices?' Don Antonio asks, whipping up a bilious mood. 'Or the German officers staying at the Novara family's grand townhouse down the road? Silver trays and Japanese porcelain espresso cups for the square-chinned bastards in their gleaming uniforms, that's what they get!'

'*Papá,* leave it with me. I shall try and find some refreshments for your visitor,' Rosalia interrupts, desperate not to hear about the Germans and Mussolini again.

'*Il Duce* has stomach trouble,' Don Antonio persists in a falsetto voice, enthusiastically riding his favourite hobby-horse. 'I might have had too much coffee and cakes,' he mocks, but Rosalia has already left. 'My visitor will be here in an hour!' her father shouts after her.

The grey stone steps outside Palazzo de' Muggifalco's front door are aged and smooth, edges rounded and slippery; in happier times, Rosalia would sit on the top one and thump down all the way to the road, step by step, as she used to do as a little girl.

Today she is in a hurry, and has a grown-up errand to run. She comes down the stairs lightly, careful not to slip, clutching a sheet of paper rolled up into a tube.

The streets are deserted. Rosalia looks left and then right: in the distance, midday light's reflection looks like puddles of water on the huge yellow stones paving the main road. An urban mirage.

Everybody is indoors, trying to avoid heat and bombs, the only thing likely to rain onto desolate Palermo during the summer of 1943.

Palazzo de' Muggifalco stands in a well-to-do district, near the harbour with its useless boats bobbing in dark blue waters. Since the Allies' bombing started, several weeks before, the fishermen have been too scared to venture out, only risking the occasional trip in the night or when hunger makes the children cry in their sleep.

The attacks on this part of Palermo have left gaping holes in ancient buildings whose owners have long since fled; Rosalia walks past façades bravely standing on the strength of one wall, rubble heaping behind window shutters.

If she doesn't look too closely, if she keeps her big brown eyes firmly trained on the pavement or the many surviving buildings in her neighbourhood, Rosalia can still fool herself into believing that Palermo is untouchable; that the whispered news about other attacks on the smaller islands just off the Sicilian coast are only *propaganda Inglese*.

She recalls a snippet of conversation overheard just the night before. One of her father's mysterious guests had dropped by. She was trying to sneak out of the house unnoticed, tip-toeing down the back stairs: a call from the *other* life that Rosalia leads when nobody is looking. The evening breeze had carried to her ears the voices of two men, deep in conversation: her father and his guest sat in the inner courtyard, surrounded by darkness and the sweet smell of potted jasmine surviving the summer.

'Did you hear the one about Don Calogero? He was on his land, checking the wheat, during daytime. Waiting for his headman to come back from the main fields, he decides to bend down and pick up a sprig to rub between his fingers, checking for disease. It's harvest time, after all, war or no war. So he's squatting on his haunches and wearing his lucky hat, the old straw one. And then he sees this airplane coming from nowhere. It's an *Inglese* aircraft, he can see it clearly. The workmen in the fields see it too, and stop to look; one or two even wave at it.'

'I'm not surprised,' answers Don Antonio heatedly. 'I would say *benvenuto* to the *Inglesi* too, given a chance. Anything is better than bloody Mussolini. It's his war, not ours. What's Sicily got to do with Italy anyway?'

'No, Antonio, listen! They wave at the airplane and the bastard starts shooting at them. In broad daylight.'

'Whom did he shoot? Don Calogero's men? Why, does he employ Germans?'

'Germans? What Germans? Antonio, don't be silly. Sicilians, like you and me.'

'*L'Inglese* must have got confused. This sun blinds you. Was he really shooting at them?'

'On my mother's soul he was. Germans, Mussolini, the *Inglesi* ... They're all shits. The government in Rome looks down on us as if we were *cacca* dangling from the tip of the boot, a wart on the nose of beautiful Italy. And now, as if we hadn't had enough trouble from our esteemed German friends, this island is being bombed by the *Inglesi*. Sicily must become independent, if you ask me.'

There had been more murmurs, lost in the zig-zag singing of the crickets. Rosalia had wanted to hear more, but she was late already and couldn't risk being spotted by her father as she left the house.

The memory of that conversation makes her feel uncomfortable. At sixteen, she has no political beliefs or knowledge. As a woman, indeed, she is not expected to. She has one passion, and she keeps it a secret. *Papá* would not approve, of course, but her secret may occasionally allow her the purchase of some luxury, make her father a little less grumpy.

So she keeps walking, still clutching her rolled-up piece of paper and following Palermo's empty streets with a light step, aimed towards a particular building.

The Novara family's home is a three-storey, sixteenth-century townhouse which has withstood two big earthquakes and numerous wars; it is now patiently putting up with the discomfort of the current conflict.

Its massive perimeter walls define two major arteries in the heart of the city, Corso Garibaldi and Via Libertá; unusually for a townhouse in Palermo, Palazzo Novara is surrounded by a large tropical garden. It is as beautiful on the outside as it is on the inside; the owners exploit its grace and convenience to survive the current political climate. The Novara family regularly entertains the top echelons of the German command. Their friendship with Italy's partners in war shields Palazzo Novara, with its immense rooms, charm and central position, from the danger of becoming just another German post. Confronted with the real danger of German soldiers using the orangery to store their guns, and the family's linen to wipe their boots, the family has opted for a more involving role. Music can be heard playing well into the night; the cellars are overflowing with foreign wines; the pantry, with cold meats

5

and potatoes. It is rumoured that Mussolini and his lover Claretta Petacci have dined there at least once.

The Novaras' only child, twenty-seven-year-old Vincenzo, has expensive tastes and rheumatoid arthritis, which doctors say will kill him before he turns forty; for the time being, the deforming illness merely stops him from fighting for his country. Vincenzo has turned Palazzo Novara's basement into his own private apartment, including a bathroom with no mirrors and an enamelled bath tub. The apartment has private use of a hidden mini-garden, completely sunk into the main grounds' tangled vegetation.

There, with the help of three stone benches retrieved from his mother's rockery and a rickety green gazebo, Vincenzo holds court, surrounding himself with beautiful people of diverse talents: artists all of them, each special in his eyes. There are Vera the painter, Laura the poet, Michele the mathematician, Roberto, the economist, and Rosalia, the youngest.

Rosalia, the sculptress.

In Vincenzo Novara's garden or – in case of bad weather or air attacks – his apartment, the young people enjoy a freedom to express themselves that would be unthinkable in public. The girls, in particular, brought up to gather their trousseau, bag a good husband and dream about baby boys, come to the hidden garden as if to meet a lover, each time with renewed passion and always leaving reluctantly, nursing their own addiction in private.

This is the place to which Rosalia comes today.

She squeezes past thick woody rows of bougainvillea, through the secret hole hacked into the bushes. A strategically positioned plant of sage, alone among the spiky flowers, covers the entrance. She knocks discreetly on Vincenzo's door at the back of the house. Shutters are firmly closed, but there is a good chance that he might just be in, sitting there on an old sofa and reading the newspaper *L'Ora*.

The door opens a fraction, two dark eyes dart this way and that, checking behind Rosalia. Then, '*Ciao, bella*. What a nice surprise. Come in.'

The door opens just a touch more and she disappears inside, relieved to leave behind the heat and possible daytime air raids. Inside, it's cool and cosy at the same time. Minimal furniture, a bachelor's pad; but the walls are covered by photos, taken by Vincenzo with his beloved camera, and pictures, mostly painted by Vera.

'Hello my friend,' says Rosalia. She pauses to look around. 'Are you on your own?'

Vincenzo smiles. 'We're not due to meet until tonight, remember, *vampirina*? It was your suggestion, as you're a creature of the night: sneak out of the house when everyone is asleep ... that not true?'

'No, no. I meant ... Maybe you're entertaining friends or ...' She cannot finish the sentence, and pauses.

Vincenzo's parents intimidate her. Dropping in on him without any notice might cause her to bump into them. Vincenzo's mother would comment on her dress ('Such a lovely colour, my dear little Rosalia, it suits you!') as if she'd never seen Rosalia wearing that very same dress before, and his father would hum and grunt in approval; Vincenzo would be formally polite to her rather than sweetly gruff as usual; all playing their roles.

Vincenzo's smile broadens. 'No, I'm alone today. My parents are upstairs playing cards with friends, and I didn't feel like company. Of course, I'm always happy to see you,' he adds quickly.

'I want to show you something,' Rosalia says, reassured, and unrolls the sheet of paper she has been holding. It is slightly damp in the middle, where her fingers have curled around it. 'I made a pencil study of a horse's head. Look.'

And Vincenzo does.

It is a beautiful drawing: the horse looks straight ahead at the viewer with veins, muscles, even the nostrils' soft tissue all meticulously detailed on paper. Rosalia has caught, with her cheap lead pencil, something else too: an air of regal pride, placidity and yet a streak of rebellion in those bulging and intelligent eyes.

'It is ... it is remarkable,' Vincenzo whispers. The lines are seductive, and it is easy to imagine the sculpture, the miracle of those clay nostrils about to breathe, a shiver in the tense neck, getting ready to run. 'Are you going to do it?' he asks, almost fearing the answer.

'Yes, I'll do it here, if you let me of course, and if you find the clay or ...' And here Rosalia stops, waiting.

'Or what?' Vincenzo is intrigued. 'Stone?'

Rosalia nods. 'Yes. I think I'm ready to try.'

'Stone,' Vincenzo repeats, slowly. 'Great. No more pushing soft matter into a shape. You can free the shape from a hard mass. I'll find the stone for you.'

'You can have the sculpture, when I finish it,' Rosalia says, quickly.

'Give it to me?' Vincenzo is bemused. 'My dear *vampirina,* if your sculpture is half as good as your sketch, it will be too beautiful for me to accept it.'

'Then I shall sell it to you,' Rosalia says. 'You're so kind to me, allowing me to do my work here, undisturbed. The clay and pencils, the paper you provide, and your encouragement. You can have it as a present, but ... there's something I very much want and you may be able to help me.'

Vincenzo laughs affectionately. 'Anything you need, my sweetest. This old Pygmalion wishes to be of assistance to his little artist.'

When Rosalia leaves Vincenzo's basement a few minutes later, she is clutching a small, yellowish paper bag.

'See you tonight,' he whispers at the door, watching the girl's slim figure crouching down and wriggling through the hidden hole. A little movement in the leaves, then stillness again. Rosalia is gone.

The aroma of coffee escaping from the paper bag follows her all the way home, and so do Vincenzo's thoughts, though Rosalia will never know.

Chapter Two
WHOSE WAR IS IT ANYWAY?

'Lampedusa and Pantelleria have been conquered, Sir.'

The young officer standing in front of his superior is sweating profusely. The small village school in San Cataldo, south of Palermo, where Colonnello Bastioni has set up his quarters, is a white, low building with two windows in each classroom. Those behind the desk of Lieutenant Zambito's boss are wide open but there is no breeze coming in. The air is absolutely still.

Lieutenant Zambito has three-day-old stubble poking through his pimples, some of which are infected and oozing a little yellow pus. He cannot remember the last time he had a proper wash or a decent meal. Despite carefully shaving his pubic hair this morning, the itching from the lice still clinging to his grey underwear is maddening.

'I know,' sighs Colonnello Bastioni. The news has reached even the sleepy village in the heartland of Sicily, travelling faster than the directives from Rome. This Italian contingent mans the only post in a fifty-mile radius and is mainly made up of Sicilian youths who had barely started to smoke when they were called to duty.

There are, as yet, no supplementary German troops to help him, only locals eyeing up his men suspiciously. Wives and daughters are under lock and key, together with any rare food supply. Potatoes are like golden nuggets; the black flour made with wheat leftovers, food for pigs during peace time, is golden dust. The pigs themselves have long gone.

'What are your orders, Sir?'

The young officer has to ask. Giuseppe Zambito could not care less about his orders, the Germans or the two little islands of Lampedusa and Pantelleria, off the Sicilian coast, which have fallen into the hands of the Allies. In fact, if the heat allowed him to think long enough to have opinions, Lieutenant Zambito would be rather envious of the little islands' population: no more bombing, hunger (there are rumours that the British forces have an endless supply of chocolate), fear, uncertainty.

'This is not your war,' say the enemy's leaflets, thousands of them regularly dropped by the Allied air force.

No more war for Lampedusa and Pantelleria. Lucky bastards.

'What are your orders, Sir?' Lieutenant Zambito repeats, doggedly.

Colonnello Bastioni thinks of the intermittent phone line service; he goes through the supplies: a handful of rifles with little ammunition, five all-wheel-drives, a scared vet who has been roped in to act as a doctor in an emergency. 'I'm waiting to hear from Rome,' he says.

It is unlikely that Colonnello Bastioni will hear from Rome today, or even tomorrow. In fact, he may not even hear from his own direct superior. He is secretly beginning to doubt the Italian government's very existence, as he is more likely to take his orders from the German forces which will be sweeping the western Sicily countryside soon.

'Are they coming here, next, Sir?' The question, simple and deadly, hangs in the air between the two men.

Then, after a moment or so, 'Yes, Lieutenant,' Colonnello Bastioni says, reluctantly. 'I believe that they are. We don't know when or where they'll be landing, but it seems highly probable. The Allies control North Africa, and the southern islands of Lampedusa and Pantelleria are taken ... Sicily should be the next move. We're a strategically important target, their passport to Italy and Rome. Do you have any relatives in America, Zambito?' he suddenly asks.

'Why, yes, Sir. One of my mother's cousins went there to find work ten years ago and has done very well for himself.'

'The American and British troops are coming, Zambito. Palermo and all the other major Sicilian cities have been bombed relentlessly for days. I suggest you dust up your English, if you know any. '

'Only "hello", Sir.'

'That'll do, Lieutenant Zambito, that'll do.'

At that very moment, the same suffocating heat that is tormenting a handful of Sicilian troops is also, democratically, besieging the most beautiful houses in the middle of Palermo, a couple of hundred kilometres away.

Rosalia's mother, Signora Muggifalco, is getting ready. In a few hours, she will hold court in her *soggiorno*, morning room, as she calls it. The irony of having a morning room too hot to sit in until late afternoon has not escaped Signora Muggifalco, but her guests, ladies from nearby *palazzi,* have the same problem. They have solved it by usually sleeping until midday, which also takes care of the inconvenience of having to skip breakfast at times of severe food shortage.

Elena Muggifalco, as stunning now as she was at sixteen, when her future husband spotted her aristocratic beauty during the Sunday service at Palermo's cathedral, misses the murmurs of appreciation that always used to follow her appearance in public. As a married woman, she satisfies her taste for the limelight by throwing sophisticated parties and patronising literary circles. A decadent hostess to high-society bored but cultured women: the *Palermo-bene,* the well-to-do Palermo. Before the war broke out, Signora Muggifalco played this role at least once a week, usually on Friday nights. She can see no reason why she shouldn't continue to have these meetings, as they are the only real alternative to spending any time at all with her husband.

Whilst Rosalia's mother is looking forward to another evening of erudite group readings and sparkling conversation, Rosalia sets out on a treasure hunt. The sketch shown to Vincenzo Novara is only one of several that she has been drawing from memory, but it would certainly be more helpful to see a real horse or, failing that, to find the book on riding that she was given as a birthday present the year before: horse-riding is a hobby suitable for a real lady. It shouldn't be too difficult to find it; a large quantity of Palazzo de' Muggifalco's furniture, ornaments, pictures and valuable items has been discreetly disposed of by Elena Muggifalco, leaving the house relatively bare, though tidy.

Ever the practical woman, and incapable, like her husband, of the many daily sacrifices that the war has meant for the majority of the Sicilian population, Signora Muggifalco has sold the most hated items first, like their wedding presents, some silver belonging to her husband's family, and the moth-eaten, dusty carpets which used to line the stone floors of the grand reception rooms. The vases, tapestries with improbable hunting scenes and sensual beauties picnicking in luxuriating forests, and ancient paintings were sold next. Pieces of furniture soon followed, though they were partly replaced by much cheaper substitutions, to avoid Don Antonio's feared dawn of comprehension. Even a lawyer's household suffers wartime deprivations.

Like the Novaras, Don Antonio could have befriended the Fascists and the German officers posted in Sicily. Like his wealthy neighbours, he could have opened the doors of his home to the people in charge of Italy's destiny, holding a glass of rare champagne.

However, Don Antonio is too Sicilian to accept the Germans and yet too used to his old privileges to face the consequences of his rejection. Therefore, whilst he complains about missing his usual summer holiday in Mondello, a beach in western Sicily popular among the rich and powerful, his wife secretly disposes of the family heirlooms.

Rosalia reaches the attic, having searched the two lower floors, empty-handed. She climbs the dusty marble steps slowly, holding the edges of her summer dress, which is starting to feel a little bit tight around the armpits. As she emerges into the servants' quarters, once alive with half a dozen plump and jovial maids, she can hear Anna, the only housekeeper still in the Muggifalcos' service, making funny clucking noises and chattering to herself.

'Anna! What are you doing?' she calls out, intrigued, and temporarily forgetting the book she has been looking for.

As Rosalia enters the room, she can see Anna's back; the maid is bending forward, encased in her long black skirt, the cotton fabric stretching across her ample behind. The housekeeper's room at the top of the stairs, with plain but clean furniture, consists of a large space interrupted in the middle by a spiral staircase, the only access to the roof rafters. Every ten years, the male servants are allowed a rare peek at the women's quarters, as they need to use the spiral staircase to reach the roof, before re-insulating it with chicken feathers and sheep's wool. In these times of war, chicken feathers and sheep's wool may be in short supply, but male servants are even rarer, having either been drawn into the military forces or simply become too much of a financial liability to justify their services in any but the wealthiest of households.

Accordingly, Anna need not worry about her colleagues requiring access to the roof rafters, as she is the only member of staff left. Nobody has bothered to climb all the way to her room for a while. Used to complete privacy, she is startled by Rosalia's voice and turns around quickly, letting go of what looks like a large cream and red ball. The ball sprouts stumpy wings before landing on the wooden floors, and runs away cackling wildly.

'Signorina, you made me jump out of my skin!' Anna says, putting a plump hand on her generous, heaving bosom.

'What have you got there, Anna? Are those ... chickens?' asks Rosalia, surprised.

'Yes, Signorina. I keep them here to be safe,' Anna replies, cheeks slightly pink.

Taking a closer look, Rosalia sees half a dozen small hens cuddled up in the far corner of the room, where an old shoe rack sits in the middle of some matted straw. There are two bowls on the floor, one with seeds and mashed crumbs, the other full of water. A strong smell of wet bread, young poultry and not-so-young flesh hangs in the air.

Rosalia opens her mouth to speak, but Anna is quicker. 'I couldn't leave them outside. They would have been stolen. The German soldiers, they come, pull their necks, put them in their bags and *arrivederci*. These are good hens, all laying eggs almost every day, Signorina. I have a cockerel too, that one over there, who prefers to hide under my bed,' and she points at the modest single bed against the far wall, a small wooden crucifix and a rosary chain hanging over the bedstead.

Rosalia suddenly remembers the omelettes and eggs à-la-coque or scrambled which regularly find their way on to the Muggifalcos' table; the rare and much welcome roast chicken pieces, the provenance of which nobody has ever queried; the stale bits of brown bread sticking out of Anna's apron, destined to be dunked in water and given to the hens; and she understands.

'At times like this, it's important to have some nutritious food in one's stomach,' says the housekeeper, a serious expression on her usually jovial face.

'Does anybody know about them?' Rosalia asks.

'No, Signorina. I am in charge of this household's meals, and couldn't risk running out of food, could I? Your mother, God bless her always, wouldn't like me to share my room with the hens, but they don't bother me, honestly they don't.'

And my father wouldn't notice their presence even if they dropped an egg on his desk, thinks Rosalia, already smiling. 'Why, Anna, how good of you! Have you got any chicks?' She cranes her neck to try and spot any yellow little heads poking through the straw.

'We had the last young chicken for dinner two weeks ago, Signorina. I try and keep them for the eggs, mostly, because you can only eat a chicken once!'

'Quite right.' And Rosalia stands there, thinking hard. She knows that Vera, the painter she meets regularly in Vincenzo Novara's flat, would kill for a yolk or two to mix with the watered-down, anaemic colours she is forced to use. Even Vincenzo struggles to find that sort of prime material. 'I've been feeling rather weak, Anna. It's this heat, I'm sure, but my legs go all wobbly and my head's spinning. Would a fresh egg help?' she ventures.

'Here you are, Signorina Rosalia,' says Anna immediately, rubbing her sweaty hands against the sides of her skirt and moving towards the shoe rack. She bends over and stretches her hand down, searching inside the straw. Her fingers cup the smooth, oval surface of a solitary egg; the petrified hens are now looking at Anna and Rosalia sideways, blinking manically with their round, glassy eyes.

'Thank you,' Rosalia whispers, as if she didn't want to startle the egg. 'I came to ask you whether you've seen my horse riding manual anywhere,' she continues, suddenly remembering why she is there. 'It used to be kept in the tall bookcase in the hall, together with my childhood books, propped against my mother's bronze figurine of a fisherman and his catch,' she adds.

Anna shakes her head slowly, trying to remember the tall bookcase, or indeed the bronze figurine, both of them now gone from the bare hall.

'Don't worry, I'll keep looking for it,' Rosalia says cheerfully, a broad smile on her lips. If she knew that this is the last time she will see Anna alive, she might say something; perhaps she would hug her, or thank her for all the ingenuity, and omelettes, which have meant she and her parents have never gone hungry. Instead, she leaves Anna to her chickens, stuffy room and matted straw without saying anything at all. She comes down the stairs carefully, clutching her precious egg, smaller than she ever thought possible but hard and real in her hand, still encrusted with the hen's effort.

She briefly considers continuing her quest for the horse riding manual, but the excitement of finding a real egg takes priority. On the spur of the moment, Rosalia decides to make the short walk to Palazzo Novara to deliver the amazing gift to her friend Vera, who at eighteen can barely read her own name but manages to paint the most amazing pictures. When she runs out of colours, Vera uses pencils and even her own bare hands, smudging the lead across the paper with the instinctive bravura of the talented.

Yes, Rosalia thinks, I'll pay Vincenzo a quick visit and leave my egg there, a little surprise for Vera.

On her way out, Rosalia pauses in her room, to try and find a suitable container for the delicate egg. All around are ornaments of varying age, each connected to a particular moment in her life; like the wooden boat that her father made for her when she was five, a scratch of red paint on the hull; the white-faced china doll, curly brown hair sticking out from under her bonnet, a present received when she had a nasty bout of flu; a porcelain jug and bowl sitting on the marble cabinet, given to Rosalia by her grandmother and religiously used every day. There is still some soapy water in the bowl from that morning's ablutions. Rosalia dabs a towel in it, and wipes her face and neck. Though she has no romantic interest in Vincenzo who, at twenty-seven, is over ten years older than her, she is woman enough to want to look pretty when she visits him. She admires his efforts to help those who need his support. There is also something else, perhaps a vague awareness of the way he looks at her when she is concentrating on working her clay. Vincenzo, whose illness imposes deformity on his life, loves beauty in every form or shape, and Rosalia instinctively knows that his appreciation of it extends to more than sculptures and paintings.

Next, she searches her drawers for a box for the egg. The maple chest of drawers in her room contains all the secrets that a girl of Rosalia's age can possibly have collected. In particular, her drawing paper, pencils, clay tools and half-used bags of powdered clay are neatly hidden in every drawer, under layers of clean linen and a few generations of lavender sachets. Her search fruitless, she looks around, biting her bottom lip as usual. Her eyes fall on a pair of stockings lying on the floor, fished out from the drawer earlier according to her mother's instructions ('Rosalia, ladies wear stockings in all seasons, it's the fashion') and discarded a few minutes later because of the unbearable heat.

'Ah! That'll do,' she says to herself. Having placed the egg in the first stocking, pushing it all the way to the toe end, she uses the second as an outer layer. With what looks like an old-fashioned sling-and-ball carefully tucked away in her pocket, Rosalia is ready to leave the house.

It is almost four o'clock on one of the hottest afternoons of the summer. Signora Muggifalco is sitting by a window in her bedroom upstairs, looking out and fanning herself, thinking of the intelligent conversation she will have with her friends later. Signora Muggifalco has a little crucifix on the golden chain nestling inside the exquisite dip in her throat. She fidgets with the pendant endlessly. Does she hear her daughter's dress whispering past her door?

Does Don Antonio spot Rosalia's black hair, tied up in a white ribbon, bobbing on her shoulders as she lightly skips down the stairs?

Rosalia reaches the ground floor, and an old lady who seems to have materialised out of nowhere emerges from the opposite shadowy corner of the courtyard, croaking 'Shoo, shoo, Rosa of my heart,' and waves both hands in front of her, as if trying to get rid of some invisible flies.

Rosalia, taken by surprise, stops. '*Nonnina*, dear Grandma, what are you doing here? It's too hot for you! Let me help you back to your room,' she cries, moving towards the figure in black.

'No, no, go away!' hisses the old woman, tugging at the black handkerchief tied upon her head that covers her white hair completely. She is not really hissing, of course, only talking through toothless gums. This is Signora Muggifalco senior, Don Antonio's formidable mother. Rosalia is her only and much beloved granddaughter.

The girl stops, unsure. Her grandmother's advanced age warrants some eccentric behaviour, certainly, but there is something about the old woman's spirited mood that indicates her determination to see Rosalia out of the house. 'Is anything the matter, *nonnina?*' she ventures again, gently, standing at the bottom of the staircase.

'Go away! *U' focu 'nta panza*, fire in the belly, Satan, demons and evils, shoo!' And with that, Signora Muggifalco senior positively pounces towards her worried granddaughter.

With a little squeal, Rosalia instinctively puts her hand in the pocket of her summer dress, to cocoon the egg, runs across the courtyard and squeezes through the patio doors. Without looking behind her, she lets herself out of the house.

In the late afternoon sunlight, slow carts, rusty bikes and rare groups of young people populate Palermo's old stone streets, now turning a darker shade of orange. There are girls with white hair bands and boys proud to show off the rare and immensely desirable cigarette stub. They talk quietly among themselves, of past and future meals and dances, deliberately ignoring the present. Back home, their older brothers' photographs, in military cap and official uniform, smile thinly from the mantelpiece.

Rosalia walks fast, eyes down on the pavement, the little egg heavy in her pocket. Her adolescent conscience sees greedy, hungry eyes everywhere, ready to spot her little secret; that single egg is meant to nourish rather than blend colours.

Vincenzo Novara's house appears suddenly, with its neo-Classical marble columns and wrought-iron balconies. The secret tunnel's bushes yield softly to Rosalia's dress. A knock on the familiar door, today as good a day as many others before. Vincenzo's familiar face in the crack that opens. Her smile, as usual. The habitual greeting, the same smells.

As Rosalia is standing in front of the basement door, beaming with expectation, her hand round the surprise egg, a distant noise, like a swarm of angry wasps, thrusts its way into her ears, and reaches her brain a couple of seconds later.

'Quick, get in,' urges Vincenzo, grabbing her bare arm and pulling her in.

A daytime raid, and no warning sirens, Rosalia thinks, puzzled and confused.

'Follow me,' Vincenzo says, and he is already hobbling across the large sitting room, as quickly as his illness will allow. When she hesitates, his hand shoots out to take hers, and he pulls her along towards a little door on the opposite wall.

The buzzing noise grows into a deep rumble. If they looked out of the windows, they would see an unusually compact formation of Wellington bombers scratching the cloudless sky above the city, so low that their crew must be able to see their aircraft's shadow running along the suddenly deserted streets of Palermo.

There is no immediate reaction from the sleepy, surprised Sicilian defence quarters around the city harbour. The forty-three British planes are flying lower than Sicilian radar would be able to pick up, though they are easily spotted in the bright daylight.

When the hissing noises start, both Rosalia and Vincenzo feel as if time will stop; as if between releasing the bombs and their hitting the target an invisible hand can take hold of 100,000 pounds of explosives and suspend the cargo in the air. It is that feeling which makes them hesitate at the door to the basement's cellar, long enough to hear the first bomb load hit the city, not too far away from the Novaras' house.

Suddenly, light seems no longer to flood into the room; it is replaced by the deafening noise coming from what Vincenzo's father, by now already in his purpose-built bunker with his wife and dog, knows to be the Wellingtons' Bristol Pegasus engines.

Vincenzo virtually pushes Rosalia down the damp, dark stairs that lead to one of the cellars. A separate door in the main kitchens leads to it too, so the two young people join a small group of scared servants, huddled under a single bare light-bulb.

There they stand or sit on a few empty barrels, in silence, waiting, listening. Most of the girls, still in their strappy summer dresses under greying aprons, are shivering from the cold, but unaware of it. 'Who's bombing us this time?' asks one of the young maids, her teeth chattering loudly in the echoing vaults of the cellar.

'The Allies, my dear. The Allies,' sighs Vincenzo, checking his wristwatch. 'The Brits and their stupid colonies, their overseas mates, all ready to jump on pathetic planes and dump their bombs here, where the most dangerous being you'll ever see is a hungry peasant.'

'The radio said the Germans were sending aircraft and manpower to the west of Sicily yesterday,' ventures the old butler, kicking a lone cork around on the dusty floor.

'Dream on!' Vincenzo says, heatedly. 'We're exposed and alone! The Germans think the invasion will come from North Africa, so they're concentrating the bulk of their forces in the south. They may be right, but we're doomed.'

Instinctively, the servants draw closer to each other. Although nobody would dare admit it in front of the young master, whose family regularly dines with the Germans, they all secretly hope for the tall, handsome American marines to come and rescue them.

Rosalia says nothing, still holding the egg inside its home-made sling. As the engines' roar, muffled by the thick walls of the Novaras' beautiful house, is drowned by the explosions, she thinks of her grandmother's words: '*focu 'nta panza,* fire in the belly!' and wonders how the old lady knew.

Chapter Three
NO TEARS

Vincenzo wraps a reassuring arm around Rosalia's shoulders. They are both sitting on a wrought-iron rose climber, complete with lovers' seat, which has been left in the cellar since the last major overhaul of Signora Novara's garden, a couple of years earlier.

Twice, the bombs dropped on Palermo have been so close that the ceiling of the cellar has shaken. Outside, the war's sickening monologue: the noise of a blast blending into its own eruption and immediately followed by another hiss, another blast, unconnected, irrational.

'Do they really hate us that much?' whispers Rosalia, a hand inside her pocket, toying with the egg she has not yet mentioned. 'Enough to want to kill us like ants?'

'Sweetie, sweetie. Don't worry about this,' Vincenzo's voice is soothing, his arm rocking Rosalia's shoulders from side to side. 'Don't let your little head worry about men's arguments. The strongest will win.'

'My father, my family ...' Rosalia starts, too upset to finish the sentence.

'They'll be all right, sweetie. You do you have a shelter, don't you?'

'The communal one is just fifty metres away. But they prefer to hide under the main staircase. Our cellar got flooded when the well was damaged at the beginning of this year. The pipes froze and cracked during that very cold week, remember?'

Vincenzo nods, pretending to remember. The central heating in the Novaras' palazzo had been on continuously throughout the winter, and it is difficult to single out a particularly cold week when one has not felt the cold at all. Even the basement had been equipped with three *stufette*, the kind of small stove which gives out fierce heat from two tungsten bars, covered by a safety metallic net. Many a time Rosalia, visiting Vincenzo's

19

flat, has sat in front of one of those, rubbing her hands together, too cold to mould clay.

'Was your family indoors?' Vincenzo asks, thinking of his own mother and father and wondering whether they are all right.

'Yes. When I left, my father was in his study as usual, and my mother was in her room upstairs. The same for Anna, our housekeeper, but *Nonna*, well, she was in the courtyard, shouting at me. She wanted me to leave the house. It was odd. Like ...'

'Old people never stop amazing me. She probably had a feeling that something was up. You'll see, she'll have dragged everybody out of the house before the raid started.' Vincenzo doesn't know whether he means it.

Finally, as suddenly as it began, the air raid is over. The cellar falls into sudden silence. The maids look at each other and then at Vincenzo, as if expecting him to decide what to do. The cellar's dampness has seeped into his joints and limbs, already sore and swollen from his disease. He rises from his seat and stretches carefully. 'Come on, let's go out. I'm pretty sure that the old house is still in one piece, but I must look for my folks and make sure they are too,' he says with a rueful smile.

A little reluctantly, everybody gets up and aims for the servants' stairs. They whisper to each other, as though raising their voices might result in the bombers coming back.

'Come with me, Rosalia,' says Vincenzo, holding his hand out. 'I'll walk you home.'

'Don't worry,' she replies, pulling her summer dress down and smoothing out the creases. The little bulge in her pocket is still there, but she doesn't notice it. 'You look for your mother and father. I'll be all right.' Her eyes are cast down, lips pursed. She is sorry about refusing his offer, but she must go back to her family, and quickly. He cannot run fast and would slow her down.

Vincenzo seems to hesitate a second or so. 'Very well. You know where to find me if you need me. By the way,' he adds, as if only just remembering, 'Was there a particular reason why you came earlier? The meeting's tomorrow.'

'Ah, that. Yes. I have something for Vera. Look.' And Rosalia takes the egg out and puts it in Vincenzo's hand. 'She can mix her own egg-based colours now, at least for a little while.'

Before Vincenzo can take the egg out of the stockings, or say anything, she has left the room, happy not to worry about the egg's safety any more and keen to run as fast as her legs, still a little stiff, will carry her.

A couple of hours before, Rosalia had left the pleasant, albeit hot summer afternoon, with its orange shades of light playing on the stone streets: she emerges from Vincenzo's basement door expecting the same warm air and a slightly softer light, given the later hour of the day. The first thing she notices is the amount of dust in the air – which is heavy and suffocating – and the sickly grey hue that seems to tinge all things, including the air itself. She has been through a raid before, of course, but

20

they have tended to be further afield, hitting the outskirts of Palermo rather than targeting the older part of the city. There have been other occasions, when the bombing has been much closer to her home, but they have only lasted a short time. On those occasions, whilst the Muggifalcos and their neighbours had been hiding in the communal shelter, some of the patrician houses built of porous limestone had merely crumbled with silent dignity, haughtily resigned to die without much fuss. By the time Palermo's shell-shocked aristocrats of old had crawled out of their refuges, some carrying their jewels in wooden boxes, the topography of the city might have been changed forever, but discreetly. Some house fronts would still stand, defining the old streets, but there would be gutted rooms behind locked front doors.

Today's wreckage and ruin is on a different scale altogether, affecting everything around her, including the sunset itself. Within seconds, her light summer dress is caked with a combination of sweat and the minute debris still suspended in the air. Rosalia finds herself on the main street, and can't recall how and when she has lost one of her shoes.

As she starts running, coughing and keeping her hands over her mouth and nose to stop the dust getting in, part of her thinks of her mother's advice about real ladies wearing stockings even in the summer. 'Caro papá, are you all right? Is everybody safe and sound? Would stockings have protected my feet from this rubble? Have the bombers gone now?' More running, gasping for air. It's this way, isn't it? No, it's the next turn. Where's the road? Rosalia stops, in order to give her heart a chance to slow down and her thoughts a chance to disentangle. With horror, she realises that her confusion over which way to go back is because the streets and the buildings themselves are unrecognisable. Entire quarters have been erased from the map. Side streets don't exist any more, and are covered by ruins; bricks, stones and contents merged in the preternatural silence.

The silence, of course, is only in Rosalia's head. For among the crackling of several huge fires engulfing the destroyed buildings, the pitiful howling of survivors dragging lifeless bodies of relatives and friends from the ruins, the anguished moaning of those still trapped, it will take Rosalia several minutes to realise that she is accompanied by a screeching, unnerving, high-pitched noise. It will take her even longer to understand that the noise comes from her. A long continuous scream, only occasionally interrupted by her forced inhaling of the foul air.

Rosalia's screaming joins the others', and races ahead: beyond the broken pavement, the occasional pieces of white paper floating in the air and broken glass still held together by undamaged window frames, that screaming beats Rosalia's mind to its final destination. There, in front of what was once Palazzo de' Muggifalco, her screaming stops and waits for her mind to catch up.

The stone steps that Rosalia used to come bumping down are intact, and so is the front door of her family home; but except for two stumps of wall, towards the rear of the house, the entire ground floor is gone: the inner courtyard, no longer protected by the three front reception rooms, merges with the street outside. Rubble with rubble, fragments of antique stone mixing with the common road slabs. Rosalia searches the scene in front of her.

A wisp of green emerges at an odd angle from the pile of shapeless ruins. Through the air thick with dust, she recognises the top of the palm tree that used to grace the courtyard. Instinctively, her eyes go up to her father's study, its window and balcony; the upper landing's windows; the second floor, the attic, the roof. Beyond the stumps still supporting part of the upper floors, there is a gaping hole, the clear emptiness of which stuns her. From where she stands, she can see the bright colours of the majolica ceramic tiles that once covered the main bedrooms' floors. Now that her eyes are more accustomed to the dirty light of a cruel sunset, she can see her father's books, scattered and forlorn, some still on the shelves of an upturned bookcase.

'*Papá! Papá!*' she cries, stumbling over the steps, and running across the empty space that was once the inner hall. '*Mamma! Aiuto!* Anybody, help me! *Mamma!*' she calls, clambering over the stuccoed ceilings that have joined the broken floors. Within seconds, Rosalia's fingernails are torn and bleeding; she flings stone, debris and pieces of crockery behind her, digging for a few minutes here, turning to another spot over there, where she thinks she last saw her grandmother. Everywhere, in the heat of fires still burning, other buildings quickly turn into blackened heaps of nothing. Around her, quartered and tattered pages of her father's books float like ghosts rising from the body of Don Antonio Muggifalco's well stocked library. On her knees, Rosalia scrapes and scoops, punches the ground and starts again somewhere else, deranged and maddened with grief. Under her right knee, something softer than the broken pieces of the marble banister scattered all around: yet another book, this one still shut, undamaged.

She picks it up, and turns it over: it is her Horse Riding Manual for Ladies, the book she had been looking for. It must have been sitting in her father's library all along. Pointlessly, she dusts it off and puts it in her pocket, without thinking. '*Papá,*' she whispers, looking around.

Suddenly, two hands grab her shoulders, a move that turns into a hug before Rosalia has a chance to turn. 'Sweetheart, *mia cara,* come away from here. That portion of the ceiling is about to collapse.' A familiar voice, with an urgency that is not familiar at all. Vincenzo is standing behind her, holding the girl whose eyes are still dry. 'Come away, Rosalia. It's dangerous to stay here. Let me help you.' A hand stretches out, as in other, happier, times.

'I must find my parents, my *nonna* and Anna. I must find everybody,' Rosalia says, and she is calm now, sitting on the floor, one shoe still on. The other foot, exposed to the fire and debris, is black and swollen.

'I know, I know, and I'll help you, *tesoro,* my darling, but now is not the time. They may not be here at all. Perhaps they managed to make their way to the bunker and are still there, worrying about you. Come away.' Vincenzo detects a glimpse of hope on her face and a little hesitation. Then her body relaxes and slumps forward. Luckily for him, she is slim and petite, and he does not waver under her weight.

'My poor girl. You'll be all right with me,' he whispers into her matted hair, and he half-carries, half-drags her down the steps and onto the road again. Her body is fragile and bony, yet he feels the wonder of those hips, the smooth curve of her waist under his fingers, her adolescent breasts hard against his chest. Vincenzo tries to push away images that have been tormenting him since Rosalia had grown her sensual mouth and eyes, almost overnight.

Around them, Palermo is populated by the bodiless voices of those still under the rubble, crying out in pain and for help. Scared and lone volunteers respond by shouting questions, searching and digging.

'We're going to look for your family at the Quattro Canti square, where many people are still gathered. If they're not there we'll look elsewhere. Do you know of any neighbours who'd have had them during a raid? What about the Finazzos?' Vincenzo asks, his eyes darting everywhere. Rosalia has started to limp on her good foot, and every step is agony for both of them.

'The Finazzos fled to their mountain villa last week,' she says, feebly. 'They asked my father whether we wanted to go with them, but he had business to deal with over here and refused. Anyway, my mother wouldn't have liked to go because Signora Finazzo is half-German.'

Despite the circumstances, Vincenzo smiles weakly: Rosalia has very little sense of their political position and this war in general. On another occasion, he may have chided her gently, reminding her of Italy's loyalty to its German friends. Today, he merely looks around at the destruction, and mutters something about hell, the British air force and innocent civilians.

Quattro Canti is heaving with people. Miraculously untouched by the heavy attacks, it is a natural meeting point because of its central position in the city. Those who have spent the last few hours underground have gone back to their homes, if the bricks are still there, to grab the radio. There is a hunger for details, a desperate need to know which areas have been targeted by the bombers, a collective worry about the absent and the far away.

Before Vincenzo and Rosalia reach the square, they have gathered enough information to know that the quarters of Palazzo de' Muggifalco and its neighbouring buildings have been the most severely hit, because of their relative proximity to the harbour: the *Marina Italiana,* the Italian Navy posted in Palermo and anchored there, has been completely destroyed. The harbour itself miraculously shows little damage, with the north docks – jutting out and embracing the bay – largely unspoilt.

The shock electrifies the civilian population and hearsay rides high above sense: 'They're organising a human chain to bring water to the burning buildings, to kill the fire, or it may travel abreast of the *vento di mare*, the sea breeze, and grow unmanageable.'

'The Italian Navy was bought off! They knew the British were coming, but gave no warning.'

'The Germans say there'll be hell to pay.'

'The boats are all alight in the water; the water itself is burning!' People make the sign of the cross several times.

'The devil is here, the devil is responsible.'

Whispers rise and fall within the crowd. Some green and grey uniforms watch over the gathering. The soldiers speak to each other in a foreign language, fidgeting with their rifles. Confusion and perplexity on their young faces are half-hidden under the hard helmets.

Rosalia is intent on searching among the anonymous faces, all sharing the same look of grief, horror and worry. A couple of times she spots a black foulard. Perhaps it will have her grandmother's wrinkles under it – but no, it is someone else's. There, a beautiful face, perhaps her mother's proud features ... no, not Signora Muggifalco at all.

She smells the many bodies, and the collective indignity. 'I want to go back home, Vincenzo,' she says, and the words come out naturally, as if home were still there to go to.

'Wait,' he says, softly. 'There are more people coming out from their shelters. Keep looking. I'm not leaving you.'

'They're not here. They're not here,' she replies, each time louder and more desperate. 'Why don't you stay behind? I'll go back to the house to keep looking. When you arrived I hadn't had the time to check everywhere, and the first floor is still ... still ...' The words die on her lips. The first floor is still what, exactly? Half-destroyed or half-standing? If they are still there, why did they not answer her when she called their names?

'Let me take you to my house, Rosalia *mia*,' Vincenzo says, talking this time a little more sternly. 'My parents will be very happy to look after you, and I'll keep searching for yours. This isn't a good place for a lady to wander about on her own. Not at the moment. And you need some rest.'

Rosalia shakes her head. 'I must find my family. My father can't move very fast because of his gout, so he wouldn't have been able to leave the house when the bombing started. And my mother was upstairs when I left, so there's a chance she may be trapped in one of the rooms at the back of the house. And Anna was in the attic, but the attic ... Is the attic still there? I'm sure it is.' She gets up from where she has been sitting, in the middle of the dusty road, her dress the colour of the road itself. The blood from broken fingernails and cuts on her legs has congealed into dark patches. When she tries to stand up on both feet, her knees buckle.

'Let's walk back towards my house, then,' Vincenzo suggests. 'On the way we can stop and have another look at yours. Soon this place will be full of medical staff and jeeps. They may bring more wounded people here. The evening's drawing in. I can't let you spend the night without a roof over your head. What kind of friend would I be if I did?'

So they limp back, Vincenzo aching in his sick limbs, still supporting the girl who refuses to accept. They don't yet know that the main communal shelter, made of wooden planks and not built underground, has been hit by two explosions and destroyed almost completely. Survivors will open the wooden doors, check inside, see the mountain of debris dotted by the occasional colourful piece of fabric, listen to the silence and bolt the doors, never to open them again. A mass grave.

'When this war is over, I'll help you open a gallery. You'll become a famous artist and go to Rome to meet the Pope,' Vincenzo says. 'Rosalia Muggifalco, the Sicilian sculptress.' And he makes a wide, panel-like gesture with his right hand, signifying the newspapers' headlines. The other hand is still supporting Rosalia under her arm. His hand's vicinity to her breast takes his breath away.

They approach the Muggifalcos' palazzo, this time from the north side of the main street, and Rosalia notices that the back walls, always affected by rising damp because of their proximity to the humid soil of the little back garden, are still standing, partially supporting the roof and the upper terrace with its marble banister. The top terrace, with its rectangular shape, white ceramic tiles and white marble banister, would have stood out from above.

Rosalia thinks of the harbour, a dark blue marina sprinkled with boats, surrounded by the cream-coloured stones from inner Sicily's quarries. The easiest of targets. 'I can understand them sinking our boats, but why the houses? We're innocent civilians!' She would like to shout, but her lips won't move.

Around them, people walk in the slow motion of dreams, taking in the individual tragedies, pulling strangers from under collapsed staircases and dusting them off as if they had taken an inconsequential tumble.

As Vincenzo and Rosalia climb up the mound where most of her house used to be, they come face to face with the massive oak dresser which used to guard the dining room; it stands, surrounded by splintered pieces of wood and an upturned table.

On the floor above, Vincenzo can still see, through a torn partition wall, the old-fashioned enamel bathtub and the chain from a toilet cistern, hanging above an empty space. Against his will, his mind conjures up images of Rosalia taking an evening bath, her hands moist with soap to soak the hardened bits of clay stuck to them; her hair loosely pinned on the top of her head. He looks down to negotiate the safest path over the debris and thinks of a long, exquisite neck glistening with water.

A little shred of colour catches his attention. Once it might have been yellow, though it's hard to tell now. Vincenzo crouches down to have a better look, and stretches his hand out. It is a piece of fabric, soft among the stones, silk perhaps. He pulls it out, and a grey hand obediently follows.

'*Papá,*' says a little voice behind him. '*Papá.*'
'Rosalia,' Vincenzo starts, not quite sure, protesting when he tries to get up

quickly, wanting to take her as far as possible from the place. She must not see.

'Don't touch me. Don't. Let me be. I want to get him out of there', she whispers, pushing him away gently.

Chapter Four
THE LANDING

Bastardi.' The insult is muttered under the man's breath.

In the days after the worst air raid Palermo's inner boroughs have experienced so far, the shocked civilians have had to cope with the loss of either their home or relatives, or both. Confusion is borne out of the usual darkness in which the Sicilians are kept: both the national and local press are wary of disseminating information about enemy intelligence, and the German presence keeps a tight lid on the population's real feelings. Mussolini despises panic almost as much as southern Italy. To warn Sicily publicly about its valuable geographical position and its intrinsic worth to the British and American forces would backfire, stirring up Sicilian pockets of ideology against the central power. Instead, *Il Duce* has expressed surprise at the capitulation of Lampedusa and Pantelleria, little islands more concerned with the quantity of fish caught daily than the war. When Palermo is hit this badly, Mussolini asks whether the dignity of the local air force and navy is still intact.

In the meantime, Palermo, usually stretching with Arabic languidness, throbs like a wounded limb. Twenty hours after the raid, both Italian and German troops have finally arrived from nearby posts to boost the local forces. The former mourn the disaster; the latter set about gathering intelligence from the locals, making sure that the tired Italian military does not buckle under the Allies' attacks. Intelligence is not the only asset that needs gathering: food supplies need constant replenishing, and that's why the Germans pay regular visits to the civilians.

'*Bastardi Tedeschi*,' the man repeats, qualifying the insult; he kicks the floppy nylon sacks strewn on the floor as he steals a look at his bare larder. Only a few minutes earlier, the little cupboard had stored some brown rice, *sale marino*, crude salt from the western coast, salami, a leg of pork and a few packets of cheap but rare dried pasta. The sacks had contained black potatoes, his family's supply.

A father of four, the little Italian man watches with increasing resentment the feverish military activity taking place outside. The streets are teeming with khaki uniforms. 'God only knows what they say,' he seethes, mocking the guttural sounds made by the German soldiers who are now leaving his house, rucksacks full of his family's food. One of them looks at him, his face young and hard. The Italian man pretends to clear his throat and spits sideways on the pavement. He catches sight of Rosalia, walking past. As she passes them, the young German soldier with a hard face also notices her, and his pace slows down as he stares. The others laugh meanly, teasing him.

Rosalia is heading for the ruins of Palazzo de' Muggifalco. For the past twenty-four hours she has dug out the bodies of her mother and father, gently dusting debris off their clothes and hair; her mother and Anna, the maid, were the most difficult to find and get to, buried under two metres of rubble. She and Vincenzo have dragged the bodies out of the collapsed building and onto a wheelbarrow, covered with a large blanket provided by Vincenzo's mother. Rosalia has taken them, one by one, to the only holy place she can think of: Palermo's cathedral. Once sumptuous and elegant, the cathedral has been turned into a repository of dead bodies and the living's grief. The Muggifalco couple, estranged in life, find themselves united in death in the place where they took their matrimonial vows.

Anna's black skirt and top, now white with dust, hide underneath the sheets, but her thick ankles stick out, feet blackened and blistered.

On her way back from the cathedral, Rosalia fleetingly wonders about the fate of the chickens. Soon, her thoughts turn back to her grandmother. *'Dove sei, Nonna?'* Despite her best efforts, *Nonna* Muggifalco has eluded her; the old lady's frail body could be anywhere, if she has not been disintegrated by the force of the blast. Rosalia does not know but will keep looking.

The sunset brings with it a little respite from both light and heat. Rosalia calculates that she has a few hours' work before the night sets in. In her search for *Nonna*, she has come across many objects that have survived: two table lamps, the kitchen table, framed pictures, the odd shoe. Methodically, she has put them on one side, meaning to store them in the two rooms at the back that have withstood the bombing. Her sore foot and bleeding knees afford enough pain to keep Rosalia focused on her task, but she is completely unaware of anything else around her, apart from the need to find her grandmother.

A little flash of white and blue amongst the grey mass: the bowl and jug from her bedroom, miraculously undamaged, bar two tiny spidery hairlines on the bowl itself. Rosalia picks up the crockery set and walks towards the back of the ruins, tripping a couple of times. A rickety door, still hinged to its frame, opens into the utility room where Anna used to do the laundry. The room is intact. The wooden board on which Anna pummelled and wrung out the washing is still sitting on the butler's sink. Rosalia turns on the tap: a trickle of water comes out, and she quickly collects it into the jug. She does not hear the steps behind her, or the jiggling noise of his backpack's straps clunking together. When he touches her shoulder, she turns around with a little smile, expecting to see Anna or her father. For a fraction of a second, Rosalia is back home and all is well.

The German's crew-cut is rough and spiky under her fingers, his cheekbones high and hard as she instinctively lifts her arms to push him away. The soldier does not budge. With one hand he slaps her hard across the face, making her fall backwards onto the utility room's floor, whilst with the other he shakes off the backpack.

Neither of them utters a sound. Rosalia does not have the time to gather her thoughts or her limbs before he is on top of her. The coarse material of his uniform and the buckle of his belt are all her body is aware of, the man as faceless and anonymous as he feels. He grabs her hair and pulls it hard backwards, determined to control her body if he cannot control her will. Rosalia's head hits the floor hard, and he senses her slacken under his weight. Eager hands crawl up her dress, up her bare legs, dirty fingers into her cotton panties, too big for her. He doesn't feel the girl's soft pubic hair or the smooth flat stomach. He has no time for exploring. One arm contains Rosalia's shoulders and chest, the other hand travels to his trousers, undoing the belt and the zip. In her state of half-consciousness, Rosalia feels his hardness through the fabric, then the shock of skin against skin, as her legs are forced open by a knee thrusting upwards. A soft ripping sound, her panties torn on one side and pushed down around an ankle. He smells of earth and gunpowder, of animal hunger and cigarettes. Rosalia looks into his light blue eyes, so close to hers, and sees no soul at all.

Suddenly, the German soldier's eyes become alive for a fraction of a second. They lock on to Rosalia's in a mixture of surprise and childish irritation. She feels his grip relax, his body between her legs jerk. A warm, wet feeling spreads out on her, her thighs, her tummy, her naked sex.

Oh my God, so this is it. This is what it is supposed to feel like ... and then I die, she thinks, blinking quickly, suddenly sad and oddly lonely.

'Bastardo tedesco.' Another face, creased by many years of Sicilian sun and hearty laughter, leans above her, behind the German's head buried on her chest. 'Are you all right? I got him in time, didn't I? He hasn't hurt you?'

Signor Radici cannot bring himself to ask the real, important question to the young girl still lying under the dead soldier. Shaking with a rage accumulated over the last few months, he tries to recover his kitchen knife from the back of the German soldier. 'I have killed this man, but if you are still intact then it will be worth burning in hell.' He grits his teeth and pulls and twists, anchoring his slim frame by pinning a booted foot against the dead man's back. With a final effort the blade comes out, and the German's body rolls over to one side. Rosalia scrambles to her knees, pulling her summer dress down on her bruised legs. It is soaked with a large dark patch, from armpits down to the hem.

Signor Radici hisses with relief. 'The bastard pissed himself. Come, Signorina. Let me help you up.' A knotty hand, weathered and stringy, takes Rosalia's and pulls her to her feet. It is still shaking and is dotted with brown patches. The fingernails are dirty and long. 'I saw you, and then him following you. What's your name, young lady?' he asks, gently.

'Rosalia.'

'Some water will make you feel better, Rosalia.'

The jug is still in the sink. Signor Radici picks it up and passes it to the girl, helping her lift it to her lips.

More steps on the rubble, rushed. 'What's going on here?' There is alarm in Vincenzo's strangulated voice, and something else too. Desperation, perhaps, or is it fear? Instinctively, Rosalia and the man huddle together, stepping in front of the dead soldier. 'The Germans are coming this way! Is he dead? Are you all right? Never mind, they'll see him. We're screwed! They'll execute us all on the spot.'

Rosalia holds the older man's hand tighter. 'This man tried to save me. The German ...'

'We don't have time, no time at all. You,' Vincenzo says to Signor Radici, who has not uttered a sound but is now shaking, 'come with me. We'll stand outside pretending we're waiting for our turn, or just checking that nobody's disturbing them.' He points at the dead body, the large patch of dark blood on his back already staining the dust. 'Rosalia, lie on the floor, but sideways, and pull him on top of you. Quick, you've got no choice. Position him so that they can see his face but not his back, like that.'

With some effort, Vincenzo drags the body by his armpits, and drops him unceremoniously onto Rosalia. He opens her legs, and pulls one up to a right angle, to support the dead weight of the man. The head he cradles between Rosalia's face and her shoulder, ignoring her revulsion. 'Yank your dress up all the way to your hips,' he urges. 'Moan. Shut your eyes if you have to, and move him from side to side. Rock him with your legs. Do it, Rosalia, or we're all dead!'

With that, he pulls Signor Radici with him, walking back to the front. Rosalia can hear her breath blowing hot into the dead man's blond crop. She moves away a little, and his arm flops onto the floor. There is no time. Rosalia lifts it up, pulling by the man's shirt, and puts the arm around her free shoulder. She grits her teeth to stop herself from gagging.

The German ground personnel coming towards Palazzo de' Muggifalco have just received orders to head for the harbour as fast as they can. Having followed their colleague from a distance, they are not quite sure behind which broken façade he has disappeared, chasing after that dirty little Italian girl. They had hoped to join in the fun after he finishes but orders are orders, and they resign to going back, calling his name.

'Heil Hitler!' says Vincenzo, loud and clear to Rosalia's ears, on seeing the group approaching. 'If you're looking for your friend, he's entertaining a young girl, and wants some privacy. We're just waiting and making sure that they're not disturbed.' An airy note of sarcasm, lost on the Germans.

One of them elbows the youngest of the group, motioning him to move forward and check things out. Vincenzo and Signor Radici look on as the soldier scrambles over the ruins and disappears into the back rooms. The rest wait in the street, guns at the ready, black boots dusty but properly buckled at the calves.

A couple of long seconds later, the young German re-emerges, a little flustered. A brief exchange with his colleagues.

'Tell him to come to the base at the harbour as soon as he's done. We may be under attack soon,' the older German soldier says to Vincenzo. A hard look, the strong jaw twitching.

Vincenzo holds his stare. 'Will do!' he says, jutting his arm forward again.

The German does the same. The group breaks into a jog, swishing their guns in front of them. Vincenzo and the old man wait until they can no longer see their uniforms. Only then do they go back to Rosalia and her *danse macabre*.

She is still lying on the floor, rocking her hips and her dead companion, a silent tear streaking her dirty face.

'Sweetie, Rosalia dearest,' says Vincenzo, kneeling by her side. 'It's over. You can stop now. Look at me, Rosalia. They've gone, and won't come back. The Allies are coming. They landed near Gela this morning, and it won't take them long to get here.'

Rosalia rocks the man and stares into the distance.

'Sweetie, it's over,' Vincenzo repeats. He rolls the dead man over to one side, and strokes her face and her hair, pulling the dress's straps up. 'I pity our soldiers,' he mutters. 'Damned if they fight and damned if they don't.'

'Thank you,' he says to Signor Radici, who is watching them, hands in his pockets.

'*Di niente*, don't mention it,' the old man replies, kicking a stone. 'They raided my cupboard this morning. I have four children. Actually, two now. The other two were executed by the Germans last month for desertion. My boys had heard that their mum was ill and wanted to come back to Palermo to see her one last time. They died before she did.'

'What will happen to me? And to you?' Rosalia talks dreamily, as if she has just realised that Vincenzo is sitting next to her. She wipes her eyes with the back of her hand, careful not to touch anything at all with the palm, which she has used to hold the German's chin against hers. She can almost feel the imprint of dead flesh on it.

'Don't worry. We'll be fine. My mother and I have decided to take a little holiday and go to our countryside house in Casteldaccia for a while. We'll stay there long enough to weather the invasion. My father will stay put, as the house needs looking after or it'll be looted. The motor car's waiting for me and my mother's packing her bags. Now, listen to me.' Vincenzo cups her face in his hands and draws her closer. He looks into her eyes and feels the usual crack in his soul, the pain of loss without having had. 'I want to help you before I go. You're welcome to use Palazzo Novara, live there for a while. Nobody will disturb you. I have the key to my basement for you. Unless ... unless you want to come with us.'

But Rosalia is shaking her head. She can see the strain in his eyes and a pain she does not understand.

'Don't worry,' he repeats. 'They'll never find the country house. Too many cacti!'

'What'll happen to my mother and father, and Anna? They're at the cathedral. What about my grandmother? I haven't found her yet.'

'I'll help you find your *nonna*. Don't worry about your parents. The Emergency Planning Commission in Palermo is organising burials within the holy grounds. You only have to provide their picture, if you have one, and confirm their name and surname. For the crosses.'

'*Signor* ...' Rosalia says to the old man. 'I'm so grateful. I shan't forget.'

'So you have your villa to run to?' Signor Radici suddenly asks Vincenzo, ignoring Rosalia. 'I despise you and your lot! Our land has been suffering, our children have been starving. My boys will never come back. Winners and losers ... Where are my potatoes? In the Germans' bellies, that's where. The countryside is full of the rich people's villas and cemeteries with young boys, who didn't even know where Germany is and fought for nothing; the generation that should have been Sicily's future is buried under white crosses, no name on them. I hate you all!' With that, the old man steps back into the street, and walks away.

'I'll dig a hole for this German son of a bitch,' Vincenzo says quietly. 'Then I'll look for your grandmother. From tonight you'll go back to my basement; it'll become your home for the time being. Leave the rest to me. Go, now. Go!'

Rosalia leaves, clutching the key to Vincenzo's flat in her hand. Her head is full of confused thoughts. In a far recess of her mind, she finds herself harbouring a secret feeling that she refuses to dwell on: a vague excitement, as if her insides had been scrambled by her first encounter with a man's body, however unwelcome. 'I need a shower,' she says to herself, dismissing all memories.

Back at Palazzo de' Muggifalco, Vincenzo mutters to the dead body. 'I'm very sorry, my good friend, but I fear you shan't be having a holy burial after all.' Grabbing the feet, he starts dragging the German across the alley at the back of the building and onto another heap of ruins. Having found a relatively discreet spot, he dumps it there, giving it one last kick. Vincenzo has no time, and other priorities: looking for Rosalia's grandmother is not one of them. Back at the ruins of Palazzo Muggifalco, he tries to work out the exact location of Don Antonio Muggifalco's study. Then he sets about retrieving as much of Don Antonio's documents, books and paperwork as he can, continually checking over his shoulder. The

Germans or, worse, Rosalia may come back.

In the meantime, two miles away, the Germans are busily setting up a temporary base using whatever is left of the local facilities after the raid; their back-up plan, in case they should be defeated by the Allies, is to prepare to abandon Palermo before the American troops arrive. Therefore, the German commander is determined to leave behind the dead weight of un-cooperative Italian forces, or to punish the general hostility with public executions: the still air is filled with the regular sound of gunfire from the firing squads.

In the middle of what sounds like faraway, sinister fireworks, Vincenzo works the patch he has chosen with alacrity, separating books from paperwork, combining sheets of paper, searching for any drawers and shelves that have not been completely destroyed. It is because of the background noise that he does not immediately register an odd sound somewhere inside the gutted house: a sound as chilling as a flake of snow suddenly fluttering onto the nape of his neck. Somebody, or something, whispering. A groan. Vincenzo does not stop his search straight away. Part of him dismisses the sound as a fervid imagination playing stupid games with his tired body. He does, however, slow down, ears straining to catch another sound, looking for a sensible explanation.

The creepy sunset creates dancing shadows between the few standing walls and the surviving ceilings supporting the upper floor. Vincenzo finally decides to stop digging and have a good look round; unlikely as it may be, perhaps the German soldier is not dead after all. Or maybe it is one of the chickens that Rosalia, in her hysterical state, was talking about after they had found her dead parents.

There! Another sound, clear and real. A little scratchy sound, which seems to freeze the air around Vincenzo, and knocks the air out of his lungs. Weakened by the physical and emotional strain he has endured during the last day or so, he shudders and takes a few steps backwards. When he sees a tiny light flickering in the rubble, a small flame licking the stones around it, fear takes hold of his legs, which carry him very fast out of Palazzo de' Muggifalco and onto the main road outside. Even when he feels he has put enough distance between himself and the Palazzo, Vincenzo barely slows down. His heart is still beating too fast when he comes across a party of dirty Italian soldiers, with baggy trousers and their cheekbones showing the pinched look of hunger.

Lieutenant Zambito and his colleagues have been sent to the capital city by German troops scooping up those confused and leaderless Italian forces who are squandering the summer away in sleepy inland villages. Having left San Cataldo, to the relief of the locals, they have driven across the eerily empty countryside for a few hours, the heat hammering through the roof of their clapped-out camouflage jeeps and the smelly, thick uniforms. They have just disembarked from their jeep, and are trying to find their bearings and their barracks, when they stop Vincenzo to ask for directions.

'I'll walk you there,' he offers. He looks at them, one by one, into their tired, gaunt faces. 'What's the latest?'

'The British are attacking the east of Sicily, towards Messina and Catania. The Americans are marching this way. We've been told to help out here at the harbour, but there's no defence around the city at all. The villages to the south and west of here have all been abandoned,' one soldier says, scratching his head.

'Which village do you come from?'

'San Cataldo. The Germans have asked us to leave, and destroy the armaments and military posts. But they've mined the roads that lead to the village and the nearby ones too. A present for the American troops, they said. Only two little boys from the village have been caught by the "present" and lost their legs. Their parents and relatives almost lynched us. They chased us out with rakes and shotguns.'

'I hear that General Guzzoni has been ordered to mine the north docks of the harbour,' Vincenzo says.

'Yes, to avoid the Allies using it if their naval forces should attack from the sea. You'd better watch out. As for the Germans ... Well, they're not very happy with us, so watch out for them as well.'

They keep walking for a while, in silence, smelling the thick stench of fear.

Chapter Five
THE MIDNIGHT MISSION

L ieutenant Zambito adjusts the straps of his backpack, spreading the weight of it more equally between his shoulders. It is one of those murky, muggy nights during the longest Sicilian summer he can remember. The heat, still lingering despite the late hour, is sticky with salt and humidity from the sea.

Zambito and his colleague, young Roberto Vincisvalle of the Italian Aosta Division, are silently treading the slippery rocks at the feet of Monte Pellegrino, a solitary mountain that watches over the *Conca D'oro*, Palermo's fertile bay, and the town itself.

It is a moonless night, carefully chosen for its friendly cover of darkness. The soldiers are on a mission. Across the damp, thick grass, Vincisvalle negotiates the well-oiled wheel of a rusty wheelbarrow around Buddha-shaped boulders meditating under the sky. The wheelbarrow is full of explosives, on top of which Zambito has placed a map of the terrain around him; it is a military map, and shows entries, tunnels and underground mazes unknown to many. He pauses momentarily, casting an eye over where he guesses the sea must be. To his right, he can hear the water disintegrating against tongues of sand, just under the rocks projecting into the Mediterranean. His torch stays steadily on the chosen path, following the map.

The orders are simple and straightforward: find the entrances to the depot; divert the pipes; drain the underground reservoir into the sea; blow up exits and entrances; cover up; carefully mark work carried out on the map supplied. The young Italians are proud of being asked to perform this very secret and important task. They have little experience of explosives, even less knowledge of the area, but the orders come from the very top: discretion, maximum discretion. Not that Zambito or Vincisvalle would tell anyone, anyway. Military secrets must be kept, or their families might suffer the consequences. Their mothers have been crying long enough.

'We're close to Entrance B, which opens up just off the south side of the mountain,' whispers Zambito to Vincisvalle and the crickets around them.

'Good,' grunts the young man. 'My hands are already covered in blisters, courtesy of Signora *carriola*, Madam Wheelbarrow.'

The wooden trapdoor is hidden behind a wild heather bush, as per instructions. When Zambito manages to lift it up, the entrance behind it opens into a long, dark corridor, down some rustic stone steps. If the Italian soldiers thought this was a dark night, peering into the solid blackness of the hole puts things into a different perspective.

'You'll have to lift the wheelbarrow and pass it on to me,' says Zambito, already slipping into the entrance and feeling the steps with his feet. As he turns to face Vincisvalle, his head is almost level with the wheelbarrow. He puts the torch in his mouth, and raises his hands to support the barrow's wheel. 'Slowly!' he warns.

It takes the two men a few minutes of cursing and panting to negotiate everybody's entry to the underground network. Zambito can feel droplets of sweat rolling down his forehead all the way to his dirty collar, hot and cold flushes down his back. He can't stop thinking about the explosives, no matter how much he despises himself for being scared instead of rejoicing at having been chosen for the task. His companion moans and curses in the darkness. Eventually, they manage to squeeze past the initial bottleneck, and start the trek into the guts of Monte Pellegrino.

A million barrels of oil are stored under the mountain, Sicily's own secret depot and a thorny problem for both the Italian and the German forces. Everybody knows that the Americans of General Patton are close; were there a full moon casting its silver glint onto the sea below, Lieutenant Zambito would be able to see, against the dark grey mass of the Mediterranean, the silhouettes of the enemy's ships, their hulks lurking offshore.

The orders are clear: release the oil supply into the sea. Sacrifice it all to protect the mountain and the cities around it. Don't let it fall into the hands of the Allies.

'What would happen if the Germans knew we are going to divert the pipes into the sea? Would we be arrested for high treason, or would we be all right because we're following the Italian general's orders?' asks Vincisvalle after a while.

'I don't know, Roberto. Our German friends would want to blow the entire bloody place, and take no chances with the Americans. We must keep *la bocca cucita*, our mouths sewn up. Just as well we're Sicilians and *ommi 'i panza*, real men,' answers Zambito, and his heart tugs a little in his chest.

There have been times, many times, when Giuseppe Zambito has not felt as if he were an '*ommo i' panza*' at all, but a quivering wreck or, worse, a useless hungry soldier disintegrating under the heat and forced inactivity. At such times, the motherland has seemed very far away indeed and a hazy concept. But now he has a chance: his first opportunity to make a difference. A little fear kneads the small of his back. Tonight, twenty-two-year-old Zambito is no longer just a Sicilian boy: for the first time, he feels Italian, grown-up and whole.

'We're following the main pipes, which carry the oil to the port and the airport; they run parallel to this path. What we need to do when we get here,' and he stabs at the map with a dirty finger, 'is to dig a cavity at sixty-five degrees north of the main pipe's flow, and make sure it's a good four metres away from it. We'll prepare the new course for the oil to ebb away from the principal cistern and into the sea below.'

'How do we know we're not going to blow ourselves up, together with a million barrels of crude?' mutters Vincisvalle, wiping his forehead. He is kneeling down next to Zambito, holding the map in front of the torch.

'We don't. We follow orders. We've already blocked entrance A and C, here and here, the other side of Monte Pellegrino. This is the only way in now. Not far to go. Besides, we'll only put the explosives behind the armoured door just off the path. Come on, let's get moving.'

For a while, the only noise they can hear besides the faint squeaking of the wheelbarrow is the thumping of their heavy boots echoing down the tunnels.

How many heavy boots, exactly?

Zambito stops suddenly, puzzled. The noises stop with him.

'What's the matter?' asks Vincisvalle, his eyes suddenly very round and white in the surrounding half-darkness.

'Nothing,' replies Zambito. But he doesn't move. The instinct of a soldier. He tries to look beyond his colleague, whose body frame fills up the cramped space in which they are standing. He shines the torch into the underground intestines they have just walked through.

'What's the fucking matter?' Vincisvalle asks again, frazzled and suddenly overcome with an immense tiredness, as if he were a rag doll whose limbs have come undone. His brain has the time to register a little burning jab somewhere in his chest, before plunging into complete darkness and silence.

Lieutenant Giuseppe Zambito's sudden rush of adrenalin, unfortunately for him, sharpens his senses: before his colleague has even started to flop onto the floor, he notices, as if in slow motion, the smell of damp earth around him, the extinguishing flash of the gun just a few feet away, the cocking of the trigger, recharging; he regrets the vicinity of the wheelbarrow with its explosives, the late hour, his past loneliness and futile youth. For the first time in his life, however, Giuseppe Zambito is proud of being where he is, and sorry to have no witnesses to confirm that he died with dignity. He contemplates the overwhelming possibility that he shall have failed in completing the task, but feels no fear or anger. 'The instinct of a soldier,' he says, with a little smile.

If anybody had been standing outside entrance B, covered by the undergrowth at the foot of Monte Pellegrino, they would have heard a muffled sound like a far-away explosion, followed by the soft thud of stones and earth twirling. A sound trying to escape, to no avail.

Chapter Six
ANDREAS KHUKLAKIS

In those frantic days of confusion and despair, with no time to care or understand, Zambito and Vincisvalle's failure to return to their barracks stirs no interest, draws no attention. Within a day or two, Palermo turns from a beacon of resistance into a defeated ghost town, left behind by the retreating Axis troops; sparse, disillusioned defence watches the menacing British fleet from the harbour docks.

Palermo, sitting languidly in a gorgeous bay on the west coast, collapses as the Germans decide to channel men and resources towards the east coast, leaving docks and city unmanned and at the mercy of the advancing Americans. First the Aosta and then the Assietta divisions give in to General Patton's troops. They leave behind tortured, donkey-beaten paths and the very mountain passes they had been meant to protect.

Avanti! Avanti! Gather up the flasks and the rifles, and move east, whilst looking back longingly at the tiny stone houses where the women have been waiting forever. Follow the Germans! They must know what they are doing.

Within four days, western Sicily is stripped of any substantial military power, relying on only a few isolated Italian defenders to stem the Allies' advance. Soon, the balconies of decadent Bourbon Palermo are dotted with many white handkerchiefs waved at the American chocolate, hailed and acclaimed. Down the main streets forlorn, malnourished and shackled Italian prisoners of war walk on: the Allies have gathered the remnants of the island's army on their way to the capital, and release them to the civilians' indifference.

Rosalia folds up her uniform as neatly as she can, and puts it on the shelf allocated to voluntary helpers in the communal changing room. Her shift is over.

'Walk together to the canteen?' says a female voice behind her.

Walking may be a little difficult for the middle-aged woman addressing Rosalia. Clarissa is leaning heavily on a set of crutches. Under the long black skirt there is only one leg to support her. Two months earlier, surprised in her courtyard by one of the bombings, she ran to grab her grandson, still playing on his wooden cart, when one of the walls came crashing down, burying her alive. The little boy, who was not even three, sat there quietly for two days until the medics arrived. He pointed at the heap of stones, dust and mangled ironwork and said: '*Nonna* sleeping there under the stones.' Severely dehydrated, he died shortly afterwards.

Gangrene had seeped all the way up to her thigh. Taken to the Civico Hospital in Palermo, Clarissa had been given brandy and a dirty rag with two drops of chloroform. 'We've run out of syringes,' somebody said. A nun held her hand. Throughout the operation, Clarissa had looked at a strand of grey and greasy hair escaping from the nun's dirty blue head covering, and listened to endless Paternosters chewed between her toothless gums.

Rosalia smiles, hiding her tiredness. 'I can't come to the canteen. I've got things to do at home. But I'll help you before I go.'

She goes to the airless office next door, and takes the files of paperwork sitting on the desk. 'You shouldn't sit here all day. It's not good for your blood circulation.'

'What circulation?' Clarissa answers with a bitter laugh. 'The job keeps me busy.'

'Me too.'

They move towards the marble staircase, and negotiate the steps slowly. Rosalia is carrying the files for her friend. Up and down the staircase, auxiliaries fuss over wounded soldiers, holding drips, supporting bandaged heads.

'No smoking in this hospital!' Rosalia says to two uniformed young American officers huddled in the far corner of the sweeping stairs, lighting Marlboros.

'Signorina! One look from those fiery eyes and I'll go up in flames!' answers one of them, theatrically. His Italian is a little stilted.

Almost every Sicilian has a relative in '*Ammerica*', as they call the United States. Some twenty or thirty years before, a mass emigration from Sicily to the dreamland had created the strongest bond between countries: a blood tie. The young and strong fled poverty and a life with no future to battle it out in post-Great War America. They took with them a suitcase held together with string and the ambition to come back rich. America welcomed hard-working Sicilians, who were soon surrounding themselves with olive jars, oil, wine and the odour of mafia from their homeland. An American accent coloured the ancient Sicilian dialect, which, far away from Sicily, stopped evolving. Many of General Patton's troops were brought up speaking a bastardised Sicilian dialect.

Undaunted by his long march to Palermo, the American soldier holds his cigarette unlit, and loses himself in this beauty's dark eyes.

The invaders confuse Rosalia. In the air, enemy planes looked like giant mechanical birds carrying an alien who would kill and destroy. On the ground, the men flying them look almost ordinary, and some even speak the same language as she does.

'I'm putting it out, see?' the young man calls to her, and his friend chuckles. 'I'd do anything for a kiss from you, Signorina.'

'What are you up to?' Clarissa asks Rosalia, struggling to keep up with her suddenly quickened step.

'Oh, the usual,' she replies. The soldier's comment has just reminded her of two cold blue eyes, short blond hair, and the pressure of a man's desire between her legs.

'Are you still looking for your grandmother?'

The two women stop at the bottom of the staircase. Rosalia looks ahead. 'Well, you know ... I keep trying. I managed to bury my parents in holy grounds, under a wooden cross. Our housekeeper's there too. But my grandmother's still missing.'

Rosalia doesn't say that going back to the ruins of her family home makes her physically sick. She can no longer dig around, half-wishing and half-fearing that a blackened mummified hand may suddenly poke out of the rubble. She is still using Vincenzo's basement flat, where there is enough silence and enough comforts to enjoy her own company. Unfortunately, silence and solitude stir images that Rosalia does not want to remember. Her father's soiled dressing gown. Her mother's detached beauty under the rubble. And the German soldier's eyes. They follow her everywhere. They float above her when she lies on Vincenzo's hard single bed, staring at the ceiling and trying to get to sleep.

The days at the hospital are emotionally draining, and Rosalia has been working round the clock for over twelve hours. Her hands are sticky with sick patients' sweat. Suddenly, Vincenzo's little bed seems to be worth looking forward to. Maybe the German soldier's eyes will not haunt her today.

'Miss Muggifalco! Miss Muggifalco!' a male voice calls from above their heads. 'Please be kind enough to come upstairs again.' The hospital chief, sounding as exhausted as ever.

'I've finished my shift, Mr Buttitta,' she says, looking up the marble staircase at the grey face.

'I know. But I need you. Please.'

Rosalia and the older woman exchange a look. The latter slowly shakes her head, as if to suggest the appropriate answer.

'No,' Rosalia says softly. To be needed is best.

'I'm coming,' she says loudly. 'See you tomorrow, Clarissa.'

Clarissa shrugs, and turns to leave. 'Yeah. See you tomorrow. Don't work yourself into the ground. Get some rest.'

'What's the matter, Mr Buttitta?' Rosalia can hear the American soldiers on the floor above, talking in their language but laughing in Italian.

'You speak Greek, don't you?'

'Not particularly well ... I had a Greek governess for a few years when I was a child, and she didn't speak much Italian so I learnt some Greek. Why?'

'We have a pilot in the burns unit on the top floor. Second degree burns to his right leg and concussion. He won't talk to any of us, not even in English. He's just lying on his bed and refusing to eat. They pulled him out of his plane's wreckage near Enna and drove him all the way here – no local hospitals left there. The burn won't kill him, but that trip on the back of a pick-up, under the sun and with no fluids, might.'

'You want me to try and speak to him?'

'We worked out he's Greek by his uniform and badges. Perhaps Cypriot. He's not very ... co-operative. The nurses are struggling to change his bandages.'

Rosalia suddenly remembers, on one of her rare visits to that floor to borrow clean bandages or more glass syringes, seeing a thin body under the grey sheets of a stretcher, its face to the wall. It was two days earlier, perhaps three. The burns unit is the hospital's top floor, a large room with no screens or curtains, and one toilet for fifty stretchers. She is not usually on duty there, as fire damage requires more advanced expertise and a strong stomach.

'OK. I'll go. What do you want me to find out?'

'Tell him we only want to look after him. We're not at war any more, at least not in Sicily. There are no Germans or Italians to kill. Convince him to have a wash. He's not allowed any of the nurses to touch him, not even to change his bandages, and he won't be helped to a basin or bathtub. Frankly, he's going to get an infection from dirt. The smell is incredible.'

Rosalia sighs. She should go back to her locker, get changed again into her uniform. A thought stops her. Perhaps Mr Smelly Pilot will be more inclined to speak to her if he doesn't think she's a nurse. She climbs two more flights of stairs, passing the Americans on the first floor. The one who spoke to her before is still holding a cigarette in his hand, between thumb and index finger, unlit. They exchange a glance, but she carries on without stopping.

The sunset pierces through the dirt on the huge windows' glass panes. It floods the top floor, mercilessly searching the tortured bodies, the weeping wounds. A couple of patients are sitting on the same stretcher, facing each other. They are playing cards, their hands oddly hidden, though the sun behind them cuts their profiles neatly. It's only when she gets closer and they turn to look at her that Rosalia notices the mangled ears and missing nose. They push the cards with fingerless stumps.

The air in the room is stagnant and heavy with the persistent smell of white spirit and sweat. For a moment, Rosalia thinks she can detect another smell too: that of rotting flesh.

Over in the far corner, the stretcher tucked against the wall seems almost empty, apart from the faintest shape under the sheets. When

Rosalia draws closer, the shape moves slightly; the covers slip to one side, showing a head with short light brown hair. Dirty bandages. The delicate, almost feminine, nape of the neck. When the figure turns to look at her, Rosalia's heart flutters, as if a butterfly had landed on it. For the man lying on the stretcher has exquisite features, despite his pallor and the bandage around his forehead.

'*Yasou*,' she says, timidly. She has not spoken Greek for many years, and she stammers the word out awkwardly. '*Ciao. Ti ineh toh onoma sou*? What's your name?'

Rosalia is very surprised when the answer comes after a moment's silence. 'Andreas. Andreas Khuklakis.'

Chapter Seven
THE CYPRIOT PILOT

My name is Andreas. I'm nineteen years old. I fly a British Wellington bomber and I'm in charge of four crew members. My name is Andreas. Andreas, like my grandfather. I must remember that. The memories of the last six months of my life have started leaking out everywhere. Once I go to sleep on the hard military camp bed, I fall head first into the deepest, blackest unconsciousness. When I wake up, I check the thin pillow to see whether my memories might have seeped from my nose, or my ears perhaps, onto the rough sackcloth. I'm petrified of forgetting myself.

I fly a 235 miles per hour death machine, which can carry a 4,500-pound bomb-load. Only a few years ago I used to spend my days playing with my twin sister in sunny Cyprus, on my uncle's farm. My sister's name is Maria. Maria, like the Virgin. I repeat the details to myself, obsessively, desperate to hang onto reality. It's easier for me to remember my childhood years than the last six months.

I'm four years old. It's a particularly hot summer in Cyprus. We children have been chasing each other round the apple trees, hiding behind the glasshouse, wrenching my auntie's red plum tomatoes from their little green crowns and wedging them in our mouths. When we bite they burst, and a little juice dribbles down our chins.

'What have I got in my hand?' My hand's closed tight into a fist and I show it to the others.

'Give us a clue! Give us a clue!' they all shout, laughing. The farmhouse's whitewashed walls almost shimmer in the sun. The other children raise their hands to their foreheads, to keep the glaring light away, and scrunch up their eyes.

'It's something beginning with t!' I say.

45

'Tooth!'

'Tassel!'

'Train!'

'How can a whole train be in such a small hand?' asks one of the older children, my cousin Adonis, laughing louder than ever.

'No!' I shout, shaking my little fist. 'None of those! Do you give up?'

'Yes! Show us, go on!' They chant, jumping up and down.

I open my fist carefully. The little stones are stuck to my sweaty palm.

'Two stones! I have two stones!' I scream, delighted.

'Silly! Silly!' And they chase me, pretending to be cross. It takes me a few years to understand why.

The roar of my plane covers the laughter, but not completely. No matter how much I try to concentrate, it is hard to believe that Cyprus is not all about farmhouses and orchards, but helping another country win the war.

The switches on the control panel are hard and cold to the touch. Over 6,000 feet, everything is hard and cold, including my soul. My cousins make rifles out of tree branches and sticks. The turret machine gun is useless. As I fly the bomber, I keep repeating to myself: my name is Andreas. Andreas Khuklakis.

I took off on the morning of 8 July 1943, from a little airfield in North Africa. We had been posted there three weeks before and had been attacking the islands of Lampedusa and Pantelleria, in the Mediterranean, and the bigger island of Sicily, for days. Lampedusa and Pantelleria look like two tiny dots in the middle of the dark blue sea, as if they are just floating there temporarily. But Sicily stretches solidly below my plane, with rippling mountains in the middle of it and miles of beaches blending into the sea.

I am one of only six Cypriot personnel in North Africa. We're relieved to be able to talk to each other in our mother tongue, which makes it easier for everybody to understand the others over the intercom during a flight, but scared of the deeper bond we have: Cypriots within the British. I volunteered to join the RAF about a year ago. I don't regret it: I really didn't have a choice.

Besides, I feel euphoric at the responsibility I've been given. When I fly what we aircrew affectionately call the 'Wimpy', I secretly marvel at the power I have over such a large mechanical bird. Or I did until 8 July.

The brief was clear: northern coast of Sicily, urban areas. I'm not proud of it. Hit the urban areas, and the people will revolt against their own heads of state. Easy job: no Germans at all, and certainly no Italians. The latter are so poor and disorganised that they don't even own eyes to cry. We owned the sky. Afterwards, I steered south-west, returning to base.

I don't exactly know what happened, or how. Bang! Bang! The port engine caught fire. I saw it: orange and blue tongues licking the wing, flicking rearwards. I was flying too low to dive down quickly, hoping to extinguish it. Panic among the all-British crew. They were very suspicious of me, a Greek Cypriot. I was the youngest, and not their usual pilot. I felt their eyes boring into my back, the fear in their voices. I thought of my cousins' wooden rifles: 'Bang, bang, you're dead!'

'I'll try. Prepare for emergency landing,' I said through the intercom. Below us, the dry expanse of Sicilian failed crops in the middle of nowhere. 'I am Andreas Khuklakis, and I can do it,' I thought, and squeezed my fists hard around the controls.

I no longer had two little stones in my child's fist, but squeezed hard all the same, the ground coming towards my face very fast. I heard shouting at the back; not the mildly amused teasing of my cousin Adonis. The screams of young men who wanted to live.

'What am I doing here?' I thought, and then smacked hard into darkness.

I saw the sky above me and felt the heat stabbing my legs and face when I woke up. My head ached dully. The pick-up was moving fast, without avoiding potholes in the road. The sun came through the branches of the lemon trees, hitting me as I lay on the vehicle's hard back, a dirty rug under me. I wiggled my toes and my fingers. I touched my face, and felt my teeth inside my mouth. Only then did I allow myself to pass out again.

Now, if I shut my eyes, I can pretend I'm back in Cyprus. Just don't touch me. Don't make me conscious of my existence again.

'*Yasou*,' the voice says. It drags me back to reality. '*Ti ineh toh onoma sou*?'

The easiest question in the world, if you know the answer. My Cypriot self replies automatically. Has this girl spoken to the individual, or has she asked the pilot? They're both here within me. 'Andreas Khuklakis'.

I become aware of her big eyes, the sadness and quiet horror within them. An Italian civilian in an Italian hospital.

Why did they not kill me? I've been dropping death over their little houses, with the red roofs and the black balconies, minuscule from above.

I don't want to come back to existing. She'll remind me that there are people inside those houses. People with eyes as big as hers, and perhaps a bigger grief.

'*Imeh i* Rosalia.'

I turn my head towards the wall again. I'm thirsty, but try to delay drinking from the glass near my bed as much as I can because it'll make me pee. Sometimes I reach under the bed for the bedpan; sometimes I'm too weak and don't care. Then I lie in it for a while. I'm no longer aware of the smell, but the bedsores sting. I don't allow anyone to touch my body.

'Do you understand me if I speak in Italian? English? I'm a voluntary *infermiera ausiliaria*. You're at the Civico Hospital in Palermo. Are you Greek?'

She seems very young, even younger than me. I nod, still looking at the wall. A baby cockroach is crawling on it, a dark red dot with eager feelers moving carefully ahead. I follow its progress and feel the disgust mounting, for it and for me.

Suddenly she is closer. A hand touches my shoulder. 'Let us look after you, Andreas. You need a good clean. Can you move? Can you stand?'

Yes, yes. I should ask where the rest of the crew is. Are they in this hospital too? I'm so tired that I don't really care whose bed I'm lying on, which country I'm in and whose war it is.

'I have an idea. If you can stand and feel strong enough, I'll help you to the bathroom and fill a tub with warm water for you. I have some lavender oil and salt we could put in it. The salt may sting a bit, but you'll feel better for it afterwards. If you want to wash by yourself, I'll wait outside the door. Please don't lock yourself in.'

If I wash I'll remember I'm a human being. It's easier to stick to what I wish to remember. My name is Andreas Khuklakis. If I get a wash will I still be Andreas Khuklakis?

'That's it then. It's decided. I'm going to sort it out. Maybe I can even find a clean set of pyjamas. I'll be back presently.'

With that, Rosalia the Italian auxiliary nurse leaves. The little cockroach has now climbed as high as my bedstead. I want to squash it to the wall, a little red mark sprawling into a larger patch of the same colour. What shall I squash it with, though? Bombs?

I must have fallen asleep for a little while, because when I open my eyes again she's back, with a bag of salt, a little bottle of something, towels and grey shirt and trousers, so large that my Wellington would fit in them, wings and all.

'All right, Mr Silent Pilot. Lean on me and I'll take you to the bathroom. The ward knows it's your turn. Nobody will disturb you. Here, let me help.'

She's surprisingly strong and lean, the little nurse. I lean on her. I notice the briefest snarl of revulsion on her face when I get up and lift my arm to cup her shoulder. I'm rotting alive on that bed.

'Slowly. Here, to the right. This door here.'

I have to let her go as she struggles to open the door of the bathroom, still carrying the salt and the new clothes. The smell of white spirit is more overpowering than ever. I lean on the door frame, suddenly dizzy. Is that the distant rumble of a squadron bearing down on us, or is it just my imagination? The toilet's cistern is high up and leaking. Water gurgles through the pipes. The basin's enamel is chipped. The dormer window on the ceiling lets the sun in, generous scoops of sunrays. I shiver at the thought of the light touching me.

Rosalia puts the towel down on a rickety metal chair, which must have been white once. The steam in the bathroom has rusted it beyond repair. 'Now, the tub is full of warm water. This', she shows me the ampoule, 'will make all the difference. It's lavender oil. Not too sweet. It's a gentle disinfectant, but with a lovely smell.' Then she opens the bag of salt and pours the contents in the water. She's left before I can worry about the bandages or my wounds. The door shuts behind her.

It's her respect for my privacy that does it. Or maybe the fumes from the disinfectant, I don't know. I start crying silently, sitting on the floor and hugging my knees. And I'm still crying when I manage to lower myself into the lukewarm water.

The sudden sting from the salty bath takes my breath away. I study the damage to my leg; the skin, bubbled up in blisters, has eventually yielded. There are bloody strips under which shreds of raw flesh look like chewed up meat. Deeper, darker marks, making out a rectangular pattern, an indentation in the middle. I strain to remember what on the aircraft would have burnt my leg through the military trousers, leaving this imprint. It looks like a handle. The emergency door panel? The bandages I've discarded on the floor are stained yellow, partly because of the antiseptic cream that's been applied to the leg and partly because of the pus. I pour some lavender-scented water on my raised leg, and muffle a scream.

I stay in the tub until the water turns cold and is murky with dead skin, blood and dirt. When I emerge from the bathroom she's still there, waiting. I give her a nod and let myself be helped back to the bed. I was wrong. She hasn't been waiting outside all this time: the linen has been changed, down to the plastic mattress cover and bottom sheet.

'Linen is best for burns,' she whispers. 'It doesn't stick to damaged flesh, and keeps you cool.'

That linen, yellowed with age but fresh and clean, takes me back home in a flash. My mother's dowry, kept in a massive trunk. Her own bed linen. I switch off the memories and lie on the stretcher again. She rolls up my trouser leg to apply new cream and put on clean bandages. Without complaining, I let her light fingers work.

At least my crash has saved me another trip to Palermo. I received the instructions for my next mission before the last flight. A guide to the city would be most useful. I look at Rosalia, the young nurse, and smile at her. I'm most surprised when she returns the smile.

Chapter Eight
THE THINGS WE DO NOT SAY

It is late afternoon when Rosalia finally leaves the hospital. She feels strangely light-headed. As she makes her way back to the basement, she longs for a little privacy, a chance to hold her thoughts in a tidy bunch. Home, if Vincenzo's flat can be called such, is a good twenty minutes away on foot. Walking briskly, Rosalia picks up the first of her fresh memories, lovingly admiring its features: the memory of Andreas's face.

No, not his face as such, of course, with nose, eyes and mouth; she can't recall those details, not yet. The artist in her knows that she must possess that face by reducing it, if necessary, to the stark lines of a pencil sketch. Perhaps she will draw that face, feverishly, under the weak light of a single bare bulb, when she is alone in her room.

That can wait, of course. What cannot wait, however, is her recollection of what she felt; the very idea of attraction, in the mind and soul of an artist.

Rosalia re-enacts, in her imagination, the moment when Andreas turned his head towards her. Again and again she thinks of the way his eyes reached out and touched her heart. Which part of his face was responsible for the emotional upheaval? Was it the eyes, so fiery and yet so resigned? Or the high cheekbones, sporting a bruise near the temple? And the small cut just below the right eye. How could it make her heart beat that little bit faster?

All around Rosalia is the quiet bustle of Palermo, a city full of women and older people. Young men have been sent to the north of Italy, where they still fight the lost war; many others, having been swallowed up by the armed forces in Sicily, either populate the faceless cemeteries or hide in their parents' stables.

The invaders have released the prisoners of war: there are not enough supplies to feed them as well as their own troops. Back home, the losers sit in their ripped sleeveless vests, looking out on the almond trees festooning the burnt countryside. Here in town, though, as Rosalia walks home, groups of jovial Americans drive their dusty jeeps down the road, one of Palermo's main arteries that cut the city, longitudinally and vertically, into four neat quarters. When the Arabs ruled Sicily there was a castle on that very road, hence the name *Cássaro*, an Arab word for castle. The manor is long gone but the buildings retain some of their exotic flavour, with spiralling turrets, black and white ceramic tiled walls and narrow windows.

The American soldiers spot the girl and whistle appreciatively at her slender waist, the black ribbon holding back her dark hair. Rosalia keeps her eyes down. The Americans aim to stop a mile or so up the road, beyond the centre, where they are eagerly awaited by a few Sicilian women who are tired of hunger and loneliness.

Rosalia keeps walking towards the harbour. The docks, spared by Generale Guzzoni's decision not to blow them up before retreating further east, are buzzing with activity: ships coming and going, men loading and unloading. The victors are here to stay.

It is not his face, she suddenly decides. Nor the thin body, whose bones Rosalia still feels under her busy fingers, as she changed his bandages, and all over her shoulder, where he leant to support himself on the way to the bathroom. No. Andreas Khuklakis's features and demeanour remind her of her childhood's magic afternoons spent chasing lizards along the crumbling low walls of Palazzo de' Muggifalco's back garden; trying to catch tadpoles in the neglected little pond with broken twigs. He makes her long for stolen kisses tasting like lemon grass.

Suddenly, the basement she is heading for loses its attraction; despite the rapid descent of darkness, Rosalia is no longer eager to go home. It occurs to her that the borough through which she is walking is almost completely inhabited by the Americans: it will be their vehicles and their uniforms that she will see on her way home; their laughter and language that she will hear as she passes the smoking ruins they have left behind. She will have to walk past Palazzo de' Muggifalco, or rather the hole where her family home had been until a few weeks earlier.

Behind her, the *Cássaro* is flooded by sunset. Palermo's cathedral is just off the same street, a mile or so from where she stands. Were Rosalia's mother and father still alive, she would not have talked to them about meeting an intriguing young man, especially a foreign pilot. The idea of her father listening to a rapturous description of Andreas makes Rosalia smile a little. As for her mother, she would not have had enough interest to listen at all. However, standing in the middle of vanquished Palermo, with no-one to speak to, no home or plans, Rosalia feels the cruel pinch of loneliness, and the unbearable idea of only having her imagination for company. I'll talk to my parents, even if they can't answer. Or *because* they can't answer, she thinks. Rosalia turns back, heading for the medieval cathedral.

Opposite the south side of the Norman-built cathedral, with its riot of different styles layered on top of each other, the main square opens up. In the fifteenth century it was used as the cathedral's cemetery. Three hundred years later, it was enclosed by a marble balustrade, on top of which sixteen statues of various saints have been positioned, standing as eternal guards. In the middle of the square a neo-Classical statue of Saint Rosalia stands proud. Behind the balustrade, thick with plain crosses and delimited by a wooden fence, lies a quiet slice of land where Palermo's victims rest; a corner of the old cemetery has been restored to its original function. Rosalia knows every mound, every blade of grass, the gnarled knots on tree trunks. There, marked by anonymous wooden crosses, are her parents' graves. She is familiar with the heavy smell of jasmine bushes and the fleshy plants of hibiscus. Indeed, were it not for the stern, angular shape of the crosses, the place would look very much like a botanical garden, cut into rectangular-shaped tombs.

As she approaches the place where her mother and father lie together for the first time in many years, she notices that she is not alone. A male figure, dressed in black, stands in front of the Muggifalcos' graves, hands behind his back. Rosalia hesitates a moment, then joins him. He speaks softly. 'Rosalia, *mia cara*, what a terrible tragedy. I would like to express my sincere regret at the awful news. Is there anything I can do to help you?' An apologetic frown; but the eyes of Vincenzo's father are cold.

'Signor Novara, it's very kind of you to visit my parents' grave. Don't fret over me, sir. I spend most of my time working at the Civico Hospital, and your son's already shown me immense kindness in allowing me to stay at his flat.'

Signor Novara waves his hand as if to swat an annoying fly. '*Di nulla, bambina.* The house is empty. As you know, we're staying in Casteldaccia, at our country villa. I've come to Palermo today to attend to some business, but I'm on my way back. Your father was a very honourable man, Rosalia. We'd known each other for many, many years. I believe I was his first client, in fact.'

'Yes, sir. My father always spoke very highly of you. Thank you.' She looks at the fresh mound of earth, still moist and dark, notices the fresh flowers.

'How's Vincenzo?' Signor Novara's features remind her of his son, but the man next to her is lean and strong, despite his grey hair.

'Fine, fine. He was going with his mother to the countryside, but changed his mind and is now staying with friends. I expect you'll see him soon enough. What about you? Are you all right? I mean ... If you need any help sorting out your parents' paperwork or anything like that ... Signor Novara bends over a little and looks into Rosalia's eyes. His voice becomes a whisper. 'Your father, *bon'anima*, bless his soul, looked after my affairs. I am obliged to make sure his only daughter comes to no harm.'

'I'm very grateful, Signor Novara, but I don't really know. Everything is so ... confusing at the moment. I don't know whether I need anything yet.' Rosalia hears the childish fear and anguish in her voice, and hates it. She has always tried to avoid the haughty Novaras, because they make her feel small and insignificant; today is no exception.

'Any news of your grandmother?' Signor Novara straightens up again, perhaps bored with their conversation.

'Not yet, sir. The mobile aid units are busy, and I'm not a priority.'

'Ah. That's something I can help you with. I'll send someone. My men can go to your … house and search around properly. You may not want to be there when they do. You don't have to.'

'Thank you. I'd very much like to be there, sir. I'm the last of the Muggifalcos. My grandmother brought me up. Were she alive and well, I'd have found her by now.'

'Very honourable, young lady. Very. You've looked after your parents, and no doubt you'll look after your grandmother too.'

Rosalia smiles and feels her cheeks grow hot; a compliment from Signor Novara is rare. She pauses, battling against the temptation to have the compliment just for herself. 'Vincenzo helped me. Together we took my mother and father and Anna here. They'll have proper crosses when this is all over. And we'll find room for *Nonna* Antonia.'

Signor Novara produces a flat silver box from the back pocket of his trousers, and takes a cigarette out. He taps the end of it on the box, looking pensive. 'Promise me something, young Rosalia. Don't get close to the Americans. They came as invaders, not friends. We can look after each other. We belong to this land. We love our country, and die for it. Look at the pictures of our soldiers in the *Corriere della Sera*. That determined look on their sun-burnt faces. What do the Americans know about us? Are you a patriot, girl?'

Rosalia's cheeks are burning more than ever. What does this man mean? The pilot isn't American, he's Greek-Cypriot. And she is only a girl. The war has taken her parents away, and that's all she knows.

'It'll be down to us to rebuild this country and to pick up the pieces. When the ships and the planes and the barracks are gone, Sicily will be alone again, against everybody. We must look after each other, do you hear?'

'Yes, sir.' She nods, twisting a lock of hair around her index finger.

'Very well. I must go now, but I'll send my men to Palazzo de' Muggifalco presently. I hope to be of help in any way I can, Rosalia. Just send for me if you need anything at all.'

He leaves suddenly, heading for the path between the graves. Rosalia watches the tall figure walk out of the little cemetery, and across the square. Looking up, she notices that the sky is getting darker and darker; and she is a long way from Vincenzo's basement. Rosalia thinks of Andreas's handsome face, which had given her a few moments' happiness after so much grief. Now it must no longer float in her imagination. She looks down at her parents' graves.

'*Papá*. Our family home is destroyed. It would make you so angry to see our belongings among the rubble. But don't worry: I've gathered all I could. In a wheelbarrow. Books, ornaments, outfits, small pieces of furniture, your fountain pen, the paintings that used to hang on the walls of your study. I am alive, *Papá*, but I'm ashamed of being alive when so many people are dead.'

Rosalia's thoughts about death remind her something about the cathedral nearby. Now stretching towards the empty skies, the cathedral holds the mortal remains of Palermo's patron, after whom Rosalia is named.

Rosalia's mother, trying to fulfil the Muggifalco family's desire for an heir, had repeatedly failed to produce the much longed-for boy, or indeed any child at all. In desperation, she went to the cathedral to touch the sacred urn, the contents of which are said to be some eight hundred years old. 'Saint Rosalia,' she whispered, 'This blessed baby doesn't want to come. If you help me I promise I'll call him Rosario, after you. We'll always remember your grace and generosity.' She had found out that she was expecting soon afterwards. She kept her promise, although she never stopped resenting the baby for being a girl. After the child was born, Elena Muggifalco went all the way to the sanctuary of Saint Rosalia on top of Monte Pellegrino, pinned a pair of hand-knitted booties to the rock wall as a symbol of gratitude, then promptly went back to her life as if the little girl had never arrived, and willingly relinquished her maternal role to Rosalia's grandmother.

Rosalia looks at the silent shadows of the trees around the cemetery. Far away, muffled by the distance, the roaring of American cars on the streets.

On the top floor of the Civico Hospital, Andreas Khuklakis is finally asleep.

She walks through the little cemetery and its discreet gate; beyond it, the square. The bronze eyes of Saint Rosalia seem to be following her, an almost maternal smile on the statue's face. Across the square Rosalia can see the cathedral's portico; under the complicated patterns of the arches, the massive cherry wood carved door, opening into the main building. When she reaches it, she finds that the slightest push makes the door yield softly, making no noise as it pivots on its hinges. The cathedral's silent welcome is surprisingly soothing. Inside, the smell of cheap wax from the many votive candles is mixed with incense. Despite its size and central position, the building has escaped all raids and is unscathed. The immense nave expands into two lateral aisles, studded with numerous niches and recesses, each hosting the statue of a saint or their remains, or both. Candles and bare bulbs illuminate the statues' features from below, giving them – despite the sanctity of the place – demonic grins. Shadows flicker and dance around the stuccoed nostrils, drawing circles of darkness around the eyes.

Rosalia walks alone down the nave, and the shuffling of her dusty sandals on the mosaic tiles echoes in the stone-vaulted ceiling. She has come to the cathedral countless times with her grandmother, and is used to both the regal emptiness of the place and, now, the perfect loneliness of someone who has no real home to go back to. Her steps take her to a certain niche at the back of the cathedral: the precious silver urn containing the bones of Saint Rosalia. There, many times, *Nonna* Antonia pointed at the vase and whispered the legend in the child's ear.

The legend says that in 1147, a Sicilian girl belonging to a well-to-do family, Rosalia, decided to leave all material comforts behind and retire to the top of Monte Pellegrino, the mountain dominating Palermo's bay, to live like a hermit. No more was known of her life until four centuries later, in 1624, the year of the black plague. Many thousands of people died, until a shepherd had a dream in which Rosalia appeared to be pointing at a specific place on the mountain. Her bones were found, and a sanctuary was built there. Soon, visitors were healed and the plague defeated. Rosalia was canonised, and became the city's patron. Her grandmother's words echo in Rosalia's head. 'She heals us all, and protects us from the plague.'

'This war is our plague.' The girl stands in front of the glass showcase containing the urn, and puts her hands together in prayer: 'Dear Saint Rosalia, protect us all from it. Protect me from hatred. This is the modern plague.'

She remembers something else her grandmother used to say: 'You have a great future ahead of you, my dear.'

'Ah. A great future indeed.' Rosalia smiles, despite herself, at her reflection in the glass. The thin face looking back, with those high cheekbones, has a permanently tired look.

'We Muggifalcos performed brave deeds for the Norman conquerors. For that we were given many awards. Look at the Palazzo. One day it will all be yours.'

'Yes. A heap of rubble. *Nonna,* where is my great future?'

Nonna Antonia Muggifalco does not answer. Rosalia takes an idle look at the numerous gifts to the saint, scattered around the glass case. More are to be found at the sanctuary, high up on Monte Pellegrino. These little signs of devotion left near Saint Rosalia's urn are from those who have received a *grazia,* a grace. Among the pinned photos, children's outfits, milk teeth and ribboned locks of hair, something catches Rosalia's attention, and chills her blood. A large piece of black fabric, hanging at the back of the case. A gloomy shroud. The edges of it are crocheted all the way round, apart from one corner where the handiwork is ripped. Rosalia remembers well the sound of the fabric tearing the day the shawl got caught in one of the door handles at Palazzo de' Muggifalco.

'What's *Nonna*'s shawl doing there?' she asks herself, instinctively stepping forward to take a better look.

Chapter Nine
THE THINGS THAT MUST BE SAID

Rosalia climbs the hospital's stairs with a spring in her step. For the last week or so, she has started and finished her daily shifts with a visit to the Greek Cypriot invalid on the top floor. Signor Novara's words about being a patriot and loyal to her land and people still play on her mind; but Rosalia is only sixteen and has persuaded herself that her interest for the pilot is purely that of a conscientious nurse. Besides, she was responsible for the breakthrough, managing to elicit a response from the hitherto silent Andreas, and feels that she is entitled to be personally concerned for his well-being.

The patient is doing well. Today, she finds him sitting up with a bowl of broth on his lap and a spoon that has seen better days. Under the sheets his legs stretch out; Andreas's back is supported by his pillow.

'*Buongiorno*, Andreas!' she says, and her smile lights up the room for the men on the ward. Rosalia is not aware of those who carefully turn towards her when they hear her voice, despite the pain, itching and discomfort of burnt flesh rubbing against bandages and hard mattresses. Their weepy eyes cloud over the image of a uniformed young nurse, finding her youth both moving and irritating.

'*Buongiorno*, sister Rosalia.' Andreas sips his broth and stares ahead. Behind his visitor, the matron glides between stretchers, holding a bed pan in one hand and a crucifix in the other, providing physiological and spiritual comfort.

'*Marescialla!*' calls one of the patients. 'Be sure that you don't accidentally swap them over! I wouldn't like to dip my hand into urine for a blessing and stick the crucifix between my legs!' A roar of laughter welcomes the remark, a sound so odd and unnatural in a hospital that the matron blushes, lost for words.

If Rosalia turned around, she would see the faces looking in her direction. Some men have propped themselves up on one elbow; some sit up, their skinny, hairy legs dangling out of their bed. If they were bold enough, they would shout, 'Look at us, *signorina*! Under the dirty sheets and beyond our suppurated toenails, we're just young men who want to feel alive again. We love to catch the glimpse of a small ear every time you push back a strand of your hair, and the garters' outline creasing your skirt at every step you take.' Nobody will ever tell Rosalia that her presence stirs a vague desire in long-forgotten groins.

The matron carries on with her tour, wishing her shift were over soon.

Andreas finishes his meal, leaving the empty bowl and spoon on his lap. He feels particularly vulnerable when carrying out the simplest tasks; like eating or visiting the communal bathroom. Privacy is paramount, as he keeps repeating to himself.

'Shall I take that away?' she says, gently.

'Thank you.'

In the process of scooping up the dirty crockery, she inadvertently brushes his arm with her own and blushes a little.

Andreas thinks quickly. This is a good moment. He can tune into her naïvety, make it work for him. He raises his hand and places it on her wrist. 'I mean it. Thank you.'

For a second, they stay still, Rosalia bent over Andreas with both hands around the bowl, his hand on hers. She notices the long fingers, thin pale skin, the bluish veins. Her heart does a little leap forward, loving the fragility of an intimate moment.

'You're welcome,' she says quickly. 'It must be difficult for you to be stuck here on your own all day. The hospital's been trying to get in touch with your squadron but we weren't sure whether you're with the British or the Americans. Your uniform was British, but your papers show American stamps. We only want to help.' Rosalia blurts the last sentence out, as if to justify how and why she should know all these details when nurses are only meant to dab sweaty foreheads. She slowly pulls away, feeling slightly embarrassed.

'I'm a British subject, born in Cyprus. Cyprus is a British colony and I enlisted with the British forces, like many of my friends. We lied about our age. I'd been based in North Africa until my last flight. Because I'm multilingual, the British have given me extra duties to perform once the invasion's completed, and I'll become a local liaison officer on behalf of the Allies.'

The sentences come thick and fast, as if Andreas has been waiting for a while to explain his presence in Sicily. Or maybe it is a monologue well rehearsed. Rosalia's heart starts to dance. She has no idea what Andreas is talking about, but that does not matter. 'Her' pilot, as she has secretly come to think of him, has chosen to confide in her! She's the one he trusts. The last dregs of broth start dripping on the tiled floor from the tilted bowl she's still holding.

'I'm well enough to leave the hospital now. I need to find out where the Americans and the British are billeted in Palermo. Then I can report back to base. I'm grateful for your help.'

Rosalia's heart stops dancing. 'Leave the hospital.'

'Now.'

Anger washes over her so suddenly that she cannot hold it back. NO! How can he tell her that he wants to leave, when she can still feel the weight of his fingers upon her own hand? His presence in the hospital has helped her get through the long, tiring shifts; she has cheerfully scrubbed the tired tiles of the hospital rooms, knowing that she could sneak upstairs to watch his handsome face just for a few minutes, every day. Andreas's existence has been comforting enough to endure the sighs of those about to die, sometimes in her arms, and the weight of private memories when alone. At night, dreams of a black shawl floating past her face are chased away by his voice.

In Rosalia's shaky hands the bowl tips; the metal spoon inside it falls on the floor. She bends down to pick it up, her young mind swirling with resentment. She turns to leave.

His voice calls her back. 'I should be very grateful if you'd help me find my colleagues and the British-American base. I know no one in Sicily apart from you. Stay, until I find my feet.' He tries to smile with his mouth and his eyes.

Anger evaporates into relief: she has drawn her own conclusions too quickly. He needs help. He needs her. 'Of course,' she says, and her heart is dancing again. 'I was born here and know Palermo very well. Let me find out where you're meant to be based. I'll ask the hospital manager to telegraph your details to the local government.'

Rosalia, like many Sicilians living during the Allied occupation, is only vaguely aware of the political changes affecting the region. Shortly after the invasion, the Allies took over all civil local governments. There are pressing problems, such as reconnecting the water supply and electricity, finding suitable accommodation for the thousands of homeless and stopping the looting of food and supplies. In some cases the Allies rely on existing military forces, such as the army of *Carabinieri*, to deal with emergencies and maintain the law. Overall, though, occupied Sicily is under the control of the newly formed AMGOT, (Allied Military Government of Occupied Territory), whose headquarters are in Palermo. AMGOT's temporary and overworked offices control provincial administration units, each headed by a senior civil affairs officer (SCAO) and his team.

When Rosalia mentions the local government, Andreas suppresses a grimace. The hospital will get in touch with the SCAO in charge of the Palermo province. He knows the officer in question, but volunteering his name would make her suspicious. Being accompanied to AMGOT's headquarters would not be wise either, as he cannot afford to be traced, even by a young and inexperienced civilian. Better to be told where the more mundane military base is; the latter's sprawling stations will allow him, if necessary, to disappear in the sea of grey-green uniforms, without uncovering the link with AMGOT.

'Contacting the local government won't be necessary, Rosalia. If I can just have my paperwork and any personal effects that may have survived, you can show me Palermo, I'll get acquainted with the city. You don't ...' and here Andreas hesitates, his toes twitching under the white sheets, '... have any news of my crew, do you?'

'I'm afraid I don't. We know very little about you. You arrived here on the back of a military truck and you were in very poor shape. We try to mend people, not chase paperwork, as my manager's very fond of saying. Do you remember much?' She's still holding the empty bowl and the spoon, grateful for something to carry out of the ward, and for having a reason to be there, other than Andreas's dark eyes.

The patient shakes his head slowly. 'Do you live close to this hospital, nurse Rosalia? How did you end up working here?' A banal question, but how to gain her trust other than getting to know her?

'Not too far. I lost my family during a recent bombing and the hospital work keeps me busy. Stops me from thinking too much.'

Andreas nods wisely. Isn't it ironic that Rosalia should try to run away from her memories when he spends most of his time striving to own any memories at all? Forced immobility only encourages a lack of focus; perhaps leaving the hospital bed will make a difference.

'I'll go to the office and apply for your discharge. You'll be checked over once more, and if all is well you'll be free to go. I'm afraid your uniform is completely ruined: they had to cut your trousers up. You got most upset, and the first aiders ran when you got hold of the scissors and finished the job yourself. Do you remember?'

Andreas shakes his head again and says nothing. Yet he must have endured the agony of burnt flesh stuck to his trousers and peeling away with the fabric. He can't remember much, but sees the evidence on his body every day. 'Privacy is my defence,' he says, as stubbornly now as when he thrashed about, grunting like an animal but never screaming. Screaming is for women. His eyes remain fixed on Rosalia's heart-shaped face.

'Your jacket and shirt are undamaged, though. If you like, I could find some clean civilian clothes for you to wear until you get back to your people.'

'Your people,' Andreas repeats, still looking at Rosalia. A foreign government on the island must be very hard for the Sicilians to cope with, in the same way as they may have felt the Fascist regime was an imposition from Rome. 'A little self-contained state within the state.' That's what his brief said of Sicily, didn't it?

There is a sparkle in Rosalia's fiery eyes, the passionate pursuit of young ideals. 'Her' people. 'I meant the British or the Americans, whoever's in charge of us nowadays. I don't mind any more.' There is no trace of irony or hatred in Rosalia's voice.

'Thank you,' Andreas says. 'I'd be most grateful for any clothes you may be able to spare.'

'I'll talk to the matron. Try to get some sleep now.'

Her clogs clop on the hard tiles as she leaves the ward; the noise attracts the attention of those who are awake and well enough to care. '*Ecco la cavalla!*' one whispers to his companion lying in the next bed. 'There goes the mare.'

Indeed, despite the traumatic time, her tragedy and the sheer fatigue of her work, Rosalia's body has undergone a subtle but definite change in the last few weeks. Her hips have blossomed into Mediterranean curves; the budding breasts of a month or so earlier have bloomed into a full, feminine promise under her uniform. She unconsciously tugs at her top's lapels, pulling the white fabric in to cover more of her chest. Andreas listens to her footsteps outside the ward's swinging doors, getting fainter and fainter. He sinks a little lower in his bed and sighs.

Chapter Ten
THE CELLAR

Signorina Muggifalco!'

She stops in the middle of the pavement outside the hospital and looks around, not sure where the voice is coming from. Palermo's streets are more crowded than ever, people crawling out of war-time. Many shops are open for business, though their windows are bare.

'Signorina Muggifalco!' A male voice, raspy and heavily inflected with the inland dialect. The man who has materialised behind her is short and muscular, with a black moustache and a *coppola*, the traditional Sicilian cap, pulled down on his shaven head. He must have been waiting outside for Rosalia to finish her early shift.

'Michelino Benfante at your service, Signorina Muggifalco. I work for Signor Novara. *Illustrissimo* Signor Novara sends a message. Would Signorina mind coming with me to Palazzo de' Muggifalco? There is something very important that you need to see.'

'*Nonna!*' Rosalia cries. 'She must be back.' There has been no news of the old lady since the bombing. Rosalia has persuaded herself that the black shawl spotted at the cathedral is her grandmother's way of letting her know that she is safe and waiting for the opportune moment to come back: leaving a personal object for Saint Rosalia, after all, means that a grace has been received. 'Let's go,' she replies, and follows the man without hesitation. They start walking, weaving in and out of the crowds. The heat is still unbearable, cooking up the smells of a city with no water or basic sanitation. 'It's my grandmother, Signor Benfante, isn't it?'

'Signorina, we've been digging up the debris and tidying up, following Signor Novara's orders. We don't know ... Signor Novara's there now with my team.'

As they approach the ruins of the Palazzo, Rosalia spots a few figures standing in the middle of what used to be the ground floor, leaning against the handles of their spades. On the corner of the street, surveying their work, Signor Novara looks on. 'Rosalia, *bambina*. Thank you for coming straight away. Come, child. Come.' Signor Novara looks impeccable as usual, with a panama hat and his beige summer suit. He clicks his fingers at the workers, who immediately walk away from the ruins and huddle together on the street nearby. A few light up cigarettes.

Signor Novara holds Rosalia's hand to help her through the debris. 'Here. Have a look at this.'

Rosalia casts her eye around the wreckage, unable to speak. Just after the bombing, at least, the many familiar items dotted around the ruins made her feel as if she was still at home. Now, with wood, stone and wrought iron all piled together in a shapeless heap, it looks like a building site abandoned by its workers.

A large area, roughly corresponding to the inner courtyard and the main flight of stairs to the upper floor, has been bulldozed to ground level. This exposes a neat hole where the Palazzo de' Muggifalco's entrance to the cellar would have been. In the afternoon light the top of the hole seems to shine. When Rosalia gets to the edge of it, she can see the steep stone stairs to the cellar. They are undamaged.

'Careful,' warns Signor Novara, stepping to her side. 'Look down there,' he adds, pointing into the darkness.

Rosalia bends down a little, scrunching her eyes up to see what he is pointing at. She detects a smell, slightly sweet and with a hint of decay, like a piece of meat that, left to dry in the sun, has lost the sharp smell of decomposition.

'Can you smell that?' asks Signor Novara, and his face is grave. She nods, still not understanding.

'Your cellar's full of grain. I'd say there's barley and hops, but also a few sacks of wheat. Of all the cereals, barley is the best to store because it keeps for a long time after harvest.' Rosalia is stunned. 'You have enough wheat to make all the bakers in Palermo very happy for a week. In short, *bambina*, you have a small treasure down there. The grain's rotting because of the dampness and the enclosed space, and a little fermentation seems to have taken place – hence the smell.'

'Grain?' repeats Rosalia, still lost. 'What grain? *Papá* never mentioned anything about keeping food stored there. I thought our cellar got flooded this winter!'

'It probably did. Somebody, however, and I'm not saying it was your father, knew about the grain and took great care of it. The sacks are neatly tied up and off the floor. You understand the importance of this, don't you, Rosalia?'

'I ... I'm not sure. Whose grain is this?' she stammers, still standing at the cellar's entrance. Her eyes, now accustomed to the darkness, can see the outline of numerous sacks slumped against the stone walls. Some are piled on wooden benches; others lie on a layer of sand and bricks. She turns towards the workmen who have made the discovery, but they all move a little closer to each other, surrounded by cigarette smoke, and look elsewhere.

'Well, as I've no reason to doubt that Palazzo de' Muggifalco is now yours and the grain's in your cellar, I believe that the contents of the cellar are also yours. I strongly suggest that you don't tell the Allied government.'

Rosalia's mouth feels dry; she does not dare ask any more questions. She wrings her hands in desperation but says nothing. Shortage of food is one of the first problems to be tackled in defeated Sicily. Or is it conquered? Liberated, perhaps? She does not know. War is certainly responsible for the famine, and the Germans billeted on the island had the lion's share of whatever could be found. Rosalia remembers the words of the little Sicilian man who had saved her life only a few weeks before: 'They raided my cupboard this morning'. The newly formed foreign government is keen to destroy the black market, but Rosalia hears about it all the time: lavish supplies of food stashed away by criminals who charge infinitely more for it than is fair. No one dares to speak the name of the beast that, at least temporarily under Mussolini's government, was forced to go into hiding. It is now growing stronger again: the mafia's ghost is back. Faceless criminals will take advantage of people's hunger and misery.

Rosalia thinks of the stories she has heard of locked granaries in the middle of the countryside. Farmers pretend not to know what is stored inside, then feign surprise as the local army forces its way through the chained door; sacks of grain, piled up high; food under lock and key. Jail for them, after confiscation. Here, though, in her family home's cellar? Surely not. Who would do such a thing? 'My father would never have done this. I don't know why those sacks are there, but I'm sure the cellar was empty before,' she manages to say, and swallows a tear.

'Before what, Rosalia?' asks Signor Novara, and his piercing eyes are suddenly kind and full of sadness. 'Before the war? Before the bombing? When was the last time you saw the cellar?'

She does not answer his question immediately. Her family had not used the cellar as a shelter for many months, because of the flooding the previous winter. But now it appears there was no flooding. She looks at the sacks of grain, and thinks of other people starving. 'I can't remember. I don't know. We haven't been eating it!' she blurts out, feeling like a silly little girl again.

'Maybe your father was storing it for somebody else. Nobody is accusing you or your family of anything. All I'm saying is that you'd better either get rid of it or hide it as well as you can. You might otherwise get into trouble with the AMGOT. Our new friends are very keen to redistribute supplies and look good.' Signor Novara takes Rosalia's hand and they walk away from the cellar. He looks around, examining the ruins of the palace, then he turns to the girl again, 'I'm making every effort to help the government in any way I can. Mistakes have been made,' and here

Signor Novara sighs a little theatrically, 'but I want to make sure that my country makes a full recovery. Here's what we do,' he adds, suddenly cheerful. Rosalia looks up, waiting. 'My men will rebuild the entrance to your cellar, and put a lock on it. Forget about those sacks. I'll make sure they disappear and end up in the right hands. In the meantime you're welcome to stay at my house. With Vincenzo still on the run I'm happy to have you in his flat for as long as you want. It's a comfort for us to know that the basement isn't empty. I'd also be happy to help you with rebuilding Palazzo de' Muggifalco. Your parents' will must be somewhere: you're not of age yet, and Signora Muggifalco senior has not been found. You need a patron. Let me be the one.'

Rosalia feels her head spinning. She is ashamed of her relief but cannot fight it. Perhaps Signor Novara is right: 'Thank you, sir. Yes, my father must have held these supplies on behalf of someone else.' For the first time since the end of the war in Sicily, Rosalia has a warm feeling of belonging again. Gratitude sweeps over her. Gratitude for her hospital work, no matter how menial; for Vincenzo's flat; and for the handsome stranger waiting to be looked after, who may never know of sacks of grain and flooded cellars. 'Thank you,' she says again.

Signor Novara smiles and pats her softly on the back. 'Nessun problema.'

'Any news of Vincenzo yet?'

It is hard to believe that it has been so long since she last saw him. Rosalia misses his friendship, the warmth of his laughter and the hours spent together with the others, creating the works of art that nobody knows about. Since her home has been destroyed, despite spending far more time at the basement than ever before, Rosalia has not touched clay. She briefly wonders where her other friends are; ironically, it was not the war that put a stop to the weekly meetings, but rather the end of it. Vincenzo's absence is hard to cope with, but even harder is his silence.

Signor Novara's face darkens. 'No,' he says curtly. 'He was supposed to accompany my wife to our villa in Casteldaccia. Instead he suddenly decided to change his plans and join some friends of his in Mondello. We haven't heard from him since. I had to go to Casteldaccia with Mara myself.'

'Can you not talk to his friends? Did they leave Palermo too?' Rosalia feels a pang of disappointment at the news. Vincenzo never mentioned his sudden change of plan, and she always thought that the artists, as Vincenzo used to call everyone who came to his basement searching for inspiration, were the only friends he had. That he chose to keep part of his life from her is surprisingly hurtful.

'They're not at the address he gave me before leaving and I have no way of tracing him. We'll just have to wait. Mara is getting very distressed about it.'

'Do let me know when you hear from him. I've been worrying about Vincenzo too.'

Signor Novara gives her a strange look, as if he doesn't quite believe her, or has no intention of doing what she asks. He mutters a polite 'Of course'.

If Rosalia were a little bolder, she would ask Signor Novara, who has always befriended the Germans, how he is coping with the new American government. For, despite the fact that the rest of Italy is still fighting on Hitler's side, the war is definitely over in Sicily. There are no Germans left here, and very little dignity. With her own ghosts to face, however, a long hospital shift behind her and an even longer one ahead, Rosalia keeps her questions about loyalty and politics to herself. After all, loyalty and politics will not explain the large supply of hidden food in her cellar, but silence will somehow make it disappear. Nobody will discuss with her how local government and police forces such as the *Carabinieri*, find the black market in Sicily one of the thorniest issues to resolve, and an effective way to create wealth in the mafia, though not the best. As Signor Novara knows only too well, the most powerful way to feed the mafia is for it to aim at the top government jobs in the region.

'Do you need anything at all, Rosalia?' Signor Novara asks kindly. 'What about food?'

'I'm fine, thank you. The hospital feeds me very generously.' The memory of an empty bowl of soup springs to her mind. The pilot's long and elegant hands; *'le mani di un pianista'* as her father would have said.

'Yes. We must take care of our wounded, our soldiers. Giving your time at the hospital is commendable, *bambina*.'

A little jab at her heart. Both her dearest friend and beloved grandmother are missing, and she is lavishing her care and attention on a foreigner. Not just the foreigner! I'm helping all those who are in need, she reminds herself. Nevertheless, it is the foreigner's face she fantasises about. In her dreams he kisses her passionately on her lips. She is embarrassed by her desire, yet lingers for more.

He is coming out of hospital tomorrow.

Chapter Eleven
WHAT'S LEFT

(O)n her way to work Rosalia spots occasional groups of people walking together, gesticulating wildly. She is growing used to it, although it still looks amusing to see two *carabinieri* and one civil affairs officer from the foreign government trying to find a common language.

A month or so earlier, Rosalia saw a large number of *carabinieri* from the local station being rounded up as prisoners of war by the Allied troops. It took some time for the Allied government to work out that, despite the *carabinieri*'s military uniforms, they are not soldiers but members of the Italian civic police force. The Sicilian *carabinieri* have therefore been given the authority to keep public order and work together with the foreign civil affairs officers, because of the latter's problems with the local culture and language. On the beat in Palermo, a typical group consists of one foreign policeman flanked by two local *carabinieri*.

Rosalia notices the guns dangling from the policemen's holsters, and shudders; her step quickens. Don't they say that the *carabinieri* are a stupid lot anyway? she thinks. Her father knew so many jokes about them. 'Why do they have pointy shoes? So they can squash ants in the corners of a room.' 'Why do they have red stripes down the sides of their trousers? So they know where to align their hands during a salute.'

She thinks of Andreas, surely by now getting ready to discharge himself. Her changing bag contains an apple, the key to Vincenzo's basement and a little money he left for her before disappearing. After much soul-searching she has decided to raid Vincenzo's wardrobe, and has a selection of clothes that should fit Andreas who, though much slimmer than Vincenzo, is about the same height. Her shift is not due to start for a couple of hours, but she needs the time to go through the paperwork and figure out which billet the pilot belongs to. The heads of AMGOT and the military forces have been using privately owned villas and stately homes in Palermo, a practice started by General Patton who took the regal *Palazzo dei Normanni* for his own use. The soldiers and air force have temporary accommodation spread around Palermo, with the nearest stations those erected close to the harbour: the encampment there is twinned with a few abandoned flats overlooking the bay, turned into residences for the Anglo-Americans.

She walks past Palazzo de' Muggifalco, and notices a newly swept flat surface. There is no trace of a hole or workmen. Signor Novara has kept his promise.

Most of the military vehicles are American jeeps, roaring past Rosalia and lifting little clouds of spent dust from the ruined buildings. The debris that covered the main roads has finally started to be cleared.

In front of her there is yet another trio of policemen on the beat, two Italian and one British. They walk fast along the pavement, which is already sunny despite the early hour. There is no room for Rosalia to overtake them, so she resigns herself to following them.

'Not ... just ... *scomparso*, disappeared ... *il mangiare* ... the food, *armi*, bang bang, too.' One of the Italian officers is trying to talk to the civil affairs officer, a British bobby determined to keep his uniform buttoned up to the neck despite the heat. Rosalia catches up with them, trying to eavesdrop without catching the men's attention. From where she is, only a few paces behind them, she can see spidery purple veins crawling all over the British policeman's cheeks and his neck, reddened by the sun.

Among the British police sent to Sicily after the invasion, many are bobbies who were on a regular beat in London. Despite the language barrier, they seem to be thorough and attentive. This one, walking between the two local policemen, is desperately trying to understand, but the *carabiniere*'s English is worse than his Italian.

'The weapons we confiscates from the village ... Altavilla, isn't it? They've disappeared? What, overnight? Didn't you have your men at the door? It was a bloody arsenal you lost, you fool!'

'*Arsenale, si.*' The *carabiniere* who has been talking is stocky and greying at the temples. He nods enthusiastically, happy to have conveyed the message. '*Andato.* Puff! *In fumo,* in smoke.' He swings his arm out to signal the distance the weapons must have gone by now.

'Not literally, I hope,' growls the policeman. The other *carabiniere,* younger than the one who has been speaking, smiles awkwardly. He steals a look at his colleague.

Rosalia's breathing struggles to keep up with the fast beating of her heart. She wonders... Weapons? There were no weapons. I didn't see any. Are they talking about those sacks of grain? If so, they know they've disappeared. What now? Should she go back to the house? Even if the three men were discussing the contents of the Muggifalcos' cellar, there is nothing she can do. She thinks of the urgent paperwork. What if they come to the hospital to arrest me? At every question she asks herself, each more troublesome than the one before, her pace increases. Suddenly, she is right up behind the policemen's heels, and as they slow down to cross the road she bumps into the younger *carabiniere*, the one who has not yet spoken.

'*Scusi!*' she apologises, terrified by the uniforms, the brass and the caps. Her changing bag falls to the floor, Vincenzo's shoes tumbling out with a soft thud.

'*Nessun problema, signorina.*' He is very tall and surprisingly blond for a Sicilian; his moustach is specked with red and gold. As he bends down to pick up the changing bag, his brown eyes meet Rosalia's. She notices that there is a speckle of gold in them too. 'Are you all right? Here's your bag.'

'Yes. Yes, of course. I'm sorry. I wasn't looking.'

'Maresciallo Casa! Our morning briefing starts in ten minutes!' calls the other *carabiniere*, who is now standing on the opposite side of the road with the civil affairs officer. The latter is standing very straight, hands behind his back.

Marshal Casa ignores them, intent as he is on the Sicilian beauty in front of him. 'Signorina, I am Marshal Nazario Casa, at your service.' He bows a little, then straightens up and looks at her, waiting.

'Ah, well, thank you. You're very kind.' Rosalia has pushed both Vincenzo's shoes back into the bag, which she is now holding against her chest.

'Maresciallo Casa!' The irritation in his colleague's voice is apparent. The British bobby looks on, his face impenetrable.

Nazario Casa's hand flies up to touch his forehead lightly in the military salute. He hides his disappointment behind a smile, then turns and runs across the road to join his partners.

Five minutes later, as Rosalia gets to the entrance of the Civico Hospital, she has already forgotten about the young man who would have loved to know her name. She leaves the humid heat outside the cracked pavement and takes refuge in the soothing shade of the hospital's hall. Up on the first floor, where the administration offices are, she looks for Clarissa. Instead, she finds the hospital manager, Mr Buttitta, sitting at her desk, with a face like thunder.

'Good morning, Mr Buttitta. Where's Clarissa?' she asks, looking around for her friend.

'Miss Muggifalco. Good morning. Clarissa's not here yet, as you can see. It's difficult to walk fast on one leg, I'm sure you'll agree.' His tone is slightly sarcastic. In fact, Mr Buttitta is in a filthy mood.

'I hadn't realised how early it is. I need the paperwork for the Cypriot pilot in the burns unit, Mr Buttitta. I believe he's ready to be discharged today, if the head nurse agrees.'

'Ah! The Cypriot pilot. What a sought-after young boy he is! His file is gone.'

'His file is gone,' Rosalia repeats. 'Gone where?'

'I don't know. Somebody from one of the foreign units, which have spread onto Sicily like cancer, came earlier and demanded to know whether we had an Andreas Kukus, or whatever his name is. When I said yes, he requested the file and took it away.'

'He's still here, though, isn't he?' Rosalia struggles to keep her panic at bay.

'I'm assuming so, but I haven't done the wards round yet. Anyway, he showed me some foreign credentials, something like an identity card, but I didn't have the time to read the name: it was in English. He said somebody will come and collect the pilot later. That's one less headache, Miss Muggifalco. For you and for me!' Rosalia is almost at the office door when Mr Buttitta calls out. 'Oh, and he said that the rest of the crew is dead.'

Rosalia runs up the stairs she knows so well. In her mind, the news about the dead crew mixes up unpleasantly with the possibility that Andreas may have gone already. When the swinging doors to the top floor open to let her in, she is oblivious to the curtains erected around one of the beds, a discreet reminder that a death has just occurred, and ignores the rasping sounds of those who are still asleep. Her eyes travel to the far corner of the room, searching for the shape under the sheets, the short hair, the white bandages.

He is still asleep, his hair matted and damp with perspiration, darker against the white pillow. The bandages have gone, exposing a few angry scars on the angular face. Andreas Khuklakis stirs, and opens his eyes to meet Rosalia's.

He knows that he is at his most vulnerable when asleep. Forcing himself to be alert straight away, Andreas does a quick check of his surroundings. He clings onto his official identity as it blends with the real one, emerging in those first moments of wakefulness. 'Good morning, sister Rosalia,' he says, politely.

'Good morning, Andreas. I think I spotted the breakfast trolley. It won't be long.'

'My last breakfast here, is it not?' Andreas stretches and moans softly under his breath.

'It should be. But we seem … it appears that we may have lost your file. That shouldn't be a problem, of course. I've got a change or two of clothes for you, and your personal effects are downstairs in a box.'

'My file. Never mind, sister Rosalia. It wouldn't have told you a lot. I've left all my personal documents in North Africa. It won't matter.'

'I haven't had the time to check where your station may be. There are American and British billets near the harbour, though the temporary government headquarters are a kilometre or so south of this hospital in the opposite direction. I'll leave your clothes here, under your bed. The head nurse will come and see you during the day, and I'll come up during my break. I've got rather a long shift today, I'm afraid, but I'm very happy to take you with me at the end of it.'

'All under control then, Rosalia. Thank you. I'll wait for breakfast and the end of today, then.' His voice is soft and the foreign accent weaves in and out of the words like an elegant swan amid reeds.

'See you later, Andreas.'

Rosalia does not want to stop and think about what she is planning to do. The unexpected turn of events pushes her naïvety to its limits. Is it loneliness? Fear? Sometimes at night, when all is still and even the foreigners' bivouacs are silent, she thinks she can hear voices in Vincenzo's basement. Voices she vaguely knows, familiar sounds. Could it be her parents, searching for peace and for the daughter who has not accompanied them on their last trip? Occasionally, when she finds a moment to sit in the basement and doodle a sketch in the large notebook that Vincenzo always had on the coffee table, Rosalia thinks she sees her friend open the front door and let himself in, smiling as usual. '*Vampirina*,' he calls.

She spends her days waiting for something, perhaps for a piece of her former life to be returned, undamaged. The hours spent by herself are the toughest. Awake, Rosalia either remembers her loved ones or fears seeing their ghosts. Asleep, she sinks into a black hole from which, occasionally, a lifeless hand wrapped in yellow silk emerges to haunt her.

It is too painful to accept that some bureaucratic process might take away a much-desired friendship. She is surprised by her sudden willingness to lie, but not enough to waver. Maybe the faceless man who requested the file will take Andreas away from his hospital bed and from her life. That makes her angry. Angry about the alien government, invaders, British and Americans alike, snatching men from hospitals without giving them a chance to recover fully. The rage supports her throughout her shift and hardens her determination.

She folds sheets, holds drips and empties bedpans, wondering, worrying. A couple of times she sneaks upstairs and pokes her head through the doors to satisfy herself that the pilot is still there. Yet, at the end of the longest day's work that Rosalia can remember, she suddenly wishes the clock would slow down. When there are only a few minutes left before she can go and claim Andreas for herself, she wishes that time would stretch, allowing her to think a little more.

Finally, the clock shows the end of her shift. I'm not doing anything wrong, she says to herself, resolutely. I promised I'd show him Palermo and take him to his billets, and I intend to keep my promise.

Rosalia washes her hands and face, wetting her black hair into shape. Her reflection in the mirror, with pursed lips and a frown on her forehead, stares back. Back in Clarissa's office the signed discharge form is waiting. She grabs it and climbs the three floors to the burns unit.

'Is it time, sister Rosalia?' Andreas asks, with a note of amusement in his voice. His eyes seem to have a little sparkle for the first time in days. He is wearing Vincenzo's white shirt and a pair of good cotton trousers held together by his own belt. Rosalia notices that it is pulled tight across his bony hips. He has a military satchel at his feet, stuffed, she suspects, with his dirty and ripped uniform.

'Yes.'

It is seven o'clock on a sultry early September evening. Vincenzo's friends, with whom he was supposed to have stayed, have come back to their town house in Mondello, near Palermo. They are telling a distraught Signor Novara that they have not heard from Vincenzo in over two months. Grandmother Antonia Muggifalco's body has not been recovered. The graves of Rosalia's parents have a smudge of daisies on the still fresh earth that covers them.

'Where to from here?'

'I'm not really sure. Just walk with me. I have an apple to share.'

Chapter Twelve
THE MILITARY CAMP

Andreas thinks they walk well together, as though matching one's step with the other person's pace is a special art, an activity to be enjoyed with the right person. Is that what war does to you? he wonders, stealing a look at Rosalia's soft features. Following the old *Cássaro* road will take them from the hospital to the harbour. The air is undeniably cooler than it was a few days before; the breeze from the coast pushes its way through the streets, carrying the smell of the sea with it.

As ever, the Sicilians dress according to the calendar rather than the weather: September will command a change of wardrobe, for those who have enough clothes, bringing out the long-sleeved dresses and corduroy trousers regardless of the temperature. Like many others, and for the same reason, Rosalia has dyed the few outfits she owns all black, as a mark of respect towards the dead. Sicilian women, more than men, need to display grief as if they were carrying a flag. The inexpensive black dress Rosalia is wearing today would have fitted her last year, when she was just a girl chasing geckos and climbing the palm tree in the middle of Palazzo de' Muggifalco's courtyard. She has picked at the seams to create more room and dropped the hem, but it still looks as if she has borrowed it from a younger sister.

Is that what war does to you? Andreas asks himself again, still walking in silence. War makes you appreciate the small things, like eating an apple or walking safely down the road with a friend. Yet, at the same time, it makes you almost impervious to death and loss.

People scurry along to a dinner of black market bread cooked in salty water. Suddenly, Andreas and Rosalia notice ahead of them a different kind of activity: military jeeps, loaded with men and equipment. The heavier pieces of war are being towed away to storage, or to be shipped over to the Italian mainland where the fight continues.

The segment of intense blue wedged between buildings catches Andreas unawares, despite the warning given by the sea air: he slows his pace, taking in the sight of a busy marina, with tents and temporary buildings. The sea stretches quietly behind them.

'That was our Naval Force's headquarters, to the left,' Rosalia explains, pointing at the low constructions virtually sitting on the west docks. The tents are interspersed with parking precincts, alive with military personnel and vehicles.

'*Rosso di sera, bel tempo si spera*', she quotes. 'Red at night, shepherd's delight.'

Covered military trucks trundle along, soldiers inside looking with indifference at the young couple standing by.

'See that stretch of tarmac over there?' Rosalia asks Andreas. 'It runs along the sea coast for a few kilometres. My father told me that before the war they used to run a car race here every year: the Targa Florio, named after the Florios, a very rich family that lives in Palermo. My father used to take me to watch the race start, sitting on his shoulders.'

'They're using it as a runway,' Andreas comments, dryly.

'Yes. I asked around today. Both army and air force officers are billeted in those houses over there. The owners fled a few weeks ago and don't dare come back yet.' She is referring to a crescent of white terraced houses that follows the curve around the harbour. Most of the windows have lost their glass panes; some have been replaced by blackout material or fake leaf camouflage nets, which are now billowing in the breeze.

'And where do you live?' He asks the question without looking at her, during a pause in the noises around them. Voices shouting orders, engines roaring: the encampment is getting ready for the evening.

'I'm using a basement flat which belongs to a friend of mine, for the time being. Another fifteen minutes or so from here, continuing along the road to our right. If I carry on working at the hospital I might apply for nurse accommodation, at least until ... until I know what to do. My home is completely derelict.'

Andreas does not answer. He looks at the sea in front of him melting into the sunset, and the colourful remains of Sicilian fishing boats swept up ashore in abandoned piles.

In his mind a memory forms, unpleasant and dark: another beach, another sunset, this time in North Africa; a radio in the distance playing 'Lili Marlene'; the teasing voice behind him of a burly officer who had had too much to drink before a night flight. 'Who's a pretty boy, then?' he was saying, over and over again. Cackling, pretending to be a cockerel. Andreas remembers standing on the beach and looking out across the vast expanse of sea. He had ignored the other officer, but wrapped his hand around the gun holster strapped to his shoulder. He had been stroking the small, cold press-studs, calculating the right moment to whip it out and kill a man.

'I said, I'm sorry about your file. It had your identity papers and bracelet.' She must have repeated the sentence louder this time, and Andreas lets go of yet another blurred piece of his past.

'The papers would have been fakes anyway, Rosalia. I'm four years younger than they said. Papers don't matter. Only men do.' Andreas smiles. With an effort, he pushes other thoughts away. The memory of that gun disappears.

'Do you want me to come with you to the main offices? I've been told that the administration work is carried out over here, but there are additional stations on the other side of Palermo, where the civil airport is.' Dear God, don't send him there. Please don't. Don't let him go. It's too far away from here. Don't let him leave me! A silent prayer behind her warm smile.

'No, Rosalia, thank you. I'll go on my own. Do you mind waiting here? The least I can do, after all your kindness, is to walk you home.'

She nods, overwhelmed with gratitude.

The Allies seem to spend more time dealing with administration issues than gathering their forces to get on with the fight. The war has not yet been won in the rest of Italy. If Rosalia could see inside the humid offices, where the only relief from the heat is a tired fan recycling the air, she would be amazed by the amount of paperwork generated, passed around, bickered about and finally destroyed. If she could understand the language, Rosalia would be surprised at the number of quarrels and disagreements among the many departments, the different layers of authority. Forced into cohabitation and tandem ruling of a foreign region, the British and the Americans are growing increasingly suspicious of each other's actions, motives and objectives. The personnel based at the harbour have executive power, whilst the Allied Government's headquarters in the heart of Palermo controls the region. Navy, army and air forces regularly manage to implode here, slowed down by the day-to-day grind. Losing trucks, supplies and arms to the local faceless delinquent bureaucracy wears down the toughest military forces.

As Rosalia stands waiting, she can hear men's voices carried by the sea breeze, heatedly arguing over yet another truck that has disappeared under their nose. An Italian workman who had been helping on the docks shouts obscenities in his dialect, realising, beyond the language barrier, that he is being accused of pilfering a load of sugar and flour, American supplies. 'How would I do that, you imbeciles?' he growls, his muscles rippling under the last rays of sun, shining with sweat. 'You're only picking on me because I'm Italian. Do you know what? I quit!' He takes the cap off his head and throws it on the floor, to illustrate his frustration.

'Easy, easy,' one of the others says, patting him on his broad shoulders. 'No *problema*, my friend. Take it easy.' The Italian is unmoved.

Among the workmen, Rosalia spots the only blue uniform, with red stripes and glistening badges: a young Italian civic police officer, tall and lean. The *carabiniere* is holding what appears to be a notebook in his hand

and is reading from it. 'The thing is, the truck was here yesterday evening and gone today. This morning the parking slot where it should have been was empty, and there's no paperwork to show it's gone anywhere else.'

'They say it was me, but I have nothing to do with it. Nothing!' The Italian labourer jabs his finger at one of the American soldiers. 'Can't even drive, *maresciallo*. Certainly not one of those beasts. I have three children at home, waiting for a loaf of bread. Why would I get into trouble here?'

If Rosalia could, she would leave the spot where she is standing, embarrassed by the argument just a few metres away. However, she does not wish to attract attention to herself, and fears that Andreas may not find her if she goes elsewhere; so she keeps her eyes firmly to the ground.

'Nobody is accusing you of anything,' sighs the *carabiniere*, and he sounds genuinely tired and fed-up, though Rosalia cannot work out whether that might be because of the disappearing supplies or the danger of losing yet another workman. 'Who was doing the late shift? It would be impossible for them to miss a big truck being driven out of here at night.'

Voices rise with names and suggestions. The Italian officer flips a couple of pages over the board he's holding, immersed in reading the notes. Rosalia steals a look at him and realises that she has seen him before. Not long ago. That very morning, in fact. She collided into his back on her way to the hospital. What did he say his name was? She keeps her eyes fixed on the handsome face whilst trying to remember; and so it is that Nazario Casa catches sight of the girl he has been thinking about all day, sure that he would never meet her again.

'Excuse me,' he mumbles, leaving the workmen behind as he walks towards Rosalia. They follow him with their eyes and stop arguing.

'What a coincidence, *signorina*. We meet again. Can I help you? Are you waiting for someone?'

Rosalia clutches her bag tighter; the uniform intimidates her and the memory of their previous encounter has brought back her concerns about the cellar. She tells herself that the sacks are gone and there is nothing to fear. 'No. Yes. I mean a friend. He's finding out where he's going to be sent next.'

'I see. Italian? Air or sea?' It is the second time today that Nazario Casa has had to hide his disappointment: waiting for a friend at the harbour's military base is not something a young woman would do unless that friend happened to be her sweetheart. She is probably already spoken for.

'I'm not really sure.' She knows that her answer sounds daft as soon as she utters it.

'What are you not sure of? Whether he's Italian, or which force he's in?' He speaks to her so kindly that Rosalia feels even more of a fool.

'He's Greek. Greek Cypriot.' The golden speckles in the Italian officer's eyes seem to glitter under the ordnance cap. She realises that he is smiling.

'Ah. British, then. Is he a pilot or a naval officer?'

'Pilot.' She whispers the word, oddly exhausted by the conversation and the sudden thought that, strictly speaking, Andreas should not be there but back at the hospital, waiting for the person who took his file to take him to his quarters. Wherever they might be.

'What's your name?' Nothing wrong in asking for her name, even if she's waiting for a British pilot, Nazario tells himself.

'Rosalia, sir. Rosalia Muggifalco.' She answers the officer, of course. It would never occur to her that the man behind the uniform asked the question.

Maresciallo Casa knows an opportunity when he sees one. 'Well, Miss Muggifalco, I shall have to make a little note of who you are and where you live, because I'm in charge of these premises, you see. I must know who comes and who goes.' He is still smiling kindly and hoping that she won't call his bluff.

'I'm Rosalia Muggifalco, daughter of Solicitor Antonio Bellino Muggifalco and Elena Muggifalco, now deceased, resident at Palazzo de' Muggifalco in Vittorio Emanuele Orlando Road, destroyed by bombs, sir.'

Marshal Casa solemnly takes some notes. Behind him the workmen have dispersed, returning to their stations or their vehicles. The Italian man who had been complaining is nowhere to be seen.

Rosalia instinctively decides that it might be better to give as much information about herself as she can, to keep the *carabiniere*'s attention away from Andreas. 'I'm sixteen. Seventeen next month.'

'Your home's been destroyed, you said. Have you got alternative accommodation, Miss Muggifalco?' The pen is poised on the notebook.

'I'm staying at Palazzo Novara at the moment, with friends. Same road as my home.'

'Novara as in Signor Giacomo Novara's villa? The businessman?' Marshal Casa's eyebrow rises imperceptibly.

'Yes, sir. I'm a friend of his son's, Vincenzo Novara. He's letting me stay at his flat in the basement until … until things get sorted out.'

'I see. Well, Miss Muggifalco, thank you. I'll bother you no longer. Do let me know if you, or your Cypriot pilot, needs any help at all. We Italians are meant to co-operate to the best of our abilities with our British friends.' He adds the last comment breezily, watching her face for a reaction he does not get. Marshal Casa knows that the Novara family was close to the Fascist regime and its German allies before the Allies' landing in Sicily. He might be wrong, of course, and Rosalia might be talking about a different family. He will make his enquiries. That may even mean a visit to the Novaras' house, depending on what he finds out.

He takes his leave, giving Rosalia the military salute, as he did in the morning. 'Maresciallo Nazario Casa, at your service. Goodbye, Miss Muggifalco.'

She watches him walk away briskly towards the battered green jeeps and temporary facilities erected on the tarmac. Men attending the vehicles, loading, unloading, fuelling and manoeuvring the trucks in the parking bays, occasionally look at her longingly, and think of their faraway girlfriends.

'Hello. Thank you for waiting for me.' Andreas has a musical voice, soft and not particularly deep, but Rosalia is startled by it nevertheless; she has been looking at the sea as it becomes darker and darker with the last vestiges of light disappearing between its creases. The harbour's voices suddenly seem to have abated, giving in to the distant murmur of those still waters. She had not seen him walk up to her.

'How did it go?' she asks, and shivers a little. September has brought the sudden surprise of chill air to the Sicilian evenings, but Rosalia has forgotten her knitted top in the rush to get Andreas out of the hospital.

'Fine. I'm to be put on desk duties until I recover fully, and I'll then be transferred to the airport camp, possibly to fly again from Sicily to anywhere in Italy. It's easier to use Sicily as an airbase than fly to the Alps from Northern Africa. They say that the Germans are taking ferocious revenge on their Italian allies, because they lost Sicily.'

Rosalia turns to look at the sea again, now a deep shade of violet. Lost Sicily. Until the war, she never thought of the tangible existence of her land. Now that it is being spoken of as if it were a piece of meat over which others fight, she suddenly understands how much Sicily is part of her everyday life. She feels a rush of affection for the bright colours and sweet smell of the lemon and orange orchards in the countryside surrounding Palermo; the fishermen's boats she could once see from her balcony, dotting the sea; the evening air carrying the sound of ancient songs bellowed in local dialect; the old people's wrinkles cooked by the sun, telling a thousand stories.

She looks down at her own hands, and for the first time in months misses her clay, longs to work it, mould it: she wishes to create stillness in this forever changing reality.

He watches her. 'Shall I walk you home, Rosalia?'

'Yes.'

The night will come, with its secret questions and ghastly terrors. There will be a time to wonder when she will see Vincenzo again; when Andreas will be taken away from her again, to fly, to fight; when she will have a home of her own. In the meantime, Rosalia happily heads for the Novaras' house, glad to share the walk with him.

Two keen eyes, full of resentment, follow them: they linger on the pilot's lean body, on the girl's dark hair. Andreas and Rosalia walk down the main road, turn left onto a side street yet to be completely cleared of debris, unaware of shallow breathing behind them. Many shadows dancing around them in the coming darkness hide the one who does not belong, who moves by stealth.

Chapter Thirteen
THE CLAY GHOST

I t is easy to succumb to the unhinging effects of war: it hits the very core of one's idea of stability, the family; it throws into chaos the orderly world human beings create to cocoon themselves in its cosy intimacy; it may make us doubt in a higher power of reasoning, the pure essence of justice. War is a challenge to our spirit.'

The bishop of Palermo pauses and looks down, embracing the crowd below the pulpit on which he is standing in one long, theatrical sweep of the eye. The silence in the cathedral is thick with drama; mothers pull startled infants to their chests and hug them tight, rocking and fearing an outburst of tears; men hold their battered hats between their legs, stroking the dirty hem, fingers swollen and nails blackened by newly resumed labour.

'Will your spirit rise to the challenge? As Sicily kneels down, prostrated by the misery of these last few years, will you keep still in fruitless meditation or will you stand up and praise the Lord for the opportunity we have today, to fortify our souls, rebuild rickety bridges and fortify weak resolutions?'

A murmur rises from the congregation like a timid sigh, gaining strength as people turn to look at each other and see, in their neighbour's eyes, the same will to believe. Channelling the energies of Palermo's community is not a job for the fainthearted, though Monsignor La Perla has taken to it with gusto; inhaling deeply the vapours of collective hysteria, he grabs both sides of the wooden lectern and leans towards the front pews, which groan under the weight of the city's politicians and top families. One or two of the black-suited gentlemen feel the temptation to clap. The ladies sit very straight.

'Will you let Him enter your life and show you the light? The ways of

God are infinite! Go, my blessed herd, go and sow the seeds of rebirth. God was with you during your ordeal, and has never left you. He will guide your hand! Remember how dear to Jesus true, honest labour is. Go in peace!'

The last words are almost drowned by the sound of bells ringing out the end of the two-hour long Sunday Mass. Monsignor La Perla lifts both hands in blessing. He watches impassively as, pew after pew, the cathedral empties of people galvanised by his sermon and trying to forget the empty cupboard back home. Tomorrow is another day and things will get better.

Rosalia sits at the very back of the church, waiting for almopst everyone to leave. She is wearing one of her grandmother's hats, a small black one with a veil large enough to cover her forehead and as fragile as a spider's cobweb. During the sermon she has allowed her mind to wander; it has, predictably, stopped at Saint Rosalia. From where she is sitting, Rosalia cannot see either the statue of the saint or the many objects left by those who have been granted their much-desired grace.

Nonna Muggifalco's shawl is back at Vincenzo's flat. On the day of her discovery, Rosalia had agonised over whether to leave it, draped across the wall behind Saint Rosalia's statue, or take it. In the end, she decided to remove it, in the hope that her grandmother would come back and notice its absence.

'I'm sure she wanted me to find it.' Rosalia waits until the cathedral is virtually empty before heading for Saint Rosalia's corner, as she has done every single Sunday after Mass since she discovered the shawl; not quite knowing what to hope for, but hoping nevertheless. The recess seems untouched; no-one has added or removed anything. Disappointed, she turns to leave.

'Rosalia.' Her name is whispered, as if Signor Novara were scared of waking the saints. She is startled by his gauntness; yellowish skin hangs from his cheekbones as if it had been de-fleshed. There are dark bags under his eyes. 'Rosalia.'

'What's the matter, Signor Novara? I haven't seen you or heard from you in weeks. Is anything wrong?' Before she finishes the sentence, a terrible thought has already been formulated in her brain, so terrible and disturbing that she cannot bring herself to ask the question.

'It's Vincenzo. We don't know what's happened to him.'

'Vincenzo.' She repeats the name, stupidly, and her head goes numb.

'Yes. He told us that he'd stay with some friends just after the invasion, but they've got no idea where he is. They've not heard from him for months. We're desperately worried.'

Rosalia does not reply. She stares at the man in front of her, suddenly seeing the father and understanding the enormity of his loss.

'Have you not heard from him at all?' Signor Novara is looking at her intently. She shakes her head slowly, thinking.

'When was the last time you saw him?'

The German soldier's body presses on hers once more; in her mind, his eyes look at her without seeing her fear. Behind his shaved head, a trembling hand wields a knife; she chases the images one after the other, and fast-forwards to Vincenzo, cradling and rocking her, whispering that all will be fine. It feels like a lifetime. Or a dream. Rosalia struggles to speak. 'I ... I think it was just before the Americans arrived. He said that your wife was waiting for him to take her to the countryside. I'm not sure, I'm sorry.'

'Not to worry.' Signor Novara's crushed face is painful to look at. 'I didn't think you'd have had any news from him, but I had to ask. We're trying to keep things as private as possible, in the circumstances. I don't want the temporary government to start a full-scale investigation over his son's disappearance. No foreigners. We're dealing with it.'

'I understand.' Rosalia does not understand, and is no longer listening. That Vincenzo should leave her is unconceivable. There must be another explanation: the war is over, is it not? Therefore he can't be dead. 'I'm sorry. Please excuse me.' She walks quickly out of the cathedral. Once outside, in the sunny square and cool October air, she starts running towards one of the hidden palms at the back of the building, to the right of the little cemetery. Behind the palm she stops to be sick, trying not to make too much noise. She can taste the tears at the back of her throat. Under her hands, stretched out and leaning on the palm tree to steady herself, the quilt-patterned tree trunk feels hard and immoveable. A lonely butterfly, stunned by the colder air, flutters about looking for late flowers.

Rosalia cannot remember returning to the flat. Suddenly, she finds herself inside it, looking around for signs of Vincenzo's existence. The curtains, drawn back and framing the dusty window sills, yield nothing but the occasional spider; the stained coffee table is covered in books and sketches, with a scattering of blunt pencils in the middle. The basement flat is as silent as ever. She throws her black cardigan, lacy hat and gloves on the bed, then starts going through the heavy chest of drawers in the bedroom, the wardrobe, and bathroom cabinets. Clothes, personal belongings, books and photos end up on the floor, where they stay, mute and accusing, scattered and forgotten, whilst she keeps searching in a blind fury. Her own few possessions mix with Vincenzo's, papers with occasional sketches of the garden outside, a study of someone's face.

When all the drawers are empty and the search still fruitless, she scans the room for more clues. The little door at the back of the kitchenette leads to a cupboard where coats and various implements are stored. Rosalia opens it to go through the clothes and the cupboard itself, more for comfort than to find answers, and spots on the floor, wrapped up in plastic sheets, a large amount of clay: Vincenzo's latest supply, as he had promised. It must have arrived just before his disappearance, as she had not been aware it was there.

She kneels down on the floor in front of the grey lump, slightly yielding to the touch, imagines him laughing with pleasure at her excitement and gratitude. 'A present for you, *vampirina*!' he would have exclaimed, as usual.

'How could you abandon me?' she whispers into the clay, stroking the cold plastic sheet, as if there were a breathing being living inside it.

Back to the simple bedroom, and the single, monastic bed, Rosalia opens the door to the bedside cabinet and looks under the hard mattress. She finds many samples of her own work scattered around: early statuettes moulded with timid fingers, the vague, yet recognisable profile of Vincenzo's cat, stretched languidly and fitting in the palm of her hand. I was ten when I made this one, she thinks, longing for those years of carefree joy once more. Vincenzo had always been there, encouraging and supportive.

A voice, calling her name from outside Vincenzo's basement flat, pulls her from reveries and back to reality. Who can it be? Not Signor Novara, surely. Rosalia knows that he occasionally stays at the villa because she has heard, late at night, the wheels of his Alfa Romeo grinding the gravel on the main driveway; the engine purring just before it is switched off, and then the soft thud of a car door being shut.

Rosalia has strained her ears, attuning them to catch noises other than the night screeching of the odd city cat, but nothing can be heard from the elegant rooms of Palazzo Novara. In the morning, by the time she is up and ready to walk to the hospital, the car is gone and the villa empty again. If he comes back during the day, when she is at work, Rosalia does not know, but she has sometimes wondered.

When she opens the door, Andreas is standing there, a rueful smile quickly turning into a frown when he sees her face, red and blotchy because of her crying. 'What's the matter?' he asks, and his eyes instinctively wander behind Rosalia into the flat. 'Have you been burgled?'

Most of the beautiful, decadent palaces of old Palermo that were abandoned by their owners during the war have been looted at some stage. In the early days after the last bombing, Rosalia has witnessed episodes of callous plundering even as people were trapped under rubble and unable to stop the thieves. She remembers the outstretched arms of those who thought the men climbing the ruins had come to help; the cries; the noise of the cart wheels tripping over the debris, stolen goods piled up high on it.

'Burgled? No, no, I haven't.'

'Is everything all right?'

'Come in. Sorry about the mess, but I was trying to find something.' As she utters the words, Rosalia suddenly knows what she has been looking for: a reason. A reason for Vincenzo's disappearance, of course, but even more than that; she has been looking for a reason for his silence.

'Let me help you.' Andreas looks as gaunt as ever, but tidy and neat in his foreign uniform; his hair has been cut under the military cap. There is a small gap between his neck and the shirt's collar where the tie rests. Not for the first time, Rosalia's eyes linger on the smooth throat. The artist in her registers odd details, such as the absence of a noticeable Adam's apple.

'Thank you, but there's no need. You can sit there.' She points at the old sofa.

The flat is untidy but welcoming all the same; Andreas thinks that it smells of her. He pushes away an unpleasant feeling of dismay, a vague sense of envy. For Rosalia seems to leave the mark of her own personality on belongings, objects, places. If only he could do the same, and feel a home as his own!

Colours fill the flat with inner light: Andreas looks around at the many drawings pinned onto the walls; Rosalia's own clay work is everywhere. 'Is your friend an artist?' he asks.

Rosalia pushes to one side the many papers and books, so as to make room for Andreas to sit. 'It's a little more complicated than that,' she answers with a sigh.

They sit, side by side, as they both look at life fragments on the floor. She tells him about Vincenzo: his generosity, the meetings, the other artists, her secret work, and the batch of clay waiting in the cupboard behind the kitchen door. Andreas listens in silence. It is easier for Rosalia to talk about Vincenzo to someone who does not know him and cannot share her loss and desperation. Signor Novara's pain only rekindles her own.

'So you're a sculptress.' Andreas picks up one of the early works, the figurine of an old shepherd as Rosalia saw him, climbing Monte Pellegrino with his herd; it was early morning in another hot Sicilian summer, a lifetime ago; the sun had not yet dried the dew on the dandelions which painted Monte Pellegrino's gentle slopes a bright yellow. She had been about twelve and out on a walk with her father. Their mission was to catch butterflies with a net made out of an old stocking.

The clay shepherd looks as if he is straining over an imaginary slope, one foot taking most of the man's weight. The wrinkles on the sunburnt face seem to dance around his half-shut eyes.

'Remarkable.' Andreas speaks the compliment to the statuette and Rosalia's heart gives the familiar little jolt she has come to expect whenever he says something particularly kind, or looks at her with those intense dark eyes. 'You have a real talent. Why did you work here instead of in your own home? Surely you didn't need Vincenzo's help.' He turns to face her, so close that she can see his smooth face, the oddly long eyelashes. Rosalia loves the delicate youth of his features. Andreas possesses the sort of handsomeness that does not threaten but soothes the onlooker. To sit so close to a man, alone in the flat and with no chaperone, feels no different from spending those secret afternoons with her artistic friends.

'I did ... well, I do ... I couldn't work with clay back at home. Just not the kind of thing one does.'

'What do you mean? Were you afraid of your parents' disapproval?'

Rosalia has never, before now, given an explanation of why she would not do any sculpting at home. Vincenzo and the others did not need one, and she rarely dwelt upon the issue herself: in truth, the secrecy of her other life contributed to the exhilaration and excitement on which she fed her creativity. 'We all came here to do our work because this place is so peaceful, and light. Vincenzo gave each of us the space we needed, and he's the perfect host. You can talk to him about art and he'll say the right thing, encourage you to explore and find your way. We owe everything to him.'

'What about your parents? Did they know about your artistic circle?'

The thought of her mother and father being aware of the regular meetings at Vincenzo's basement flat makes Rosalia smile. 'No, they didn't. They had no idea I knew him well. To them, he was just the Novaras' boy.'

Andreas' ears prick up. Novara. Vincenzo is a Novara. Is this a coincidence? That surname is at the centre of his current preoccupations. Has this girl unknowingly brought him straight to that family?

Rosalia continues, 'I mean, they knew him; but not the real Vincenzo.'

He puts that piece of information away, to be retrieved later. Then, with a sigh, 'Aren't we all different people according to whom we're dealing with? I'm sure that Vincenzo behaved like the Novaras' boy with your parents, but showed you and your fellow artists his other self. I say other self, because who are we to know whether there's a real, unique self at all?' He notices a shard of suspicion in her eyes, borne out of misunderstanding, and finds her readiness to defend her absent friend oddly irritating. She must surely love Vincenzo. Bitterly, he considers how strange it is that a sentiment as all-encompassing as love can make him feel left out and lonely. It is that loneliness which makes Andreas lower his defences a little, in an unconscious effort to draw her closer.

He should not even contemplate the possibility of disclosing secrets that are not his to share, but what if he gave her just a hint, perhaps a glance into the tangled reality in which he is caught? 'I'm not trying to say that Vincenzo may have been anything other than who he is, but it's in human nature to slip on one of our many identities as circumstances dictate. We all do it. You did too.'

Rosalia's expression hardens. 'I don't understand. Are you saying that I'm a fake as well as my friend?'

'No, not at all. But in showing your parents one aspect of your personality, that of a caring and dutiful daughter – as I am sure you did – weren't you reserving your artistic, creative self for your friends instead? You gave a portion of yourself to those who would understand and nurture it.'

She sits there quietly for a few moments. Then, shaking her head, 'I don't agree.' 'Wherever I was, whatever I was doing, it was still me, Rosalia, and nobody else. My hands could still mould clay even though I decided not to do so at home. When I was here in Vincenzo's flat, I chose not to speak about my love for my parents, which I nevertheless felt.'

'So, what do you feel now?' Andreas asks, not looking at her but playing with the figurine he is still holding in his hands. It is a question he has asked himself plenty of times in the last few months, locking the answer away before it took shape in his mind.

Rosalia has never been asked that before. To enquire directly after one's personal feelings is in contrast with the Sicilian way, which is to circumnavigate people's insular privacy. In fact, unprepared for the question, Rosalia struggles. At sixteen, and incapable of expressing emotive landscapes, she lies. 'Nothing.'

'How can you say that? You were crying when you opened the door to me,' he reminds her.

'Was I? I can't remember.'

Andreas looks at her clay statuettes and the many sketches, through which Rosalia tells her story more compellingly than with words. The idea comes naturally to him. Perhaps if they could find a way to filter their feelings, it might be possible to achieve some kind of intimacy. The closeness he seeks is otherwise denied to the person he must be and the person she is. 'Have you ever worked with a real model? I mean, somebody willing to pose for you.'

'No. I mould from memory. The sketches are there to help me find the features I need to transfer onto clay.'

'Would you like me to sit for you? I could come whenever you and I have some time off.'

Rosalia looks at Andreas, hardly believing her luck. To stare at him, legitimately, at leisure! She holds her breath, allowing the suggestion to sink in. 'Of course, that would be lovely. You could sit there,' she adds, already thinking ahead, pointing at the chair near the little kitchen worktop. That corner of Vincenzo's flat is always flooded with warmth: two windows open onto the unkempt garden, but at ground-floor level the sun's rays are smoothed into softer light.

'When do you want to start?' Andreas asks, still sitting on the sofa and stretching his long limbs under the coffee table. The patches of burnt skin tighten painfully under his uniform trousers. 'That new batch of clay is screaming to be put to good use.'

Rosalia does not hear him, as she has already sprung into action, running into the little porch at the back door, to the cupboard. As she crouches to grab the top of the plastic sack containing the clay, in order to drag it into the sitting room, she sees behind the stained glass of the door a familiar shadow. Seconds later there is a discreet knock on the glass, and the young girl standing outside pours herself in, hugging Rosalia tightly.

'Vera, dearest, how wonderful to see you!' Rosalia speaks into Vera's hair, which smells of hay and oil. The other girl says nothing, but squeezes her more tightly. Freeing themselves from the embrace, the two friends look at each other in the small porch, still holding hands.

Vera's bushy black hair frames a plump face, wet with tears. 'Did you hear?' she asks. 'Vincenzo is missing.'

'Yes, I know. Signor Novara told me today. It's terrible.' The pain Rosalia had managed to shut away for a while comes back, hard on her heart.

'Nobody has seen him for weeks. Why would he do that? Why would he disappear without telling us where he was going? We're his friends!' Vera wipes new tears off her eyes with the back of her hand. Rosalia notices that her fingers are stained with colour, her fingernails broken and blackened. She must have been painting, as usual.

'I don't know. I've been expecting him to turn up here every day since the war ended. He gave me the key to the flat when my home was destroyed by the bombing. He may still come back. Be strong.'

Shuffling in the background catches Vera's attention. 'Who's there?' she asks, and her voice sounds suddenly hopeful.

'Just a friend I made at the hospital where I'm working. He was in the burns unit for a while, but he's better now. Come, I shall introduce you.'

They find Andreas standing next to the window overlooking the garden, hands in his trouser pockets, gazing outside. He turns to face the two girls and smiles.

'Andreas, remember I told you about our little group of friends? This is Vera, one of us. She's a very talented painter. Vera, meet Andreas. Andreas is a Greek Cypriot pilot.'

'Hello.' Vera's hand flies to her unruly hair, smoothing it down.

'Rosalia's been telling me a little about this circle of gifted artists. Nice to meet you.'

'Have you heard from the others, Rosalia?' Vera turns to her friend, slightly embarrassed by the compliment.

'No, no-one. Michele and Laura's families were talking about leaving for the countryside, if you remember, but I'm not sure that they're back yet. Roberto's probably back now, trying to get a place at the university. He managed to avoid the army by becoming an *obiettore di coscienza*, a conscientious objector,' Rosalia adds the explanation for the benefit of Andreas, who suddenly feels the uneasiness of being a stranger among friends of old.

'I'm sure that you girls have a lot of catching up to do, and I should start wading through a pile of administration papers at AMGOT. I'll see you soon.' He picks up his hat and touches his forehead with two fingers, in a mock military salute. After that, he is gone.

'How are you?' Vera asks. She hasn't changed at all, still wearing her favourite dark green cardigan, complete with holes and stains that will not come off. It hides her overweight body, something of which she has always been ashamed.

'I'm fine. I keep myself busy. After the bombing, with Vincenzo not being here, I've just worked at the Civico Hospital as much as I could, just coming back here at night. You know, my parents ...'

'Yes. I'm sorry, darling.' Vera steps towards Rosalia and gives her another hug. 'I've been very selfish, coming here to cry about Vincenzo's disappearance, when you've lost so much more. My relatives spent all their time in the cupboard under the stairs, and they find it hard to adjust to high ceilings again. They still walk with a stoop.' She smiles, big white teeth and a dimple in her left cheek. Rosalia feels the usual pang of sisterly love. Vera squeezes both her hands. '*Coraggio, amica mia.* Be brave, my friend. I'm back now. We have each other. Come, let's sit down.' She gives a conspiratorial wink. 'Tell me all about this pilot friend of yours. He looks very handsome.'

Not far away, Marshal Nazario Casa is tempted to approach the young man in a British military uniform who is now walking down the Cassaro road, towards the harbour. From where he is, Nazario can see that there is no car parked beyond the gate on the Novaras' main driveway, which presumably means that Signor Novara is not at home. The British officer must have been there to visit the nurse from the Civico Hospital. Nazario Casa has done some homework and knows that Rosalia is a voluntary auxiliary nurse; he has been to see the place where her former house stood and is acquainted with her shift patterns and habits, such as going to Mass on Sundays at the cathedral. The British officer seems to visit the basement flat quite often.

Checking Signor Novara's movements is not as straightforward, and rather frustrating. Nazario Casa wishes that he could rule out for certain the girl's involvement with the Novaras, and whilst he knows that he could ask for the British officer's co-operation, he is nevertheless disinclined to do so: Nazario feels vaguely uneasy about how close, exactly, the young man may be to Rosalia. Moreover, as an Italian officer, Marshal Casa is privately resentful of the Allies' presence in Sicily and wary of their activities. Stretching his legs, which have gone numb from his forced immobility, he thinks, this one is probably just after our local girls. Somehow, that thought makes Marshal Casa even unhappier.

Chapter Fourteen
THE SITTINGS

The Civico Hospital's canteen is far more than just a place to eat; in the large room furnished with expanses of Formica worktops, doctors and nurses escape for a little while from the daily suffering of their patients. They end up dipping into each other's lives.

At lunchtime, the hospital radio sitting on the window sill broadcasts news of the war still raging in the rest of Italy. As the Anglo-American temporary government settles in newly conquered Sicily, there is no mention of the fact that the Allies' heaviest losses in the war have been suffered as they invaded the island. No political broadcast will dwell on their mistake of letting German troops retreat to the Italian mainland and continue the offensive from there.

'At least we got out of that mess,' comments Dr Sciortino to a couple of his younger colleagues. Wearing their stained white coats complete with stethoscope sticking out of a pocket, they are queuing for the second-rate wheat spaghetti coated in watery tomato sauce; solitary glasses of cheap wine balance on their battered canteen trays.

'Those poor buggers in Northern Italy have to choose between being executed by the Germans if they get caught, or imprisoned by the Americans if they don't fight the Germans. Nobody knows what they are meant to do.'

'Our great king, eh? Good old Vittorio Emanuele Orlando, dropping his royal pants and signing the armistice with the Allies. Unconditional surrender, that's what he's promised.'

The youngest doctor pipes up, still struggling with his tray. 'What was he supposed to do? Italy has no chance whatsoever with the Anglo-Americans closing in from all sides.' His stubborn first attempt to sport a beard has resulted in isolated in-grown hairs peppering his face.

'Ah yes, but he forgot to tell our troops, didn't he? Ran away together with our General Badoglio and left all the Italian armed forces facing both the Germans and the Allies. No briefing, no information, nothing. We've become Europe's laughing stock: our men get shot in the back by the Germans if they don't attack the Americans, and yet Italy is supposed to have ended all belligerent action! I don't envy our troops or the partisans. As I said, poor buggers.'

'Sister Rosalia,' booms Dr Sciortino, suddenly noticing the girl behind the spotty young doctor, the keen supporter of the monarchy. 'I was wondering whether you might be interested in doing some overtime for me: the other nurses have families to attend to and are cutting down on their hours.'

For the last fortnight Rosalia has declined offers to do extra hours, and has spent her working days at the hospital suspended in a state of joyous anticipation. The meetings at Vincenzo's flat with her artist friends used to fill her with a sense of excitement: those were hours stolen from her family life, a naughty secret to be shared by few. Now that she is working with clay again, it is the thought of consigning Andreas to it that sustains her throughout the day, as if she had finally found the real purpose of sculpting.

'I'm sorry, Dr Sciortino, but I'm unavailable for extra shifts at the moment,' she answers sweetly.

'What could possibly keep you from this hospital, girl?' he asks, the hint of a smile ready to be shared with his other colleagues. 'You've not found yourself a boyfriend, I hope?'

Rosalia feels as if the entire canteen had stopped to listen to their conversation. Certainly, the other two doctors are watching her expectantly. She sees, with the corner of her eye, the serving lady holding the ladle in mid-air, waiting for her answer. 'No. I'm busy, that's all.'

'They've not found young Novara yet, have they?' His eyes narrow as they scrutinise her face. As she feels the blood creeping up her cheeks, Rosalia desperately tries to fight the oncoming blushing. 'Rumour has it that he was bumped off by the Germans when they realised that his father had been doing some undercover work for the Americans. Do you know anything about that?'

As quickly as it had arrived, the heat leaves Rosalia's face, replaced by a deadly cold. She turns as pale as candle wax. Her hands' grip on the tray weakens, and crockery and cutlery crash onto the floor.

'Leave her alone.' Clarissa has moved from her place in the queue to stand next to Rosalia, defiant and straight-backed despite her precarious balancing on crutches. 'She's only a child.'

Dr Sciortino looks around harvesting support from the others; his eyes stop on Rosalia's face. He does not address Clarissa, feeling a little uneasy about the public confrontation: Clarissa works in the administration office, and could, if she wanted to, mess up the weekly wages, delaying them enough for him to feel the discomfort. The black market is as expensive as ever, and Dr Sciortino has two children and a wife to feed.

'Well, everybody knows that you live with the Novaras, so I'm only asking whether you know where the boy is. It's hearsay, I'm just repeating what I heard.'

'I don't live with the Novaras. I'm borrowing Vincenzo's flat until he … until I sort my family home out. I know nothing about Vincenzo or his father.'

Hospital staff, weary of the scene, grow keen to move on, and the queue starts moving again, imperceptibly. Rosalia picks up the tray from the floor, takes another bowl and a ladle is dunked with a splash into the broad bean soup. Conversation resumes.

She sits at one of the tables in the far corner. Clarissa joins her and they both stare, in silence, at their white enamel soup bowls, chipped and too hot to touch.

'Is it true?' Rosalia finally asks. 'Did you hear that too? Did the Germans kill Vincenzo?' In her mind, she recalls Signor Novara's tired face, and his insistence that the search for Vincenzo should be undertaken discreetly. If not killed, could Vincenzo have been kidnapped?

'I don't know, sweetheart.' Clarissa wishes she could reach out across the table and take Rosalia's hand, but she does not want to get too involved; the grandchild she lost after the bombing was all she had, and she does not feel ready to let anybody else into her lonely life. Not yet. 'There's been some talk about the Novara family, simply because they're rich and famous. People wonder why they've not been taken in for questioning; after all, they were very close to German high officials. Some say they know Mussolini personally.'

'Signor Novara has been very kind to me and is so worried about his son's disappearance. Vincenzo would never have left like that, without a word. He's a caring and loving friend and … I miss him very much. Something terrible must have happened; maybe the Germans have taken him.' Rosalia talks whilst stirring the soup with a piece of black bread, absent-mindedly. When the piece sinks into the dark liquid, she breaks another one from the roll.

Clarissa ponders. 'The Allied military government may know more. Someone from AMGOT came a few days ago; they were after that young man who was in the burns unit … the Cypriot pilot, I'm sure you remember him. It was an Englishman who made the enquiry, I think. He got the pilot's file and said that he'd be back for him the day after. Only when he did come back, the pilot was already gone. My records say he discharged himself, so I told him.'

Rosalia struggles against the onset of more blushing, and keeps her eyes down to examine the enamel bowl in great detail.

Clarissa does not seem to notice, absorbed by her recollection and the task of twirling the overcooked spaghetti onto her fork. 'At the time he left his details with us here, in case the Cypriot pilot should come back for any reason. He told me to call him straight away, should that happen. I must still have his phone number somewhere. You could call him and ask whether they know anything at all. He spoke good Italian.'

Rosalia nods, fishing the bits of soggy bread out of the soup with her spoon. Inside, she struggles. There is danger in calling the AMGOT representative – what if he found out that she was behind Andreas's hospital discharge? But the desire to find out as much as possible about Vincenzo's fate is burning her soul.

Thankfully, her shift is busy enough to peel those thoughts away. Fewer and fewer of the hospital patients are there because of the military conflict. Civilians and soldiers alike have been treated, cared for and discharged; later, they join the anonymous phalanx of wounded victims who can no longer legitimately lay a claim to any specific malaise, and must leave the hospital with able bodies and sick memories.

The new patients are, in a way, easier to deal with. Their ordinary ailments encourage Rosalia to think of life as normal again. Occasionally she wonders what her elegant mother would have thought of washing stained sheets and bandages, wiping down ulcerated wounds and stripping bare the mystery of a man's body by helping patients with their most basic physiological needs.

Nevertheless, to know that Andreas will be there at the end of her shift gives her both the excitement she only ever achieved outside Palazzo de' Muggifalco and the comfort typical of family life.

As is now routine, once Rosalia gets home, she is greeted by the murmur of a *caffettiera* on the little stove and two little porcelain cups on the table. There is a bar of chocolate to share, which Andreas has been given by his American friends at the harbour military base. The lump of clay she has been working on is on the round wooden worktop, carefully covered to avoid it drying out.

'I have two oranges,' she announces, before dropping them unceremoniously on the coffee table and running to wash her hands.

'How was your day?' He sits on the sofa and opens the fruit with his long, slim fingers. AMGOT's directives have filtered down to the military camp at the harbour, together with new shirts and underwear for the officers. Andreas is now wearing a long-sleeved khaki shirt, tucked into his ordnance trousers. Her hesitation does not go unnoticed. 'Something happened at the hospital?'

'One of the doctors told me that people think Vincenzo has been executed by the Germans.' She sighs, coming out of the little bathroom and wiping her wet hands down her dress. The towel has been used to wrap up the clay.

He looks at her with those dark eyes, an impenetrable expression on his face. 'And what do you think?' he asks. The segments of orange are tidily laid out on a plate in front of him.

'I have no idea. Vincenzo always told us that his family believed in the Germans' military power, and that Mussolini was right to position Italy on their side; and yet he never said anything about his own opinion on the matter. With our group he only discussed art, painting and poetry.'

'Well, he was your mentor, after all. Possibly he felt that politics should be left out. Did any of the others have a political view about the war?'

'No, not really. We just met here to enjoy art, exchange ideas. I suppose we came to enjoy the freedom of doing what we loved without being judged.'

Andreas gets up slowly. The burns on his legs are still bothering him: with any movement, the patches of skin not entirely healed stretch and burn, reminding him that he is still convalescing. He walks to his chair, there in the corner, as the sunset comes through the window. He sits, and stares straight at Rosalia, as he has done for the last two weeks, and clasps his hands in his lap. 'Tell me more,' he says, and falls back into the state of immobility she has insisted on, so she can capture his handsome features. When they both take a break he will gaze out of the window, at the palms and sycamore trees filtering the dying light. Vincenzo's garden, as they both refer to it, seems to be irradiating life in the cool October air.

Rosalia's hands work on the clay carefully, gently. He knows that when she concentrates hard a little vertical line will appear between her eyebrows, at the very top of her nose. That line, which he cannot see at any other time, is a sign that Rosalia is lowering her defences. A silent audience may be less threatening to someone who is not used to expressing her opinion. By modelling for her, Andreas agrees to satisfy Rosalia's artistic needs. However, his silent stillness creates a vacuum in the room that Rosalia instinctively fills with words. The information Andreas seeks may be found among them, and his attention never wanders. 'My father and Signor Novara were good friends. It was my father who looked after the Novaras' legal affairs, being a solicitor. He had an entire shelf for their paperwork in his study. Sometimes Signor Novara came to our house and they locked themselves up in there for hours. My mother would joke that if Signor Novara paid my father proper wages, we'd be richer than them.'

Andreas lets his eyes follow the curls of Rosalia's dark hair, which falls prettily onto her shoulders. He briefly wonders what she would look like without the hair band that holds it back, covering her ears. A smudge of wet clay is quickly drying on her forehead.

'Vincenzo has always been in my life, since I was a little girl. I'm an only child and so is he; he's also a few years older than me and has always looked after me, despite his disease.' Andreas looks at her quizzically. 'He has some body-wasting illness that means he's physically very weak. The Novaras dote on him, and he's always had whatever he wanted: toys, travel, books, money. Even, as you can see, this flat, which is completely separate from the rest of the house.'

As she talks, her fingers caress the neck of Andreas's bust, smoothing it, creating the illusion of movement within the clay. That little crease between her eyebrows deepens. She does not know how to say that, like her, Vincenzo had love but not in usable currency. Andreas guesses that she must have always taken comfort in her talent, whilst Vincenzo drew his from surrounding himself with gifted artists.

'You had the talent, but no-one around you saw any particular use for it. He did.' Andreas stretches his legs in front of him, slowly and carefully. October seeps into the room, claiming the legitimate darkness of an autumnal early evening.

Rosalia removes a sliver of clay from the angular jaw of her Andreas, and then stands back, the better to observe the result. The domesticity into which they seem to have fallen makes Andreas closer to her than ever before. Probing his features affords an intimacy that leaves her, after every sitting, longing for more. More time. More closeness. Inexperienced as she is, Andreas's availability during the day has necessarily started eroding her platonic fantasies later at night. His smell lingers in the flat after he is gone; Rosalia finds herself staring at the incomplete bust, gingerly touching its grey cheek with one finger, trying to imagine what it would be like to stroke the real thing. One night, feeling more than ever the weight of loneliness, Rosalia had crouched down near the bust, her mouth level with one of the ears. She could feel the warmth of her breath against its coldness; in her nostrils, the faintly musty smell of damp clay. 'I love you,' she had whispered, confused by her own desire. 'Tell me you love me too.'

The bust only stared back at her, with that supreme form of coldness which is indifference.

Rosalia had been struck by it. 'I've not managed to give my sculpture a life of its own. Why?' she had asked herself, studying the bust closely. Andreas's features were all there, meticulously reproduced and well proportioned. She was sure to have caught the constant sadness in those dark eyes, but something else was missing. 'Where are you? Are you still inside this lump of clay?' Inflamed by passion and maddened by her own solitude, Rosalia had questioned her own sanity.

She had just engaged in conversation with a statue.

Chapter Fifteen
THE BUST

Tell me about your parents.'

'No.'

'Is that because there's nothing to say, or because you don't feel like talking about them?'

It is a beautiful, cool and sunny Saturday morning. Vincenzo's garden is swathed in lashings of gold and red leaves that have fallen from the horse chestnut and cherry trees. From the kitchen window Andreas can see, here and there on the bougainvillea bushes, the sparkling tear of a lingering drop of dew.

Rosalia is wearing a little black top with three-quarter sleeves and a thin string of little pearls round her neck. Andreas wonders when she found the necklace, as he has never seen it before, and whose pearls they were. From where he is sitting he can see the back of the bust, and is once more surprised at her attention for detail: those little curls of clay hair covering the head look as if they have just been combed; the collar of his shirt, perfectly reproduced, still slightly too big for his neck. Andreas wishes he could see the face on the bust, but that will not be allowed until the work is finished. Rosalia is fussing over it, blowing an invisible speck of dust off its ears.

'I can use this study of your face to make a proper stone sculpture of it when I find the right kind of stone.'

'Do you miss them?'

She straightens up, putting her hands on the small of her back, and looks at him curiously. 'Do you miss yours?' she replies, without answering his question.

'Mine died when I was a child. I was brought up by my uncle, Christakis, one of my father's brothers. He still works at the farm where I grew up. My twin sister died last year of glandular fever. Uncle Christakis lives on his own.'

'What's it like to have a twin sister?'

Andreas struggles to keep his thoughts straight and coherent. Many memories come flooding in, overlap and disappear inside one another; he has trained himself to pick the right ones and make them work for him, but the question has caught him unawares and he hesitates, trying to gain time. 'It's rather like having two versions of yourself, one you can control and one you'd sometimes like to control but who, annoyingly, doesn't let you. We were very alike and yet incredibly dissimilar: stubborn and determined to fight for one's important causes, but in different ways. Same ideals, opposite sex. My twin complemented me. I suppose I've been searching for that part of me ever since.'

'I'm two persons too.' With her fingernails, Rosalia is carefully imprinting on the bust's face the faint reticulate of lines she can see on Andreas's own. Lines she can only see when he smiles. 'I am what I was expected to be at home: my father's loving little girl, my mother's polite and respectful daughter. I was tutored by my family and read all our Sicilian playwrights' works. I did needlework and charity visits with my grandmother.' A pause, a step back to check the overall effect on the bust; she steals a look at Andreas, sitting on his chair, waiting. 'The perfect child, faithfully fulfilling expectations of what a Sicilian girl should sound, act and look like. My family made sure that I would be well educated and mannered, a nicely wrapped present for my future husband. My bridal linen and clothes were washed, ironed, starched and folded, then put away in three iron-buckled green trunks in the loft. If you go to Palazzo de' Muggifalco, you can still see them through the missing wall on the upper floors. My parents may well be under a wooden cross at the cathedral, but my trousseau is safely tucked up in the loft.' She spits out the last sentence with bitterness. 'For all the love I felt for my father, life at home – whether my family home or my own – could never be what all my girlfriends aspired to. I wanted more, I wanted something else. I cheated and lied to my parents so that I could be the *other* person too, at times. The person I could be here.'

'Rosalia.' His voice is tender and so is his face, but he does not make any attempt to get close.

Rosalia continues, ignoring him. 'Working with clay, or stone, or wood, anything at all, drawing with coal or lead, is what I want to do. What makes me feel alive. I couldn't face my father's disapproval, his disappointment, so I hid it from him. Now he's dead and I shall never have another chance to ... atone. To explain. To make him proud of me. My parents will never have a chance to know this other part of me. Will never learn to love the whole of me. And that ... that's sad. That's my regret.'

'I'm sorry. Nevertheless, you did what you felt was right. It's not your fault that your parents have died.' Andreas flexes his hands and leans over slightly. The midday sun plays with his hair and casts a soft shadow to the side, over the chunky white marble butler sink. 'I'd say that you're rather brave to have pursued your dream. Cyprus is no different for women. Cast in their roles from a very early age, their life, too, is determined by whom they shall marry and the number of children they will be able to produce. This war exacerbates the difference between the sexes. Nobody recognises that aspirations may grow in the wrong body.'

Rosalia looks at the man in military uniform sitting in front of her as if she saw him for the first time. Not just the man she is in love with, but someone's child and brother. 'You must miss your sister very much. As an only child, I longed for company. To have someone to talk to, just like this, must be a very precious gift indeed. Even during our best meetings and afternoons together with Vincenzo and the others, we never discussed why we were here, or our aspirations. I feel ... I feel a closeness to you that I've never experienced before.' She blushes. In her fantasies she has occasionally told Andreas what she feels for him, and has then been swept up in his arms, a passionate kiss soon following. Now, standing in the kitchen, with a clay bust between them, she waits for that dream finally to become true.

Instead, Andreas remains seated, his face troubled. He ignores her confession. 'Are you close to the Novaras too? You're barely seventeen and shall need a guardian. Are they likely to step in and take you under their wing?'

Rosalia is briefly startled by the question; she has been so close to telling Andreas about her love that the sudden change of subject catches her out. Pretending to study her fingernails, dirty with dried-up clay, she gingerly walks to the sink to rinse them. Maybe Andreas has steered the conversation in that direction because he is embarrassed, she thinks, moving her fingers under the cold water. Already she regrets her forwardness, and longs for the previous silent intimacy, unharmed by words. 'Vincenzo's parents?' she asks, still at the sink, turning towards him.

She is closer than she has ever been to him. Does he know that? If only Andreas had any idea how painstakingly Rosalia has chosen her clothes that morning! She had agonised over whether to wear her mother's pearls, the same necklace Signora Muggifalco had been wearing when the bombs found her in her bedroom, getting ready for another literary meeting.

'Yes. Have you found your father's will? Is there one? He'd have provided for you, I'm sure. Have you found any documents at all?'

Documents, paperwork, books and ledgers: Rosalia thinks of all the ripped pages and loose papers dancing about the ruins of her family home, isolated fires feeding on some, the wind stealing others. 'What is it with you men?' she asks, with a sigh. That moment of mad physical proximity seems to have gone. She walks back to the table, angry with Andreas for having spoilt it. 'All you seem to be concerned with is paperwork,' she continues. 'Signor Novara asked the same question and so did Vincenzo, when we were trying to salvage what we could from the wreckage.'

'Painful as it is to confront death and your loss, Rosalia, there are implications about your future that you can't ignore,' says Andreas carefully. 'You need funds to rebuild your house; you can't stay here forever. A solicitor will ask you the same questions, but charge you for it. Your grandmother's disappearance doesn't help.'

Rosalia's heart feels the familiar squeeze; if *Nonna* were with her, loneliness would be so much more bearable. She thinks of all her grandmother's old stories about her father's childhood, the glorious past of the Muggifalcos and the bright future ahead. 'Something very odd happened a few weeks ago. I found her shawl.'

'Her shawl? Where?'

'It was at the cathedral, behind the statue of Saint Rosalia; one of the pawns given for a grace received. I'm sure it's hers; it's got a rip at the edge that I remember.'

Andreas frowns. 'Who do you think put it there? Your grandmother? Why would she do such a thing?'

'I don't really know. It's here, in my bedroom, if you want to see it. I removed it, and brought it home with me.'

'Did you find anything else? Papers, documents? I may be able to help you because of my contacts at AMGOT. The Allies are already planning to leave Sicily to its own devices and move their troops to mainland Italy. The future government might not be as helpful.'

Rosalia shakes her head. 'No, just the shawl. All the loose papers I've been able to save are in a box under Vincenzo's bed. You're welcome to have a look if you wish.' A sudden thought strikes her, and burns as sharply and as deeply as the loneliness of which she is so scared. 'The Allies are planning to leave Sicily? What will you do? Surely you're not well enough to fly again, not this soon.'

'I'm doing some … classified work on behalf of the British. That's all I can tell you. I'm not expected to resume flying duties for a couple of months at least. Let me have a look at those papers.'

'Wait. I need to cover your bust first, or you'll see it before it's finished. Only a couple more sittings and it'll be done.'

Andreas remains where he is, whilst she gently wraps the damp towel over her work. It stands on the table like a half-ghost, and even under the cover Andreas recognises his own proud stance, the perfect shape of his head. 'I can't wait to see it,' he murmurs, before moving towards the boxful of documents that Rosalia has pulled out from under the bed.

He sits on the floor, surrounded by papers relating to a family and other strangers he does not know and will never meet; pages yellowed either by time or by fire, old receipts for fancy hats and opera tickets. Amongst them, though, there are official files belonging to Antonio Muggifalco the solicitor, such as grazing agreements and dowry arrangements, property deeds and temporary wills. Other people's wishes, belongings and hopes, entire lifetimes consigned to paper.

As Rosalia embarks on her routine weekend housework, duster at the ready and a large apron to protect her best Sunday clothes, Andreas ploughs on, neatly separating the Muggifalco family files from the clients'. He is not entirely sure what he is looking for, but knows that he has the greatest chance of finding it in the dusty box in front of him. The alternative is for the document to have been lost among the ruins of the Palazzo. That cannot be helped, but all other possibilities need to be ruled out.

'Anything interesting?' she occasionally calls out from behind the kitchen worktop.

'Not yet,' he replies, truthfully.

They only take a break when Vera turns up with a loaf of proper granary bread, not the 'usual black brick', as she says smiling, and a large piece of *ricotta salata*, the hardened and seasoned goat cheese that Sicilian people grate over pasta during better times. Nowadays it is a rare treat to eat it as it is, its flavour unencumbered by sauces and sublimated by hunger.

'Are you doing a bit of clearing-up?' Vera asks, between mouthfuls. As always, she is wearing her green cardigan and a long skirt. Her fingers are stained with purple and gold, her fingernails still broken.

'Yes, I suppose so. Though I can hardly believe that this is all you found at your house, Rosalia,' Andreas says, pointing at the box.

'Oh no, that's just what I could carry with me. Vincenzo gave me a wheelbarrow and we shuttled back and forth, bringing whatever we could. The rest is still in some great big leather-bound folders that Signor Novara's men hoisted up to the second floor to keep out of the way whilst they were bulldozing some of the ground floor.'

Andreas sighs, still holding a document with one hand and a piece of cheese with the other.

'I heard that Signor Novara might become Palermo's new mayor,' says Vera. She is standing behind the kitchen worktop, trying to find a bottle opener for the home-made wine she has stolen from her uncle's cellar.

'Really?' Rosalia cannot take the surprise out of her voice. She thinks of the incident in the hospital's canteen and Dr Sciortino's words about the Novaras. 'I thought he was involved with the Germans. Why, Vincenzo was even worried about his parents' well-being after the invasion! How can this government allow him to become a mayor?' Her eyes, instinctively, go to Andreas who is still sitting on the floor, reading.

'I always thought that the German liaison was a cover-up,' Vera replies. 'The Novaras are far too cunning to put all their eggs in one basket.'

'Have you ever heard of Signor Novara over at AMGOT, Andreas?' Rosalia asks, a note of irritation in her voice. She had always thought of herself as Vincenzo's friend, his best friend even. Now she feels that she may never have known anything about him, or indeed his family. Her father had been Signor Novara's solicitor, but even he never spoke about his client and friend's political views. And now Vera, the outsider, the working-class girl who can't even read or write, seems to be up to date with the latest news.

'Sorry? Ah, maybe. The name rings a bell.' Andreas does not raise his eyes from the paper he is reading, a bored tone of studied indifference in his voice.

'Of course it would ring a bell. It's Vincenzo's surname. We're talking about his father. Surely you'd remember that.' Rosalia is clearing up the empty plates, and looks at Andreas with a frown.

'Yes, yes. Well, I don't really know. The offices are full of files on Italians with odd surnames. It's difficult for a foreigner to remember them all. I'm sorry.'

'Do you mean you might have access to information about Italians who are still missing?' Rosalia and Vera exchange a look.

'Well, I don't work in the missing persons department, if that's what you think. Anyway, do you have any idea how many people *are* still missing? Lost in battle, bombing raids, still fighting in Italy, left the country, the possibilities are endless. We deal exclusively with war-related issues and basic administration: things like running water, which we still haven't got in the east of Sicily because the pipe network has been damaged by bombing raids and the Germans, who blew up everything behind them; or food, which is still scarce and expensive. Rations should be increased but we need a central system to manage it all. Sicily is on its knees.'

'My father hated Mussolini,' says Rosalia, quietly. 'He thought that *il Duce* would send this country to hell. It's a high price to pay for someone else's dream.'

'Can I have a look at your work, dear?' Vera says, her eyes begging Rosalia.

Rosalia shakes her head, but she smiles. 'It's not finished yet,' she replies, her fingers already lifting the towel to afford Vera a private view of the bust.

Vera's eyes wander from the clay study to Andreas, still immersed in his reading, and back to Rosalia's work. 'It's beautiful,' she whispers in awe. She hesitates, then takes a breath as if to speak again.

When nothing comes, Rosalia turns to look at her friend. 'What is it?'

'Nothing.' Vera has walked to the bust and is holding up the towel herself, examining the pure line of Andreas's nose, the lips slightly open to show a glimpse of those perfectly straight teeth, the regal curve of his etched eyebrows, a small scar on the right of his forehead.

'Don't say nothing, Vera, when I know there's something. Spit it out!' Rosalia does not know why she is in such a foul mood. Perhaps it is the way Andreas has spoken about Sicily, as if it were a sick patient needing too much attention, forgetting that it is not Sicily's fault if it inconveniently stretches at the end of the Italian boot, open to all manner of abuse. Or maybe it is because Rosalia already knows what Vera is not saying: that she has unwittingly transferred her confused feelings towards Andreas into the clay model, smudging the edges of a perfect reproduction of his very essence.

'I'm sorry, Rosalia. I don't really know. It's as if ... as if ...' Vera leaves the sentence hanging in the air, unable to explain further. Her hand flies to her mouth, and she starts chewing her fingernails.

'... as if the physical features are there, but without his soul.' Rosalia finishes the sentence for her.

Vera subjects her fingernails to a renewed attack.

'There. I think this is enough for one day, Rosalia. I've sorted some of your paperwork for easier filing.' Andreas gets up from the floor with visible effort, leaning on the old sofa for extra support. He looks pleased as he points at the documents stacked in four neat piles. 'Your family papers were mixed with documents referring to several of your father's clients. If your parents made a will or some arrangement regarding your welfare, it would have been kept in your father's study, wouldn't it? Did he have his study in the house?'

'It was upstairs. Destroyed by the raid. Papers scattered everywhere.' Rosalia's answer is dispassionate.

'I know it's painful, but you must find out everything you can about your family's finances. You don't want to be working at the hospital for the rest of your life, not when you've got such a great talent.' Andreas smiles at both the girls. Only one returns his smile.

'I have no idea what to do,' replies Rosalia, smoothing the towel over the bust and still frowning. 'Palazzo de' Muggifalco will need a lot of work, and I'm not sure I want to live there anyway. Not after what's happened.' In the silence that follows Rosalia's words, she knows that the other two must be thinking of her father and mother, buried under the rubble, and *nonna* Muggifalco, evaporated into air thick with fire, smoke and screams. But something else bothers her almost as much: the cellar with that secret stash of grain: the food that Sicily is so desperately short of. What would Andreas say if he knew that? Would he still be helping her to find her parents' will? We know nothing about each other, she thinks, suddenly sure that Andreas will not, cannot, ever be hers. That perfect certainty cuts her as deeply as knowing that the bust of Andreas will never be completely finished. What on earth is missing, and where should I look for it? she wonders.

Chapter Sixteen
FAREWELL

They're all guilty of betraying the Italian people,' growls Vera. 'The Vatican, the Church as a whole, the rich industrialists of Northern Italy, the army with General Badoglio and that pathetic king we have. They've slept with the Fascists for so many years that we Italians no longer remember who we really are.'

Rosalia looks at her friend in utter amazement. They are outside AMGOT headquarters, sitting on the stone steps of the grand building in Cavallaro Street, for three hundred years a stately home belonging to a local prince and requisitioned by the Allies three months earlier. 'I didn't know you were involved in politics. This is the first time I've heard you talking about it. Since when have you felt so strongly?'

'Since always, my dear. Just because I hide myself behind canvases and colours it doesn't mean I don't feel for my country.' Vera lowers her voice, looking around to make sure they are not being overheard: 'They're all bastards, Fascists and Allies alike. The radio wouldn't mention it, as the government's keeping such tight control over the broadcasts, but up north the Allies have been bombing all the major cities, Milan, Turin, Genoa, instead of destroying the mountain passes – so the Germans keep pouring into mainland Italy! Nobody has our interests at heart; we have to defend ourselves.' She points at the *Casa Reale* building. 'Look at this. They came as liberators, but after the Armistice they took full control of everything, including our buildings and land. Let me tell you something: they've only destroyed the name of Fascism, not its essence. It's just like having the same regime without Mussolini. Can you not see *il Duce* coming out of these headquarters, military uniform tight around his fat stomach, square jaw jutting at the populace gathering outside? What's so different now? You tell me! And don't look at me like a scared rabbit. You intellectuals met at Vincenzo's to discuss paintings and sculptures, not the destiny of our country. I may not be able to read or write, but I know what's going on here.'

'So how do you ...' Rosalia stands up, shrugging off the cold that makes her limbs stiff. Autumn is well on its way, and the air bites through the thin fabric of her coat. She pulls it closer to her body.

'... keep myself up to date? I have friends who buy the *Sicilia Liberata*, the only publication allowed under this wretched government, and even that complains about the Allies' imperialist attitude.' Vera looks defiant and proud. 'I'm learning to read using the *Sicilia Liberata*. Did you know that the new Sicilian trade union centre is actually run by officers appointed by the Allies? So much for democracy! And strikes and protests aren't allowed. I ask you, what's the point of having trade unions if they can't represent workers and their rights?'

Rosalia is utterly bewildered. It is not just Vera's tirade that has shocked her, rather her referring to affairs she knows nothing about.

Vera laughs. 'Look at you, daughter of the genteel but penniless solicitor Muggifalco, brought up a real lady, wrapped up in cotton wool like a porcelain figurine. Come on, my friend, let's try to find out what they know about Vincenzo.'

The headquarters remind Rosalia of a very large beehive: officers, both in uniform and plain clothes, go in and out of the Catalan-styled building, on their own or in the three-man formation that she has come to know so well. As the girls enter the hall with its mosaic tiles and high windows, Rosalia is aware of the fact that they seem to be the only women in the building, and certainly the youngest. 'Where do we go from here?' she whispers.

'I haven't got a clue!' For all her audacity and passion, even Vera looks rather small and anxious as they approach the first flight of stairs. The click-clicking of their shoes echoes all the way up to the domed ceiling.

'Ladies! Have you got a pass? You must register here at the desk before visiting the relevant office.' The disembodied voice seems to come from under the stairs. A couple of seconds later, a middle-aged man with the obligatory moustache and plain cap emerges, having left his chair behind the reception desk. His military uniform is neat and clean, showing no badges or sign of having been put to any use other than vetting visitors.

'We don't have an appointment, sir. We're ... we're looking for a British officer. His name is Khuklakis. Andreas Khuklakis.' Rosalia tries to think quickly, annoyed that they have been caught out without a proper reason for their visit. What did we think we would do,? Just walk in? she muses. She knows that Andreas cannot possibly be here, as he is based at the other military base, near the harbour.

'Khuklakis ... Khuklakis ... Yes, of course. He's in today, I believe.

Signed in this morning as usual. His office is upstairs, second floor. Is he expecting you? Who shall I say is here?'

The surprise on Rosalia's face makes the guard suspicious. Maybe officer Khuklakis is not expecting these visitors; or rather, the visitors did not expect him. 'Just wait here, ladies,' he says, curtly. As he turns to reach for the intercom, a voice behind the girls stops him.

'Signorina, *quale onore*. I had hoped that you would do me the honour of a visit sometime.'

Rosalia manages a weak smile of relief; she recognises the handsome Italian as the *carabiniere* whom she has bumped into before, once on her way to the hospital and later at the harbour. She can't remember his name. Vera, on the other hand, looks as if she is about to melt into the floor. Her big green eyes bore into the Italian's face; a hand flies to her hair, in the usual attempt to rein it in. She looks so awe-struck that Rosalia gently nudges her.

The guard's body stiffens, hand to cap in the usual military salute. 'Maresciallo Casa. *Agli ordini*. At your service. These ladies are after officer Khuklakis, but don't seem to have an appointment with him.'

'Ah, I see. Well, Sergeant Rucolo, where is this Khuklakis's office? I'll escort the ladies myself. They'll be all right with me, I trust.' Marshal Casa points at the stairs with an outstretched hand. Vera, surveying his blue uniform with dreamy eyes, is the first to follow him.

'Yes, sir. Officer Khuklakis is on the second floor, at the end of the corridor and after the *Sala delle conferenze*. Good day, sir.' The guard clicks his heels as they climb the stairs.

'Thank you for your help, Maresciallo. We didn't think of making an appointment with anyone here. Officer Khuklakis's name was the only one that sprang to mind when we were confronted by the guard. Sorry, we've been foolish,' Rosalia says quietly.

'Not at all. So, you don't want to see him?' Marshal Casa has a smile on his lips which he will not let emerge. He has authority over these young ladies, and will use it to best effect. The seriousness of his face is betrayed by a sparkle in his eyes; Rosalia suddenly remembers the golden dust in them.

'No,' Vera answers, finally snapping out of her reverie. 'We thought this would be the right place to find a high-ranking officer to talk to. It's about a friend of ours who seems to have disappeared just before the Allies arrived. I'm Vera Lacrima, by the way.'

Rosalia raises an eyebrow. A visit to AMGOT headquarters had been her idea, and she had had to persuade Vera to accompany her. It now appears that Vera's feelings about the armed forces and Allied governments are starting to mellow, judging by the way she is looking at Nazario Casa.

'Vera Lacrima. True tear. Interesting name, Signorina Lacrima. I am Marshal Nazario Casa, at your service. What's your friend's name?'

'This is Rosalia Muggifalco, Marshal.'

'Oh, I know Signorina Muggifalco already. I meant your missing friend.'

Vera is puzzled. 'How do you two know each other?' she asks, giving Rosalia a strange look.

'We've bumped into each other a couple of times,' Marshal Casa says, and the private joke, lost on Vera, makes Rosalia laugh.

'Our friend's name is Vincenzo Novara,' says Rosalia solemnly, composing herself.

If Marshal Casa is surprised to hear the name he does not show it. 'Vincenzo Novara. We'll have to dig out a few files and see what we can find. Has he been reported missing? How long has he been gone?'

The girls look at each other, then Rosalia answers. 'We're not really sure whether he's been reported as missing or not. He disappeared on 23 July, according to his family. He said he was going to stay with friends west of Palermo, but never got there. His family assumed that he was still with these friends during the bombing raids and the invasion, so nobody worried about his absence for a few weeks.'

'I see. Have you asked the hospitals? A list of those who died in Sicilian hospitals is available for relatives who are looking for missing loved ones, but we don't have a list of wounded patients – they are discharged in time and go home. The problem is, hospitals are usually too busy and short-staffed to keep their lists up to date, so what we have on record is only the tip of the iceberg. But you're welcome to have access to the information we've got here.'

Vera nods vigorously. 'Thank you.'

As they follow the grand spiralling stairs, from which three upper floors spin off, with wide, light corridors, Marshal Casa steals a look at Rosalia, who seems lost in a reverie. She is silently pulling out of her memory strands of conversation she has had with Andreas over the last month. Did he ever mention having an office here? I don't remember. I assumed he would be based at the harbour because that's where I took him when he came out of hospital. 'What's the difference between this place and the military base at the harbour?' she finally asks.

They stop at a ceiling-to-floor window on the third floor, level with the roof terraces on the opposite side of the road. Instinctively, Rosalia looks for any sign of damage that has been sustained during the city's bombing raids, but finds none. Untouched either by the centuries or war, intricate rococo carvings support the wrought-iron balconies; the windows' wooden shutters, discreetly ajar to let in a thread of air, occasionally part enough to show a tongue of heavy silk curtains that have seen too much sun.

'Apart from the beauty of these buildings?' Marshal Casa replies, looking out of the window. On the building opposite *Casa Reale* two stone dragons crouch at the corners of its guttering, looking down with regal grace. 'See that palace there?' He points a finger at the building. 'Legend has it that those two roof dragons will fly off if someone in the house is about to die a violent death. The owners came out during the bombing raids to have a look, and when they saw the dragons still perched there they went back in and stayed put. As you can see, the whole street was spared.'

'Yes, but why did AMGOT decide to have its headquarters here and at the harbour?' insists Rosalia.

'AMGOT's headquarters are here. The military base at the harbour is an American camp which organises, among other things, the distribution of food and supplies to the areas that need them most. There's a small administration block that co-ordinates army, navy and air forces at the first point of contact, but the daily running of the temporary government happens here. We *carabinieri* are meant to keep public order whilst the British and Americans decide what to do and what kind of structure to leave in place when they go. I deal with liaison officers as well as Italian officials.'

They walk down the corridor, a musty smell of decay hanging in the air; it reminds Rosalia of her father's study. Sorrow tugs at her heart, waiting to be let in. Not yet, she promises herself. Later, when I'm alone. Then, aloud, 'Maresciallo. There's something else I'd like you to help me with.'

'Do tell, Signorina Muggifalco. I'll try my best.'

'It's my grandmother. She's ... well, she's missing too. Actually, I'm not sure whether she counts as a missing person or just as a casualty. She was at home when the house was bombed, but we couldn't find her body.' Rosalia rushes the words out before she has a chance to change her mind. Will he tell her not to waste his time, as *Nonna* must surely be dead?

'You couldn't find her body, did you say? I know this is very difficult, Signorina, but sometimes, when the damage of a building is extensive ...'

'No, it's not like that. We found my mother and father; and the house isn't completely destroyed. And ...' Both Vera and Nazario Casa look at her expectantly. They have stopped outside a door that opens onto a very large room; inside, there are many desks manned by numerous officers, both Italian and foreign, talking to each other or typing. The furious tapping is rhythmically interspersed by the ding as each typewriter arm reaches the edge of the page. The noise is extraordinary. 'There's something else too. I don't quite know how to explain it. It's rather odd, really ...'

'Maresciallo Casa! I need to talk to you about the Picione grain affair, it's *urgentissimo*! Trucks are coming back empty and the drivers have been told to get lost. I've got twelve men on the case but it's getting hairier by the day.' The lieutenant who is addressing Casa has a few decorations on his blue uniform, and a bald head under his greasy cap. He waves fingers stained by nicotine, punctuating his sentences with the robust salvos of a chesty cough. 'Picione himself is guarding the store with two shotguns and warns everyone about coming closer.' The man seems close to a nervous breakdown. Rosalia feels suddenly sure that he would pull his hair out if he had any. Marshal Casa looks at him concernedly but does not reply. Lieutenant Bartolini continues. 'Damn Picione! Do you know what he says to our boys? Look out! I have two shotguns, this one is *a palle* and this other is *a pallettoni*. Would you believe that? He's even giving the choice: bullets or buckshot. What are we to do? Let's send the Yanks and see how they take to Sicilian shotguns. I bet they'll suggest we ask the mayor of Picione's village for help, as usual.'

'Bartolini, just a minute. I'll be with you presently.' Marshal Casa looks at the two girls with regret. 'Ladies, I'll make some enquiries and come back to you about your friend. What were you saying about your grandmother, Miss Muggifalco?' He looks slightly nervous now, almost eager to finish the conversation. Some of the *carabinieri* in the room have stopped typing and are watching them curiously.

'It doesn't matter. I'm sorry about taking your time, Marshal,' says Rosalia. She clutches her little black bag tightly with one hand and adjusts the backpack containing a change of clothes for her hospital shift with the other.

'Do get in touch!' pleads Vera, turning back to address Casa on her way down the corridor.

'I promise.'

Vera struggles to keep up with Rosalia, who is striding past the various makeshift offices on the third floor of *Casa Reale*. 'What's the rush, Rosalia? Wait a minute!' The girls' kitten heels chase each other on the red and green majolica-tiled floors.

Down the flights of stairs and out of the front door: only then does Rosalia stop, panting a little.

'Whatever's the matter with you, Rosalia *cara*?' Vera puts a hand on her heaving chest, covered by the green cardigan, as if trying to stop it from wobbling. 'It looks as if you've seen a ghost!'

'I couldn't be there any longer; all those rooms, the noise and the uniforms. No more war. I can't take any more war, Vera. Even talking about my grandmother is enough to make me want to scream and run away.'

'The marshal seems very nice. Isn't it what you wanted, somebody to help us find Vincenzo? And what's this story about your *nonna*?'

Rosalia pulls her friend on one side. Uniformed officers are coming and going, indifferent to them. 'Shhh! Quiet! Before you know it, these people will come swarming all over the place. My father always said it's better to give polished badges a wide berth.'

Vera smiles. 'Well, that depends on who's wearing them, I suppose. Anyway, why the distrust now? It's not as if you're hiding something. We're here because we need their help.'

'I'm starting to think I can't trust anybody. Did you hear about Andreas? He never mentioned he had an office here.' She looks at the building towering above them. The massive statues of two rampant lions flank the bottom of the staircase outside AMGOT headquarters, and the first marble steps curl around the beasts' hind legs. Tall, unclipped yew hedges mark the perimeter of the building, an evergreen wall through which fans of ferns poke out tantalisingly. In the middle of Palermo's sorrowful desolation, this topiary extravagance strikes Rosalia like a dead note.

'What exactly does Andreas do?' They both sit down against one of the stone lions; mildew has painted a coat of dark green mould on its cold paws.

Rosalia shivers a little, hugging her knees under the thick corduroy skirt. 'He was put on administration duties until he's well enough to fly again. I think he mentioned some classified material he was working on, which he couldn't talk about, but I'm not sure.'

Vera frowns. She is condemned by her illiteracy to a world of puzzling signs. To her eyes all material is secret and forbidden. 'You may want to ask him why he did not mention working here when you see him next. I would have paid him a little visit in his office, as we're here.'

Rosalia sighs. 'I must go. My shift is due to start in half an hour.' They get up, dusting off the cold dampness that sticks to cheap clothes. Behind them, a breeze has started tormenting the yew hedges. 'See you later.'

You never told me what happened to your grandmother,' whispers Vera.

'That's because I don't really know,' is the sombre reply. They part on the pavement, with a hug and a kiss.

On her way to the hospital, a few blocks away, Rosalia has a feeling of dense premonition: in her imagination, old Mrs Muggifalco's black shawl billows menacingly in the distance; hundreds of *carabinieri* march towards her, carrying knives; Andreas's face floats dreamily above it all.

At the front door of the Civico Hospital, the feeling of dread stops her from going in and she stands there, backpack on her shoulders, thinking. '*Gesú bambino*, I can't do this.'

From the first floor of the hospital block, Clarissa is looking out, a cup of coffee resting on the window sill, crutches leaning against it; she sees Rosalia just outside the door, hesitating, as if she were making her mind up about something. A moment later, her slender silhouette starts to run away, backpack bobbing up and down on her shoulders. Clarissa checks the daily shift schedule: Rosalia is due to start in ten minutes. I wonder what she's up to, she muses, drinking her coffee before it goes cold. Maybe she's forgotten something.

The administration office is as dusty as ever; a single bulb gives out a weak naked light from the dirty ceiling. Clarissa sits down on the hard chair with an effort: she has been warned that the stump will bother her at every change of season, as if the missing leg cries to be reunited with the rest of her body, and the stump answers nostalgically. On this particular occasion, Clarissa's discomfort is probably more psychological than physical. Having seen Rosalia run so fast on her long, slim legs, she has felt a sharp tug, the cruel bite of envy. To have her youth and her body! To feel men's eyes following the contours of one's hips, staring longingly at the plunge between those full breasts! Clarissa smoothes the skirt over her lap, caressing the stump.

Rosalia runs towards the AMGOT headquarters without wondering what will happen if she is late for her shift or misses it altogether. She would be very surprised to know that her friend Clarissa will note her absence and mark it in red for Signor Buttitta to see. A gratuitous, wicked thing to do; but Clarissa will go to sleep that night and dream of her dead grandson playing with her two legs, shiny and beautiful like a mermaid's tail.

Casa Reale's stone lions cast their shadow onto the road as Rosalia approaches them. The evening is fast approaching. The dragons on the building opposite stare down at the road below, as if they are watching her. A moment to catch her breath, one foot on the first step of the staircase; at the top, barely visible in the fading light, the front door. Rosalia briefly considers going back to Marshal Casa's office, but before she has even started climbing the stairs someone comes out of the building and stops, taking in the fresh air, perhaps after a day spent in offices smelling of American cigarettes.

'Andreas!' She calls him without thinking, though later she will regret her impulsiveness; better to have followed him, to have found out where he spent his evenings and nights. Later, however, it will not matter any more.

'Andreas!' she calls again, but does not wait for him to answer. She is suddenly in front of him, at the top of the stairs, glaring.

'Rosalia. What are you doing here?' His eyes are harder in the dark. He lifts one hand to grab her arm, but changes his mind and lets it drop to his side again. She fancies that his voice is a little high pitched, with a note of worry.

'What are *you* doing here?' Rosalia spits out angrily. 'I thought you worked at the harbour, the military base I showed you when you came out of hospital. Why are you here? Why haven't you told me you have an office at the main headquarters?' She shivers a bit. One of the straps of her backpack has slipped down her shoulder and is resting in the fold of her arm.

'What does it matter? Someone came to look for me at the harbour and told me to work from here.'

'Was he British?'

'Again, why does that matter? Yes, he's British. I report to them, remember?'

'Is he the one who came to look for you at the hospital and took your file away?'

Suddenly, Andreas looks at her with infinite tenderness, as if she were his younger sister. 'Well, if you already know that, perhaps it's not me who's been hiding things.'

'I wanted you to stay with me!'

'And I do too, but I can't. Not the way you want me to. My job ...'

She interrupts, mad with grief: 'I don't mind your job. I don't care about your job or where your office is. Won't you just let me be your friend?'

Andreas sighs, then puts his arm around her shoulders, pulling her gently to one side. There they sit, side by side, on the top step. The evening has finally given in to darkness. Rosalia knows that whatever Andreas is about to say will make it impossible to go back to what they had before this conversation. For a moment, she contemplates getting up and running away, but she stays.

'It's not the job I have now that I was talking about. It's the one I had before and will go back to.'

'I'll wait.' She sniffs, in utter misery.

'Do you know what I'm talking about, Rosalia?'

'Your job as a pilot?' she ventures.

'You've never asked me what sort of pilot I am.'

'I don't know what you're talking about.'

'I'm a bomber pilot, Rosalia. A bomber pilot.' He repeats it more to himself than to the girl sitting next to him. As always, his brain immediately fills up with noises and images of his other life: the engines screaming, howling and growling; the voices of the other crew members, friends, dead or alive; flak exploding twenty feet away from his body, suspended and tantalisingly bright in the darkness of night missions; and the terrifying hissing of other aircraft materialising out of the nothingness one only finds high up in the sky. Give and receive death. That's what a bomber pilot is all about. The memories tear Andreas's mind apart, and he tries to escape them. The intense smells of a Sicilian evening, of jasmine and marine salt, mix with the unmistakable and sickening smell of burnt human flesh. 'I've bombed Sicily.'

'Sicily?' Her voice seems far away, as if she were no longer with him.

'Palermo.'

'When?'

'We flew from North Africa and targeted the area around the harbour. We left the harbour itself untouched, so it could be used by our navy, concentrating on enemy forces and supplies near it. Those were my instructions. In July, just before the Allies landed. I dropped my load and then flew back, inland. My plane developed a fault and I was forced to do an emergency landing. I can't remember much else, apart from the fact that I was thrown onto the back of a pickup and taken to Palermo. The same city I'd bombed that day.'

'Did you bomb my house?' This is the moment Andreas has been waiting for. The question he has asked himself many times and yet has no answer for. 'Did you destroy my home and kill my family?' The calm in her voice surprises Rosalia more than Andreas. Finally, she has a chance to confront the anguish, extinguish the doubts and terrible confusion that have plagued her mind. 'Did you?'

He smiles bitterly in the dark. 'I don't know. I was there, that much I can tell you.'

'That much is enough.' She shudders and thinks hard. I'll not show you my tears. You've squeezed my raw grief with your bare hands, but this pain is mine to hold, and can't be shared.

'I'm sorry, Rosalia.'

'You're a murderer.' Her ideas of war and life itself are suddenly clear. Puppets, that's all they are: human beings functioning without real humanity, loyal to their country much as a dog worships its owner beyond love, without understanding love itself. She wonders whether dogs are aware of being dogs. Would awareness increase responsibility?

'If it makes you feel better, I live with that certainty every day.'

'I hope you burn in hell.'

'That too.'

She gets up slowly, feeling neither the cold nor his eyes on her. Coming down the stairs of *Casa Reale*, Rosalia doesn't look back, even though she knows that she will never see him again.

SICILY, 1955

Chapter Seventeen
LETTING GO

(O)ccasionally, Rosalia walks to his office just to catch, on her way there, a glimpse of the building: *Casa Reale* has not changed much over the years: the same grand rococo façade, large windows and marble staircase. Perhaps the stone lions show a little wear, after exposure to the salty sea air from the harbour a mile or so down the road. The mouldy patches between their claws and around their open mouths have grown larger; while the tall hedges behind them are not clipped regularly, so the lions seem to live inside a slice of jungle within Palermo's urban landscape.

Usually she looks up at the dragons on the house opposite, to check whether they are still watching the street below. Sometimes she stops to admire the architectural beauty of those three-hundred-year-old buildings, huddled together yet separated by the narrow cobbled alleyways that neatly dissect Palermo into a Roman grid.

Rosalia's hair is fashionably cut to shoulder-length and encouraged into soft curls, secured by tortoise-shell pins to keep it away from her beautiful face. Today she has decided to walk past *Casa Reale* on her way to the art gallery where her first exhibition is due to start. She is wearing red lipstick and a flattering black suit with a fluted A-shape skirt. Her heart is beating fast with anticipation and a little dose of fear. Will it be well received? Will there be enough people? Is he going to be there in time?

The marble staircase fans down to the street; Rosalia's eyes follow the steps one by one to the very top, reaching the building's front door. As always, no matter what time of the year or day it is, in her imagination it is always cold and dark up there, two people sitting on the top step of the staircase. She waits for the hurt to fill her chest and then flow away, and, as always, accepts it as the tidal rite of passage from childhood into adult life.

Casa Reale is no longer a requisitioned building, of course. Neither is it throbbing with uniformed police. It placidly sits in the sun, showing its decadent beauty to the people walking by.

Palazzo de' Muggifalco will never have the same ambience and presence, though the lengthy and painful restoration has finally made Rosalia grow fond of it.

She smiles at the thought of seeing him at the art gallery soon. Today it feels as if the long-awaited reconciliation with the world may finally be a possibility.

'Caught you!' laughs Vera, leaping at her from behind and pushing her arm through to rest on the inside of Rosalia's elbow. They walk for a while in silence, as only really intimate friends can. 'Are you nervous?' she asks, and as usual she leans slightly towards Rosalia, whispering conspiratorially.

'A bit. The owner of the gallery told me last night that everything's fine: the sculptures are in place, the rugs have arrived, the lights are working fine. All we need is people.'

'I'm sure they'll come in droves!' Vera replies, and smiles at two men on the other side of the pavement. They touch the rims of their Sunday hats and bow slightly, returning the smile. Rosalia notices that her friend has made an effort, looking rather pretty in a long flowery dress and matching hat. 'Steady! Don't give men false hopes, Miss Lacrima,' she scolds.

'Ah, you know I'd never do that.'

'I mean you should give them real hope.' Rosalia steals a look at her friend, and a conversation they had long ago springs back into her memory.

It happened just after their first visit to the AMGOT headquarters in *Casa Reale*, twelve years before. They were sitting on Vincenzo's old sofa, side by side, when Rosalia said that Vera seemed taken by Marshal Nazario Casa. 'You were making *occhi dolci*, sweet eyes at him,' she said.

'I most certainly was not!' Vera's reaction was forceful and disconcerting.

'There's nothing wrong with fancying someone,' Rosalia continued, confused by the denial.

'No, there isn't; but I don't fancy him, that's all. I was trying to be nice to him.'

'Well, it looked as if you were absolutely besotted.'

'I'm telling you, I wasn't. I can't possibly be besotted with a man.'

'Not all men are bad, Vera.' She spat out the words, not feeling very generous towards men when one of them had just broken her heart.

'You wouldn't understand.'

'Try me.'

Vera's sultry looks darkened further. 'You're too young to understand.'

'I may be young but I've been through a lot already. What can it possibly be that I've not experienced?' Rosalia said, with seventeen-year-old insouciance.

'OK, look.' Suddenly, Vera cupped Rosalia's face in her hands and placed a passionate kiss on her lips.

Rosalia remembers the kiss well, because it was her very first and possibly the most passionate to date. Vera's lips were full and warm; she held her friend's face in her hands throughout, making it impossible for Rosalia to withdraw. She never even thought of moving away, partly because of the shock and partly because there was a strong feeling in that kiss, a private insight into Vera's soul; and not entirely unpleasant.

It only lasted a few seconds; then Vera put her hands on Rosalia's shoulders, and pushed her away gently. 'There. Do you understand that?' she asked in a husky voice Rosalia had never heard before. 'I prefer women. Don't worry, I don't fancy you, but I do love you as a friend – so consider my kiss just that: a pawn of friendship.'

Neither of the girls had ever mentioned the incident again. Vera had never found herself a boyfriend.

The walk to the art gallery takes them through Palermo's old streets, nowadays paved with the same kind of big, square tiles that buckled and shattered under the Allied bombing of 1943. Reconstruction of *la Palermo antica* has been slow and beleaguered with setbacks, but at least most of the damaged historical buildings have been restored, together with the harbour and the main roads.

Grandmother Muggifalco's will was eventually found, under clothes covered in dust in the old woman's wardrobe. Access to substantial funds that had been bequeathed by Signora Muggifalco senior to her only granddaughter had made the restoration of Palazzo de' Muggifalco possible, with the help of Signor Novara's advice and his workmen. By then he was Palermo's mayor.

'When are you going to hold an exhibition of your paintings, Vera?'

'I don't need to do one. I have loyal buyers and can work as much as I want to. I'm happy. I'm the shy type, Rosalia. Art galleries are for competitive men. Or for talented sculptresses,' she adds quickly.

'I'm not sure about the idea of having my work prodded at and exposed to people's eyes, I must confess,' Rosalia says. 'But it's a great honour to be exhibiting at the Teatro Politeama.'

They are approaching the Politeama, one of the most famous theatres in Palermo, a sober architectural beauty oddly coupled with wild statues of golden chariots and winged horses chasing one another on its roof. The majestic theatre has become a meeting place for post-war, fun-starved Sicilian upper classes. The square in front of it is the perfect backdrop to indulge in public *passeggiate*, the weekend slow walks used to show off a new hat, outfit or friendship. The western wing of the Teatro's basement is dedicated to regular art exhibitions; the theatre itself is a magic showcase of acting talents and neurotic primadonnas, with comedy and drama usually sold out every weekend. 'A celebration of beauty in epicurean Palermo,' as the press calls it.

'You're the first female artist to be granted an exhibition here, my dear. The Politeama Gallery is a masculine world. Look, the only other women allowed here today have fur collars around their necks and strings of pearls as long as a day without food,' chuckles Vera.

They go down a short flight of stairs to the basement. The arts and exhibitions general manager spots Rosalia immediately and walks over with a smile on his face. Her sculptures are dotted all over the studio, some perched on plinths, others resting by the double doors through which the girls have come in. Mostly they are on the floor, but one or two are suspended from the ceiling.

Rosalia's eyes search the studio for him, beyond the general manager's smile and weak handshake, behind the fake partition walls, among the people who have come to see her creations. When she finally sees him, standing next to a stone composition of entwined lovers, Rosalia allows herself to relax a little. 'Nazario!'

He takes both her hands and places them on his mouth, for a gallant but chaste kiss.

'I was worried your shift wouldn't end in time for you to come.'

'I wouldn't have missed your exhibition for the world.' Despite Rosalia's high heels, Nazario Casa towers over her, and he has to lean towards her to make himself heard over the noise in the art gallery. 'I'm so proud of you.'

'Thank you', she says, and means it. Nazario is the only person in the room to wear a uniform. A few men give him an odd look; a *carabiniere* always makes people feel uncomfortable. The ladies, though, let their eyes linger on his broad shoulders and handsome, open face.

'Your very own show. A woman with the talent of a man.' He says it good-naturedly, delighted to share the sculptress with others, yet knowing that the woman is his.

'Ah! The talent of a man! Vocations can sometimes grow in the wrong body.' She has not meant for her voice to sound so cold. Someone else's words. Another man. Twelve years before. She pushes the memories away with an effort. Not today, she promises herself. I won't allow him to ruin everything today. She smiles at Nazario, softly.

'Nice to see you,' Nazario turns to Vera, and shakes her hand. 'How's the painting going? You're working on a Madonna with child, aren't you?'

Vera smiles conspiratorially. 'You two are the only people who know that. I'm so bored with traditional renditions that I can't wait to finish my own interpretation. Museums everywhere are full of ladies in halo and blue cloak, with beautiful baby attached. Wait for the Sicilian version!'

The gallery's general manager emerges from behind a plinth, slightly flustered by the champagne he has been drinking since before the doors opened to the public. 'Miss Muggifalco, could I borrow you for a minute?' he whispers, and opens his arms to show Rosalia the way, apologising to her friends. 'It's going remarkably well,' he adds as they walk towards the far corner, near the entrance. There are shiny pearls of sweat on his forehead; the gallery is quickly filling up. 'The mayor himself is here,' he says, regretting the champagne and wishing that the lights were not so hot. 'He wants to keep a low profile, so he's waiting for you over there, away from the crowds.'

Signor Novara is studying a group of pencil sketches hung on the wall, hands behind his back; his minder is smoking a cigarette just outside the front doors.

Rosalia has a few seconds to look at Signor Novara before he sees her, and she is struck by how much he seems to have aged in the last few years. It is true that he has never been the same since Vincenzo's disappearance, but there is a clear deterioration in him, which makes her quite worried about his health.

'*Bambina!*' he chuckles when he finally sees her. 'Look at you, the famous sculptress! What a fine exhibition you've put together. The general manager tells me you've already got a few buyers.'

'Signor Novara. How good of you to come here today.' She stands on tiptoe and lands a peck on his withered cheek. 'How is la Signora?' Rosalia politely enquires after Signor Novara's wife, though she knows that Mrs Novara lives likes a recluse and refuses to go out of the house.

'Well, well, you know ... Mara is ... comfortable. We're getting along fine.'

'You know that all of this wouldn't have been possible without you, Signor Novara. You've been incredibly good to me, and I'm very grateful.'

'Now, now. You've done it all yourself, Rosalia. Your parents would be so proud if they could see you today.' Signor Novara fans his hand out to include in one sweeping movement the whole of the brightly lit gallery. Behind them, people mill around, whispering as they stop in front of each exhibit.

'Yes. If only they could!'

Would they really? Rosalia is not sure. Her mother would probably be surprised, but would she be proud? A sculptress, indeed. But what's a woman unless she marries into a suitable family?

That thought makes Rosalia turn around to look at Nazario. What would her father think of his only daughter with a *carabiniere*, though a high-ranking one? At the age of thirty-three, Marshal Major on Special Duties Nazario Casa has progressed meteorically in his career and is now in charge of thirty men and two offices. He is also responsible for liaising with the Italian police force and regional government, and an influential member of the community. He is also the son of a greengrocer.

Papá would ask who Nazario's parents are and what they do. He would expect his father and grandfather to have been in the army; every male member of the family, going back several generations, to have served the country with a gun or a sword.

In the gilded mirror that hangs at an angle from the ceiling coving over the double doors, she catches sight of herself and Signor Novara. The heat of the gallery has lit up her cheeks and made her eyes sparkle; she likes the sassy haircut under her new hat. Thanks to *Nonna* Muggifalco, her life is comfortable and pleasant. Her career as a sculptress seems about to take off and make her wealthy beyond her father's means, crippled by his ideals and principles.

'Where's that fine young man of yours, Rosalia?' Signor Novara's hand shakes as he puts his empty glass on a silver tray.

'He's here somewhere. He finished his shift early to come to the opening.' She stands on tiptoes the better to search in the crowded room for the crested hat.

'When are you going to marry him? He's been waiting long enough.' Signor Novara smiles, patting her shoulder; the emerald on his big ring flickers green.

Nazario has been asking the same question for a while. Not to Rosalia, as he fears the answer, but to himself. Every time they spend the night together but he drives to his own home in the morning, or they have a splendid time at the theatre or the seaside but go back to their separate lives afterwards, the question is ready to tumble out of his lips – but never quite makes it.

Always there is a certain hesitation from Rosalia. At the beginning, Nazario interpreted it as shyness and naïvety. Later, when there was no doubt about the true nature of her reluctance, he simply decided to ignore it and live by the dangerous game of waiting; though exactly what he is waiting for, Nazario has not decided.

Rosalia does not withhold her love, that's true; at times, when they lie in bed at Palazzo de' Muggifalco, listening to the house's stiff joints creaking in the dark, Nazario is sure that she has chosen him and no other to love and be happy with. However, the small part of her that is thoroughly unreachable makes it impossible fully to own the rest.

'I'm not sure that I want to be married, Signor Novara. I may be too set in my ways to impose my bad temper upon the poor man. Besides, very wisely, he's never asked.'

'Time goes by fast, my dear, and sometimes it's not generous with what you already have.'

She knows what he is referring to. Given that Vincenzo's life expectation was poor, the gift of grandchildren would have brought great consolation to Signor Novara and his wife. Time can also be too generous with what one cannot have, stretching the disappointment further.

Rosalia's work is displayed all around them and she is confident that more and better is still to come, but there is one piece that she has held back, keeping it for herself: the bust of a young man, which is sitting on the window sill at the top of the stairs in Palazzo de' Muggifalco. Only the night before, during a chat over coffee in the austere and cold kitchen, Vera asked why Rosalia would not include it in the exhibition. 'Is it because you were never happy with it?'

'No. It's because I'm still not happy with it.' Rosalia was surprised by her own answer. She had never seen Andreas again, and he had died a year or so later, in action. Always careful not to talk about him, she did not know why she replied so candidly.

'The bust is incomplete because you stopped seeing each other,' ventures Vera. 'You never told me why.'

'He stole something very important from me. I could forgive, but I don't want to. The bust is there so I don't forget either.'

'How does Nazario take it?'

Rosalia shrugs her shoulders. 'We don't talk about it. The bust is there on top of the window sill and Nazario is alive, with me. They belong to two different Rosalias.'

'I remember you telling me after a while, that Andreas had died. Was it true?'

'Yes. I got a letter from the British Embassy saying that he perished during an air raid; he must have given my address in case something happened to him. It was a formal letter of condolences, but it was attached to another one, sealed and from him.'

'What did it say?'

'I don't know. I was so mad at him that I forwarded it to the Cyprus address that appeared as his official domicile in the British Embassy letter without opening it.'

'Haven't you ever wondered what it said?'

Rosalia is silent for a while. The logs in the fireplace crackles in a not entirely friendly manner. Somewhere beyond the dark hall, a clock strikes the hour. 'Yes. I wonder about it all the time.'

'*Santa Madonna*. What are you going to do about that?'

'Nothing. I pray it'll go away.'

Chapter Eighteen
THE SANCTUARY

The front door of Palazzo de' Muggifalco, made of solid oak, has a brass knob that is always cold to the touch, no matter what the temperature outside. The firm of builders employed by Signor Novara reproduced the original door destroyed by the bombing, and followed Rosalia's own drawing. The brass knob used to be one of four on her father's bed, and was found in the rubble. There is still a little dimple in the otherwise smooth metal, a dent during its fall from the first floor.

On the outside, the Muggifalcos' home is little different from what it used to be before the war, though elsewhere a few changes have taken place. Rosalia has kept its character, not wanting to let go of the centuries breathing inside, but has tried to make it more functional: the palm in the inner courtyard, torn off its roots by the blasts, has been replaced by a large wooden workstation so that Rosalia can take advantage of the light coming from above all year round, and work well into the evenings.

Almost every corner of the palace houses a sculpture; the unfinished wet clay pieces are covered with sheets that were once part of Rosalia's trousseau. Vera jokes that she knows married women whose trousseau does not get as much use as Rosalia's.

Late at night, in the soft moonlight creeping in from the shutters left ajar, Palazzo de' Muggifalco looks like a haunted place, populated by shapes covered in dustsheets. Sacks of clay and lumps of wood pile up in the courtyard, together with various kinds of stone that arrive weekly from the quarries just outside Palermo.

Rosalia has recreated her father's study exactly where it was, at the end of the long corridor on the first floor. It is no longer the tidy room, with mahogany shelves groaning under the weight of old books and paperwork, where Antonio Muggifalco retreated from life and his family. However, when she goes in to file a document or put away a book, for a moment she still smells mould and his aftershave, lingering over ancient folders saved from the blast, and still kept closed with pieces of half-burnt string. At times, she sits on the new leather chair her father would have loved so much and looks around her, feeling almost as if part of him were still there.

Oddly, whilst she does not mind being in that room, there are others where Rosalia never goes: her mother's bedroom and the attic, which collapsed during the bombing, taking lives with them. Whenever she passes by one of those doors, she fancies feeling a cold draught that seeps deep into her bones.

It is, however, the old entrance to the cellar that makes Rosalia feel most uncomfortable. She has briefly contemplated cementing it up, but that felt like trying to suffocate something alive. Nowadays the square door in the floor under the stairs is kept locked; under it, a stone flight of stairs leads to an empty space she has not seen in almost twelve years.

'Emptiness can be more substantial than matter', she says to the lump of raw stone sitting on a turntable between her legs, waiting to be given a shape. 'Emptiness is what *defines* a shape, by cutting into it.'

'I knew you'd start talking to yourself if you were left alone long enough!' Nazario laughs, poking his head out of a window on the floor above. 'You have stone dust all over your hair, I can see it from here; and only half an hour to get ready to go to church.'

'I'm not talking to myself. I'm addressing a naked woman who's still locked into this stone.'

'Well, I can only see one naked woman at the moment, and I suggest she hurries up, or I'm coming downstairs to take advantage of her.'

Rosalia smiles at the stone. She likes its slightly pink hue, which gives depth to the granite texture. It feels cool to the touch but also full of promise, ready to turn into the perfect shape it was destined for. 'I'll see you later,' she whispers.

Half an hour later, anyone walking by Palazzo de' Muggifalco on that sunny and clear Sunday morning would see a young woman and a senior marshal of *carabinieri* coming out of the oak front door, hand in hand. They would probably be struck by the beauty of the woman, who is wearing a silk top with a large collar and a vertical row of little buttons covered by the same fabric, a sombre pattern in grey and black; a black skirt with fishnet stockings complete her outfit. Because of the woman's very high heels, black with a little strap across the foot, onlookers would not immediately notice the difference in height between the woman and her dashing companion; Rosalia is not very tall but perfectly proportioned.

'You do realise we must be the only church-going couple who are living together without being married?' says Nazario, who walks slowly to match Rosalia's step, restrained by her tight skirt.

'We're not living together,' Rosalia reminds him. 'You just happen to spend a lot of time at my place. Anyway, we're adults and free to behave as we please. I trust you'd tell me if we were doing anything illegal.' She loves teasing him, knowing that his affection for her is enduring; and that her own for him, though deep and heartfelt, is something she can control. Rosalia is aware that controlling one's passion has the immense benefit of shifting the balance of power in a relationship, but is careful to use such an advantage discreetly.

'It depends on who's judging us. Don't you think it's hypocritical of us to attend the service every Sunday if we live as man and wife for the rest of the week?'

'I'd argue that God knows your heart and mine and doesn't judge. Anyway, the important thing is not to tell the vicar,' she adds mischievously. 'Then we'd definitively be in trouble.'

Nazario does not reply, knowing that the entire congregation is aware of their relationship and disapproves. His superior has tactfully hinted at how inappropriate it is, in his position of trust and responsibility, to cohabit.

'*Carabinieri* are meant to give the good example to civilians. I'm sure you keep that in mind at all times, Marshal Major Casa!'

Marshal Major Casa does keep that in mind. All the time. He has a handsome three-storey house in the middle of Palermo, which miraculously survived two air raids. On occasion, he goes back home to collect the post and air the rooms. Would Rosalia be more willing to relinquish her independence if he made himself less available and spent more time in his own house?

Once in the church, they slide across one of the creaking pews at the back, rubbed to a shine by years of old women's clothes against the ancient wood. Nazario takes his hat off and tucks it under his right arm. His blond wavy hair retains a ghost of the hat's shape. Rosalia will sit, as usual, her back very straight, looking ahead at the pulpit. Absorbed in the sermon, she will be very quiet unless there is any mention of the war: in that case a little hand will crawl out of her lap to find his, and Nazario's will always be ready to squeeze it.

Today, Rosalia looks a touch unsettled. She kicks the hand-woven knee cushion at her feet out of the way before dropping her bag on the immaculate black marble tiles. Looking around her, she cranes her neck towards the pews nearer to the altar, flanked by marble statues of various saints and martyrs. Beyond the neo-Classical columns that support the nave, two aisles house more niches, sarcophagi and chapels, rich with holy relics and fresh flowers. The devilishly sweet smell of *La Violetta di Parma*, the most popular and cheapest ladies' perfume, mixes with that of the flowers and burnt wax.

'What's the matter, sweetheart?' whispers Nazario, watching her. 'Are you all right?'

'Yes, yes. I just want to see if there are any empty spaces towards the front.' She answers impatiently, as if she expected him to know.

The front pews are usually packed with the senior members of Palermo's social and political community: the pearls and furs of Sicily's upper class painted with the colours of devotion and piety. The vicar knows that most of the cathedral's weekly offerings will come from the first four or five pews, and makes an effort to address them specifically. 'Might as well get the show as they bought the ticket' is Father Tommaso Caltagirone's philosophy. Even at the front there will be empty spaces between the compact clusters of families and friends, because of old and unspoken feuds, or fresh love affair scandals, forbidding people to sit next to one another. Gossips are reflected in the Sunday morning seating arrangements.

'Why do you want to sit at the front today?' Nazario is puzzled.

'Not at the very front, just further ahead, towards Saint Rosalia's chapel. Let's go.'

They walk quietly down the aisle on the north side, holding hands.

'Excuse me,' whispers Nazario, apologising to people who are already seated and leading Rosalia to two empty centre seats on a pew that is otherwise fully occupied. To their left, just visible beyond two columns, Saint Rosalia's chapel sprawls out of the nave, with a little brass gate separating it from the aisle. It is no longer allowed to leave faith and grace pawns at the feet of the saint's mortal remains.

Once the opening remarks have been voiced from the pulpit, and the vicar has launched into a vigorous condemnation of modern times, and television as the mother of all evils, Nazario turns towards Rosalia to comment about a church that criticises modern technology instead of old sins. Noticing that she seems to be more interested in the chapel, he gazes over to the same place, wondering what is so intriguing, and is struck dumb. Nazario catches a glimpse of rosy cheeks and dark, curly hair: the young girl with fresh flowers adorning her smooth forehead is looking up at the sky with a sweet smile of gratitude and joy. It is, of course, a large painting of Saint Rosalia, heavily framed in gilded stucco. For reasons that he can't explain, Nazario has never seen the painting before. How can that be? Like most people living in Palermo, he is well acquainted with the grand cathedral and its contents. With Rosalia, he has been attending the *Messa Domenicale,* the Sunday Mass, for many years. It is true that they usually sit at the back and thus would not have the opportunity to study Saint Rosalia's chapel in great detail, but even so Nazario is perplexed. Surely he would have noticed it – for the young saint in the painting looks very much like the Rosalia he knows. Not exactly the same, no, but with a remarkable similarity in the hair colour, the shape of her face and those eyes. Looking up at the sky for some hidden truth, they remind him of Rosalia's when she looks intensely at her clay, looking for inspiration. 'Look at the painting, Rosalia,' he murmurs, lightly squeezing her knee. 'I don't think I've seen that before. Who does it remind you of?'

'It's by Velasquez,' Rosalia whispers. 'Last century. You must have seen it before; it used to hang at the back of the chapel, behind the statue and the silver urn containing the saint's bones. Now that it's been restored, they've placed it more prominently.'

'Yes, but who does she look like?'

Rosalia leans to her left in order to gain a better view. 'I suppose … I'm not sure. Ah! You don't mean … me?'

Nazario squeezes her knee harder in agreement. 'Yes. Isn't it an amazing coincidence? Is that why you wanted to sit over here?'

People around them shift uncomfortably, clearly unhappy at having their sermon spoilt by the conversation.

The hour and a half befor ethe end of the service is pure torture for Nazario Casa, who spends it contemplating plausible explanations and finding none. 'Let's go and have a closer look,' he suggests when Mass is over.

They negotiate their way through the crowd leaving the cathedral, going in the opposite direction. They stand, side by side, just outside the chapel's brass gate. The hum of people around them is soon forgotten.

'Did you know that the painting would be displayed there today?'

'Yes. I heard someone say that Velasquez's St Rosalia had been returned to the chapel. I was curious to see it. I remember during the war, when people were allowed to go through the gate here and pin their pawns behind the statue and the urn. That's where I found my grandmother's shawl.'

Nazario's brain registers the last piece of information and logs it next to his own private collection of memories: it finds an empty space and fits there snugly. 'Ah, of course! Your grandmother's shawl. You never told me the full story.'

Rosalia shrugs. 'There isn't much to tell. After the bombing, we couldn't find my grandmother anywhere. She disappeared into thin air. Then, some time later, I came here for a prayer after tending my parents' graves outside the cathedral. Do you remember? They were in the little cemetery behind the main square.'

'Yes, I do.' He puts his arm round her shoulders protectively.

'Well, I came to the cathedral that afternoon on my own, and came here, as I used to do with my grandmother when I was a child. Every time, she pointed at the urn and told me the saint's story. I saw a few pawns scattered around, as usual. One caught my attention, because it was her shawl. I'm sure of it. She was wearing it the last time I saw her alive. It was hanging over there.' She points at the wall behind the urn and the statue. 'So I walked around the urn and took it.'

'Who put it there?' From where he is, Nazario can make out old marks on the wall, left by nails that were used to pin personal items. Each a symbol of grace, received or requested.

'I've never found out. The shawl's in our bedroom, hanging behind the wardrobe door. It's her wardrobe … I rescued it from the ruins and had it restored.'

Our bedroom. Nazario's heart lifts with a song; he looks at Saint

Rosalia's painting and feels oddly at peace, awash with gratitude. The intimacy of those two words make him happy. Our bedroom. She said our bedroom.

'Where are the pawns nowadays? Do people still offer them?'

'Of course they do. They go to the sanctuary on Monte Pellegrino, where Saint Rosalia's calcified bones were found in the fifteenth century. Have you never been?'

'No ... sweetheart. I know where the sanctuary is, of course, but the mountain's more significant for me in national and political terms.'

'Why?'

'Well, since there are no documents showing otherwise, it's assumed that Monte Pellegrino is part of the Sicilian government estate. It's not privately owned. During the war the port and airfields' fuel was stored underground there. During the last days before the Allied invasion the military command at the port had instructions to blow the whole place up, releasing a million barrels of oil into the Mediterranean, so the supplies wouldn't fall into the Allies' hands.'

'I don't remember it.' Rosalia frowns, and wonders whether she has forgotten the incident because she was only sixteen and had just lost her family.

'No, you don't ... it never happened.'

'Did the Allies arrive before we had a chance to blow the reservoir up?'

'No one knows. There was utter confusion: the American forces were advancing from the west, the British were closing in from the east, different departments issued contradictory orders, military heads were being executed at random. It was a mess. The orders were probably aborted or misunderstood. The entrances to the network of tunnels might have been obliterated by air raids or bombings: they can't be found any more.'

'My children. If you'd be so kind as to make your way to the door, the cathedral's to close for housekeeping before the afternoon service.' A gentle voice from the choir's pews addresses Nazario and Rosalia.

'Of course, Padre. We'll go presently.' Nazario takes Rosalia's arm and turns towards the front door. To the left, two churchwardens wait in the vestibule, by the *aquasantiera*, the font.

Rosalia throws a last look at the marble arch crowning Saint Rosalia's chapel, with the huge eagle sprawled in the middle of it – the symbol of Palermo. 'Surely there must have been maps showing the underground site.' She resumes their conversation on the way out.

'There must have been, but they're lost. Lost or destroyed, together with thousands of other documents that the Allies would have liked to get their hands on.'

'Let's go and eat,' Nazario suggests when they reach the main square. He puts his hat on, suddenly feeling ravenous. It is lunchtime; the sun has kept its earlier promise and, despite it being November, there is not a single cloud in sight. The cathedral's principal dome, rich in baroque detail, looks splendid against the piercing blue sky.

'Aren't we lucky to be here today, enjoying this sun and just being alive?' Rosalia opens her arms and does a little twirl. If she had roses in her hair and was holding a lily like Velasquez's Saint Rosalia, the likeness would be even more remarkable.

'Marry me.'

She stops in mid-twirl, as if she had been hit. Her suddenly serious face makes Nazario's stomach turn with apprehension. The words rolled out of his mouth before he could stop them, and there is no way back. He stands straight and waits, knowing that things will never be the same between them, no matter what the answer is. His jaw twitches.

'Don't ruin everything.'

'Why would marrying me ruin anything?'

'No. Don't ruin everything by asking me to marry you.'

'That's unfair and cruel, Rosalia. All around us people have fallen in love and got married. Your girlfriends have already had their second child. You have a career, a life and … me. As you just said, we're lucky. Why not get married?' Before the question has left his lips, he fears the answer more than anything else in the world.

'Because I'm not ready to get married.'

At least she did not say, 'Because I don't love you.' There is still time. Time to enjoy the sun.

'I have an idea,' she continues, as though nothing had happened. 'Let's go to Saint Rosalia's sanctuary, on Monte Pellegrino. I've not been there for years, but I'd like to show it to you. I was fond of the place when I was younger. My father and I used to climb up the Monte in the early morning in the summer, before the sun became too hot. It'll be good to go back.'

'All right, but I need to eat first.'

Monte Pellegrino rises abruptly from the sea, with sharp edges and vertical drops; to visitors coming from Palermo there is only one route, from the south, where a scattering of little houses is buried at its feet. Nazario's Fiat 1900 struggles on the narrow paved road that climbs, following the mountain's contours and going up in a corkscrew. At each bend a little more is revealed of Palermo and the *Conca d'Oro*, the 'golden bay' in which the city lies; a breathtaking view into a distance that blurs the coastal line between sky and sea. Tall chestnut and olive trees stretch their branches at each other across the road; in the sunset everything seems to be soaked in glittering autumnal reds and golden lights, as if God himself had decided to dip his fingers in the horizon and smear them across the land.

'The days are drawing in,' remarks Nazario, looking out of the window. 'It'll be dark soon.'

They park in the little belvedere at the top of the Monte, just outside the sanctuary. Beyond the steep cliffs and stubborn shrubs hanging onto the rocks, the city lights wink in the distance.

'Let's go in, before it gets too dark.'

The sanctuary is bolted onto the rock, a large part of it a cave inside the mountain. On the outside, its sober, restrained lines would not attract the attention of a fleeting visitor seeking thrills. Rosalia weighs up the dull, yellowish façade, the unassuming door, and suddenly feels apprehensive. 'Perhaps we've done enough pilgrimage for today,' she says in a low tone. 'Two hours listening to Padre Caltagirone's sermon should buy us some absolution.'

Nazario takes her hand. 'Don't be silly. I've never been here. Come with me. She's only a girl – she can't be that fearsome!'

The warm, soft light outside is abruptly extinguished in the sanctuary. In the sudden semi-darkness, Rosalia instinctively squeezes Nazario's hand and draws closer. It takes a few minutes for their eyes to adapt, by which time they are walking towards the heart of the cave, holding to the rails to avoid slipping on the damp floor.

'Look at that case, Nazario. The statue's gold.' The glass case lying on a plinth is splendidly lit from the inside, and shows the statue of a young girl stretched upon a bed, a hand lifted high towards the sky and her God.

In a second, Nazario realises that Velasquez's Saint Rosalia back at the cathedral relies heavily on this statue's features: again, the same soft face, smooth forehead and dreamy eyes Nazario wakes next to almost every day. 'How old is this?' he asks, taken by its beauty.

'About five hundred years old,' Rosalia answers. She has crouched down to caress the cold frame. Her face is almost level with the statue's own, and the light inside the glass sarcophagus illuminates hers too, with a touch of gold.

'So it pre-dates Velasquez's painting.' He stands behind her, amazed. It occurs to him that neither the original Rosalia, the young girl who fled a life of comforts to live like a hermit on this mountain, nor the real one who is crouching down in front of him, show typical Sicilian traits, with their tall forehead, dark, curly hair, large eyes and perfect heart-shaped face.

'I thought your family was Sicilian!' he exclaims, and his comment sounds odd even to his own ears.

'Who gave you that idea?' She turns to face him. When her eyes look up, she is a perfect copy of the saint behind her. 'The Normans gave my family our land for services rendered during the Crusades. The original building was destroyed during the plague of 1624, which is when Saint Rosalia's bones were found on this mountain. She's of Norman descent too. The Norman ancestry will die with me, I fear. I'm the last of the Muggifalcos.'

'Let's go home. It's a long way down to Palermo again, and I don't trust my car's headlights, or its brakes.' Nazario offers his hand to help her up. They make their way out of the sanctuary. In the antechamber, Rosalia stops to look at the hundreds of votive pawns hanging from the cave's walls. The rock is covered in photographs, ribbons, bandages, babies' rattles and items of clothing. There are notes of thanks and recommendation, pleas and promises.

'People's unhappiness always saddens me,' says Nazario.

'But these aren't signs of unhappiness. These are offerings to the saint, thank-yous for performing a miracle. Look how many there are!' She swings around to take in the colourful exhibition of the fragments of people's lives. Then her heart goes cold.

In the days to come she will wonder how on earth she managed to spot it, in that delirium of objects, notes and photographs. It is almost as if it called her, forced her to look its way.

For right there in front of her, stuck to the rock in Saint Rosalia's sanctuary, she sees a photo of Andreas Khuklakis.

Chapter Nineteen
ANDREAS'S PHOTOGRAPH

It is an anonymous rectangle of paper among hundreds, neither bigger nor smaller than the rest of them. It has a little white strip framing it, and its slightly faded colours are unremarkable. It should have gone unnoticed.

Nazario does not notice that the colour has drained from her cheeks. He is searching for his car key. But when he turns towards Rosalia to spur her on, he is amazed by the change on her face. For a moment, he worries that she has lost her mind: her frozen features are horribly contorted as if she were in a great deal of pain. He calls her name, but receives no reply.

For Rosalia, twelve years are obliterated in a heartbeat: she is sixteen again, working on the clay bust of a man who has long gone. She is back in that kitchen with the white Formica worktops and the tall straw chair, on which he is sitting.

'Rosalia!'

There are three poppies in a glass vase on the window sill to his right. He brought them this morning, found the vase and blew the dust off it before popping the flowers in, forgetting the water.

'Rosalia!'

She knows that under the rough fabric of his uniform his legs are scarred by fire. Forced immobility makes him twitch with discomfort occasionally, but he never complains.

'Rosalia! You look as if you've seen a ghost. Are you all right?' Nazario is irritated by her silence. His eyes follow hers, trying to work out what is absorbing her attention, but all he sees is a wall covered in pictures. Strangers, and stories he will never know.

Tell him the truth or protect him from it? It occurs to Rosalia that she may be wrong, that she has been caught out by an amazing resemblance.

135

How can there be a photograph of Andreas proudly standing in front of Palazzo de' Muggifalco, if he must have been dead by the time her home was rebuilt? She can just about make out the brass knob on the front door behind him, the same knob that was on her father's bed before the bombing. How can her heart so readily accept the photo when her brain clearly refuses to do so? 'There's a picture of Andreas.' She finally utters the words.

'What are you talking about? Which one?' Nazario walks closer to the wall but he does not know what he is looking for. Hearing the name has brought back unpleasant memories that he would rather forget. Surely not that Andreas! The Cypriot pilot? The young man who was visiting the Novaras' house, intriguing him personally and professionally, until curiosity was overcome by jealousy?

She won't move any closer to it. 'That one.' She points at one of the photos in the middle of the wall. Nazario starts to study them one by one, searching for a face he is sure to know well, because every day the clay bust reminds him of it. Most of the photos are of smiling people, with a note at the bottom that explains why they are there. Spidery writing, elegant notes, tentative words: little stories of ordinary families blessed with extraordinary grace. Finally, he finds it. It is just a sepia photograph, but there is nothing ordinary about it: Andreas looks straight into the camera. He is wearing a high neck jumper and black slacks. His hair is combed back showing, even in a picture that small, the little scar on his forehead. Defiance and sadness are in his eyes. 'I thought you said this man was dead.' There is a slight note of childish irritation in his voice, one that he cannot control.

'He is. He was. I mean, I know he is. The official letter said so.'

'Then this isn't him. How can it be? Has he ever got in touch?'

'No. Certainly not. I'd have told you. It's him.' She tries to get a proper look at the photo, which is too high up for her.

Nazario looks around and, satisfied that they are alone, lifts his hand to touch the photo. His fingers stroke the slightly glossy surface, the sharp corners. Quickly, he tugs at the pins that keep it in place, and catches them deftly in one hand. The photo falls into the palm of his other hand.

They stand as close as possible to the front door to take advantage of what's left of the light. Nazario holds the photo with two fingers, flicking it this way and that as if its meaning can be shaken out of it.

'Let me see.' Rosalia takes it from his hand and bends over it, checking the face, the clothes and the house. 'It's him. I'm sure.'

'That's impossible. Unless ... Maybe it's an old photograph that you took, and forgot about.'

'No, that doesn't make any sense. I didn't meet him until after the air raid, when I was working at the hospital. He couldn't have posed outside the house: it was just a pile of rubble.'

'Maybe it's a similar building.'

'See that door knob?' She stabs the photo with her finger. 'I had that put on the front door two years after the bombing.' The photo in her hand seems to pulsate with life. 'Put it back,' she says, and it is the hardest thing to do. To relinquish that picture, to let it return to the cold wall in a cave so far away from her home is almost unbearable. Nazario looks at the photo, unconvinced, then takes it and pins it back where it was.

He feels the photo's effect straightaway, as it wedges itself between them. Rather than coming out of the sanctuary in a tender embrace, like so many other couples who have shared an intimate and spiritual experience, they walk into the fresh early evening air apart and in silence. She waits for him to open the car door and gets in without a smile. They both want the same privacy and solitude, a chance to think about the photo and make sense of it.

Once in the driver's seat, Nazario hesitates before switching on the ignition. When the Fiat's engine springs to life in the deserted belvedere, he says, 'You know it's impossible, don't you? It must be someone else.'

Rosalia smiles bitterly in the dark. 'Must it? Why? I know it's him.'

The policeman in Nazario struggles to understand her stubbornness. 'Look, I know that this man bears a strong resemblance to Andreas, but unless the official letter about his death was a mistake and he's been loitering around your house ever since, how can you believe that the person in the photo and Andreas are one and the same?'

'Why does it bother you whether I believe the man to be Andreas or not? I'm entitled to my opinion, aren't I?' Rosalia feels the heat of anger rising fast inside her, a fury that she has not experienced for a long time. She breathes deeply, hanging onto a thin thread of control.

Nazario switches the engine off and stares at the steering wheel, motionless. 'Let's say you're right. We've found a recent photo of Andreas, who appears to be well. Once we rule out the impossible, all that's left is the truth. Could the British government have been wrong? I suppose mistakes have been made. I can check it out. Is it possible that Andreas, alive and well, might have posted a picture of himself as a pawn of gratitude to Saint Rosalia? Is he a believer?'

'I don't know. We never discussed religion.' She hates herself for sulking and hates Nazario even more for being reasonable.

'It stands to reason that Andreas would try to get in touch with you.'

'Not necessarily.'

Nazario ponders carefully. He remembers that the Cypriot pilot suddenly disappeared from her life. After Rosalia's visit to his office, he made a few enquiries about her grandmother, but did not find out anything significant. As for the case of Vincenzo Novara, he worked on it a great deal more than Rosalia ever realised. Using the little he knew as a reason and his position as an excuse, he had started to go to her flat regularly, partly to investigate the Novaras and partly to see the girl who had stolen his heart. Shortly afterwards, he noticed that Andreas's office had been vacated; its occupant had been transferred to northern Italy, resuming flying duties. Nazario was wonderfully relieved. 'You once said there'd been a special person in your life and that he'd left. I remember you pointed at the bust on the window sill, and told me that was all you had of Andreas. What happened? Did you ask him to leave?'

'Yes. He may have killed my family. He was one of the bombers who attacked Palermo and destroyed my home and all I loved. You know the rest.'

'What's upsetting you now, then? The fact he might be alive, or the idea that he's not bothered to tell you?' Nazario knows the question has hit the spot, and feels sorry for both Rosalia, who seems to be a captive of her memories, and himself, for not being a good enough alternative to them.

Two lamp-posts direct their cone of light towards the simple wooden door to the sanctuary. In the encroaching darkness, even Nazario feels uncomfortable at their complete isolation. The thought of ancient powers, collective prayers and supernatural forces locked away behind that plain door makes the usually sensible and rational *carabiniere* wish he were safely home, with a glass of wine and his companion by his side.

Rosalia must have read his mind, for she turns to look at the sanctuary and shivers a little. 'There's something quite powerful about this place. Whether you believe in God or not, it's hard to dismiss Saint Rosalia's attraction,' she says quietly.

'She's a powerful influence in people's lives.'

'Nazario.'

He reaches for the car key, willing to go, emotionally exhausted.

'A votive offering is a grace received or asked. If that picture is there, strictly speaking it may not be a reflection of reality, but a desire for it.'

Nazario slumps back on his seat, running his hands through his hair. Tonight, the woman he thought he knew so intimately has shown him a glimpse of abyssal unfamiliarity. 'I want to go home. You can tell me more whilst I'm driving.'

The only way down is via the same narrow road which snakes around the mountain. Palermo's lights twinkle attractively in the distance, as if they belong to a far away world. As Nazario drives back through shadowy woods, the car's weak headlights catch glimpses of precarious guardrails and stray branches.

'What if the photo expresses Andreas's wish to come back?'

If Nazario had not been concentrating hard on driving, he would probably have lost control. 'Come back where?' he asks, exasperated.

'Here. To this life. Life in Sicily.'

'Rosalia ... I deal with crime at the highest level. Every day I'm exposed to people's wickedness and treachery. I've never come across anything that suggests a supernatural will strong enough to influence this world, but I've had plenty of opportunity to experience first-hand what men are capable of. Sometimes the most obvious explanation is the right one, sweetheart.'

'How do you know?' Her voice is shrill. 'You've just witnessed how many people are grateful to Saint Rosalia for her help. She listens to prayers.'

'So you're suggesting that Andreas is dead but has somehow managed to send a picture of himself standing in front of your house. A big grace indeed, to be able to come back from the dead. You're an intelligent girl, Rosalia. Does that make sense to you?'

The silence in the car is heavy. A couple of times, Rosalia draws in her breath noisily, as if about to speak again, but thinks better of it.

It has taken one photo to stir up a multitude of feelings that have been lying dormant for twelve years. As a sculptress, Rosalia's world is very much a physical, tangible and visible one. Every time she has had the temptation to dwell on her memories of Andreas, it has been easy to push them back and lock them away. The bust has been a reminder of her pain rather than of the person who caused it. What she cannot explain to Nazario without hurting him is her theory about whose wish it might be to have Andreas returned to the land of the living. Confronted with Andreas's face again after so many years, a small part of Rosalia knows beyond doubt that she has always been mourning his absence; and that her secret, desperate longing to see him again may be so strong as to …

'Do you actually wish that he were alive, and here?' Nazario has stopped at some traffic lights. Engine idle, he reaches for a cigarette and lights it, holding the steering wheel with one hand. He inhales noisily. The tiny glow seems to move magically in the dark.

'Are you that cross with me?' she says, referring to the cigarette and their tacit agreement that he should not smoke in the car.

'I only wish you were honest with me, Rosalia. We can look at this together and in many different ways, but whatever the truth about the photograph we won't survive as a couple unless you're clear about your reasons for believing what you believe.'

'All right.' She sighs, and feels the smoke tickling the back of her throat.

'What did Andreas mean to you?'

Rosalia resents the tone of voice, which she is sure Nazario usually reserves for the criminals he apprehends. With an effort, she answers. 'I suppose I was in love with him. I'd never felt like that about a boy and it blew my mind away.'

'Why? What did he do to you?'

'We were so young and he was … so quiet and reserved. When I met him at the hospital, it looked as if he was willing to let himself die. Not of the physical wounds, I think, but because of some sort of mental anguish. He spoke three languages but had trouble communicating. Occasionally, he asked me questions about my family or me, but didn't say much about himself. Oh, and he was handsome.' Handsome, she thinks. Not like Nazario, of a masculine, primeval kind of attractiveness, of solid build and awkward big hands. Women turn to look at Nazario and barely hide their lust. In the picture Andreas still looks fragile and lonely, but with a steely resolution in his eyes. 'I never even kissed him.' For a mad moment, Rosalia considers telling Nazario about her passionate teenage kiss with

Vera, of its tenderness and depth, intimacy and passion. She quickly discards the idea, and the memory itself.

The crossroads is deserted; not a single vehicle passes before the lights turn green. The Fiat lurches forward when Nazario puts it in gear. Empty houses and disused buildings run past their eyes as he drives through Palermo's inner boroughs. The occasional light smirks from ground-floor windows with no curtains.

'Andreas Khuklakis was working for the British Military Intelligence service, Rosalia.'

'You know his surname?'

'That day, when you and Vera came to visit AMGOT headquarters at *Casa Reale*, do you remember? You asked for him at the reception desk. When I enquired where Khuklakis's office was, he said it was on the second floor. I knew that only British Intelligence services operated from that floor, but you seemed surprised to find him there.'

'That's because I thought he worked at the harbour. I told you, Andreas said very little about himself – but he did mention he was doing some classified work.'

'So you two just turned up at AMGOT, with no idea how to get in or whom to see?'

'We were young ...' She shakes her head. 'You've never told me what you knew about him. Surely you must have realised that I'd been in love with him.'

Nazario throws his cigarette stub out of the window. He recalls seeing Andreas's slim figure walking out of the Novaras' home, through the unclipped hedge in Vincenzo's garden, during his endless surveillance hours. He remembers studying paperwork, checking the trucks full of American supplies, retracing lost cargoes of local supplies. He fought his own personal war. It's not over yet, he thinks. 'You never told me about him either.'

They pull up opposite Palazzo de' Muggifalco. He parks, but does not switch the engine off. 'Do you want me to stay, or shall I go to my place tonight? You may want to do some thinking of your own, without this *carabiniere* policing your heart.'

Rosalia looks straight ahead, knees together, handbag in her lap. Her profile under the streetlamps is like that of a china doll, with a perfect little nose and full mouth.

A lone passer-by emerges from a side street, hat on, and passes between the streetlamp and the Palazzo's stone walls. It is dinnertime.

'No. I don't want to be alone tonight. Please stay. Let's talk about it.'

'All right.'

'If I'd asked you to steal that photo for me, would you have done it?' Suddenly, her tone is mischievous again.

Nazario gets out and walks around the car to open her door. 'Signorina Muggifalco, you know I'd do almost anything for you, but I'm still a civil police officer with social and legal responsibilities. I couldn't remove any property belonging to Miss Saint Rosalia, not even for the most beautiful woman on earth.'

They laugh as they climb the three stone steps leading to the front door. Rosalia puts her hand around the brass knob and feels for the dimple with one finger.

Not far away, someone paces up and down a cold, damp place; in the echoing silence, stoops, wondering, hoping, with a heart full of hatred and violence.

Chapter Twenty
A QUEST

I think we should go back to the sanctuary as soon as we can.'
'Mmmm.' He pulls the blankets across his chest and all the way up to cover his head. Early mornings have become much colder, and Palazzo de' Muggifalco does not get warm until the fire is going simultaneously in most of the living rooms downstairs. The coal stove in the bathroom will be doing its job, heating up the enamel bathtub behind the lacy curtains.

Rosalia's new bed is made of two mattresses, one on top of the other for extra comfort, filled with sheep's wool that will need to be aired and untangled every spring. When that time comes, the *matazzare* women will come and knock on every door of her street, offering their services: they will spend several days sitting on the floor, unstitching the mattresses and pulling out the wool.

When Rosalia was a little girl, her grandmother used to supervise that job; the women took the wool up to Palazzo de' Muggifalco's big terrace to wash and dry it on the flat surface under the generous Sicilian sun. Even now, Rosalia cannot turn the bed out at night, folding the bedspread out of the way, without remembering those days and her formidable grandmother. She sits up in bed with two pillows behind her back; she has already been downstairs to get the fire going and into the bathroom to light the stove. In the semi-darkness her eyes shine with feverish excitement. 'My grandmother believed in Saint Rosalia's power. She said that when my father was a baby he almost died of a chest infection, but was saved by the saint. Ask and you will be given, *Nonna* used to say.'

'All right. I'm asking you to let me sleep a little longer!' groans Nazario. 'I've got a busy day ahead. The head of the Separatist movement is presenting the regional government with an official petition to cut all ties with the rest of Italy. I've been asked to keep things under control.'

'What needs to be kept under control?'

Nazario sighs and emerges from the covers, resigned to an early start. 'Tempers flare up at the regional assembly. Your mayor Novara stirs discontent amongst the easily swayed. He wants to be the champion of an independent Sicily. Independent, that is, but under his control.'

'He's not my mayor, Nazario, he's everyone's mayor. Don't talk about him like that. You've never liked him, but if you took the time to get to know him you'd change your mind.'

'I've taken a lot of time to get to know him,' replies Nazario darkly, 'and I still don't like what I know. Political figures behave very differently when they're acting as family friends.'

'If only you knew how much he helped me when I lost my parents!' Rosalia says. 'Despite being worried about his son's disappearance, he still found the time to look after me. He said my father had been very loyal to him and he wouldn't abandon me.'

Nazario feels a nasty longing for a cigarette. It's unusual for him to get the craving so early in the morning and he is puzzled by it, but then realises that even a private conversation about the mayor is likely to make him feel tense. 'What exactly did your father do for him? I gather he looked after Novara's legal affairs.'

'Oh yes, for years. In my father's study there was an entire set of shelves dedicated to his affairs. They spent hours locked up in the room to talk about business. I wasn't allowed to go in, apart from bringing a tray with coffee and biscuits when Signor Novara arrived.'

'What's Signora Novara like?'

A memory of Mrs Novara forms in Rosalia's mind; the stiff corset and large hat, the immaculate cream-coloured gloves, the brooch with a cameo representing a lady's profile, surrounded by a set of emeralds. 'She's a proper lady, very formal. My mother used to invite Mrs Novara to her literary circles every month, but she declined each time. It was usually migraines, or charity work that Mrs Novara needed to attend. Regardless, my mother kept inviting her to show that her own social life was as active as anybody's. She's a recluse now: no one's seen her for years.' Rosalia pauses. 'She always made me feel as if I was a child from the impoverished part of town that she visited so often.'

'Ah! Not all good and pleasant then. Finally, a chink in the astounding Novara armour!' exults Nazario, thinking of his own poor upbringing and his father's sacrifices to send him to school.

Rosalia is particularly talkative early in the morning, when a day's work has not taken its toll on her temper. Nazario loves the intimacy and warmth of those last moments before daily duties call. That is perhaps why the words come out of her mouth unguarded. 'No, Nazario. That might have been the case before, but after the air raid the Novaras' attitude changed. He rescued me from a bad situation, and I've been in his debt ever since.'

'Really?' The policeman in Nazario raises his head. The cigarette craving is stronger. He has a packet of tobacco in the inside pocket of his corduroy jacket, which is tidily hanging on the back of an upholstered chair a few yards from the bed. Next to it, in a neat pile, is his uniform with the hat sitting on top. 'Tidy mind, tidy gain,' as his father used to say, putting prickly pears, apples and apricots out on display in order of size and grouped by colour.

'What was it?' he asks, trying not to think of cigarettes or his greengrocer father.

Rosalia considers the question briefly. Would it really matter now? Would it hurt anyone if she told the secret? The people involved have long gone and food is no longer rationed. She has not even seen the cellar since: the builders restoring the Palazzo bolted up the original entrance square door, positioned flush with the floor under the stairs.

When Rosalia initially accepted Nazario's courting, it had been with fondness rather than love. Their relationship has had time to flourish without the inevitable blows of reciprocal passion, as a slow-growing plant gains strength in the shade. It is Rosalia's composed fondness and trust in Nazario that persuades her to talk now; a more passionate love on her part would have prohibited a confidence that might tarnish his perception of her. 'After the bombing, Signor Novara sent his men to try and clear up some of the debris. We'd found the bodies of my parents and the maid under the rubble, but not my grandmother's. I was trying to rescue as much as possible from looting, and it was hard work carrying heavy items over to Vincenzo's flat or putting them in their cellar.'

The large clock on his bedside table reminds Nazario that it is time to get ready for work, but he ignores it.

'The blast had blown away the entrance door to the cellar, but amongst the debris and the dust I didn't notice anything odd. Most of those first days are hazy memories.' Hazy, that is, apart from her recollection of the German soldier. She has never mentioned that to Nazario either. Irrelevant, she tells herself. Move on. 'I came out of the hospital after my shift to find one of Signor Novara's men waiting. They'd found something in the cellar, and Signor Novara wanted to talk to me about it.' Nazario's silence makes Rosalia think that he might have gone to sleep again. When she turns to look at him, though, he is listening attentively, eyes wide open. 'I walked to the cellar entrance, and Signor Novara showed me what was stored inside.'

A pause. Nazario is tempted to spur her on, but decides against it.

'There was grain, Nazario. Lots of sacks, all neatly stacked up. A very large quantity. The room was full.'

'Hiding food during the war was a criminal offence! I spent most of my time retracing stolen supplies and arresting farmers who didn't co-operate. The black market was squeezing the poorest like lemons. Whose grain was it?' His voice is sterner now.

Rosalia shakes her head, already regretting her confidence. 'I don't know. Signor Novara said that finding wheat in our cellar didn't make my father the owner. Maybe he was just holding it for someone else. Anyway, Signor Novara told me not to worry, that he'd take care of it. When I went back the next day, the cellar was empty, and so it's remained.'

'If your father allowed someone to use his cellar to store those supplies, that would have made him equally guilty. There's only one reason why anyone would have kept such a large amount of grain stashed away, and that's to supply the black market. Big money earned on the back of desperate families.'

'Don't you dare insult my poor father's memory, Nazario Casa!' she shouts, furious. Ah, to be able to take it all back, forget she ever said it. Her father's secret, exposed and vilified. What was she thinking? Isn't Nazario a *carabiniere*, after all? All *carabinieri* are stupid, as her father used to say.

'You're being childish. I'm only stating an obvious fact. The truth may not be what it seems, but there must always be a sensible explanation. Did you open and check every single sack? How do you know that what looked like a huge supply of food wasn't actually a cover-up? Besides, you'd have been better off reporting it to the police, rather than allowing Signor Novara to take it away. You don't know what he did with it, do you?'

'No, of course not. I was just glad he got rid of it.'

Nazario feels an odd excitement rising inside him, the feeling he has when he gets a hunch. It is an increasingly rare feeling nowadays and may amount to nothing, so he resolves to wait for it to go. 'I must get ready for work, sweetheart. Can we continue this tonight?' He swings his legs out of bed, feeling with his feet for the slippers on the hard, cold floor. Once up, he reaches for his dressing gown.

'No, I don't want to. I want to discuss it now. And I want to go back to the sanctuary and speak to the monks. Maybe they know who put the photo up.'

'I'm afraid everything will have to wait. If I'm late for this meeting, and something happens, I'll be demoted to directing the traffic at Politeama Square.'

'There isn't any traffic at Politeama Square. Cars aren't allowed there,' she cries. Suddenly, the mystery of those sacks in her cellar has become the most important thing in the world.

'Exactly. There's no traffic there ...' is Nazario's sombre answer. He runs downstairs, holding his hat in one hand and the banister in the other. Rosalia listens, in the following couple of minutes, for the silence to be broken by the usual thud of the front door shutting. He seems to be taking longer than usual to leave, and when he does, the house sounds eerily quiet.

The stone with its pink reflection sits alluringly in the middle of the courtyard. Rosalia looks at it from above, biting her bottom lip, thinking. I'm afraid that work will have to today, she resolves. She slips quickly into some comfortable clothes and pins her hair back with a large hair band, the way she does when she embarks on another sculpting session. Only instead of walking downstairs and sitting at her turntable, tools at hand, Rosalia goes to her father's study, down the corridor.

Hot water flowing in brass pipes whines occasionally as it is pumped from the water tank in the kitchen up to the first floor. Rosalia remembers when the tank used to sit directly above the large fireplace, before the pipes were installed. The maid used to bring the hot water to the bathroom using large enamel buckets, with thin handles and rusty edges. When the new system was put in, it took Rosalia, who was only a little girl, a few weeks to get used to the noise. Early in the morning, the gurgling of water being forced through the pipes became monsters hiding in the walls, howling for fresh blood. She had been frightened by the well in the cellar, from which the maid pumped the water into the tank above. Nowadays an electric pump did that job. During the war, one particularly cold winter, the pipes burst; she remembers talking to Vincenzo about it during the fatal air raid. The cellar had flooded, or at least that was what her father had told his family. Had he lied?

'Thank God for electric pumps,' she shivers, opening the door to her father's study. Many people had gone through her father's papers, trying to help her find his will and anything else that might be legally useful to an orphan; but they had been looking for a certain kind of official document, ignoring all others. No document pertaining to Rosalia had ever been found, apart from her grandmother's will many months after her disappearance. The Italian law had taken the view that, as the only surviving Muggifalco, her family home should *ipso facto* pass to her, together with the slim savings books with her father's and mother's names on them.

Rosalia is moved whenever she comes across her father's handwriting, whether it be on the spine of a folder or on a piece of paper. It is simple and elegant, just a fragile reminder of his past existence. Here, a note about extra monies due to the servants for Christmas; there, a legal point about shared perimeters and duties in land litigation.

Of course, a large part of the study's contents were destroyed, but Rosalia recalls a particular box that was mercifully spared by the fire. Where is it? she wonders, looking around her. Dust is quick to settle on dead papers that are not handled often. She blows on the top of a few leather-bound cases, fidgets with stubborn clasps, pulls many heavy folders from their shelves. She finds the box she is looking for behind another one. It is made of heavy duty carton, with holes on each side at the front through which flat beige ribbon has been threaded. The receipt box. Hand-written reminders or receipts of the many transactions carried out by Antonio Bellino Muggifalco, 'ABM' as he signs himself.

A hoarder, that's what my father was. Rosalia smiles affectionately at the ocean of white pieces of paper, mostly scrunched up, none in chronological order. The proper, official receipts would have been recorded on the ledger book, but that had been lost in the blast. If he was storing the supplies on behalf of somebody else, there'd be a record of the number of sacks and their contents. It stands to reason, she thinks, arms up to the elbows in the big box. And if he was storing them for himself he'd have kept a list of quantities and the kind of grain, maybe dates and possibly sales. 'Why didn't I think of it before?' Rosalia mutters to herself.

Hours go by, until she loses her sense of time and space, and her back hurts from the forced immobility. Virtually every receipt tells a story. A few remind her of particular occasions. It is lunchtime when Rosalia starts feeling the sharp pangs of hunger. She is working methodically, setting aside receipts that shed light on her parents as individuals, and discarding the rest. Her legs are stiff, and she unfolds them with difficulty. She pushes the box to one side, proposing to go back to it after a trip to the kitchen. That movement, which tips the box slightly, disturbs its contents; one or two of the larger sheets, folded into quarters, float to the surface. Rosalia gingerly picks up one and flattens it. It is a reminder to give one lira to Natalino Contumace for services of translation, from *Ammericano* to Italian. What was he translating? Rosalia checks the date: it is 1 May 1941, during the war. She reads the note in its entirety, and her heart skips a beat: '... an eight page document submitted by Giacomo Alessandro Novara, and to be kept in safe storage by myself'.

Rosalia remembers perfectly well her father's attitude towards Mussolini and the Fascists; his refusal to submit to the political regime had cost him and his family many benefits and comforts during the war. Nevertheless, solicitor Muggifalco and Signor Novara had been the best of friends, not allowing a divergence in political opinion to spoil their relationship. In May 1941, the United States would not have been involved in the conflict, but would have started supplying military equipment and goods to the Allies as they watched the Italo-German coalition with suspicion. Why would an enthusiastic Fascist like Signor Novara have anything to do with a country so far away, and a potential enemy? Unless ... Rosalia remembers gossip at the hospital after the Allied invasion; the theory about what really happened to Vincenzo, and Signor Novara's rise to power, becoming Palermo's mayor just before the Anglo-Americans left the island. He's always come up trumps, she thinks to herself, whether under the Germans and Mussolini or the Allies, changing allegiances as it suited him.

The document must be a legally binding one, or solicitor Muggifalco would not have stored it on Signor Novara's behalf. Why is the reminder here rather than in the official receipt folder? Rosalia is tempted to ask Signor Novara for an explanation, but something tells her that it would be a mistake to do so. Must keep searching ...

That is how Nazario finds her that evening: in the study, surrounded by those *pizzini*: her father's little pieces of paper, each containing a nugget of his life.

'How was your day, darling?' she asks. The irony in her voice is not missed on him.

'As bad as I imagined,' he sighs. 'What are you doing? I thought paperwork wasn't your forte.'

'Did Signor Novara put his point across well?'

'Incredibly well. There were grown-up people crying when he rose to speak. It was all quite emotional. You'd have been proud of him.'

'Have a look at this.' She is calm and her eyes are darker than usual. Nazario had suspected that she was still angry at him, but now realises there must be something else.

The piece of paper changes hands. Nazario reads it, and his hunch grows stronger. He sits down on the rug next to Rosalia and reads it again. His hat has left a red mark across his forehead, where it must have been sitting all day. 'You've never seen this before?' he asks, trying to keep his excitement under control and his voice steady.

'No. Vincenzo went through my papers and Andreas did too, but they didn't find it. I'd forgotten my father's habit of keeping these little notes to himself. He had a poor memory.'

Andreas checked the papers? An alarm bell rings in Nazario's ears; he carefully silences it. 'Why did Andreas look at your papers?' He makes the question sound as casual as he can.

'Oh, because he was trying to find my father's will. I was sixteen and I really didn't know anything about these things.'

'A foreign pilot going through Italian papers! He must have been pretty confident to know what he was looking for. Anyway, what are you doing digging up all this?'

'I was trying to find a record of the contents of our cellar. It's important to me.'

'More important than finding Andreas?' Nazario can't help smiling. He has learned over the years about Rosalia's affection for her father.

'My father was an honest man, Marshal Major Casa.' She is serious now. 'It feels out of character for him to hoard in the cellar when our maid had to keep chickens in the loft to feed us the occasional omelette. Something's wrong.'

Nazario nods. 'When I went downstairs this morning I tried to open the hatch to the cellar, but couldn't. It's stuck.'

Rosalia knows he is telling the truth; she remembers the lapse of time between hearing him on the stairs and the front door shutting behind him. 'Yes, I told you. They bolted it during the works and I've not been in there since. The thought of it scares me.'

'Perhaps we should join forces, you and I: what you know of your parents and their habits, and my policeman's nose.'

'What are we looking for?'

'Don't you think it strange that your father wouldn't make ample provision for the well-being of his beloved only daughter, in case something happened to him and your mother? That no document about your future has ever been found? That the only will concerning you was somewhere else, in your grandmother's wardrobe of all unlikely places!'

'Well, my grandmother was old. Maybe she just wanted to keep it safe, like her money under the mattress.'

'Yes, but if I remember correctly the will was properly drawn and typed up, with witnesses and the Sicilian government stamp to endorse it. Hardly something a little old lady would do if she had no clue about legal documents. Besides, why not give it to her son, a solicitor? No, I think we're missing something, Rosalia. I've been thinking about it all day, whilst Signor Novara was thundering about the emancipation of the Sicilian people.'

'What about Andreas? Shouldn't we find out where he is?'

'Andreas may be not a separate issue. Do you know what he was doing at AMGOT? His office specialised in monitoring relationships between locals and Americans. CIC, Counter Intelligence Corps. Very classified information.'

'Why the Americans?' The words in her father's note spring to mind again: an eight page document ... a translation from American to Italian.

'During the first few months after the Allied invasion of Sicily, I was working with both the British and the Americans. They set up a local government in an effort to control the region, but they were very suspicious of each other's motives. We *carabinieri* were chosen by AMGOT to deal with the civilians, because they perceived us as a military authority and trusted us more than the Anglo-American forces. Anyway, the British thought the Americans were cashing in on their good relationship with Sicily, as thousands of us have emigrated to the States since the beginning of the century; and the Americans were worried that the British would use Sicily as a foothold in the Mediterranean to expand their Empire.'

'I don't understand,' Rosalia whispers. The hard floor is cold under her feet. Something in her father's study creaks every so often; perhaps the shelves or the shutters complaining about the unwanted visitors.

'I think we're looking for a document that outlines Signor Novara's involvement with the American government. There are powerful links between the American mafia and our own home-grown variety.'

'Signor Novara isn't a Mafioso, Nazario. He wouldn't have been appointed Palermo's mayor, and he wouldn't still be mayor now, surely. Wouldn't you have made sure that he didn't enjoy such a position of power? You *carabinieri* and the police forces, I mean. You're supposed to defend us.'

Nazario laughs. 'Women! You have the most romantic notion about politics and crime. It isn't as easy as you think. Our forces keep public order, but we don't create or topple government figureheads. Look at me, Rosalia: today, Signor Novara discussed the bright future of our country in front of hundreds of people. I stood there as stiff as a knife, with my badges on and my shoes polished to a shine, charged with the responsibility of making sure that no-one got up to shoot him.'

'So what has all this got to do with Andreas?'

Nazario ponders the question for a few seconds. 'I don't know, sweetheart. It might be that he was investigating your relationship with the Novaras.'

'You mean, instead of seeing me as a ...' She struggles to say the word. Girlfriend. Did Andreas ever consider her his girlfriend? Rosalia somehow doubts it; but the thought that he might have used their friendship for investigation purposes burns her soul.

'We could just put everything away. Let sleeping dogs lie.' He folds the piece of paper in two, neatly.

A moment of silence, whilst Rosalia considers the alternative. The shutters in the study let out a moan like a woman's. 'I think Andreas was trying to tell me something after he left, but I didn't allow him. He sent me a letter, which was delivered together with the document of official condolences from the British Ministry of Defence. I never opened it. I wanted to destroy it but somehow I couldn't bring myself to do that, so I forwarded it to Cyprus as a piece of him that I felt his family was entitled to.'

Nazario looks in the direction of the shutters, and the window that gives out onto the inner courtyard and Rosalia's workshop. It is a dark, moonless night. 'I could take a few days' leave, if you can bear to be parted from your work. Cyprus isn't a peaceful country at the moment, but we could go.'

'What do you mean, not peaceful?'

Nazario sighs, getting up and helping her to her feet. 'Some sort of military conflict, apparently. With the British, of course, who are refusing to give Cyprus independence.'

'Perhaps we should send Signor Novara there, to orate about freedom for the people.'

'I never thought I'd hear you say anything sarcastic about Signor Novara, Rosalia.' He kisses her on the lips, and his hands travel to her hips, then up to the small waist and soft breasts.

'I've never been on a plane.'

'Me neither.'

Chapter Twenty-One
CYPRUS

Among the coming and going of porters shouting at each other and sullen passengers dragging brown carton suitcases, she looks stunning. The long flight and stopover at Athens, baffling check-in desks and tiring queues seem not to have taken their toll on Rosalia's uncreased silk dress and matching red hat.

After landing, as they climb down the aircraft steps and directly onto the airfield's cooked tarmac, Nazario follows that hat, a little dot of colour swaying amongst the crowds. The relief of passengers touching *terra firma* again is almost palpable, but Rosalia seems to be immune to physical strain or the novelty of flying.

Once in the air, they settled into their hard seats and talked little, each lost in their own thoughts. Several times during the flight, Nazario checked inside the folder for their tickets, identity cards and the address he had been able to retrieve using his contacts and his access to war-time records. Rosalia persuaded herself that the thick layer of clouds, looking like cotton wool and stretching under the aircraft, would be enough to cushion a crash.

Carrying her vanity case and a small hold-all, Nazario follows Rosalia through the dusty and noisy airport of Nicosia, jealous of her earlier silence. He guesses that, looking out of the small window, she must have thought about Andreas, flying his wartime machine. Nazario wonders what the pilot must have felt as he flew to a height at which exhilaration might be the product of both rarefied air and reckless youth. Supreme power, perhaps, woven with a touch of fear? What had he done during the same war? He had spent the years pushing paper and keeping watch over dubious characters. Not exactly an exciting career.

Waiting outside for a taxi, Nazario suddenly hopes that this trip might hold all the answers, that whatever information they obtain will put Andreas to rest in Rosalia's heart once and for all. He hopes their visit to the obscure village whose name is written on his piece of paper may make Andreas's death a tangible reality, instead of his glorification.

'Are you all right?' she asks, once in the taxi. She has re-applied her lipstick using the mirror inside the vanity case and looks serene.

He eyes her up suspiciously. 'Yes, of course. How about you?'

'Nervous.'

'You don't look it.'

'I'm trying not to think about what can go wrong. Will the farmhouse still be there? Will his uncle still be alive and willing to talk to us? The Italians were Germany's friends, so technically speaking we're the enemy.'

'I'm not really sure who the Cypriots think the enemy is any more. They certainly seem to dislike the British.'

'Why? I thought Andreas fought with the British.'

'He did. Cyprus is a British colony. They were promised independence during the war, but that promise hasn't been honoured.'

'It must be an island's destiny. Mussolini, according to my poor father, never thought of Sicily as an integral part of Italy, though he expected us to fight the invasion better than the Germans. He most certainly wouldn't have approved of the separatist movement Signor Novara is so fond of.'

'That's because at least with Mussolini the mafia had a hard time raising its ugly head. In contrast, it schemed and planned its own revival despite the Allied temporary government.'

'I wish you didn't accuse Signor Novara of being a mafioso without any proof. He's always told me to be proud of being Sicilian – and that when all else is failing, one should look to one's country for inspiration and support.'

'Yes, especially if that means power to the individual, and control of the entire region. Believe me, the Sicilian black market during the war was ruled by the same class who went around preaching about pride and principles. In the meantime, we end up trying to protect the weak and the poor against their own people.'

'Vera's been saying for years that if the state can't do its job, the Sicilian people must look after themselves.'

'And I say that different regions can only thrive by being equal partners of a larger political organism. Individual laws lead to anarchy or dictatorship. You know what happened to Mussolini!'

Rosalia does not reply. Through the dirty windows of their clapped-out taxi a strangely familiar countryside rolls past, as indolent and sensual as the Sicilian landscape she knows so well. Nazario lets his eyes rest on her neck, framed by the round lapel collar; Rosalia's tweed dress has short cap-gathered sleeves, a daring choice for November. He now wishes he had had faith in the Cypriot weather; instead, he is wearing a warm long-sleeved polo shirt and sensible trousers. The local taxi driver occasionally checks in the broken rear view mirror, not quite believing the rimmed red hat and matching lipstick.

White rendered houses are scattered everywhere, long and flat and seemingly inhabited by the animals that linger around them, enjoying the bright midday sun. Multicoloured patches of harvested crops randomly alternate with dark brown rectangles of land scratched by ploughs. They pass through the occasional village, on a road overlooked by neat little houses whose front doors open directly onto the narrow pavement. Several women, carrying their age around their eyes, sit on straw chairs embroidering immaculate white sheets.

Suddenly, the road climbs up hill after hill; the taxi's engine wheezing, and the driver softly swears under his breath in a language that Nazario and Rosalia have never heard before.

'Are you sure he knows where to take us?' she whispers, though she remembers that the driver cannot understand her. It is hot in the car and she has not spoken for so long that her mouth feels dry and dusty.

'I showed him the address and he nodded as if he knew. Perhaps he's taking us to some God-forsaken cave where the guerrillas are hiding, armed to the teeth,' laughs Nazario, feeling uncomfortable all the same.

'Guerrillas?' She looks scared now, a little pale under the rouge carefully applied on her smooth face. Why has she bothered with all that makeup?

'Don't worry. If anything, I'm the one they'd seize immediately, being a man and a member of an official police force, albeit a foreign one. These people are said to be rather gallant with the ladies.'

'Stop teasing me, Nazario.' She catches sight of two black eyes greedily staring at her in the rear view mirror, and forgets to sulk.

'That's why you're all dolled up, isn't it? To impress the Cypriot men.'

She does not reply.

Nazario has not even reached the end of the sentence when he realises that he has been a fool. Of course she has made an effort. Not for the local population, or in celebration of their first trip together, or even for herself. 'I'm wrong. It's not to impress the Cypriot men, or not all of them. Just the one.'

Nazario wishes she would answer and challenge his accusation, although he knows that he is correct. If Rosalia made an attempt to rebuff the charge, at least it would show him that his opinion counts, that she cares enough to lie. But his words are met with a silence that is only interrupted by the unhappy buzzing of a fly, trapped somewhere inside the car.

The taxi slows down shortly after a long, sweeping bend, at the top of a dusty hill. Everywhere around them olive trees seem to be stretching their gnarled branches at each other, like holding hands under the early afternoon sun. When the car stops, the driver turns round to face them, leaning his arm across the greasy back of the passenger seat. Rosalia notices how hairy his arm is; the hand too, with dirty fingernails and tufts of hair sprouting from the base of each finger.

The driver points at a large farmhouse sprawling in the middle of a patchy field, a stocky central construction from which several outbuildings emerge and roll out in different directions. From a distance, it looks as if a large spider has taken great pains to spin a cobweb of outdoor stairs connecting the main house to the raised upper floor and several little terraces. White- and orange-striped curtains are draped across a balcony and over its wooden banister.

'Here we are.' Nazario nods to the driver in acknowledgement. He jumps out of the car, expecting a warmer temperature: they are quite high, and the breeze carries with it a sweetish smell of wild olives cooked by the sun and the sound of far away goats' bells.

Whilst Nazario rummages through his bag for some money, Rosalia gets out of the car and stops at the edge of the road, looking towards the farmhouse. It is exactly as she had expected from Andreas's description. A few brown hens peck in the dust and a donkey brays nearby, but there is no one around.

'Wait for us here,' says Nazario to the driver loudly, as if by shouting the meaning of his sentence is clearer. 'Here,' he repeats, pointing at the road. 'We need to find out if there's anyone in that house,' he adds. The driver smiles and nods, his elbow out of the window.

When Nazario and Rosalia turn to face the farmhouse, bags in hand, the engine suddenly springs to life again and, before Nazario can stop him, the driver has reversed into a little lay-by. The taxi careers back down the empty road, lifting a cloud of dust mixed with gravel.

'It looks like we can't go back.' She carefully straightens her red hat on those dark curls.

'Let's hope it's the right house and that someone's in,' Nazario replies, with a little sarcasm in his voice.

He helps her find a path through the lavender plumes and thorny broom clusters. Nearby, pines and junipers cast their friendly shadows over a few sheep. In the still air of an afternoon like many others, the click of a gun's hammer being raised sounds oddly out of place. Nazario recognises it straight away and instinctively pulls Rosalia down to the ground. There they remain, faces buried in camomile and thyme bushes. Rosalia's red hat has tumbled away onto the grass near her feet.

'Are you insane?' she hisses through gritted teeth. 'What's the matter with you?'

'Shhh ... Keep your head down. We've got a gun trained on us.' Nazario rolls on his side and peeks through the dry and yellow blades of long grass.

'Don't shoot!' he shouts in Italian. 'We're unarmed!'

A middle-aged man is standing in the middle of the courtyard where, a minute earlier, the brown hens had been pecking away happily. He is holding a double-barrelled shotgun with an ease that only comes with habit. '*Italiani?*' The man shouts back in their language, and does not sound surprised or angry. He lowers his gun.

'Yes! We mean no harm.'

'Stand up. Let me look at you.' His voice is calm, like his demeanour.

Rosalia remembers Andreas saying that he had learnt Italian from his uncle, who was multilingual. There is something familiar about the voice's inflexion, but it could just be the Greek undertone. She furiously brushes straw and grass off her dress, smoothing the fabric down with sweaty hands, then retrieves her hat.

'Come up.' A hand rises in a gesture of welcome.

Sitting at the top of a gentle hill, the farmhouse affords a panoramic view. Approaching the building, Nazario and Rosalia notice the low perimeter wall, made of sun-dried bricks, and the narrow windows.

'*Yasou*,' she says. Greetings, the same word with which she addressed Andreas twelve years earlier. '*Imeh i* Rosalia.' Her thoughts tumble around her head. My name is Rosalia; this man is Nazario, my friend. Tell me that you're Christakis Khuklakis, Andreas's uncle. Tell me that he's alive and well, maybe sleeping in one of the cool bedrooms upstairs. Its shutters will be slightly ajar to let in this breeze, scented with camomile and lavender. He'll be hearing my voice soon and will come out on the balcony behind you. I've seen the whitewashed walls of this farmhouse in my dreams. There, too, Andreas has held me tight, kissed and made love to me. We've had children and grown old together. She wishes she could say this in the man's own language, quickly and clearly. Her eyes travel to the balcony and the stoneware pots peeping through its iron bars. There is no sign of Andreas.

'I'm Nazario Casa. We're sorry to pay you such an unexpected visit, sir, but we're looking for Christakis Khuklakis. Is this his farm?' Nazario looks at the man in front of him and has the sudden certainty that their visit might not be a total surprise.

The man's white open shirt is creased but clean; his short hair is greying, the bushy eyebrows still dark. 'I thought you'd come sooner or later. I'm Christakis. Come in.' He moves with the fluidity of a feline, jumping off the low wall without a noise. His shotgun swings from its leather strap, hanging from his shoulder. Christakis lifts the cotton curtain and pushes the front door open to let his visitors in. Nazario and Rosalia walk straight into the ground-floor kitchen with its large floor tiles and chestnut lava inner walls. The clay oven in the far corner keeps the large room warm. Nazario remembers several vineyards carpeting the hilly landscape on their way: a stoneware jug filled with young wine sits invitingly on the battered kitchen table near the window. Christakis motions them to sit on a couple of cane chairs. Without a word, he moves around the kitchen nimbly, fetching glasses, bread, olives and goat cheese.

From the inside, the farmhouse reveals itself to be much bigger than they had expected; a number of doors lead to different parts of the house, tantalisingly half shut. It is quiet but with an air of expectation, as if whoever lives there is waiting for something, or someone. This house is in a state of permanent alert, Nazario thinks, a policeman again. It is impossible not to look around and wonder: the oven tools hanging on the wall next to the clay oven's door, the buckets of wood amassed in one corner, the blackened grill positioned across the in-built stove. It all seems too well organised if just one man is living there.

'I met Andreas during the war,' Rosalia says to her glass of wine. 'He was injured and spent some time at the hospital I was working at.' The wine has deep red tones like melted rubies. A couple of sips are enough to imagine a donkey's head poking through the front door, inquisitively. The heavy breathing from those large and wet nostrils sounds very real.

'Shoo, shoo,' chants Christakis, but he pats the animal's large head affectionately before it withdraws.

'Do you live on your own?' asks Nazario when their host finally sits down at the table.

'That depends.' Christakis's face is a parchment of lines in which the eyes sparkle with life and energy. His grey moustache matches his thick short hair in colour. Rosalia tries to find Andreas's delicate features within the older man's, but fails. But there is a flash of sadness in Christakis's eyes, as sharp as a splinter, and something else that Nazario and Rosalia are too young to recognise: a deep sense of pride. 'There was a time when this farmhouse was full of life and voices, children at play and laughter. It was a long time ago, but the memories are enough to last a lifetime.'

Rosalia keeps looking at her glass, fearful that Nazario might read similar feelings in her face. 'Greeting strangers with a gun isn't in the Cypriot tradition, though?'

'No,' Christakis admits, sipping his wine. 'But these are dangerous times. I wouldn't expect the Italians to know about us; the Greek Cypriots, I mean. The people you may think of as liberators are, to us, a selfish country denying our freedom.'

'You're talking about the British government.'

'I don't know you. You may be a spy.' Christakis smiles, and Rosalia finally sees something of Andreas in his face. 'You', he continues, turning to Rosalia, 'must be the Sicilian sculptress.'

'Is Andreas here?' Why wait any longer? This is the person to ask, the man with the answers, the memories and that letter that is legitimately hers. Now she is ready to read it.

'My dear girl, you know that he's dead. You received the official note from the Ministry of Defence, did you not? It was kind of you to forward it to me.'

'Yes, I read that; but we have reason to believe that he may still be alive. You see, there's a photo ...' She is willing to continue, but something in Christakis's eyes kills the words that are about to come out.

'He's buried in a little cemetery in northern Italy, near where his plane crashed in July 1944. He rests there with his crew. I've been to see his grave. Andreas isn't in this house, at least not physically.'

'We've seen a recent photo of Andreas,' she insists.

Christakis shakes his head. 'I'm afraid that, much as I'd love to believe it, this isn't possible.'

'How do you know?' Rosalia is trying very hard not to raise her voice. 'I'm telling you that the photo exists and the person in it is Andreas.'

'Andreas would have come back here if he'd survived the war and the last plane crash. This is where he belongs. His grave in Italy is the thing that upsets me the most; to be buried in a foreign country is much worse than fighting on behalf of one.'

'Were you Andreas's guardian? Where are his parents?' Nazario asks. Under the table, his hand has finally found Rosalia's and is holding it tight.

'They died when the children were very young. Yes, I suppose you could say that I was his guardian, and his sister's too. The rest of the family is buried over that hill, in the old cemetery. He wanted to join the British forces during the war, to fight for freedom and justice. I don';t know what he'd have made of what's going on in Cyprus at the moment.'

'Why such bitterness against the British now? After all, didn't you fight side by side?' Nazario thinks of the Italians' war, and their disappointment in post-war local government. Would the Italians have kept on fighting if their own liberty had been at stake?

'They took a brilliant, talented and brave student and put him on a plane after about nine weeks' training. He was too young to fly, too young to do their dirty work and certainly too young to die. The rights and principles that Great Britain was so keen to defend during the war are the same rights we Greek Cypriots are being refused by their government.' Christakis turns to Rosalia. 'I thought you'd come here one day to retrieve what is yours.'

'The letter.'

'I never opened it. It was addressed to you personally, and I thought you might have a good reason to send it to me without reading it – perhaps safekeeping? In any case, I took great care of it. If you'd like it now ...'

'Thank you.'

Christakis gets up, dragging the feet of his chair across the tiled floor. He goes to the stove to add some wood, then to the clay oven to feed it a log or two. The fire inside gurgles happily. 'Have some wine. I'll be baking some more bread as soon as the oven is hot enough.'

The silence that follows his departure from the room is heavy. Outside, the brown hens cackle wildly.

'They're very noisy, don't you think?' he says, eventually. 'I never realised how loud chickens can be.'

'Not usually,' she replies. Memories of Anna's captive chickens sharing her loft room make Rosalia emotional all of a sudden. 'They only get rowdy when they're scared.' A single tear falls down her cheek, but she does not seem to know that it is there.

'You may well be right.' Nazario's tense voice makes Rosalia turn towards him. From where he is sitting, near the kitchen's only large window, he can see a large slice of sky, the hill slopes and a good view of the road. In the distance four or five military jeeps are driving up towards the farmhouse, heavy with uniformed men. A few yards away, outside the low perimeter wall, the first soldiers are already climbing up, holding their guns; their black boots sink in the soft scented herbs and lavender bushes.

From the courtyard the donkey starts braying.

'What's going on?' Rosalia's eyes are wide with fear. She struggles to get up, as if she were tied up to the chair.

Nazario has gone to the window to take a closer look, trying not to be spotted, but comes back straight away. 'British soldiers. Stay still. Don't make sudden movements.' She opens her mouth to say something. 'No. Quiet.' He puts his finger on his mouth and then walks behind her chair, where he stands, his hands on her shoulders, waiting.

Christakis comes back into the kitchen. His demeanour does not seem to have changed, but his eyes are steely with resolution. 'Pray don't be frightened. They're not after you, and won't hurt anyone here. Let me deal with this.' He lifts his hands to indicate calm. Rosalia notices that they are empty but steady.

When the officer in charge bursts into the kitchen, he finds the three of them sharing the last of the olives and cheese. The bottle of wine is empty. Outside, his men look around, poking the stable doors open with their rifles. Some go to the back of the farmhouse and stay there. More vehicles stop at the foot of the hill, men pouring out of them.

'*Kalispera.*' Christakis greets the officer, then switches to English. 'Do let yourself in. My door is always open, as even my donkey knows.'

Chapter Twenty-Two
THE MAP

I'd use sarcasm more carefully, if I were you.' The officer's badges and decorations shine on his chest; his uniform is well cut and the cap suggests his high rank.

'Would you rather I complained formally about your invasion of my privacy and disregard for my property? Your men are trundling all over my land, scaring the animals and destroying the crops at the back, no doubt. My guests are frightened. Your uniform suggests that you're an officer, but I've no idea why you're here with such a large display of military force. I'd be flattered if you think an old man like me is dangerous!'

Nazario observes the two men weighing each other up, the young one in full uniform, pistol dangling from his ordnance belt, the other in his white shirt, unbuttoned to the middle of his chest, a Greek cross pendant threaded through a thick gold chain around his neck.

The British officer ponders, hesitating. The girl sitting at the table is dressed like a lady and looks concerned. Perhaps an overt use of authority won't be necessary. 'All right,' he says. He pokes his head out of the front door, and shouts at the soldiers outside to wait for his orders. 'I'm Captain K.J. Robinson, here on behalf of the British government. I must remind you that it is your duty, as a British subject, to respect public safety and obedience to the law.'

'First of all, Captain K.J. Robinson, I respect public safety and obey the law as a Greek Cypriot. This is my land. My name is Christakis Khuklakis and these are my Italian guests. How can I help you and your men?'

'We're in receipt of important information about a group of individuals who have embarked on a campaign of consistent and continuing sabotage of British infrastructure and property. You must know it by the name of EOKA. I don't need to remind you that EOKA is a danger to the peace and harmony that this country has enjoyed for many years under the benevolent eye of the British government. It seems determined to undermine the mutual respect and consideration that the Cypriots and British have built up over a long time. They must be eradicated as soon as possible.'

Nazario and Rosalia sit at the table, listening attentively. The tone of the British officer leaves them in no doubt about the seriousness of his demands, though the full meaning of his speech escapes them. Nazario tries to recall the little English learnt during his months of close contact with the British and American forces, but with no success. Frustrated, he looks at Rosalia, who seems to be on the verge of tears.

'This intelligence you've gathered points at my land and my home?' Christakis looks perplexed. 'Or do we look like brigands to you?'

The officer pauses. The young foreigners puzzle him. A likely female rebel plotting to overthrow the current regime would not sit at the table, politely eating olives with hands too smooth ever to have held a shotgun; and the man has something of the military himself. Still, isn't George Grivas, the head of EOKA, a general himself? A military man, who should know better than to become an agitator of the populace. Appearances can be deceptive. 'Sir,' he starts, addressing Christakis, 'I must ask you to let my men search your house. We're looking for guerrillas who may need shelter, food and support. The village down the road has been surrounded too. This is the only house in the area that we haven't looked at yet.'

'I see.' Christakis turns to his guests and opens his arms in a sign of personal defeat. Rosalia's eyes are wide with fear. The exchange between the two men has left her none the wiser, and even Nazario looks uncertain. 'This man needs to search the house. They're looking for a contingent of guerrillas who are wanted by the British government. Please don't be afraid. I can deal with this.' Then, to the British officer, 'You can ask your men to start their search. I'm at your disposal. Don't inconvenience my guests by subjecting them to an interrogation. They don't speak your language.'

'Ah, yes. They're Italian.' In the officer's eyes, Nazario recognises the spiteful look of the victor. A look he has seen before and has endured since the end of the war. Eyes that say the same thing over and over again. Italians! Of course: they're the ones who couldn't fight and yielded to the enemy immediately. Cowards. Hitler's servants. A sudden rush of anger washes over him and tenses the hand still holding Rosalia's. She squeezes it back, misunderstanding his emotional turmoil. Nazario gets ready to pounce, his body leaning across the table.

Fortunately, Christakis understands. He deftly leaps up to the British officer and gently turns him towards the front door. 'Go on, call them. I'll guide you myself around the ground floor.'

As the officer shouts his orders to the men still loitering outside, Nazario regains his composure. He exchanges a look with Christakis that means several things to both of them. Mainly, it is a tacit way of saying thank you. It is also recognition of a similar love for one's country.

Ten, fifteen armed men swarm into the kitchen; an equal number remain outside checking the stables and the other outbuildings. Rosalia withdraws into the far corner, as more and more uniforms come in; the smells of guns, barrel oil and human sweat come with them. To Rosalia, the soldiers look like dogs standing on their hind legs, sniffing and searching like animals maddened by the scent of blood. There must be a very fine line between mankind and the rest of Nature's kingdom, she thinks, as the men open doors, move curtains and look inside cupboards not big enough for a child to hide in. How else to explain this thoughtless hunt for other human beings?

'Come!' says Nazario, 'Let's follow Christakis and the Englishman. I don't want to be left here whilst the bloodhounds are unleashed.'

She walks behind him, trying not to look at the soldiers. The indifference in their eyes scares her more than the hunt itself.

Through the wooden door to their right, left open by Christakis, they see some more formal furniture, two leather sofas and a coffee table; on the opposite wall is an imposing mahogany dresser displaying pretty blue and white crockery. On the walls there are a few portraits, mainly photos. As they walk into the room, Christakis is standing in the middle of it, watching the officer check behind the full-length window shutters, still wearing his military gloves. His boots clomp heavily on the stone floor.

Captain Robinson turns towards Christakis and opens his mouth to say that he is satisfied, and that he wants to move on to another room, when something on the wall in front of him, over the vast red-brick fireplace, catches his attention. The photograph on the wall is large and in a simple wooden frame. It is right in the middle of the wall, where one would ordinarily expect to see a mirror. Rosalia's sigh, when she sees the photo, is loud enough to be heard by everybody in the room, but no one pays any attention to her. The British officer stares at the photograph, in silence.

Andreas is looking into the distance, his face serious under the pilot's hat with its flying eagle and crown badge; in his crisp uniform he looks well scrubbed, as if the photograph had been taken to commemorate an official occasion. Only his eyes have the pensive look that Rosalia remembers so well.

'Who is this officer, Mr Khuklakis?' Captain Robinson asks the question without taking his eyes off the photograph.

'That, sir, is my nephew, Andreas. Pilot officer Andreas Khuklakis, to be correct; 40 Squadron, Royal Air Force Volunteer Reserve.' Christakis sounds immensely proud as the words roll out of his mouth. 'He flew Wellingtons during the war from bases in England and the Middle East. Enlisted in 1942.'

The British officer's face is impenetrable. 'Where is he now?'

'Padua, sir. Northern Italy.'

'Padua?'

'Yes. The war cemetery. Died in action on 13 July 1944 whilst on a mission, an air-raid over northern Italy. He was twenty. God rest his soul.'

'And these Italian people, are they here for any reason related to Pilot Officer Khuklakis?' He turns to look at Rosalia curiously, as if he were seeing her for the first time.

'Yes. They knew him. Andreas was wounded in 1943 and spent a few months in Sicily, convalescing. At the time, he was part of CIC, the Counter Intelligence Corps. I'm sure you're aware of the organisation.'

Captain Robinson studies the photograph a little longer, in silence. Then, suddenly, he stands to attention and gives it the military salute. Turning to Christakis, he repeats the salute. 'I'm very sorry to have disturbed you, sir. My profound apologies for putting you through the inconvenience of a house search. Had I been aware of your nephew's personal sacrifice for our country and Europe's freedom, I wouldn't be here.'

A curt nod of his head towards Nazario and Rosalia and he leaves the room, walking perhaps a little stiffly.

The three people look at each other. Christakis makes a sign to them to suggest they wait, but no-one talks. Rosalia lets her eye wander across the walls, and she lingers on smaller photos she had not noticed before. Family pictures: a child, standing near a man who, Rosalia is sure, must be his father; the latter sits on a chair, a straw hat on his knee, a walking stick in his hand. He seems to be wearing his best clothes, a white shirt, a buttoned -up waistcoat from which the gold chain of a pocket watch can be seen. His knee-high boots are well worn, like his son's. Rosalia takes a few steps towards the photograph, to look at the child. His face is familiar to her, but there is something else that she cannot recognise. He is wearing a little peaked cap with a white band; his jacket is buttoned up all the way to the neck. Rosalia easily imagines a loving mother's fingers working through the buttons and smoothing the jacket down to make her son look as neat as a pin.

'Who is this boy?' she whispers.

'That's Andreas, when he was about ten,' is Christakis's distracted answer.

'Ah. I didn't think it was him,' she says, with odd regret. She does not know why she should be apologetic about not recognising him as a child. People change over the years, don't they? Yet she knows those features as well as his mother would. Why did she not see Andreas in the child? Nazario looks at her and the picture, but says nothing.

Raised voices outside catch their attention. Captain Robinson is gathering all his men in the courtyard; they hear the heavy steps of the last soldiers hurrying back downstairs, responding to the order to leave.

'Are they going?' Rosalia turns to Christakis, who is concentrating on listening to what is happening outside. He nods. 'Why? I thought they wanted to search the house!'

Nazario answers for Christakis. 'That's because the man in command saw that photo of Andreas. He's withdrawing his men as a mark of respect towards a Greek Cypriot who fought and died for Great Britain. He's reasoned that the house of a war hero couldn't be hiding guerrillas who are fighting against Britain. Isn't that correct?' he asks their host, who seems distracted by a noise above them rather than what is happening in his courtyard.

'Yes. This house has seen a lot of death. When I received news of Andreas's death I hated the British even more.' Christakis walks to one of the windows, which gives onto the western side of the farmhouse where the fields lie. There are no soldiers out there.

After a minute or so, engines fire up on the road.

'Do you know anything about the crash that killed Andreas?' Nazario asks as they follow Christakis back into the kitchen.

'Nothing at all,' is the angry answer. 'If I knew of his last moments, how it happened, what he was thinking, how he felt, I'd be more at peace with myself.'

'Surely you had no personal involvement in Andreas's decision to join the RAF and fight against the Axis forces,' replies Nazario. 'I remember feeling the urge to do something for my country, and I'm sure that Andreas must have felt the same.'

'That's certainly true,' Christakis says. He sits at the table, suddenly looking grey and tired. He has put away his public defiant face, as it is no longer needed, and what Nazario and Rosalia can see is the exposed and lonely man who is living with too many ghosts. 'I'll go and retrieve your letter, Rosalia,' Christakis says suddenly, as if he had just remembered. He shuffles over to the door, and shuts it behind him.

'What was that all about? Who are these guerrillas?' Rosalia looks around as if she were expecting somebody to jump through one of the doors, armed to their teeth.

'I suspect they're ordinary people fighting for this country's freedom against the British government. They can't have a full-blown war against a major power, so they've decided on a more subtle, covert approach. But they need shelter and food as they continue their campaign. Those officers were probably looking for a cell of, say, four or five men working together.'

A little noise from outside the door stops Nazario, who looks round suspiciously. A few seconds later, Christakis emerges, clutching an envelope that has often featured in Rosalia's dreams. She would recognise it anywhere: the neat handwriting on top, with her name and address; an Italian stamp on the right-hand side; smooth and clean as if it had been delivered that very day.

'I took great care of it, Rosalia. Here it is.'

The two men look at her with interest: Christakis meeting her excitement with the worn envy of those who no longer receive letters; Nazario searching her face for a sign of his own death.

'Excuse me,' Rosalia says, knowing she must be alone before she can open it.

'Of course,' Christakis nods. He points at the door that leads to the sitting room with Andreas's portrait, but she shakes her head.

'I need air.'

Outside, the brown hens must have decided that it is safe to resume their pecking and dust baths. In the late autumnal afternoon the countryside is vibrant with darker colours; heavy, musky scents mix with the dampness of a fast approaching evening. She chooses the only corner of the courtyard still lightly kissed by the sunset, and sits on a stone. The envelope throbs in her hands as if it is alive.

'Will they be all right?' asks Nazario, once Rosalia is outside, as he accepts another glass of wine from Christakis.

'Who?' Christakis looks at his guest over the top of his glass, curiously.

'You know who. Your friends.'

'What friends?'

Nazario puts his glass down slowly. 'The ones you're hiding.'

'What makes you think I have anybody hiding here?'

'I'm a policeman, Christakis. You live on your own, isolated from the rest of the village, but does that justify walking around with a shotgun and pointing it at visitors? The way you held the weapon showed familiarity with it. You don't get that just by shooting the occasional rabbit.'

Christakis nods. His glass is empty and he pours himself another. He shakes the bottle gently. 'Would you care for some more?'

'No,' Nazario replies, and shows him his own half-full glass. 'And when we arrived you had a batch of bread freshly baked; it was too much for one. Even though Rosalia and I ate plenty, there was still some left when you mentioned you'd bake a second batch later. Also, all the doors were ajar. You didn't want us to see the other rooms, but you needed to allow whoever's upstairs to listen to conversations, or perhaps be alerted by the noise of unexpected visits.'

'Perhaps the British should consider employing you to help with their random searches. They wouldn't be such hit-and-miss affairs.'

'Who are they?'

Christakis sighs. He cranes his neck towards the front door, trying to see whether Rosalia is coming back from the courtyard. The curtain hanging from the top of the door frame swings gently in the breeze. 'She doesn't need to be involved.'

'No,' Nazario agrees. She has her own chimaeras to chase, he thinks, and that terrible sadness he usually keeps at bay bites him again.

'Do you know Georgios Grivas and EOKA?' Christakis's voice is a whisper.

'I've heard of him, and EOKA.'

'I'll come back to EOKA. Grivas is a Cypriot-born general who fought in Greece when your Mussolini invaded it with his German friends, during the Second World War. A brave man, who was decorated for his efforts and has the love and respect of both Greek and Cypriot people.' Christakis gets up to put another log in the stove. It is now noticeably colder even in the

166

kitchen. Nazario worries about Rosalia. He briefly considers joining her but pushes the thought to one side. 'Grivas leads EOKA, the guerrilla organisation whose aim is to free this country from British colonial rule. It's made up of a handful of incredibly courageous men with limited resources; but they've got the local people's complete faith and support.' Christakis is standing in front of the wood-burning stove and seems to be talking to the fire. 'As Grivas says, "you don't need a tank to catch field mice; a cat will do the job nicely." This country wants to be free to join Greece and be part of an independent Greek state. The guerrillas hit little and often, demoralising this foreign government and ultimately destabilising it. They want to draw the other nations' attention to the Cyprus problem. I like to think that if Andreas were alive he'd have joined EOKA.'

'Have you got Grivas upstairs?'

'No. His right-hand man, Gregoris Afxentiou, with three other men. When the captain gave his men orders to withdraw, some of the soldiers were just outside the room where they're hiding. It was a close call. Gregoris wouldn't have given himself up, I know. It could have been a bloodbath. Andreas saved us from the grave.'

Nazario's thoughts are grimmer. Andreas is luring my girl to him, from the grave. Even time and death haven't softened his hold on her. I can't compete with a man who has died to defend other people's freedom and whose family risks it all to protect their own.

'I know you're scared.' Christakis is so close to Nazario that their faces almost touch. With a jolt, Nazario realises that he has been staring into his empty glass, lost in his thoughts. He opens his mouth to protest but no sound comes. 'Don't be. Look at us. Do you think this is the first visit I've ever had from the British? Today they almost caught us, but we won't give up. Fight for what is yours to keep.' The older man whispers in Nazario's ear.

At this moment, Rosalia comes back, bringing with her a chill breath of air from outside. She is no longer clutching the envelope but a piece of paper; Nazario spots the edge of the envelope poking from her dress's front pocket. Her face is hardened by the cold and pale with distress. Her hair hangs limply, curls long forgotten. 'Nazario. Look at this.' She gives him a large single-page document, double folded. He takes it mechanically, Christakis's words resounding in his brain. 'Fight for what is yours to keep.'

When he opens the piece of paper, though, his senses come back to him sharply: suddenly, he is a policeman again. The document he stretches out on the kitchen table is a map. A detailed map of Monte Pellegrino. It was not drawn to satisfy a geographical interest, nor is it a recent rendition of those ragged and wild spaces. It is a military map of the area and its network of tunnels, yellowed by time and a little torn at the corners. Nazario gazes at it in utter amazement. 'For the last twelve years everyone's been searching for this map. There used to be two, but neither of them has ever been found.' He traces his finger across the drawing. 'Until now.'

'Look at the back. There's a note from Andreas.'

Nazario turns the map over, making a supreme effort to stop his hands shaking. He reads the words 'You will need this when the time comes.'

'What does that mean?' he asks Rosalia, confused. 'Is it his handwriting?'

'I think so. It looks the same as the writing on the envelope.'

Christakis leans over the table to look at the note. 'Yes, it's Andreas's writing. I taught him and his sister calligraphy when they were four.'

You will need this when the time comes. What time? After the war? After Andreas's death? With an effort, Nazario takes his eyes off the map to address Rosalia. 'You must know what he's talking about. Have you seen this map before? Do you know how valuable it is?'

'No, not at all. What are those tunnels? I recognise Monte Pellegrino, but what are these strange marks?' She stabs the map with her long fingernails.

'They show the entrance and exit points to the largest wartime Italian fuel depot. Until now, it was thought to have been lost forever. Monte Pellegrino sits on a treasure, and a time bomb.'

'Why would Andreas send it to me?'

'He must have thought you were involved in some way. He probably planned to give it to you when the war was over, if he came back. He must have put it in an envelope to be sent to you in case he died. Was there anything else in the envelope?'

The silence that follows forces the two men to look up at Rosalia. A log in the stove crumbles, fizzing. From upstairs comes the faintest noise, perhaps a whisper or some discreet shuffling.

'Yes, there was. A letter. It's got nothing to do with this map, I promise you. It says nothing at all about it. It's just a letter to me, a very personal one.'

'Can I see it?' For the first time in all these years, Nazario does not care that he sounds like a policeman, nor is he ashamed of his unbearable curiosity. He would do anything, anything at all, to read what Andreas has written to Rosalia. It clearly still matters, even after such a long time.

'No. It's personal. You'll have to trust me that there's no explanation why the map was put in the same envelope.'

'Very well.' Nazario swallows hard. A thin blade of suspicion wedges itself between them. 'You may want to hold on to your map as well. As it says, you'll need it when the time comes.'

'Arguing over this won't help you find the truth,' says Christakis. 'You'll have to work as a team to get to the bottom of this. My nephew would have known what he was doing.' He looks at Rosalia with regret. 'I'm sure Andreas would have wanted you to do something with it.'

She takes the map and puts it back in her pocket, carefully

following the existing folds. 'You have no reason to be upset, Nazario. He's just trying to help us.'

'From the grave,' Nazario murmurs.

Chapter Twenty-Three
MONTE PELLEGRINO

Gregoris Afxentiou will thank Christakis Khuklakis when he leaves under the cover of darkness later that day. He will not be so lucky a month later: surrounded by the British military up on the same Troodos mountains, he will order the other members of his cell to surrender and come out of their underground hideout, but will not do so himself. Eventually, as the British forces cannot dig him out of his hiding hole, they resort to setting fire to the place, burning him alive.

Nazario and Rosalia will never know. Over the following months, news from Cyprus will trickle back to Italy, but the country is still too busy concentrating on its own recovery to take much notice of what happens abroad. However, Rosalia will often think about Christakis and his isolated farmhouse, and wonder about the rooms upstairs; the men hiding in those rooms, prepared to die for their principles; an old man who cannot grieve properly.

Back home, an odd coldness has settled between them. Rosalia is perfectly aware of Nazario's resentment over not being allowed to read Andreas's letter, but that makes her even more determined to keep it for herself.

The map, on the other hand, is a different issue altogether. Rosalia has put it away in one of the mahogany desk's drawers, in her father's study. Occasionally, she opens the drawer carefully to look at it, as if she fears it will somehow escape. The lines dance on the paper, animated by her imagination. 'You will need this when the time comes.'

One night, a week or so after their trip to Cyprus, Nazario comes back home to find her in the study, sitting on the floor and surrounded by her father's papers as usual. The lump of stone is still patiently waiting downstairs for Rosalia's inspiration to return. She has not been able to concentrate on her work for many days.

'Going over the same papers won't help,' he says gently. 'We ought to find the American document.'

'I know.'

'Do you think it's still here, in one of the folders? It may be lost forever.'

'No. I don't think it's here.' She sighs. 'But looking through these papers is easier than opening the hatch to the cellar.'

'Why would you want to do that?'

'I have a feeling that there's something down there, the missing piece to the puzzle.'

'Before you do that, listen to this. I've been doing some searching myself. I've got access to the official archives and war records.'

'Go on.'

Nazario sits on the leather chair in front of the desk and leans over, resting his elbows on his knees. His face is almost level with Rosalia's. 'What did Andreas write on the back of the map, which, incidentally, he must have removed from General Guzzoni's old office? "You will need this when the time comes." I'm assuming that "you" means you, Rosalia, personally. You "need" a map to look for something; needing the map itself doesn't make much sense. Do you follow me so far?'

'Yes.'

'That's the easy part. Now for "when the time comes". What time is he talking about? Does he mean after the war's ended, or is it something more personal, like "when I come back"?' Nazario pauses to gather his thoughts. 'I think he intended to say "when it's appropriate for you to do something". This suggests a more personal interpretation, rather than a general one: you must act upon this map or unlock the information in it.'

Rosalia shakes her head. 'I don't know what I should be doing with a map of Monte Pellegrino. I've got nothing to do with it.'

'Well, that's not entirely true, is it? For a start, there's a sanctuary up there dedicated to a saint who shares her name with you. If I'm not mistaken, Saint Rosalia was a girl belonging to a rich Norman family who lived during the time of the Crusades.'

'Meaning ...'

'Look around you. How old are the grounds on which Palazzo de' Muggifalco stands? Seven, eight hundred years? How did your family come to own this property?'

Rosalia bites her bottom lip, trying to remember exactly what her grandmother used to tell her. 'Nonna boasted that this house was given to the Muggifalcos for their bravery and for the help they gaveto the Normans during the Crusades. The old house was burnt down in the seventeenth century, to stop the Black Death spreading ...'

'... which is more or less when the legend says Saint Rosalia's bones were found up Monte Pellegrino.'

'I don't understand the connection, Nazario. What's Monte Pellegrino got to do with this house?'

'It's a remarkable coincidence, but I think the connection's with you personally.'

'Me?'

'Yes. If we forget about the fuel depot and the entrances to the tunnels, the only other thing that's on the map is the mountain itself. Andreas wouldn't have expected you to need the map to the fuel depot, but the map on its own shows a link between the place and your family. He didn't steal this document for its military value, although that's obviously an aspect of it. He sent it to you as a sign.'

A sign. Rosalia suddenly remembers what her grandmother used to say: 'Look at the Palazzo. The signs are there: one day it will all be yours.'

'How would he know anything at all about the Monte, Saint Rosalia and this house? He was only a pilot, after all.'

'I've told you before, Rosalia. He wasn't just a simple pilot. Didn't you hear his uncle? Andreas was extremely bright and gifted with languages. He worked for the CIC; perhaps he came across other documents which shed a light on this map, and saw something we still can't see. I think CIC was investigating the Americans and their policies in Sicily during the AMGOT months. Monte Pellegrino is part of the government estate, and its importance would have trebled because of the underground fuel depot.'

'You're trying to tell me that Palazzo de' Muggifalco will turn out to be part of the government estate too, aren't you? Perhaps we should let things be.'

'We should have given the map to the authorities by now. Strictly speaking it's not ours. Access to the fuel depot will give Sicily enormous financial assistance, unexpectedly so as the underground supplies are thought to have been lost forever, but I think we may hang onto it a little longer. I'll be doing some detective work tomorrow. I've been given permission to go through the deeds and any paperwork concerning public estate properties.'

Rosalia thinks of Andreas and the secret he kept until after his death, and wonders whether other people might have done the same. 'I have a feeling that what we're looking for isn't in this room', she adds. 'But it may still be in the house.'

'What about Andreas? Is he still here?' Nazario has never asked such a direct question about Andreas before. Rosalia knows that the lingering presence of the dead pilot has always bothered him, but Nazario seemed to have learnt to live with it, until their trip to Cyprus.

'Why do you ask?' She tries to make her voice as kind as possible. Sharing the letter is not an option, at least not now, whilst she is still digesting its contents; but Rosalia is aware that denying him access to it only makes the distance between them all the more real.

'His bust isn't on the window sill any more,' is the sober reply.

'Yes. I took it down. Something has been missing, but I think I know what it is now. I won't be able to do any more work until I deal with it.'

'What is it?'

'I'll tell you when I've made the new bust. I don't like leaving things unfinished.'

'Yes,' agrees Nazario, and his face is dead serious again. 'Unfinished business has a nasty habit of coming back to haunt you. Better confront it. Are you glad we went to Cyprus? Are you persuaded that Andreas is dead now?'

'Dead? Yes. Andreas is dead. I kept him alive inside me all these years simply because he didn't leave me properly. It wasn't me who refused to let him go; it was him who stayed.' Still sitting on the floor, Rosalia hugs her knees and puts her heart-shaped face on them. Nazario's hazel eyes look straight at her. The gold dust sprinkled over them has never stopped amazing her. She is about to tell him that she loves him, when he speaks first. 'My God. I think I know what the link is!'

'Tell me.'

'No! I must check a few things first. You'll have to wait. It's a bit far fetched, but when you rule out everything else it's the only possible option.'

'You're impossible!' she cries, frustrated.

'Come to bed, Rosalia.' He whispers in her hair, near the perfect ear lobe. A sudden tenderness, borne out of relief and excitement: relief that the past does not stare at him from the top of a window sill; excitement at the thought of being close to solving a mystery that has been taunting them for years.

The little table lamp in the bedroom casts a discreet shadow and is barely visible from the street outside Palazzo de' Muggifalco, especially when the curtains are drawn. However, its weak light can still be seen flickering through the window. The person who stands in the dark street opposite the house, that evening as on many others before, looks at it for a long time with a tortured heart.

In the early morning, when Nazario leaves the Palazzo, he sees nobody outside. The mist breathing out of the old stones is starting to lift; on his way to work, despite the dampness and cold, Nazario tucks his hands inside the uniform trousers and whistles happily. In his mind there are only thoughts of old tunnels, barrels of oil and a saint waiting in her sanctuary on top of the mountain. 'Saint Rosalia,' he finds himself praying, 'keep love in her heart and make room there for me.' He recalls Christakis's words once again: 'fight for what is yours to keep.'

Rosalia, in the meantime, has decided to pay the saint's sanctuary another visit. She must look at that picture with her new eyes. Under the worktop table, covered by one of her dowry's embroidered sheets, is the bust that must no longer remind her of a lie. As she runs downstairs, ready to leave, an odd noise stops her in her tracks: a scratchy, slow noise at odds with the ringing steps of someone in a hurry. Looking around her, Rosalia waits in silence, trying to work out where the sound is coming from. A few seconds later, there it is again, slow and discreet like a mouse digging for food. Sounds chase each other, room after room, ricocheting from Palazzo de' Muggifalco's high ceilings to the wide curved staircases and roofless courtyard. I'm going mad, she thinks. It sounds as if someone else is in the house, but I know I'm the only one here. Nazario left half an hour ago. What is it?

And there it goes again. Does it come from upstairs? Rosalia looks up the staircase, a hand still on the banister. Slowly, she climbs back up, step by step, ears straining to pick up anything apart from the hard beating of her heart against her ribcage. On the landing upstairs she looks at the closed doors to rooms where she very rarely ventures, populated with people she has not seen for a long time. The room at the end of the corridor is her father's study. Surely she closed the oak door before coming downstairs? It is now slightly ajar. 'You're being silly,' she says to herself.

To her right there is an expanse of glass windows that tilt open into the empty courtyard; to her left are three or four doors she never opens. Behind her is the safety of her bedroom: memories of last night and Nazario's warm body against hers. She allowed him to climax inside her for the first time: a sign of newly found and implicit intimacy.

She lifts her hand towards the nearest door handle. The scratching noise again, this time more distant. Rosalia's hand falls by her side: whatever it may be, it is not on this floor. She hears a fly buzzing somewhere in the house, looking for a place to die before the winter. It reminds her of the one trapped in a dirty taxi back in Cyprus, their drive up the Troodos mountains and Christakis's farmhouse.

Behind the buzzing is a whisper, more like a sigh. Unable to take the strain any longer, Rosalia walks the few steps to her grandmother's room quickly, yanks the door open and walks in. The room looks quiet and unruffled, very much as it did the last time she went in, to air it during the summer. The sheets covering the old furniture are undisturbed, the shapes under them innocent in the semi-darkness. The window shutters are closed. A mirror, hanging on the opposite wall returns her reflection: a young woman with an amethyst-coloured furry collar framing her long neck, spirited eyes and a pale face. Why didn't I cover that mirror? she wonders. Gingerly, Rosalia walks further into the room, lifting a corner of each cover to reveal what is underneath. The wrought-iron single bed with its stiff mattress, a chaise longue, the monastic bedside table, a little armchair and trunk – items retrieved from the blast and carefully restored.

Up against the wall is an antique bookcase that used to stand in the hall. She remembers being a child and looking up at books she would like to read with her tutor. During the war, the bookcase, once surrounded by priceless ornaments and heirlooms, had looked rather lonely in the vast entrance. When Rosalia lifts the sheet the bookcase is there, looking exactly the same as it appeared to her as a child, just smaller and shorter. The mahogany shelves hold the few books that survived the blast. She runs a finger across the long-forgotten spines. The red and green covers with the unique smell of old glue and decaying string holding the pages together. Maupassant, Tolstoy, Sartre: foreign authors translated by local professors.

At the end of one shelf, hidden behind the supporting frame, Rosalia spots the corner of a book she has not seen for many years. It is the Horse-Riding Manual for Ladies, the book she had been looking for just before the air raid and the first thing she had spotted among the debris. She remembers picking it up and putting it into the front pocket of her torn summer dress. Her bloody fingers had left smears on the cover. My manual! Rosalia thinks, and smiles, knowing now as she did then that there is no chance of her learning how to ride a horse. She pulls the book out of its place, and opens it, expecting to see the many illustrations that fascinated her as a young girl. She had meant to flick through it, but realises that the pages will not turn quickly, as if something has been wedged between them: a document, a few sheets stapled together. The document is neatly folded in half. Who can have put it there? Her father perhaps, who would have known that the book had little chance of being read or needed. Rosalia removes the sheets carefully. She hates her hesitation before unfolding the document, and her trembling fingers.

'... 1 May 1941 ... an agreement of co-operation to pursue the best interests of both our countries ... Giacomo Alessandro Novara ...' Rosalia stops her cursory glance at the document to look around the room, allowing her heart to slow down. The document they had been looking for! Here, now! She holds the pages so tightly that her knuckles turn white. Breathe deeply, breathe slowly, she tells herself, her mind galloping ahead. '... will undertake to gather secret information from the enemy by befriending ... Giacomo Novara will have access to unlimited funds used for the sole purpose to lure ... German top officers ... classified information will immediately be reported to the agreed point of contact ...' So this was why Signor and Signora Novara had been entertaining German top officers and Fascist representatives of the local government at their beautiful house throughout the war. '... particularly with regard to the German Navy's plans in the Mediterranean; concentration of forces, location and strategies ... an American representative will process the information.' All the time they were wining and dining the Germans, they were planning to overthrow the regime and were working with the American government. A dangerous game.

But how, and why? America did not have had an active part in the conflict until the end of 1941. Were they already gathering information to be used against the Axis forces? She reads on, trying not to skim. According to the agreement, Signor Novara was to file a regular report with any information gained via a network of secret agents. Rosalia notes an Italian name that recurs throughout the document: Signor Tony Mancini. An old memory resurfaces, of Vincenzo telling her about some family friends in New York, the Mancinis, who had emigrated from Sicily in the late thirties. There is something else linked to that name, but she can't recall what it is.

It is the last part of the document that really captures Rosalia's attention. It is an outline of the Novaras' recompense for services rendered to the country: 'as suggested by Mr Giacomo Alessandro Novara, the American government will do all that is in its power to appoint Mr Giacomo Alessandro Novara to a position of power within the local government and ... re-assign, after the end of the conflict, the territory ... part of the Sicilian government's estate ... for private use ... the whole of Monte Pellegrino excluding all urban settlement and adjacent villages unless an integral part of the land in question.' Dear God! That's what Signor Novara had in his sights! Monte Pellegrino itself. Panic grabs hold of Rosalia so suddenly that it leaves her out of breath. For, if this document is legally binding, and she has no reason to think otherwise, why is it hidden inside her horse-riding manual rather than carefully stored in one of Signor Novara's official folders?

Solicitor Muggifalco would have approved of America's involvement with locals who were working against the Germans from the inside; so why would her father remove this document from its proper place in his study? Unless ... unless, for some reason, he did not want it to be found easily, and certainly not by Signor Novara. But if that were true, why agree to carry out the legalities in the first place? The answer comes to Rosalia easily, as if it had been lodged in her brain all the time. Because he would have preferred to be kept informed about the agreement, rather than allow outsiders to carry it through. Keep your friends close, and your enemies closer. Another thought increases her sense of panic and danger: if the document has been hidden until now, and Monte Pellegrino still seems to be part of the public estate, it is inevitable that Signor Novara does not have a copy of it. 'He's still looking for the original,' says Rosalia to herself. 'He was looking for it after the blast, among the rubble. Vincenzo was searching for it too!' She feels a terrible sense of betrayal and loss. When she thought Signor Novara was being kind and helpful during the worst time in her life, he was pursuing his personal interests. She leans against the bookcase, half of which is still under the white dustsheet. In her hand, scrunched up, is the document that Signor Novara must have been desperate to find.

A new and even more terrible thought replaces all others: the memory of a cellar full of grain and sacks, which, Rosalia is now sure, did not and could not possibly have belonged to her father. 'He lied to me.' Signor Novara's pinched look floats up to the surface of her earlier recollections; his men, gathered in the street opposite where Palazzo de' Muggifalco stood in all its glory before the bombing, waiting for Signor Novara to deliver the news about the stolen grain to a sixteen-year-old girl whose parents were not there to defend themselves. The look on the workmen's faces had been of pity and embarrassment, not, as Rosalia had thought at the time, of condemnation.

Did her father know about the food supply in his cellar? Rosalia fears that she will never find out. The cellar has been boarded up for twelve years. Signor Novara's men did the work when most of her home was a pile of rubble. What will Signor Novara have done with the grain? Perhaps he sold it on the black market, profited out of it. 'If the cellar hadn't been flooded, my parents would have been able to take cover. The hatch door was bolted because of the flood.' Who told the Muggifalcos that the cellar was unusable? Signor Novara, who sent his men to check it the winter before. Who locked the door, claiming it was unsafe? Signor Novara. Antonio Muggifalco had accepted his advice without question: they were friends. But were they really friends? Why would solicitor Muggifalco hide his friend's entitlement to property and riches? A pattern of deception emerges in Rosalia's head as she stands in the silent room full of dustsheets and answers.

Of course, there is one question for which there seems to be no answer at all. If Signor Novara was keen to convince the Muggifalcos that the cellar was unusable, in order to store his own food supply, how did he fill the place up with dozens of heavy sacks without anybody noticing? The only entrances were the one under the stairs, or a secondary door through the laundry room. Anything destined for the cellar would have had to go through the main house. 'I refuse to believe my father knew about it.' She says it aloud to the covered furniture around her. But a little voice whispers in her ear: this is a man who acted as the legal adviser for Signor Novara and then hid the document. Solicitor Muggifalco had a legal and moral responsibility towards his client and friend, and ignored it. Maybe they were in this together. There is only one thing to do. Open the cellar. Now.

At that very moment, the door bell rings, echoing all the way up the stairs and into her grandmother's bedroom. Rosalia is so startled that she drops the document. She stuffs it into the manual again, and puts it back in the bookcase. Lastly, she drapes the dustsheet across it and walks out of the room, shutting the door behind her.

Coming down the stairs towards the front door slowly, to try to compose herself, Rosalia remembers that she had asked Vera to go with her to the sanctuary, partly for company and partly because she feels the need for an outsider's opinion. Somebody who has no emotional involvement in the matter could look at that photograph objectively.

'Good morning, my friend,' Vera says, happy as always. Ever the artist, her uncombed hair seems to be impermeable to fashion or people's disapproving looks. Today she is wearing a man's coat and emerald green gloves. 'Mmmm, huge eyes, startled expression, pale skin ... you look as if you've finally given in to opium, my dear!' she says.

Rosalia smiles. They couldn't be more different, and yet they share this all-consuming pursuit of beauty through art, which pulls them close together.

'You know I've never taken opium, and I'm unlikely to start now, thank you. I can produce a glazed stare without any help.' She motions Vera in and shuts the door behind her.

'What a shame! You don't know what you're missing, my dear.'

'I'll regret it later.'

'Are you ready to go? I can't wait to see this famous photo of Andreas.

I bet you and Nazario are wrong. The light in the sanctuary can play nasty tricks on your eyes and brain. But the trip to Cyprus sounds fascinating.'

Rosalia hesitates. She desperately wants to see the photo again, but even more desperately wants to see the cellar. Vera would be welcome company; she knows she would be too scared to go down there on her own.

'Do you mind a change of plan?'

'Does it involve Cyprus? I've never left Sicily and I'd love to travel.'

'No. Well, yes. A little trip to the centre of the earth. Only joking,' she adds quickly, seeing in Vera's face a little shadow of disappointment.

'I've found something by chance. A document.' Rosalia bites her bottom lip as Vera looks at her with renewed curiosity.

'What kind of document? Not another photograph?'

'No. A proper, legal document. I can't tell you what it is yet, but I was wondering whether you'd come with me for a little exploration. I need to check things out.'

'All right. Where are we going?' Vera has not removed her coat or the gloves, feeling the cold in the draughty hall and expecting to go straight out.

'I'd like to go down into our cellar, but I need your help: the hatch door is bolted shut. Nazario tried to open it a couple of days ago but couldn't lift it. The latch must be stuck.'

'Where is it?' Vera looks around her as if she were expecting the door to be somewhere in the hall or on the walls.

'It's under the stairs, over there. Come.' Rosalia takes Vera's hand and pulls her gently towards the entrance.

'Do you have any tools? If a man can't lift the door, we certainly won't be able to.'

'I've got the hatchet I use for work, of course, and a large file, knives, possibly some pliers.'

'Rosalia's arsenal! Let's get to work. Tell me what we're looking for. Don't you know what's in your cellar? When was the last time you went down there? Surely you must check the well every so often.'

'No, I don't. The cellar was locked just after the war ended and the workmen who upgraded the hot water system went underground from the old laundry room, and that passage was then filled. The electric pump is in the kitchen so there's no need for me to use the cellar at all.'

'Let's have a look at this hatch. Go and get me all the tools you can lay your hands on.' Vera smiles and pulls her gloves off, throwing them carelessly onto the floor. Her coat joins them.

Whilst Rosalia hunts for her tools, Vera ducks under the flight of stairs. There she finds a round hatch opening, flush with the rest of the surface and made of the same stone. Camouflaged like that, it is hard to distinguish it from the rest of the floor. On one side of it a large ring sits inside a groove carefully carved into the stone, a metal ridge around it. Vera scrapes and digs around the groove, trying to get a grip on the ring, to no avail.

'Have you got something like a spatula?' she asks when she hears Rosalia return.

'Of course.' The large flat tool that Rosalia uses to smooth down the rough edges of drying clay is passed over Vera's shoulder.

'It's too thick. I need something thin and sharp but strong – and a light would be helpful.'

'Try this one. I'll go and get a candle or two.'

The next tool to be passed to Vera is a long, thin steel pointer. She grunts in approval.

Head to head, the women kneel by the hatch door, trying to prise the ring out of its groove. A candle burns on top of an old tin.

A click in the semi-darkness is closely followed by Vera's triumphant scream. 'Yes!'

The metal ring stands up, stiff and cold to the touch. 'Now all we have to do is get some leverage. If we find a piece of wood thin enough to go through the ring and strong enough to hold the weight of the hatch, we can lift both ends, just hoping it doesn't snap.' Vera puts a finger through the ring and pulls it as if to show how the idea would work.

Rosalia looks at that finger, still hooked onto the ring, fascinated. The nail is cut to the quick and dirty. Vera's other fingernails are in no better shape. 'You'reare so practical. I'm glad you agreed to help me. I wouldn't have known what to do.'

'Don't mention it. A little underground adventure is too romantic to resist. Curiosity is a strong incentive.'

Five minutes later, they are bent over the hatch, one at each end of a piece of broomstick, either side of the ring.

'Ready, Rosalia. One, two, three, pull!' The broomstick groans and flexes but does not break. Slowly, the hatch moves, sounding like a tombstone being removed from its bed. As it lifts and rotates on its hinges, Rosalia notices its thickness and weight and is scared. 'Ease it back until it rests on the floor,' suggests Vera, still holding the broomstick.

For a moment, until their eyes are used to the darkness, it seems to both women that a black, perfectly round hole has been opened in the floor. The candle on the tin flickers worriedly.

'Are you sure about this?' Vera looks very grave. 'You may not like what we find in there.'

Rosalia looks into the hole, a sixteen-year-old girl again, looking at potatoes, grain and flour. 'Of course I'm sure. If you're willing to come with me.'

'What are friends for? Let's go,' Vera says. She gropes for the first rung of the rickety steps that are attached to the lower rim of the hatch. 'Pass me the candle.'

Twenty-Four
THE LOST ESTATE

'Nei secoli fedele.'

Nazario walks into the *carabinieri*'s headquarters in Palermo and, as usual, looks up at the front door which is surmounted by a plaque with the Army's motto: 'Loyal through the centuries'. He wanted to join the *carabinieri* when he was a child, and still remembers his father's pride when, aged seventeen, he was accepted into the best known and most loved Italian police force. During his years of service, his affection and respect for it has never wavered. The *carabinieri*'s military authority is widespread: the army is split into various areas of responsibilities, from armed defence of the Italian state to general control of public order, environmental and cultural assets.

During the war, as a liaison officer between local police and the Allied government, Nazario was exposed to privileged information. He was also given the kind of authority that either damages a young man's perception of self-worth or gives him a taste for the relentless pursuit of truth. Today he feels the long-forgotten excitement of the hunt fill him with renewed energy. He remembers the days spent investigating Signor Novara. His dossier on the person who soon became Palermo's mayor was as thick as it was inconclusive.

Nazario sits at his desk, mentally going through the only factual information he has ever been able to collate about the Novaras: a rich Sicilian family business, steel dealers, old money. They were known Fascists, though Giacomo Novara was rumoured to be an opportunist and hypocrite when, after the invasion, instead of fleeing like so many other supporters of the Nazi regime, he had stayed, had wined and dined the American top command; proposed himself as the new champion of defeated Palermo. Nazario knows perfectly well that there was no real competition to stop his rise to power, and that the Americans were very happy to have a ready-made *podestá*, a local figurehead to take on the headache of governing a wild foreign land. Nevertheless, whilst looking into the mysterious and recurrent disappearance of both American and local food supplies, Nazario came across some faint but audible voices that pointed at Novara as in some way implicated. No hard evidence. Always above suspicion.

Before starting his search on Monte Pellegrino, Nazario pulls out the old file on Giacomo Novara, which had been stored in the judiciary police archives for over ten years. His discreet investigation stalled and eventually withered, but Nazario has remained convinced that there is more to the Novaras than everyone was led to believe. The family tree, for example. The Novaras, although of substantial social importance, abruptly appear in the census papers and among the birth and death certificates that Nazario has access to, as if were not in Sicily earlier than the seventeenth century. By contrast, all the other genteel families living in the best areas of Palermo have a documented history that goes back many centuries. Like the Muggifalcos. When Nazario met Rosalia for the first time, he went back to work and made a few enquiries into her name and family, to discover they are mentioned in official documents time and time again: their history is interwoven with that of Sicily.

Nazario sits at his desk, biting the end of his pencil. Ancient books, documents and folders are piled up in front of him. A faint smell of old paper lingers in the air, mixed with cigarette smoke. Fighting in the Crusades would have meant rich pickings for the Normans' allies back at home, and Palazzo de' Muggifalco was a good way to thank them for their support. But where is the land? Traditionally, there would have been acres and acres of it, given at the same time as the house, but the Palazzo doesn't even have a proper garden like the Novaras' home.

Who owned Monte Pellegrino before it became part of the government estate? Rosalia's heart-shaped face smiles in Nazario's imagination. The Arabs who conquered Sicily and lived there for many centuries before the Norman invasion left few signs of their passage: Arab places of worship and buildings were either destroyed by the Christians who came after them, or were adapted; and yet the exotic survives in the language, words, places, rivers and landmarks, in Arabic traits such as strong features and black hair, so common in Sicilian people. However, Rosalia's dark hair is not coarse and thick; her skin is fair and as smooth as porcelain. Nazario remembers his surprise when he noticed the resemblance between Rosalia and her namesake saint.

Loud voices, cheering and laughter filter through the door to his office from the big room behind it. With Nazario's promotion to marshal major on special duties has come a bigger private office and a team of thirty-two *carabinieri*; one of them has just become a father and is being applauded by his colleagues. Nazario's attention wavers a little. What does the legend say? He tries to remember from his catechism lessons and Sunday school:

Saint Rosalia was born into a rich family, but left everything to live a life of contemplation and prayer in one of the caves of Monte Pellegrino. Which family did she belong to? More cheering; the unmistakable noise of a bottle of champagne being uncorked. 'It was a Norman family. Saint Rosalia is Norman. She chose to live like a hermit, but her bones weren't found until four hundred years later, during the Black Death.'

'Marshal Major!' A happy voice behind the door. 'Can I come in, sir?'

Nazario looks out of the window. It is nearing midday and the sun is making an effort to cheer up a grey November. 'Not yet, Catalano. Not yet. I'm busy. My congratulations to you and your wife. I'll call you presently.'

'Yes, sir.' A note of disappointment in the man's voice. Catalano is young and enthusiastic; married last year, in a new job and with a new baby. He likes all things new and is in awe of technology. An unlikely *carabiniere*.

Rosalia Muggifalco's family descends from the Normans who invaded Sicily in medieval times, who fought in the Crusades and stayed on for five hundred years. Why did Saint Rosalia choose Monte Pellegrino? Was it because it was wild and far away from everything? But there are taller, wilder mountains.

Owning the place. Nazario smacks his forehead hard with the palm of his right hand. His hat flies across the back of the desk and hits the wall. 'Catalano! Catalano!'

'Yes, sir. At your service, sir.' The door opens and Catalano's slim figure appears, a happy smile on his smooth face. His shoes are shiny and so is the badge in the centre of his hat. He is impeccable.

'Catalano. I need the land register file for Monte Pellegrino. Be kind enough to fetch it for me. Ground floor, archives. Ask Mrs Pintacuda, the secretary. She'll show you where it is.'

Catalano clicks his heels together and touches the tip of his hat with his right hand. He is not impeccable after all, Nazario thinks with a sneer: his fingernails are in a terrible state, broken and dirty.

Waiting for the land register, Nazario briefly considers telephoning Rosalia but discards the idea. I don't know for sure, and this may just be a very shaky theory, he thinks. I'll wait till I have more information. Suddenly, he remembers Rosalia telling him of her intention to go to the sanctuary again that morning with Vera. At least she's not on her own, he reasons. Vera, for all her eccentric looks, is rather sensible. They won't be back yet.'

Idly, Nazario reads the sparse notes about the Novara family again; he flicks once more through the documents in chronological order, going back as far as he can, to the first mention of their name.

'Novara ... Novara ... Nov ... Nova, Latin for *nuovo*, 'new'. A new name,' he says to himself, splinters of Latin coming back to him from school, when he learnt the ancient language like all Italian children. 'A new name.'

Nazario freezes. Then, frantically, he goes through his file on Giacomo

Novara, a terrible thought forming in his mind as he pulls at the pages, scanning the highlighted paragraphs and looking at the words in a different context, uncovering a different meaning. There's always been a building on the spot where the Novara house is, but the records of families inhabiting it over the years are confusing. Before the Novaras there may not have been anyone there, which would be very odd. Unless ... unless the Novaras' surname isn't their original one. They must have changed it. Why? What did they have to hide? There it is: first mentioned in the sixteenth century, the Novaras of Palermo. 'Historical building of great importance which ... later withstood the earthquake of 1677 ... untouched by the passing of time ...' Would it be the same family? With no record of who lived in the house before the Novaras, Nazario has no way of finding out, but he has a strong hunch that he may finally be on the right track. There are only a few reasons why anyone changes their surname: if they were attached to a crime, say, or if they wanted to delete any traces of a past identity.

Nazario holds his pencil so hard that it breaks in two, but he barely notices. Of course: the seventeenth century, the prosecutions. It all started in Spain, didn't it? The Spanish Catholic royals keen to get rid of that minority of the population which owned a majority of the wealth in Spain, as in most parts of Europe and elsewhere. They're Jews. The Novaras are Jews. Nazario has absolutely no evidence but he is sure he is right. What line of business are they in? Steel making. Traditionally, that's a Jewish business. Tens of thousands of Jews offered to go away into exile, leaving all their wealth behind, or they renounced their faith and stayed.' Nazario recalls the pages of Sicilian history he studied during his apprenticeship, in order to understand the historical reasons for the persecution of the Jews. They were forced to be the executioners of people of their own kind; everything they owned was stolen, and the state swallowed their estates. Once upon a time they lived peacefully alongside the Normans, but after the Spanish ruled against them there was nowhere for them to go.

So the Novaras chose to die and be reborn in their new faith, but they did not leave. Nazario knows that Signor Novara rarely attends Mass at the cathedral; when he does, he hovers in an aisle, as if uncomfortable to be so close to the Jesus in whom he doesn't believe. It was a very dangerous game to play, to have one's home full of Nazis and Fascists during the war; they could have been found out at any time! It would have demanded nerves of steel, which Mrs Novara obviously didn't have, hence her rare social appearances. Vincenzo, too, living in a separate part of the house, kept his exposure to a minimum. But Signor Novara must have had a plan. A plan so important that it justified continual danger for the whole family.

Nazario wonders about looking at the oldest topographic maps of Palermo to pinpoint the Novaras' property, then looking it up on the *cespite catastale*, the small 'private interest' part of the land register, instead of looking at their family history. It might yield more information. He gets up from his desk in such a hurry that he forgets to retrieve his hat.

On his way out he sees Catalano coming back, balancing a large tome across his arms. 'Sir! I have your information here, as you asked.'

'Never mind, Catalano. Put it on my desk. I'll be back in a minute.' Then a sudden thought stops Nazario on his tracks. 'Wait a minute! What letter does that book cover?'

'M, sir.'

'Give it to me.'

'Yes, sir.'

'Go back and get the topographic maps of Palermo, dating back as far as you can. And the land register for the letter N.'

Catalano looks puzzled but says nothing, turning round and disappearing down the corridor.

In his office, Nazario feverishly pores over the pages for what feels like only a few minutes. Even when Catalano is back with the documents he requested, he does not lift his eyes, hardly registering the thump of more papers landing on his desk. When he looks up again, the sunset is upon him. The large room behind the office door is much quieter.

The volumes cover both the history of Monte Pellegrino's legal ownership and information about the Muggifalco property. The Novara house, five hundred yards down the same street, is comprehensively pictured in the maps and described in the land register. It is there that finally Marshal Major Nazario Casa finds the link he has been looking for. 'I've been an idiot.' The clock on the wall shows a fast-approaching four o'clock. 'Catalano!'

The door opens slowly. Catalano pokes his head through carefully, as if scared that his superior might give him another errand to run, which would make him late. 'Sir!'

'You passed your judiciary and legal exams recently, did you not?'

'Yes, sir. Just last month.'

'Would you say that a legal document pertaining to a private interest in a public property, which must be passed down from generation to generation to be acknowledged, would still be valid after four hundred years, even without the relevant signature? Can a private individual claim ownership based on an ancient contract between himself and the state, though the current state has a different statute?'

Catalano stands at the door, holding on to its frame, thinking. 'Well, sir, most Italian law goes back to Roman times and has survived untouched for about two thousand years. The state has a separate legal identity regardless of time and changes if it relates to the same land. I'd say that property law would be no different, especially as the nature of the land, if not the property itself, doesn't change. But if a signature's required, then its absence would constitute a legal problem for the claimant.'

Nazario nods. His eyes are bloodshot and he has a headache. 'Yes, I agree with you. I must leave now, Catalano. An urgent matter has just come to my attention. My congratulations again about your new baby. What is it, by the way?'

'A boy, Marshal Major. We named him Gualtiero. Would you like to see the photograph?' Catalano seems to be bursting with pride. 'I took it and developed the film myself. We've got a new camera, bought with the money from the wedding presents. Shame about my fingernails, but it's worth it.'

Nazario feels as if a thousand alarm bells have gone off in his head all at once. His eyes narrow. 'What about your fingernails?' he asks, urgently.

'Well, sir, the bromide acid I use as a developer for the exposed film is very strong. If you don't use gloves, the acid will destroy your fingernails and crack your skin. Even with gloves on, prolonged use causes the rubber to burn and split. These black particles here aren't dirt but melted rubber, which is stuck under the broken fingernails.'

There is one person whose fingernails look very similar to Catalano's. She has never mentioned an interest in photography and is with Rosalia now, at Saint Rosalia's sanctuary, discussing a mysterious photograph of Andreas.

He is running before Catalano has finished his sentence.

Twenty-Five
UNDERGROUND

The oldest part of Palermo stands on calcareous rock, inside which, over the centuries, an entire network of natural and artificial tunnels, wells, rooms and cavities has expanded at the same rate as the above-ground city. The Arabs may have been the first in Sicily to introduce the idea of channelling natural underground water-courses to benefit the ever-growing city; in such an arid and hot climate the Arab *qanat*, a complicated water management system based on vertical wells connected to a passageway through which water runs freely, was paramount for the survival of the settlement. Earlier, tunnels and natural caves, suitably altered, would have fulfilled burial functions, as with the Christian catacombs. After the Arabs, the secret and invisible underground world continued to grow, sometimes serving the same religious purpose for which it was originally born.

The vast properties huddled together in the centre of old Palermo, home to nobles and royals, boast the most intricate network below ground, with extensive cellars and secret passageways dug as a refuge and a safe way to move around the city in less peaceful times.

Vera starts her descent into the hole. When her head is level with the floor of Palazzo de' Muggifalco, she stretches her hand towards her friend. 'Pass me a candle. It's rather dark down here.'

Rosalia hesitates. 'Are you absolutely sure about this?' The two candles flicker. She reaches for one of them. 'All right, let's do it. Wait for me at the bottom of the stairs.'

'Don't forget the matches,' says Vera's disembodied voice.

Once Rosalia has joined her inside the cellar, they stand at the bottom of the stairs from where the hatch opening is a reassuring roundel of light. 'There must be a light switch somewhere,' whispers Rosalia as she looks

187

around her, trying to cast some light with her candle. The cellar is rectangular and half as large as Palazzo de' Muggifalco's ground floor. There is a faint smell of mould and decay, but the cellar does not feel at all stuffy. 'There!' Rosalia has spotted a string dangling from the ceiling; a single weak bulb in the far corner seems startled to be put into use – and it immediately blows. 'I haven't been in this cellar since I was a child.' She shivers a little. She had expected the cellar to be completely silent and is amazed by the many noises that fill it up, most of which she is well familiar with: the water and heating pipes gurgling away; the creaking and moaning of old joists; even the muffled rumbling of cars passing the front door. Waiting for her eyes to adjust to the artificial light, Rosalia listens to the noises as if they were a language she knows, spoken with a foreign accent: the cellar picks up sounds but filters them through its thick stone walls, adding long, wheezy whistles like an old man struggling to breathe. 'What's that?' she asks Vera.

'What's what?'

'I can hear a strange sound like an airflow, but there's no wind here.'

'Really? Look at your candle.' Vera points at Rosalia's flickering flame. 'Of course it's the wind: we're underground. There's a system of ventilation here that goes back a few hundred years.'

'But this is an enclosed cellar. Four walls, a floor and a ceiling. Where's the draught coming from?'

Vera sighs. 'I don't know. Check everything quickly. I don't want to stay long enough to discover your cellar's inhabited by rats.'

In the faint candlelight they see the solitary electric pump sitting on the right-hand side of the stairs. A set of bricks grouped to make a circular shape marks the position of the well that serves Palazzo de' Muggifalco. From its centre a large pipe emerges, then bends towards the wall behind it, where it climbs up steadily until it disappears through the ceiling.

'It's absolutely empty.' Rosalia cannot hide her disappointment. Old cobwebs dangle in a dead grey triangle between the pillars and the cellar's ceiling.

'What were you expecting to find, an Aladdin's cave? If you've not been in here for the last twelve years, it stands to reason that it should look like this. But ...'

'What?'

'Does it look right to you? The size, I mean. Do you remember the way it was when you were a child?'

'Now you mention it, it looks rather smaller; but that's probably because I was little and it would have appeared enormous to a scared child.'

'Or it could have shrunk. Let's have a proper look.'

They start walking slowly along the walls, Rosalia behind Vera. Their feet shuffle along no more than a couple of inches from the base of the stones. For a while, neither of them speaks. Suddenly, Rosalia notices that Vera's candle is spluttering, as if an invisible force were trying to put it out.

'Watch out!' she exclaims, and at the same time she puts her hand protectively around her candle.

'There's a strong draught here,' Vera whispers, focusing on the wall directly opposite the stairs.

Under the flickering light of two candles, some of the wall's calcareous stones seem to bulge in and out. 'Look! The wall's not sealed here. The stones are just piled up to fill a door!' Instinctively, Rosalia pulls closer to Vera. Then, holding her candle in one hand, she pushes in a rectangular stone. There is a grinding noise when the stone rubs against the others as it travels further into the wall. It falls on the other side with a dull thud. Vera puts her mouth to the hole and shouts; the echo that follows tells them all they need to know.

'There's another room,' says Rosalia. 'This side is hollow!'

'That's hardly surprising. I expect they were interconnected rooms at some stage. I bet we'll find something similar on the opposite side. Come on.'

Rosalia looks longingly at the hole, wanting to explore, then reluctantly follows her friend.

Before she reaches her, Vera cries triumphantly, 'What did I tell you? Another door. Your cellar's one room sandwiched between two others. They're probably part of a much bigger network. How old is this house?'

'My grandmother used to tell me that it goes back to the early sixteenth century.'

Vera strokes the wobbly stones with her free hand. 'I reckon these rooms are a lot older than that. They'd have been very useful to hide in. Or ... to worship undisturbed.' Her face, framed by her bushy hair, has taken on the yellowish colour of the stone and the candlelight; she speaks the last words almost dreamily.

'What are you talking about? You make it sound like an evil religious sect performing human sacrifices.' Rosalia giggles unconvincingly. 'Come on, let's get to work. Don't you want to see what's behind the walls?'

'Yes, of course. Let's start with this one.'

They put their candles down on the floor, and start pushing the stones until they come across one that slides willingly through the thick wall and falls through. A giant puzzle. Soon they have created an aperture large enough for them to get through: ahead of them there is a dark expanse of unknown space.

'What are you waiting for?' Vera says gravely. 'Your mystery tour's about to start. You're not scared, are you?'

'No, it's just that ...' Rosalia bites her bottom lip. 'The thing is, this is the way towards Signor Novara's house, to the west.'

'It doesn't matter, does it? Nothing's going to stop you from going through now.'

'I guess not.'

They step through the gap, struggling to lift their skirts whilst holding the candles. They realise that they are not entering a room at all, rather a passage with a high ceiling.

'It's a tunnel. They'd have used it to move from one room to the next.'

'Who's "they"?' Rosalia makes an effort not to sound petulant, but her voice comes out at a higher pitch than she had intended.

'Whoever built the network. Did your father know about this passage? Let me through; I'll go first.'

'If he did, he never told me about it.' Rosalia squeezes herself against the curved wall of the tunnel. At regular intervals at shoulder level, little niches are carved into the rock.

'See those?' Vera points at the recesses. 'They're to rest your candle or your lantern on.'

Rosalia walks behind her friend, more than ever aware of the whistling noises of circulating air. 'That's the noise I heard when we first came down into the cellar.'

At every step, Rosalia feels her resolution disintegrate under the pressure of something that feels close to fear. 'Perhaps we ought to stop and think about what we're going to do. This tunnel's obviously leading somewhere, but we don't know how long it is or where it's going. If we go back now, we could come back with Nazario later.'

'Ah! Do we need a man? Are you scared of an old tunnel? I want to know where it leads. You're right – it's heading towards the Novaras' house. Perhaps the houses are linked.'

Rosalia feels anger rise, pushing away her fears. If Vera is right, then Signor Novara could have stored food in her father's cellar; a passageway would have made it possible for others to use the cellar for storage without gaining access from the main house.

They walk for what feels like a long time, following a straight line under the rough ceiling. A faint gurgling of water flowing somewhere near the path accompanies them.

Eventually Vera slows down and lifts her candle. 'There's a door. We've reached the end of the tunnel.'

A wooden door with metal hinges and a primitive lock, but no handle. Rosalia looks at it with surprise, mixed with a vague recollection. 'I've seen this door before', she whispers. Their candles are reduced to half their size, but the little flames are strong. 'There's not a lot of draught here.' She pulls at the lock, expecting the door to be bolted, and is surprised when it yields. Behind the door lies a room that she recognises. 'For the love of God, Vera! I've been here before. It's Vincenzo's cellar ... he brought me down here when the air raid started. The day I lost my family.'

They step into the cellar, which looks as if it has not been used for a long time. A faint daylight comes through a series of grids where the walls meet the ceiling.

'Are you sure?' Vera's voice is coarse and low.

Rosalia looks at the door they have just come through. 'Yes. That door was covered by a curtain when we were here last. I didn't know there was an entrance at all.'

'Did Vincenzo ever tell you about this secret passage?'

'Are you serious? Of course not.'

'Maybe he didn't know about it. The door could have been kept locked when he lived here. Anyway, it doesn't matter. You haven't told me what we're looking for yet.'

'Let's go. This place is full of bad memories; I can't stand it.' Rosalia walks past Vera and through the door, ready to retrace her steps.

'As you wish.' Vera gently pushes the door shut.

Their return trip seems much shorter. When they come to the broken wall and step through, Vera turns to Rosalia. 'You've barely said a word since we left Vincenzo's cellar. Come on, what is it? I can't help if you won't tell me what we should be looking for.'

'I don't really know myself.'

'Didn't you find what Andreas had stolen from you in Cyprus? I thought that's what you went for.'

'What? Andreas didn't steal anything from me.'

'But you said ... In the kitchen, we were in the kitchen, don't you remember? I asked you why you never talked about Andreas and the reason why he left, and you said he'd stolen something from you. Something very precious.' Vera frowns, confused.

'I didn't mean it literally.' Rosalia feels a little pain in her heart and cannot tell whether it is remorse or regret. Should she tell her friend? Why not? Silence will not bring her parents back but she may hold on to the good memories of Andreas by exorcising the bad ones. 'What I meant was that he took my parents' life. He bombed Palermo the day this house was hit. I couldn't forgive him then, but I'm trying to now.'

'So what else are you chasing down here?'

Rosalia pauses. Her father's secret is more painful than Andreas's memory. 'All right, I'll tell you. It happened just after the war ended. My father appeared to be storing some ... something that didn't belong to him, and I suppose I'd like to prove that he wasn't guilty. We didn't even use this cellar as a shelter during air raids because we thought it had flooded and was unsafe. Signor Novara helped me by emptying the cellar, but it's been haunting me for years.'

Vera gives a little smile. 'My parents used to tell me lots of stories about Palermo's tunnels. Our generation didn't have much use for them, but your father would have been aware of whatever's below Palazzo de' Muggifalco. Shall we leave it now and bolt the hatch for good? Would it make you happier?'

'No.' Rosalia points at the opposite wall. 'How can I close the door on that? We've got to see what's there as well. And I didn't tell you the whole story. Only today I came across something hidden in my grandmother's room, a document, and it makes me wonder what really happened. Let's go and get some fresh candles. If you still want to, of course.'

'I'll come with you, Rosalia Muggifalco. Wherever you want to go.'

In the meantime, Nazario is driving very fast towards Monte Pellegrino, not knowing what to fear.

Twenty-Six
THE DEAD'S BED

R osalia grabs a couple more candles from the kitchen drawer, and stuffs them into her pockets. Then she remembers the two little oil lamps that were used in Palazzo de' Muggifalco during the long winter evening curfews, or when air raids temporarily cut off the electricity supply. She fetches them from the cupboard with the bleak feeling of someone who must leave comfort to confront a ghost.

The fire is happily stirring among the coals in the brazier; clothes are stretched onto its dome-shaped wood and wire cover to dry. Remnants of her breakfast are still strewn on the kitchen table. The smell of domesticity makes her long for a life without questions. With an effort, she leaves the warm kitchen and goes back to the hatch, where Vera is waiting. On the edge of the hole lies a little hatchet from her workshop, which had helped to open the cellar hatch; it joins the candles, poking out of her coat pocket as she descends once again.

'Let's hack at the stones,' Rosalia says with fake enthusiasm, not wanting Vera to sense her dismay. Above them, Palazzo de' Muggifalco seems to wait serene for their return. She positions the lamps on the staircase, lifting the glass covers to reach their oil-soaked wicks with a match.

For a while, the cellar is full of sounds as Vera and Rosalia widen the hole in the wall before stepping through. They find themselves in a natural cave that has been hollowed out to create a larger room. Ahead of them, the cavity narrows again into a passage.

'What do you think this is?' Rosalia asks. 'The floor seems to be sloping towards that corridor.'

'I'm not sure, but I think it might be a drainage room, which would have collected the overflowing water and channelled it. Can you smell the mould?'

Rosalia looks up. Above her head the yellow stone is brittle and slightly shiny, but the darker surface under her feet feels slippery.

'Dare follow the corridor?' Vera says. When Rosalia looks at her friend, the little flame inside the lamp seems to shine directly into Vera's very dark eyes, which shimmer oddly. She is not smiling.

'All right. I go first.'

Rosalia quickly realises that they are sinking further into the earth's bowels; the noise of flowing water that has been in the background since they came down the cellar seems to grow closer.

'It's rather ironic, isn't it? On the surface, the continuous drought from which Sicily has suffered since the beginning of time; under it, the mighty force of the water table. The Arabs knew how to exploit natural resources better than we do.'

A few minutes go by before Rosalia asks, 'How do you know all this?' The corridor is wider than the other one, but her coat still brushes against both high walls. She stuffs her hand in her pocket, looking for the hatchet, and is surprised to find it empty. Vera does not answer. The silence is only interrupted by the murmur of water, and their steps echo. Something in the depth of her memory clicks. 'How did you know about the well and the water level? You asked if I ever came down to check the well's water level, but you'd never been in the cellar before!'

'Look to your left, Rosalia.' Vera's voice is more urgent now. Suddenly, the high, smooth walls of the corridor have ripped into a large tear. The rock dips and opens up to show a man-made wide staircase dropping down. They stop at the top, candles held low. 'This staircase leads to two antechambers and then pure water. The two rooms by the pool are for disrobing: one for the women, one for the men.'

Rosalia feels as if she is slipping into a state of dreamy confusion. Part of her is glad to hear Vera's confident voice, to know that her friend is in charge; somewhere inside her, though, the germ of fear grows.

'This is one of the very few left; we're right under the *Giudecca* quarter in Palermo. The ancient Hebrew quarter. This is a *miqvah*, a Jewish bath, for religious purposes and especially for purification. Women bathed in it once a month, after their period, or after birth, to wash away impurities. If you go all the way down the stairs you turn right or left, leave your clothes and then continue to the sacred pools. We no longer use it. We.' She mouths the word to herself.

Rosalia tries to think fast, but her brain is stuck in idle. I want to turn around now, run back to the cellar. I've seen enough. I want to go home. Vera must have researched this place; she must have her reasons. But I don't want to be here any more. A sudden urge to run, but Rosalia's arms feel heavy, legs rooted to the floor. Shake the terror off, run! she tells herself, but she can't move. 'I'm leaving now, Vera. I want to go back home.' When the words come out of her parched mouth, her voice sounds as if it comes from another person.

'My dearest, that's simply not possible any more. Don't you find this underground world fascinating? Safe and pure, so close to the water table. People of all religious denominations have been drawn to this. In our case, we had to learn about it.'

'Why are you talking like this? Who's "we"?'

'Why, the Jewish people, of course. The ones who've been persecuted everywhere, always. Do you know how long we've lived in Sicily? Six, seven hundred years. Longer than the self-righteous Normans, primitive Spaniards and lascivious Bourbons. The Jews have brought wealth to this mean country. We gave it riches, instead of gallivanting around masquerading as God's soldiers in the Crusades.' With an ugly laugh, she continues. 'Yes, the holy Crusaders who slaughtered innocent Jews on their way to Jerusalem and when they were conquering the city. The same Crusaders who came back to Sicily and were rewarded with property and wealth. We, the hard-working people, were spurned and turned away. Sicily had done that before, when the Mediterranean countries rejected the Jews during the Inquisition. Then again, when the Italians decided to befriend the Germans during the war.'

'I didn't know you were a Jew.' Rosalia steps back from the top of the stairs, feeling the rock behind her back, slippery underneath her sweaty hands.

'No, you didn't. Neither did the Germans. My real parents left for America before the war broke out. The people I call mother and father are non-Jewish distant relatives. Giacomo Novara's family officially renounced their faith more than four hundred years ago in order to stay. They changed their name but not their way of life.'

'How do you know about my cellar and these rooms?'

'The food that Vincenzo kept in the cellar underneath his basement flat wasn't safe, because during air raids the servants could have used it as a shelter. Signor Novara pumped the water up to your cellar, faking a flood, and your father had no choice but to accept his help. Within eight hours the water had flowed back into the earth's natural folds. We boarded the cellar up and stored the supplies in it. After your house was bombed, Signor Novara built up your trust in him. He temporarily removed the supplies, then put them back in your cellar. There was always access to it from his house. It was during the black market times.'

Rosalia's mouth is filled with something sickeningly sweet. It takes her a few seconds to realise she has bitten her lip.

'Come with me, little Rosalia. You always were Vincenzo's favourite, although I was the chosen one: dumpy, shy and ignorant Vera, the Jewish painter.' The hatchet has magically appeared in Vera's hand; she motions Rosalia to step ahead of her so they both face the passageway, with the Jewish bath behind them.

'Where are we going? I've done nothing to you. Let me go back home. We can forget about the black market; it's in the past. I'm sure Signor

Novara knew what he was doing. I just want to get on with life.' Rosalia looks over her shoulder, shivering. The hatchet shines in the candlelight.

Vera laughs bitterly. 'You want to get on with your life? How about mine? You spend your life crushing other people's feelings and don't even notice. Vincenzo only had eyes for you but you ignored him. I was left behind to pick up the crumbs of a love that should legitimately have been wholly mine, as a Jew. You're a spoilt little girl who doesn't appreciate anything. Now move. It's not far.'

They resume their walk. Rosalia is aware of the hatchet. Is the place they are heading for more terrible than being hacked to pieces? That kiss, all those years ago. The warmth of Vera's lips as her tongue explored Rosalia's mouth. How could she fake it?

'I didn't realise that you were in love with Vincenzo. I thought you were ...'

'You thought what I wanted you to think. Walk!'

'Where are we going?'

'I'm taking you to see someone you've missed a great deal.' Vera's coldness chills Rosalia's blood. She tries to think quickly.

'I have something ... something that may mean a lot to the Novaras. If we go back home I can give it to you.'

Vera hisses into her ear. 'Yes, I know. You told me earlier, don't you remember? You said that it's in your grandmother's room. I can go and help myself when I'm finished with you.'

'You don't know what it is.' Rosalia's torpor has dissolved, replaced by panic. She tells herself to breathe slowly.

'I think I do. The Novaras were robbed by your father of what had been promised to them, and which they risked everything for. '

'Monte Pellegrino.'

'Yes. The document gives the Novaras absolute control over that land. Vincenzo tried his best to find it among the ruins of your grand house, but failed. Your father hid it because he was jealous. Envious of a Jewish family owning a little slice of Sicily.'

'My father didn't even know that the Novaras were Jewish!' cries Rosalia. Her words sound clearer and sharper than she expected.

'Shut up!' Vera snaps. For the first time, her voice is shaky. 'Monte Pellegrino would have been small compensation for the many centuries of injustice. Instead, I lost Vincenzo inside it.'

Rosalia stops and turns to face Vera, despite her fear. Completely surrounded by darkness but for the light of their two lanterns, she braces herself, expecting to see a satanic sneer on her tormentor's face. Instead she finds anguish.

'What are you saying? What happened to Vincenzo?' At that precise moment, Rosalia realises that they may have spent years hiding pain from each other; that their incapacity to mourn freely has simply prolonged the agony for both of them. She briefly fears that Vera's hatred may never allow her to know the truth.

A few seconds pass in silence. Then, to her surprise, Vera replies. 'In the last days before the end of the war he found out that the fuel depot under Monte Pellegrino would be blown up to stop the Allies using it. The Italian general had given orders to destroy a million barrels of oil, a priceless treasure. Vincenzo felt he had a duty to protect what belonged to his family, according to the agreement with the American government. I went with him that night, as climbing the mountain in the dark and on his own would have been too physically demanding for him. Two Italian soldiers were carrying the explosives. They had a map of the entrance and exit points to the underground depot. We followed them from a distance.' Vera pushes her hair back with the hand holding the hatchet. There is a smear of dirt mixed with tears on her cheek. 'Over the years I've tried to recall the route they took, but we were behind them and in the dark we couldn't see landmarks. All we needed to do was to stop them from using the explosives. It was a small amount. Little danger.'

'You blew them all up?' Rosalia leans against the damp wall to support herself; her shaky legs are buckling under her weight.

'No! I loved him. I wanted to help him, that's why I went too. We'd have got married and I'd have contributed to the family's wealth. My family. All we had to do was stop them.'

'Something went wrong though.' Rosalia says gently. She recalls Signor Novara's face, grey and dull with pain outside the cathedral. He did not know then what had happened to his son, she is sure of it.

'Yes. Vincenzo was about twenty metres ahead of me in the tunnel. I saw him shoot both of them, but he must have hit the wheelbarrow carrying the explosives. I can't remember much apart from the noise, and then soil and stones blasting everywhere inside the tunnel. I had to turn and run. All around me the mountain seemed to crumble down. Vincenzo was doomed. He was too weak and couldn't run as fast.'

'Didn't you tell Signor Novara?'

Vera laughs bitterly. 'No. How could I? He's suffered a suspended sentence, never knowing what happened to Vincenzo, and I've endured my silence and the memories. The depot's still there but the government hasn't even bothered to open it up. I've lost Vincenzo for nothing.'

'It wasn't your fault, Vera. We can still work this out.' She persuades herself that she can see a little sparkle of hope in Vera's eyes, full of tears.

'You're right. It's not my fault. It's your fault. The rich girl with big eyes and a palace. That oil depot could have been my dowry. Vincenzo would have been proud of me. I wanted his family to be my family. My father recommended Signor Novara to the American government as a man they could rely on for information about the Germans' plans in the Mediterranean. We wanted to help.'

Rosalia remembers a name in the document. What was it? Mancini? Yes, it was Mancini, the man in America who proposed Signor Novara as the person to be granted ownership of Monte Pellegrino in exchange for his espionage activities. A mafia deal, masquerading as the Jewish community's effort to help the good guys against the bad Germans and Italians.

'I loved Vincenzo, Vera, but only as a brother. Surely you could see that.'

'You destroyed everything I ever wanted. First it was Vincenzo. Then you stole Nazario out of spite, not because you really wanted him. You were in love with the Cypriot pilot and only grabbed Nazario because I wanted him!' Vera is screaming. Her lantern swings violently from side to side, and in an effort to avoid it Rosalia takes a step back, only to hit the rock with the heel of her foot, which makes her lose her balance. She slips onto the floor, letting go of her lantern, which lands on the hard surface. The blow smashes the glass and extinguishes the light. Vera grabs her by the elbow with a strength that Rosalia didn't know she had, twisting and pulling it savagely.

'You knew I liked him!' she screams. 'You said so yourself that day when we left the AMGOT headquarters. I had to hide my feelings from you again, you filthy thief.'

'You're insane! Let go of my arm!' Rosalia sobs, crouching on her knees and beside herself with pain and fear. When she tries to prop herself against the floor with her free hand it meets the shards of broken glass, which sink into her palm and slice through the flesh.

'I'll let you go. Don't worry.' Vera's tone is suddenly icy cold. She pulls Rosalia up and motions her to start walking again: Rosalia in front, Vera right behind, holding her companion's arm at an angle.

With only one light left, they continue in semi-darkness and silence. Occasionally, Rosalia tries to pull away, only for Vera's hold to tighten. Eventually, they come to a vestibule; to their right, closed with a latch and a modern padlock, stands a wooden door framed by the surrounding rock, thick wood stained by damp and age.

'We've arrived. Stand over there and don't play any tricks.' Vera lets go of Rosalia to search with one hand inside a pouch tied to her waist. With the other she keeps the lantern up, stealing frequent looks at Rosalia. She seems perfectly at ease.

'Where are we?'

'This, my dearest friend, is the back door to the Catacombs. You know it, surely, as the place where, in the olden days, holy Christians retired to rest their weary bones.' Palermo's Catacombs: the underground cemetery built by the Franciscan order of the Cappuccini monks in the sixteenth century, below the Chiesa dei Cappuccini, their church. The church itself is a couple of miles away from Palazzo de' Muggifalco, north of the cathedral, as the crow flies. The large hole into which the monks threw their dead brothers' bodies, clad in a white sheet, grew into a gallery large enough to store, over three hundred years, thousands of bodies. Most were monks, but the Cappuccini also allowed members of the noblest families in Palermo to use the Catacombs as their final rest place. The Catacombs stretch out into a corridor several hundred yards long, dug into the porous tuff rock. The volcanic nature of the rock provides the ideal environment for fast mummification.

'Are we in the Cappuccini's church?'

'No, their cemetery.'

'But the underground gallery's been shut since the last century!'

Vera's expressionless face is briefly lit by the lantern she lifts to the padlock as she inserts the key. It opens with a click. 'In that case I'm sure you'll consider it a privilege to gain such an intimate knowledge of it. Let me escort you. There's someone here who's dying to see you again.'

Rosalia's brain tells her to break free and run away; her legs, however, obediently follow Vera.

Immediately, they are hit by a different kind of air, heavier and stiller than in the passageway. The very narrow corridor has walls that are neatly built of stone.

'This would have been the Cappuccini's secret way out of the cemetery and into Palermo's underground system, should they feel the need to spill out of the area the Catholic Church allocated them. You see? Everybody got their own portion of land: even the dead.'

Another door, shut but unlocked, leads into a square antechamber, bare but for white and green majolica tiles and two wall lights. It is so silent that Rosalia can hear Vera's shallow breathing.

'Straight ahead.' Something sharp pokes Rosalia's back; the wound to her hand, where the glass pierced the flesh to the bone, throbs incessantly.

The second door is slightly more modern, with a round brass knob; Rosalia uses her good hand to turn it. When the door opens, she realises that they are entering the Catacombs' gallery through a stone arch, flanked by black drapes. Here the air is warmer still, with a slightly sweetish smell of parchment or old leather. There are dim wall lights positioned at regular intervals, casting a ghostly halo on the place's residents. Both walls of the long corridor are covered in hundreds and hundreds of mummified bodies, hanging vertically side by side, dressed in their best clothes. Heads are sometimes turned towards each other, as if they are having a discussion with the neighbour they have been given for eternity.

There is something in the air of the underground cemetery that, as the Cappuccini noticed in the sixteenth century, delays decay indefinitely. None of the bodies are enclosed in any kind of coffin or glass case: they simply hang like old marionettes with skin as hard as leather and patches of hair attached to polished scalps. The Cappuccini monks perfected the art of mummification by letting bodily fluids drain away from the corpses; they also placed bodies in an oxygen-poor environment, so that flesh would dry without much visual damage.

'*Gesú, aiutami tu!* Sweet Jesus help me,' Rosalia whispers as she walks along the corridor in front of Vera; the mummies' hollow eye sockets seem to follow the women with curiosity.

'Jesus has little to do with this, Rosalia.'

Halfway along the corridor, the bodies change their pattern. Now they are stacked up from floor to ceiling and built into the walls on both sides, there are rows and rows of shelves packed with fully dressed residents, each resting horizontally in its own crypt. The heads are turned towards the corridor, as if the dead are looking at visitors.

'If you hated me so much, why have you waiteed for so long to exact your revenge?' Rosalia's pity for the bodies is mixed with revulsion, but she keeps her eyes firmly on them, unable to look at Vera.

'Because I wanted to return that document to its rightful owner. You had a better chance than anybody to retrieve it. If you'd already found it you'd have confronted Signor Novara, perhaps even turned him in. Your Cypriot pilot might have stolen it when he left, but I knew it hadn't been destroyed by the air raid. Your grandmother told me.'

'My grandmother!' Rosalia forgets her fear. 'When did you last speak to my grandmother?'

'Vincenzo heard your grandmother, though he didn't realise it at the time. He was rummaging through the debris of your house when he saw a little flame dancing over the rubble, more or less where the opening to the cellar is located. He heard moaning. Poor love ... he thought the spirits of the dead had taken possession of the place and that he'd seen a will-o'-the-wisp. I told him that the flame was probably methane escaping from the grain, which was partly fermenting. Vincenzo wouldn't be persuaded, so I went to see for myself later that evening. I found your grandmother lying in the cellar. The blast had blown the hatch open and she'd stepped into it. The sacks of grain softened her fall, but she was nearly gone. When she saw me, she started hissing and spitting and growling. She'd seen the stored supplies and guessed the truth. She said that Signor Novara wasn't going to get away with it and that he'd never find his document because your father had hidden it.' Vera purses her lips. 'That upset me somewhat.'

'What did you do to my grandmother?' The image of the old woman's frail body forms in Rosalia's mind. 'You put the shawl in the cathedral, didn't you? To taunt me.'

'Not exactly. I put it there to taunt your Saint Rosalia. You're a lot of heretics. What does the first commandment say? "Thou shalt have no other gods before me." But you spend your lives worshipping common mortals, like the saints and Jesus's mother. I thought I'd give the shawl as a sign of your commitment to statues made of stucco and plaster.'

'Where's my grandmother?' Rosalia repeats. Cold fury begins to fill her with desperate energy.

'Keep walking. We're not far.'

'Far from where?'

'You're in no position to ask questions!' Vera suddenly raises her voice. 'Turn and follow the corridor till it branches to the left. I'm right behind you.'

'Nazario will wonder where I am; you'll not get away with this. If I find out that you've harmed my grandmother ...'

'... Then what? Your Saint Rosalia will come down from the plinth and

200

haunt me? Why the anger? I'm taking you to see someone who's been waiting for you a long time. Have faith.'

The corridor continues straight but two narrower passages lead off it, both to the left. More mummified bodies cloaked in monks' habits cover the high walls, following the natural curve of the rock. They go down a few steps. There are fewer lights, and Vera's lamp seems to be weaker.

When Rosalia comes to another door a cold hand presses a key into hers. 'Open it, then give me the key back,' Vera hisses.

Another antechamber lies ahead, illuminated by just one bulb. The smell of age is overpowering. Rosalia stands there, struggling to breathe. There seems to be little or no oxygen left in the low-ceilinged room; in front of her, heavy iron grates with latches cover two stone arches in the wall.

'Goodbye, Rosalia. Remember, it's not life that ebbs away, just bodily fluids.'

'Vera! Vera! What are you doing?' Rosalia leaps to the door, but too late to stop it from closing. A soft click in the silence confirms that Vera has locked it from the other side. 'Let me out!' Rosalia bangs her fists on the door, screaming in agony when her wounded hand hits the hard wood. A shard of glass penetrates deeper into her palm. Her sobs dry up quickly, as the limited amount of air in the room sucks out her breathing. Forced to take shallow intakes of air, she looks dizzily around for an escape route. The arches! There might be a way out through there, she thinks in a panic.

Looking through the narrowly spaced-out bars, Rosalia squints into the semi-darkness of the space behind the grates. It cannot be larger than the room she is in, but it is worth exploring. She lifts the latch and pushes the grate at the same time; she is relieved when it gives easily, pivoting on its rusty hinges. When she steps into the lower chamber, the smell of death is unbearable. Then something in the middle of the room catches her attention: a rectangular slab, slightly raised off the floor and placed on a perforated grid. Something is lying on top of the slab, wrapped in dark fabric. Despite herself, Rosalia moves closer: the shape is familiar. Dear God, protect me from all evil, for I am truly powerless against it. The thought forms in her mind even though her mouth refuses to speak.

There, in front of her, lies the lifeless body of Signora Muggifalco senior, in the clothes she was wearing when Rosalia last saw her. 'Fire in the belly, fire in the belly!' cries her grandmother in Rosalia's memory, pushing her out of Palazzo de' Muggifalco, as vividly now as she did twelve years earlier.

The slab has drainage channels carved around its edges. *Nonna* Muggifalco's bodily fluids would have collected in those and trickled down, through the grid, into the soil below. Her brownish, leathery features have tightened around her teeth, bared in a final silent scream. The horror slashes Rosalia's legs from under her. She slides onto the damp ground, urinating into her skirt. Her grandmother's black top is barely visible against the shadows, covering a bony ribcage that sticks out like a bird's chest. There, among the folds of ripped and old lace, Rosalia sees the white corner of a piece of paper, maybe a document, before she passes out.

At that very moment, Nazario is driving back towards Palazzo de' Muggifalco. He considers radioing his station for some backup but discards the idea. At the sanctuary he could find neither the girls nor the photograph, which has left no mark or empty space. He presumes that they must have been there but left before he arrived. A sense of foreboding grips him. When he drives past the building with the winged gargoyles, he looks up automatically as if expecting to see the creatures fly away, warning of impending disaster.

As Vera retraces her steps to the Muggifalco's cellar, she moves with ease, holding her lamp low to light the path. Neither silence nor the murmur of water distract or worry her. Her pace is quick and confident until she approaches the *miqvah*. She stands there for a while, very still. The *miqvah* has not been used for over a hundred years, Vera reckons. In her imagination, there are clothes piled neatly in the ante-room, and faceless women immerse their naked bodies in the sacred bath, closing their eyes in relief.

The oil lamp sits obediently in a hole carved inside the rock as Vera disrobes. In the semi-darkness she feels her fingers one by one, carefully removing her rings. Her tiny earrings join them on the hard rocky ledge. Nothing is allowed in the *miqvah* apart from her naked body. Vera shivers a little as she approaches the underground pool. 'Purify. Cleanse. Wash away. Be gone.' Her knees buckle as the icy water laps at her ankles, first inviting and then hypnotic in its uncomfortable embrace. It is an absolutely private experience, she thinks. The intensity of it brings a stillness of its own. Deep underground and suspended in perfect peace, she ducks under the water's surface the prescribed three times, whispering her blessings; thus she does not hear either Nazario's hurried steps or his anguished breathing as he runs past the entrance to the *miqvah*, holding in his hand the scared flame of a solitary candle.

EPILOGUE

Christakis Khuklakis looks at the marble bust with fearsome intensity. The resemblance is so strong that it takes him a few minutes to fight back his tears, before he feels confident enough to address the two young people in front of him. 'It's the most thoughtful present I've ever received, and it's a masterpiece. Are you sure you don't want to keep it?'

She shakes her head, smiling. 'No, it's yours. Your house is the right place for it.'

The bust's finely chiselled face looks pensively ahead, its intelligent eyes lost in distant thoughts and the long search for private memories; the mouth, slightly open and hinting a sad smile, is so vibrant with life that it seems about to speak.

'I've been working on these features for the last twelve years, but only now have I managed to catch and hold the spirit inside. Whatever was missing before I've found. It makes sense that it should be where it belongs.'

'Thank you.' The older man puts the bust carefully back into its box and closes the wooden lid.

It is a bitterly cold winter day in Padua, northern Italy. White swirls of snow whip the war cemetery, and dance among the rows of whiter headstones.

Christakis's eyes sweep across the desolate landscape and stop at the headstone in front of them. He speaks quietly. 'Some six hundred Cypriot volunteers died during the war. A higher proportion of Cypriots died than from any other Commonwealth country.'

They stand, side by side, to read the epitaph. 'In memory of Pilot Officer Andreas Khuklakis, 162971, 40 Sqdn, Royal Air Force Volunteer Reserve, who died aged 20 on 13 July 1944. Remembered with honour,

PADUA WAR CEMETERY. Stranger, tell Mother Cyprus here a son died for her own glory and liberty.'

Nazario holds Rosalia's hand. Nobody speaks for a while, apart from the wind.

'Are you all right now?' Christakis gently pats a gloved hand on Rosalia's arm.

'Yes, I am, thank you.'

'Haven't you found her yet?' he asks Nazario, who has wrapped a protective arm around Rosalia's shoulders.

'No. The cellar's hatch was open when I got to the house and I didn't see her when I went in to look for Rosalia. My men have been searching everywhere but Ms Mancini, also known as Ms "Lacrima", seems to have vanished. The photo was gone from the sanctuary, so I'm assuming she retrieved it before going to Palazzo de' Muggifalco that morning. It was very clever of her: she took a photograph of Rosalia's home and a portrait of Andreas that she must have painted – she's an extremely talented painter – and then juxtaposed them.' Rosalia winces at the thought. 'After locking Rosalia up in the Catacombs she must have gone back to the house, because Signor Novara's document was no longer in the book. When I came back carrying Rosalia I found the hatch locked shut, so I had to walk all the way to Vincenzo's cellar to get out via his flat. We'll find her, Christakis.'

'It's rather strange,' adds Rosalia with a frown. 'For a start, her fingernails have always been broken and in a bad state, for as long as I can remember. She can't have recently started dabbling in photography, which is the theory that explains the find at the sanctuary. And she was at my house quite early that day. She wouldn't have had the time to go to the sanctuary, take the photo and come back. Maybe ...'

'Maybe?' Christakis raises an eyebrow.

'Maybe the photo was never meant to stay there for longer than necessary. Once its purpose was fulfilled it was no longer a wish, a desperate desire.'

Christakis nods gravely, as if what Rosalia is saying makes perfect sense. Nazario hides his scepticism behind an indifferent glance at the willows surrounding the cemetery. 'What about Signor Novara? Are you going to press charges?'

'What for?' says Rosalia. 'I've got no proof. The document's gone, the grain's no longer there. He can't claim Monte Pellegrino because of the Muggifalcos' codicil, and he's an old man no longer at peace with himself. His son died in vain, his wife is mad with grief. I think Signor Novara has been punished enough.'

'How did you work everything out, Nazario? Why did Andreas have that map?'

'We'll never know for sure, but I think your nephew was investigating Signor Novara, like I was, but on behalf of the British government. The British and the Americans didn't always see eye to eye during the AMGOT days, and perhaps Andreas was searching for evidence of Americans supporting our mafia in their quest for positions of power, so the Americans could retain some influence in Sicily. A foothold in the Mediterranean would have been highly desirable for both Allies, but America had the advantage of their links with the local mafia, making Sicily very appealing indeed.'

'So you're going to be the Lady of Monte Pellegrino? Judging from the map I saw in Cyprus, it's a pretty large estate.'

'Yes,' laughs Nazario, 'and it comes with its own fuel reservoir!'

Rosalia smiles. 'There's an old law buried in the Sicilian land register and never made public, stating that ownership of the Monte is passed to the last female member of the Muggifalco family on her eighteenth birthday, all the way from Norman-born Saint Rosalia. Every woman married to a Muggifalco, generation after generation, has had to sign a disclaimer when a son is produced, but my mother didn't because I'm an only daughter. My grandmother had the responsibility of keeping the document safe, and my father held onto Signor Novara's secret American agreement, knowing it was invalid: the Sicilian government couldn't give to a private individual something that wasn't part of its estate. He wanted Signor Novara to do the job he was being paid to do, but knew the final prize was unavailable.' Rosalia pauses. 'But as it's now mine to dispose of as I like, I'm negotiating with the Sicilian government. What I want is an agreement by which I remain the ultimate owner but the estate is made available to the public, and the fuel depot is returned to the government, on the understanding that it won't be pumped out into the sea. For whatever reason, Vincenzo died to avoid the oil being wasted, and I owe that to him, even if just out of respect for the dead.'

'That's very commendable, *signorina*. I'm not sure I'd be that generous if I were you.' Christakis winks at her.

'I don't need that kind of money. Besides, it's wealth linked to war and death, and I'll have nothing to do with it.'

'What about you, young man? Do you agree?'

Nazario looks at the headstone as if he can read the right answer on it. 'Rosalia is a free spirit, Christakis. I agree with her, but even if I didn't it would make no difference.'

Christakis's eyes meet hers; she gives an imperceptible nod. 'Young people, do you mind if I spend some time on my own here? I've been meaning to come and visit the grave for years, and now that I'm here I need some private time.'

'Of course. Come with me, Nazario.'

They walk down the path, which is watched by sombre oak trees and lined with tombstones. The short grass dressed in frost cracks under their boots. There is no-one in the cemetery apart from them, and an old man bent over a simple white stone in meditation.

'I'd like you to read this.' She produces a page filled with angular handwriting, which Nazario recognises immediately.

'That's ... That's Andreas's letter to you. Are you sure?'

'Absolutely sure.'

There is a bench nearby, groaning with age. They brush the snow off its wooden planks before sitting down to face the cemetery. The letter billows in Nazario's hands.

Dearest Rosalia,

It is painful to know that if you are reading this letter I can only reach you from further away than I ever feared. However, it is easier to write these few words than utter them to your beautiful face.

I have not ignored your love, nor dismissed it behind the hypocrisy of blaming your extreme youth. On the contrary, it is to that youth I appeal now, asking for your forgiveness: as you are still impervious to human cruelty and deceit, I shall talk to you about moral values and principles, knowing that you will attach to them the same sacred meaning as I.

In the short time we were given to spend together I saw on your face the simple happiness that I was longing for, knowing that I was never meant to feel it. I was not the person you thought I was and had no right to mislead you.

I shall not use the war to justify my behaviour; let us just say that circumstances forced me to wear a face which did not belong to me.

My parents had two children. Twins: Andreas and Maria. Twins of opposite sex can never be identical, but we were very similar in looks, build and complexion. Maria was hungry for life, pursuing dreams and believing in a higher purpose, confident in her spiritual essence. Andreas was handsome, in love with knowledge and culture. He had a more introverted attitude towards the world. Despite their differences, the children grew close to each other, and the tragedy of losing both parents pulled them closer still.

The war fascinated Andreas, who felt that the relentless chase for justice and peace could, and should, be achieved by observing the universal laws of freedom and equality. He abhorred using death and destruction to achieve peace, but was undeterred in his pursuit for justice. He decided he would give the most precious thing he owned, himself, to see wronged people vindicated and freedom reinstated.

Andreas fell ill five days before he was due to join the Royal Air Force, having lied about his age in order to be accepted. I stayed at his bedside day and night, willing him to get better, knowing that if the opportunity to make a difference should pass him by he would never be the same person again.

On the last day he opened his eyes to find me, as usual, sitting there. 'I am dying,' he said. He pronounced the words with disappointment, like a child who feels he is being cheated out of a treat. 'They will fight on without me.' I tried to reassure him but he was drifting in and out of consciousness. Then, suddenly, he was lucid again. 'Would you do it for me?' he asked. 'Would you take over from where I may be forced to leave?'

I understood him completely: if he could not give himself totally, absolutely to the cause, then he would offer as an alternative the next most precious thing in his life: me.

There was my very own chance to make a difference. As a woman, I would never otherwise have been given the option. I said 'yes' just before he closed his eyes. I would carry out the task as well as I could, living out my dreams and by my ideals.

We were incredibly similar in height, looks and hair colour. I was always the tomboy, in spirit as in looks. Andreas had just passed his medical; nobody in the village knew that he was gravely ill, because our old doctor had himself just passed away. My uncle cried when I asked him to cut my long hair. We sat at the kitchen table talking about what we would do when the war ended, and my hair fell on the floor without a sound.

I had duties to fulfil and the legacy of a man's responsibilities. However, for all Andreas's intellectual stance about the war and his reasoned decision to give his personal contribution, I knew that my ideals burnt the steadier flame.

I could have been your best friend, loved you affectionately and loyally. Instead, I had to hide my real identity for reasons beyond my control. How could we become true friends if I held back such a large part of the person you thought you knew? I struggled daily with the effort to push back memories of Maria and hold on to Andreas. Often I resented a simple headstone with my name on it, back at the village, when I fought under my brother's name. It is hard to achieve glory through sacrifice when even the glory itself must be sacrificed. Sometimes I begrudged Andreas his untimely departure. When I finally accepted and embraced my role wholeheartedly, I realised that principles and ideals give results that are higher than individuals, whatever their gender. Bombing cities is something that goes against the grain of any decent human being; but when you are up there, and the fate of many countries depends on how you fly your aircraft, you no longer look down at the houses and see people: you see maps and markers. I left the individual back at home with my uncle and my dead brother.

You have a chance to be true to yourself and live and love as you wish. Remember me when you have choices and are free to make them.

Will you ever forgive me? I promised myself that if I should survive the war I would come and ask you in person. I never told you, but when we were together you made me more of a person than the war could ever do.

With love,
Maria

Nazario's jaw twitches. Rosalia thinks she sees something sparkle beyond the dusting of gold in his hazel eyes. He folds the letter neatly and holds it in his hands.

'Did you ever suspect?' he asks her after a while.

A memory floats up again, that of Vera's unexpected kiss. Rosalia does not know why, but she suddenly regrets never touching Maria's delicate face.

'No. I was only sixteen. She never allowed anyone at the hospital to remove her clothes. There was something very fragile about her, but I'd never have guessed. What I loved, I realise now, was not Andreas himself but the very special bond only two girls can have. As an only child, I missed intimacy and longed for it. My sculpture of Andreas's face, therefore, was an impossible task. The essence that eluded me was something I wasn't aware of: her femininity, hidden behind the uniform. 'This letter doesn't just give me an explanation; it also gives me freedom to remember without anger and love the memories for what they are.'

Rosalia looks away. The ghost of Vera's single kiss still glows, proud and solitary, in her private memories. Was it not Maria's femininity that attracted her in the first place? The absence of bulging muscles under her military shirt? Working with clay left her strangely unfulfilled because she expected fullness and found delicate lines. And yet her perception of Maria must have been subconsciously in tune with the same desire that Vera appealed to.

'You spent many weeks with her,' says Nazario. He remembers how oddly quaint Officer Khuklakis looked, even from a distance and yet ... and yet, how could anybody guess? All he saw was the uniform. From where they are, they can see Christakis crouching over the headstone, stroking it gently. 'You saw no clues.' His voice is flat.

Not for the first time, Rosalia recalls a conversation she had with Maria about women in life and at war. What had she said? 'This war only exacerbates the difference between the sexes. Nobody recognises that aspirations may grow in the wrong body.' Aspirations or attractions? And does that matter now?

Rosalia sighs. 'I think she offered some; but I didn't spot them. And now ... now you know that we must part ...'

Neither of them notices the snow as it falls harder than before. In looking for Andreas, she has found herself.

ABOUT THE AUTHOR

Newly graduated, Italian-born Angie Voluti came to the UK in 1991, attracted by the capricious weather and the island's challenging cuisine; even her young age and a first-class degree in English Language and Literature did not mitigate the shock of a self-inflicted and brutally sudden immersion into a different culture and country. However, she never looked back, though at times – when she can't face another plateful of sausage and mash or the usual three-hour traffic jam on the M1 – she becomes rather nostalgic about sunny, juicy and desperately poor Sicily, where her parents kept dreaming of their daughter returning to her destiny as a part-time teacher and full-time wide-hipped *mamma*.

Angie feels very much like a modern Little Red Riding Hood, living in a village in the middle of a Northamptonshire forest with her two young boys: despite the occasional sub-zero temperature in her study, she has never suffered from writer's arthritis or block.

Lightning Source UK Ltd.
Milton Keynes UK

177285UK00003B/9/P